A SAMMI EVANS
MYSTERY

EVIL THOUGHTS KILL DREAMS

By

JEANNE L. DROUILLARD

Evil Thoughts Kill Dreams© 2013.

A-Argus Better Book Publishers, LLC

For information:
A-Argus Better Book Publishers, LLC
9001 Ridge Hill Street
Kernersville, North Carolina 27285
www.a-argusbooks.com

ISBN: 978-0-6158458-9-2
ISBN: 0-6158458-9-3

Book Cover designed by Dubya

Printed in the United States of America

DEDICATED TO:

YOUR THOUGHTS

Thoughts Are Everything – Keep Them Your
Best Friends and Not Your Enemies

Special Thanks to:

Cathie Omilian – your editing expertise is very
much appreciated. Thanks for your friendship.

My mom and dad – whose thought processes
strengthened and guided me on my journey, each in
their own way.

My Angels on the other side whose constant
help keep my thoughts on the positive side of the
universe.

CHAPTER I

Sammi Evans Patterson was mesmerized while reading a news article that had all of the sensational ingredients necessary for a popular movie. Her undivided focus centered on the story of an unstable, homeless man arrested for killing a beloved state senator in the city of Hartford, Connecticut. The article said that the itinerant hobo, arrested within a few days of the horrendous murder, still had the alleged weapon on his person. He seemed totally oblivious to any reasonable questions officials asked him.

Although the police were attempting to make him aware of helpful facts that could assist him in his defense, his ability to concentrate even for a few moments hindered him at every turn. His Miranda rights were repeated slowly and explained several times before officers believed that he understood them, at least to an acceptable degree. Sammi wondered if he was faking or not. The arresting officers alleged that he'd never be fit to stand trial and somewhat compassionately observed a pathetic, oblivious creature struggling to remain reasonable. Yet, both the city and state were reeling from the slaughter of one of their favorite and most celebrated senators and no kind-hearted emotions were being extended to anyone, whether blatantly sane or obviously needing some type of empathetic understanding.

On and on the story went eventually determining that the citizens of Hartford didn't want a vagrant getting away with this crime and prosecutors were pushing hard for an arraignment as soon as possible. Many of the populace were outraged at the possibility of an insanity plea, a ploy used by many suspects to get away with serious offenses.

Yet the only time the police got any significant focus or any semblance of a lucid conversation with this hobo was when he proclaimed that he didn't kill anyone and then returned to uttering certain words and sentences that he kept repeating over and over, much to the displeasure of anyone around him. He seemed to be babbling words that didn't make any sense or even convey a complete thought. Sammi was living every word of the story, and wondering what the real facts would turn out to be.

When her husband, Detective Dave Patterson entered and left the room at several intervals, she was oblivious to him, so intense was her absorption. Her focus was complete and forceful and couldn't be penetrated except by the determined effort of another person.

"Sammi, what are you reading? You haven't looked up for twenty minutes." His first attempt didn't shake her from her inner world. He tried again, a little more forceful than the first time. "Sammi, that must be a good one."

"Oh hi, honey," she said looking up in a hesitant manner as she realized gradually that she had been involved totally in another world for some time. "Yes, I guess I got caught up in this one." She started connecting with Dave slowly still trying to eradicate herself from the undeniable spell she had just experienced. "Have you heard about ..." and she repeated the story.

"Yeah, there was talk about it around the station recently. I think it only happened last week and it took no more than a few days to find this homeless person with the gun and something else quite telling in his pocket. That's all I can remember, but it'll be interesting to see how this one plays out."

"But a homeless man with a gun? That seems strange to me. I would guess if he'd found a gun he would have pawned it for food or drink or something, don't you think? Don't homeless people search for things they can pawn or sell?"

Dave smiled as he looked down at a face that was trying to understand a puzzling set of clues. "Don't go getting logical here. Many homeless people do illogical things because their minds aren't quite right anymore. You know that."

"That's true," she said somewhat in a daze as she turned back to finish the article. When that was completed, she slowly put down the paper, but kept it on her lap with her hands across the article in a more or less protective gesture. She was increasingly thoughtful and her mind couldn't quite let it go.

"Something's getting to you about this one, right?"

"It is," she answered thoughtfully as if her mind was still in another place. And it was. "Of course it's just one article, but so much is left out."

"They don't put everything in the paper, and besides it happened in another city. I'm surprised they revealed that many facts anyway."

"Probably because it was a senator who got killed."

Dave agreed. "Yes and I heard he was one of the favorites around there, very well liked with strong family ties in the community. That usually conjures up tons of publicity from the start."

"Still," she began in a slow and preoccupied tone, "you've got to wonder what motive a homeless man would have to kill a senator. In fact, you've got to wonder what their relationship could have possibly been or if they even knew each other."

"That's a thought," he said realizing Sammi did have a good point.

"Want some coffee? I could use some."

"Sure," he said. He watched her walk into the kitchen knowing that her mind was still trying to figure out more possibilities. She had a certain walk and a unique way she carried her body when she was in deep thought. He was about to mention that more evidence would probably be forthcoming in the next few days, but the phone rang.

"Dave, it's Roy Dawson."

Roy was one of the newer officers that worked in his group. He was a hard worker, totally dedicated and seemed happy to have finally found a niche where he fit in.

"Hey buddy, what's up?"

"I didn't get a chance to talk to you today, but tomorrow the sarge wanted me to get down to Sweet Valley and check out the area where they've had so many car thefts and break-ins lately. I wonder if you'd have time to come with me. I know you're familiar with that scene and it would help."

"I think I'd probably have time later tomorrow morning and to tell you the truth, I'd like to check on that one myself."

"That's what the sarge thought. He wanted me to let you know I was going."

"Okay, let's plan on it, but I have a few things to straighten out first thing in the morning, then I can join you."

"Great, you let me know when you're available. Thanks."

"Bye," said Dave smiling, as he put the phone down.

"He seems to be working out rather well," said Sammi.

"He's so committed. It was a shame what happened to him, but we've got him back now."

Roy Dawson was blackballed early in his career because some uneasy politicians thought he had seen something that would put them in a precarious position. It took years to straighten everything out and during that time, he'd been ignored, overlooked and disregarded wherever he went. Finally, he was charged with murder in a bizarre incident, much to the delight and instigation of the same anxious politicians and while solving that crime the true killers were seized and he was finally exonerated. Now that everything was solved, he was at last being treated as the valuable and dedicated police officer that he was, and he finally got acceptance as part of Dave's group.

Sammi said, "I think that party we gave him did a lot to renew his belief in people and his hopes that he had a future in the police force. It's nice to see the change in him. And to think that he knew our friend Billy G from way back, it's so uncanny …"

The phone rang for a second time. Sammi answered.

"Hi, Ben. It's always a pleasant surprise to hear from you."

"And I can hear the wheels turning already because you're wondering what could he possibly want now?" answered Ben, keeping his tone on a light note.

Sammi laughed aloud, which caused Dave to pay attention. "That's true; I can't deny it." Sammi heard some disturbing thoughts on Ben's mind. He had a huge worry covering his thought atmosphere and he was constantly thinking, *God, I hope they'll be able to help us. I need Sammi and Dave in on this one. I'm really lost.*

Ben Collier worked for the FBI in Pittsburgh and both Dave and Sammi had worked with him in the past on several cases. He always looked for Sammi's help in difficult situations. He'd never figured out how she could find out information when everyone else failed, but then she'd never taken him into her confidence. It kept him in a state of amazement and always looking for opportunities to work with her. In time, he hoped to solve the puzzle of her talent.

Her husband Dave and a few of her trusted friends were the only ones she had confided the fact that she could hear other people's thoughts. Certainly, it was a strange occurrence, but true, nonetheless. It had started when she was seven years old and nothing she'd practiced. Her Grandpa Logan could do it, too, and they both felt it was a gift, and as such, it was not to be misused for selfish gain or for recognition. To this end, all Sammi had to do was stand close to someone and concentrate and she could hear what they were thinking. She felt that she worked better furtively and that's why she'd only revealed her secret to eight people in her entire life and didn't plan to tell anymore.

A while back, there came a time when necessity made it essential to welcome a few loyal confidantes into her circle, but she had reached her limit now. Others confused by her prowess, still questioned her ingenious ability, but she neither confirmed nor denied their suspicions. Actually, she had to admit that she liked their constant and sometimes prying curiosity. It made some of her heavy responsibility a little lighter and kept her from becoming too bogged down in the quagmire of unstable people.

"Is Dave with you?"

"Yes, he's here with me now. Do you want him on the phone, too?"

"Yes, I'd like to talk to the two of you."

Dave joined them and when the greetings were finished, you could hear the change in the tone and quality of Ben's voice. He talked softer and more purposeful, yet quite clear and couldn't withhold some of the emotion that came across the phone line without any intention on his part.

"I don't know if you've heard about Senator Mike Stedman from Hartford, Connecticut; he was killed a few days ago."

Both confirmed in definite words that they knew about the murder, had discussed some of the scanty details and were interested in further information.

"I can tell you for sure that it wasn't an accident, and I need to tell you right off that he was a personal friend of mine."

Dave sighed, "We're sorry, Ben. We understand it was horrendous and more like an execution. That must be tough for you. What do you know about the murder?"

"Not a lot, but I'm going over there for the funeral and I want to see what I can find out. Right now, they've arrested a homeless man whom they're trying to pin this one on and honestly, it smells bad to me. I don't buy it at all. It's just a gut feeling right now, but it doesn't make sense to me."

Sammi agreed. "I was reading an article in the paper earlier tonight about this murder and I thought the same thing. You wouldn't think he'd be in the same circle of friends as the senator."

"And they want a quick solution to this, I hear. He was a good man and a very honest and effective senator. There was never any scandal around him and he was a dedicated family man ..." Ben stopped for a moment. His emotions occasionally slipped ahead of him.

"Sorry," he continued. "Anyway I want to see what I can find out, but was wondering if I could get the two of you out there later on, just for your perspective. I don't want to narrow the possibilities at the beginning like others seem to want to do and I could use Sammi's expertise on this one."

They nodded to each other and Dave said, "Sure Ben. We'd be glad to help out. I'm sure Sergeant Brady would give me the time off."

"Oh, I'd clear it with him for sure. It's just that I'll be going out there alone, and even though I'm FBI, that doesn't always get me a welcoming committee. It can be tough going solo and one person doesn't always see all of the possibilities around him. Besides, I have to admit that I'm too close to this one. If I was on the case officially, that's one thing, but I'd just like to see what the facts are and what really happened. I mean I know I could push it and get involved and I may do that later if I don't feel satisfied, but ... I don't know."

Dave said, "Tell you what. After you get out there and nose around, call us back. If you'd like us to assist you, if you think it's necessary and we could help, let us know; we're willing."

Ben's thoughts were coming through very clear to Sammi. He was thinking, *There's more to it than a homeless man who doesn't seem to be right in the head. He's just an opportune scapegoat. I want to make sure that we get Mike's killer, and I don't think we've got him yet.*

"Thanks a lot you two. I guess that's what I needed to hear right now. I'm glad we can all work together."

"Of course," said Dave. "Sammi's curiosity had already peaked when she read the story. I think I'd like to get a closer look at this one as well."

"Thanks a lot, really, thanks a lot. I'll be in touch."

When Dave put down the phone, Sammi had a faraway look that bothered him. He looked at her with an inquiring look.

"Oh nothing really. Yet it does seem funny that the article had me totally engrossed and then Ben calls asking for our help."

"Yeah, I see what you mean. I think I'll sit down and read that article as well."

Later he felt that he'd found out all he could for now. They weren't even sure that they'd get involved, but it seemed there was a good chance.

"Hartford, Connecticut. Have you ever been there?" asked Sammi.

"No, that's one state I haven't visited yet. Why?"

"Just curious."

"How about you? Ever been to Connecticut?"

"No, I haven't either."

Dave let out a telling yawn. "If the phone doesn't ring again I'm heading for bed. I'm tired and I've got a lot of work to get done in the morning before I join Roy on those auto thefts."

"What's that all about?"

"It seems for the last few months there have been an unreasonably high amount of auto break-ins and thefts over by Sweet Valley. In fact, Kingston has asked for our help since they've had their hands full with this same problem as well. A few of the suspects have been traced back to Scranton so I guess we're all in this one together."

"So they break into cars and take valuables or they steal the entire car?"

"Both. It's hard to believe with all the warnings we put out, that people still leave valuables in unlocked cars. Mind-boggling, isn't it? I can't believe they do that. Don't they know they're just asking for it? I guess all we can do is warn them and make them aware. Still, it's a crime and we have to look into it. But the number of cars stolen has risen dramatically in that area so we need to figure out why."

"Any ideas?"

"Sometimes gangs work certain areas for a while and then they move on. Sweet Valley has been a target area for several months. A few cars were broken into in their own garage, so that puts a new twist to it. They must really need the parts or items stolen."

"Seems like a big chance to take."

"It is. It's more likely they'd get detected because a lot of people have alarms on their garage doors for that exact reason, but they still seem to think it's worth taking the chance. Makes you wonder why."

"This is out of your realm as a rule, isn't it?"

"Yeah, but the sarge wanted me to go with Roy a few times until he gets more familiar with our procedures and I don't mind getting my feet into this mixture once in a while. Sort of keeps my hand into things I used to handle all the time."

Sammi smiled.

"So nothing's going on at the bank?"

"Things are pretty smooth right now. That's good. I hope it stays that way in case Ben needs us. That case really has my interest for some reason. I can't put my finger on it, just a gut feeling, but I think this case will prove very different than the way we see it now."

"You and Ben both."

"That's it for me; I'm turning in," she said.

"I'm right behind you."

Sammi had other thoughts occupying her mind. Ben was in extreme distress on this one. Apparently, Mike had played an important role in his earlier years and Ben was mourning him like a close brother, which is the way he thought of him. Sammi realized some secret was involved between the two of them that they hadn't shared with anyone else. Ben's thoughts were delicate on the subject in lieu of his friend's death, but he seemed intent on keeping the secret, at least at this time.

* * *

The next morning Dave was finishing up on his never-ending paperwork at the station while grumbling under his breath at the amount of time it took him to satisfy Sergeant Brady. Nevertheless, it was part of his job to have the details of crimes documented correctly and it was always valuable in future times when they needed information at a moment's notice. He was satisfied as he saw his paperwork dwindling about the same time that Roy Dawson approached.

"When do you think you'd like to leave?"

"I'll be done in about fifteen minutes. You seem anxious, why?"

"I've been thinking about these car thefts all night. I hate it when there's no single clue that jumps out at me. I know it's probably a theft ring using the parts for sale or converting them into metal for some other purpose, but that doesn't get us any closer to anything. This is like a blank wall."

Dave said, "And that's why we're going over there today. Sometimes just looking around the scene can show a pattern better than anything else."

"This has only been car thefts, right? What I mean is," Roy paused trying to get his thoughts in order, "I haven't heard of anyone getting hurt so far."

"I've heard nothing about that, why?"

"Well, I was just thinking that unless there's something else going on, this will be hard to pinpoint."

"Again, wait until we get out there. We'll survey everything and maybe come up with something more solid."

"Okay, I'll grab some coffee and leave you alone to get your paperwork done. You want some?"

"No, thanks Roy; I'm fine."

As Roy walked away, Dave realized that he was an inclusive thinker. He probably really had stayed up late last night trying to figure out every angle of this situation, and that was good. Sometimes when you least expected it another thought would jump out at you and get you going in a better direction.

"Hey Dave, what are you up to today?"

That was Jim Mucci, another of his group. Dave told him where he was heading.

"Those thefts are getting worse I hear; be careful. I'm off on a domestic dispute and Tom's coming with me."

Dave sensed something inside of him react to those words. Jim didn't usually give any warnings, casual or otherwise. He shrugged it off. Probably he was sensitive today. He hadn't had a tough case for a while, not since they'd gotten Roy Dawson off on that murder charge and found the real killers. Now Roy was one of their group, and a more solid and hard-working officer he'd never seen. He fit in very well and Dave was happy to be around to see the positive change in him and watched as he finally etched out a new beginning and a more encouraging future.

Closing out his books, he went in search of Roy and they headed out toward Sweet Valley. They had the addresses of several places where thefts had occurred and wanted to see the crime scenes for themselves. As expected, several homes were in the same general area, close enough to each other so that the thieves could hit them all at once on the same day or night. It was a moderate, unpretentious area, certainly not rich, but most had garages for extra safety. There were some cars parked on the streets and Dave, with Roy alongside checked them out to find a few of them unlocked. Some of the owners came running out suspicious of the police investigating their cars.

"Sir, did you know that your car is unlocked?"

"Oh yeah, I guess I forgot. Why? Is that against the law?"

"No, it's not, but are you aware that your area has been targeted in the last few months as a great place for stealing cars or taking items in unlocked cars?"

"Yeah, yeah, I know. I thought that was over now. You mean it isn't?"

"We don't know," said Dave. "But it's always better to keep your car locked and not leave valuables in it."

"Right, right, I agree," said the owner. He reached into his car and took out a cell phone and an IPod before locking it. "I know you're right. I get in a hurry sometimes."

"We understand, but this will only help you."

"Thanks officer," he said as he headed back toward his front door.

About this time, a white sedan with dark windows squealed around the corner speeding up the residential street at a very high rate of speed. One could smell the rubber burning and hear the engine revving loudly as if in an open race. Suddenly it screeched to an abrupt stop nearly in front of them. Dave and Roy barely had the time to turn around before some shots were fired. The car owner that was heading back to his house was shot in the back and he went down fast. The crime vehicle had stopped in the middle of the street and three guys got out, guns drawn and began shooting at Roy, who had managed to crouch down behind a parked car. Dave, who'd made it behind a large oak tree, was safe enough with decent protection.

Dave got one of them immediately in the upper arm and he went down groaning, and Roy got a second one in the leg, which incapacitated him instantly. From behind the tree, Dave called for backup immediately as they began doing a carefully choreographed dance with the third gunmen. When he was out of Dave's vision, he began running blindly without a gun and came around the same tree that protected Dave for the moment. As he rounded the tree for protection himself, he was shocked to see an officer there. His eyes went wild with fear and shock until instant panic could be his only response. He lunged at Dave and tackled him to the ground, but Roy was there in an instant and it was over fast. Backup was already pulling up and they tended to the ones on the street. Dave went straight away over to the guy who'd been gunned down in front of his home. He was still breathing and an ambulance was on the way. At this point, Dave went down and Roy was at his side at once.

"Dave, Dave, did you get hit? I thought we both cleared them."

Dave grabbed Roy's arm with his right hand and said, "No, I didn't get hit, but this last guy punched me incredibly hard in my left shoulder. I think he triggered an old injury."

Suddenly Dave was wincing in pain. Involuntary tears were escaping his eyes as Roy looked on helplessly. He seemed to be in and out of consciousness quickly and it all happened in a fleeting moment. First, he lay limp and then he perked up and began talking again unaware of what had just happened to him. Roy got help to get him sitting in their squad car.

"Everyone's alive, but the homeowner's in critical condition. Apparently he's been shot in his middle back and seems unable to move his legs." Dave carried on a conversation with his voice going in and out of clarity.

"Are you okay?" asked Roy tremendously concerned at what he was seeing. This upright officer was not making any sense and Roy wasn't aware of the history involved.

"Yeah, I'm fine. Don't worry. I want to know what the hell this was all about?" asked Dave.

An officer from the Sweet Valley police station overheard and came over for a moment. "You okay, Dave?" he asked anxious as he assessed his physical appearance.

"I'm fine you guys, but what the hell just happened here?"

"We've been trying to get these guys for a while now. This wasn't about stealing cars. They're part of a group that hates authority, especially police officers and all they stand for. Good thing they're bad shots or I don't think you two would have made it. At least we can get them off the streets now. They've already killed two of our officers, but we haven't been able to find them."

"What's their problem?" asked Roy.

"They hate cops, hate the establishment, and hate anything legal and right that stops them from doing what they want. We've had problems with this group for a few years now. They call themselves, The Right Side Group," said the officer.

"Are they part of any mob activity?" asked Dave.

"Not in the usual sense of the word. They don't officially belong to the mob, as we know it, but they seem to be their own little group and they've been rather dangerous around here for a few years now."

About this time, Dave grabbed his shoulder and bent over again. He was in tremendous pain and it showed. He winced and almost passed out again. Roy grabbed him and they called for another rescue unit. Dave came out of it showing embarrassment.

"I'm sure it'll be okay. I was shot in that same shoulder over two years ago, and it's been fine for a while now. But that last guy tackled me and punched me hard right in that exact spot. I know there's been some damage."

"We need to get you checked out right now."

"Okay, okay," he said, "but I'd rather get back to Mercy Hospital in Scranton. The doctors there have everything on file."

"Then I'm driving you there personally," said Roy. "Now are you going to call Sergeant Brady or shall I?"

Dave laughed. "Well, I see you've caught on to our protocol real fast."

"This is no laughing matter, Dave."

It was obvious that Roy was upset. Dave nodded and Roy got into the driver's seat, and started the seemingly long drive back to Mercy Hospital in Scranton.

Dave said, "Who would have known this would happen today? Hell, we were just checking out an area for car thefts. I didn't even know about this Right Side Group. Well, I'd heard of them a while back, I must admit, but didn't know they were still active in this area. Striking right in the middle of the day for no obvious reason; it sure seems like a mob hit."

"Apparently they saw uniforms and decided to go for it. But why did they shoot that home owner?"

"I've got a feeling that he may have been the real reason why they were in this area in the first place."

Then Dave put his head back and tried to relax.

Roy said, "You haven't called the sarge yet, do you want me to? We've got to call him right away."

There was no answer from Dave.

"Dave, Dave, are you alright?"

There was no answer.

Roy took a deep breath, put the siren on, called the sarge and exhibited his best effort to get over to Mercy Hospital in paramount speed.

CHAPTER II

Sergeant Brady hung up the phone just as he spotted Jim Mucci and Tom Harrington returning from a domestic dispute problem. He called them in immediately and relayed all of the available information to two very shocked and concerned officers.

"Word has it that Dave's fine; he didn't get shot. However, he was attacked fiercely in that same shoulder where he was shot two years ago and it must have fired up everything again. Roy said he passed out in the car on the way to the hospital and was shaky before that as well. They should be arriving at Mercy Hospital any minute."

"What the hell happened? They were only checking out the vicinity of those car thefts. That's all, right?"

The sarge told them about The Right Side Group and they were both familiar with some of their previous activity.

"No shit," said Jim. "They've already killed some cops in the past. Hope this will go a long way to get them off the streets for years to come."

"We're leaving for the hospital now sarge. We'll keep you informed." Jim paused for a moment to tell his wife about Dave and also asked her not to call Sammi. He wanted to check out Dave in person first, have the story straight and then he'd go tell Sammi directly and in person. She nodded and watched them as they hurried out the door.

Julie noted that this was one of the calamities always awaiting an officer. You never knew when they were going into a dangerous situation and their uniforms alone could get them in unforeseen trouble. Today, Jim and Tom went to check out a domestic dispute and those situations always scared her. That kind of duty could be so unpredictable. She was forever holding her breath until she knew that Jim returned unscathed.

Reminiscing a little, Julie remembered that she had been with Sammi at her home when Dave, Tom and Jim had gone on a sting operation a few years back. At that time, she'd had but a few dates with Jim and had not yet begun a serious relationship with him. She and Sammi had been waiting for a phone call from Dave. The hour was getting late and Sammi, believing he should have already called, was growing increasingly alarmed. Suddenly there was a knock on the door and it was Jim. Sammi knew immediately that something dreadful had happened. But Julie remembered the first targeted words out of Jim's mouth.

"Dave's alive, but he's been shot and it's serious. I'll take you to him right away. He'll be asking for you when he wakes up."

As it happened, it took Dave almost five days to wake up out of that coma. He'd been shot twice in his left shoulder and one bullet came dangerously close to his heart. At first, the doctors weren't sure if he was going to live or die. Thankfully, he survived, although he faced a long recuperation period. Nearly six months later, he was still on desk duty, but slowly beginning to reclaim his earlier proficiency. Julie remembered the toughness that Sammi showed and was glad her inner strength had grown over the years. She'd need it again even with strong support at her side.

* * *

Sammi looked down at her dwindling workload and smiled. She was happy that the boring part of her job was almost behind her and she looked forward to some new more interesting assignments. She was thoughtful about the predicament that Ben Collier was in and remembered his anxious unnerving thoughts. She hoped they could be of assistance should he want them involved. Purposeful, senseless murders bothered her even more than accidental ones.

She was almost in a dream arena at her desk as dark worrisome thoughts kept crossing her mind. She tried to shake them off, but only succeeded in making them more vivid than before. She couldn't believe that it was connected with that senator's death; she wasn't even involved in that yet. Of course, she had deep sympathy for the homeless man who'd been accused of the crime. Somehow, her senses confirmed that they had the wrong man. Something didn't seem to fit with her and if this scenario continued, she hoped to be involved in some way to set her mind at ease. Again, dire thoughts crossed her mind pestering her attention. She had the impression of dark colors slowly closing in on her and she felt nervously on edge for a moment. She tried again unsuccessfully to shrug it off.

"Sammi," called one of the co-workers. "You have someone at the front desk waiting for you."

"Oh," she said surprised, "who is it?"

"I've no idea but they want you down there right away."

As she entered the lobby and saw Jim looking at her, her footsteps faltered some. Tears were escaping her eyes by the time she got close to him. She knew what was on his mind immediately and he knew it as well. She felt this might be a replay of a few years ago. But he explained quickly.

"He's going to be fine, Sammi. He didn't get shot." And he meticulously explained the details that he knew. "I just left him at the hospital and he was talking to me like always. He's in a lot of pain though; it's the same shoulder. He wanted me to come and get you."

She gave him a quick affectionate hug knowing that Jim's presence made her somewhat comfortable in this trying situation. He put his arm around her helping to instigate steadiness.

"Give me a few minutes. I need to close up my desk, grab my purse and I'll be right back. Can I call him right now?"

"Let's try."

Jim put through a call and got one of the nurses in his room. "Mr. Patterson just went down to x-ray but he's doing quite well. We've put him on pain medication and that's helped a lot. He should be back in his room within the hour."

"Thanks," said Jim and together they decided to head over to the hospital immediately. They'd wait for him in his room.

* * *

Sitting in Dave's hospital room, impatiently waiting and fighting off worrisome thoughts didn't do much to alleviate Sammi's increasingly troublesome feelings. She remembered the other time Dave was in a precarious condition and although she tried repeatedly to blank it out of her mind, it remained. It seemed that Jim knew what she was thinking.

"Kind of reminds me of that last time he was in this hospital," Jim said.

"Yeah, exactly what I was thinking."

Jim nodded. "But he's okay. It was just damn bad luck that he was smacked in the same shoulder. I'll bet he'll need more therapy and Dave's gonna hate that."

"For sure, but I'll make certain that he goes for every session that's needed."

"Even if he fights it all the way?" he asked jokingly.

"Especially if he fights it all the way," she replied with purpose.

Sammi got up and started to walk around the room. She was fidgety and couldn't sit down. Within ten minutes Roy Dawson appeared in the doorway. He was the one who could tell them exactly what happened, and he did.

"I've never heard of that group, The Right Side," said Sammi.

"We've heard of them," said Jim, "but they've been lying low for a while. They killed two cops last year and we've been trying to find them. But these guys will definitely be off the streets for a long time now. We know that this is only a small part of them; still, it's a beginning."

"So Dave passed out twice?" she asked.

"Yeah, but he came to again just before we got here. He said the pain was intense and soon they gave him some pain medication and he was much better after that. I know he was worried about your reaction, Sammi."

"Of course he would be. I'm just glad that it wasn't worse for either one of you. Did the doctors say anything about what the injury might be?"

"Not really. I heard one of them speculate about tearing of muscle tissue and hoped it wasn't too close to the heart." As he saw Sammi's worried reaction, he added quickly. "He said that if it had injured the tissue close to the heart that it would take a little longer to heal, that's all."

Sammi took a deep breath. She stayed in her own world for a few moments. She had picked up a little information from the universe and there were white lights coming forward around Dave's name. That was a good sign; it calmed her down even more.

She was about to say something when Dave was wheeled back into the room, and he was awake. Sammi was next to his side in a second.

Dave grabbed her hand and said, "I love you, Sammi and I'm going to be okay. I don't like the worried look on your face; you look worse than I do."

She laughed knowing as usual he was making light of the situation. When he saw both Jim and Roy there he said, "And who's minding the store?"

They answered in unison, "The sarge."

That lightened up the situation. "Okay," said Dave, "here's what they've told me. I have some very small tears in several areas of my shoulder, but it's very minor. I knew it right away; I felt it. But it's already swelled quite a bit so I'll be starting with ice packs right away for a few days and then it'll be more x-rays so they can really see what damage there is. That guy really plowed into me and then tried to hit me in the jaw but missed and smacked right into my shoulder. He was shocked when he came around that tree and saw that I was there with my gun drawn. Actually, he did the only thing he could do. I must say that you got over there fast, Roy. God, buddy you were there in a second."

"I saw him heading toward the tree and I was right behind him. Another few seconds and I might have caught him before he got to you."

"I think you did fantastic," said Dave. "Thanks a lot."

Roy smiled proudly. "I only wish ..."

Dave cut him off. "You did all anyone could do and probably saved my life. I'm somewhat fuzzy after that. Did we get them?"

"Oh yeah, all three of them. The other two were shot, remember? I got one and you got the other. They'll both be fine, but the third one hit his head when I wrestled him away from you and the doctors say he's still unconscious. They don't think it's serious, but he did go down rather hard."

Dave nodded. "Boy this pain stuff sure helps a lot. They told me the results of the first x-rays should be here within a few hours, but with the swelling, they might not show what they need to see. I sort of know anyway; it hurts like crazy."

Jim said, "Might be a slow go, but it sounds like it's fixable, so that's good."

"That seems to be the word around here."

"I'm going to head back to the office," said Jim. Roy mentioned that he'd join him. "Let me know when you want to get home," Jim said to Sammi. "Julie or I'll come and get you."

* * *

Sammi smiled and turned to give Dave her full attention as the others left the room. She wouldn't let go of his hand and just stared at him in blessed relief.

"You know what this reminds me of?" Dave asked.

"No, what?"

"Some mornings when I wake up and you're lying there staring at me."

Sammi laughed. "I know. I like to watch you sleep sometimes."

"It used to drive me nuts, but right now, I rather like it. The important thing is that I'll be just fine, but probably more damn therapy. And I wonder for how long?"

"And you're going for every session that's required."

"Yes, ma'am," he said teasingly. "But I will because I need to get this shoulder in working order again."

Just then, Doctor Ken Freedman stuck his head in the door.

"I see you've been at it again," he said smiling.

"Wrong place at the wrong time, I fear," he answered.

Dr. Freedman had been one of the doctors on duty that notable night when Dave was wheeled into the Emergency Room with two gunshot wounds to his left chest and shoulder area. He teetered between life and death for several days and Dr. Freedman oversaw his case, offered encouragement to Sammi and the others while walking each step of the way with each one of them at the needed time. That was more than two years ago and with time Dave had healed nicely. Sammi remembered Dr. Freedman as the doctor whose thoughts told her when the crisis was over and his caring and understanding manner went a long way to keep everyone steady and hopeful.

"And how are you, Sammi?"

"Good and thanks again for all your help in the past. I hope we can have a repeat performance of those great results again."

"I'm quite sure we can. You did take quite a blow to the pectoralis major muscle in your left shoulder, which is the exact one where the bullets landed before. Although you've had good strength in that area for a while now, it's still a little weaker than before all this happened. So it's a particular insult to have it injured again. If this attack had happened in your right shoulder, I'd be sending you home today with instructions and ongoing therapy for a while. But since it's in the same area as before, I have to keep you around for now. The x-rays didn't show much. I couldn't tell for sure if it was simply aggravated, merely a bad bruise or a tear or what. I hope it wasn't a tear, but we can deal with that, too."

Dave jumped on that one right away. "And what would that mean?"

"Okay, let's not get ahead of ourselves right now. A tear would definitely require minor surgery, depending on the damage done. But the good news is that with our modern surgical ability, we can repair them and with therapy you'll be like new again, but the therapy will be important."

"When will you know what should be done?"

"There was a lot of swelling like I've mentioned to you and I couldn't get a clear sight of what I needed to see. You'll be on ice packs most of the evening and by late tomorrow I hope the swelling is down enough so that I can see what I need. Then I'll be able to tell you exactly."

Dave nodded but looked very worried.

"No sad look, Dave. You're gonna be fine one way or another. Even if you need surgery it will be minor, but that would ensure that you'd get full strength back again in that arm and shoulder area. And I know that's the end result that we both want."

"Of course. I guess it's the waiting that's hard."

"That's true, but the waiting is only to tell us what path to take. Either one will get us to the finish line, one a little sooner than the other."

Sammi said, "We should be thankful, Dave. Really, it's good news."

"It is at that," he said.

"I'll be stopping in later tonight to poke at you again, but I've got a feeling that the damage was relatively minor. It's the bruising of an old injury that's causing you pain, but we'll see."

"Thanks again, doctor," Dave said as he watched him nod and smile as he left on a positive note.

Turning to Sammi he said, "You don't have to stay here all night, you know. You're looking tired yourself."

"A little, but I needed to be sure you'd be okay."

"And I will. What he said was a relief. I'll mend again; it's just a matter of knowing what they need to do. But it also means that I get to eat hospital food again," he joked.

"And I'm happy about that," she said. "It could have been a lot worse."

"That's very true," said Dave and then gave out an involuntary yawn. "Gees, sorry. Guess I'm getting a little tired now; maybe I'll take a nap. Probably this is the medication kicking in. Listen, Sammi, I want you to go home, take a rest and not worry."

Sammi laughed, "Fat chance of that. I always worry about the people I love."

Dave had to laugh. He had used that same line on her in the past.

* * *

While waiting for Julie to pick her up, Sammi walked around the outside of the Emergency Room entrance and had a vivid flashback. It was only a few years ago she remembered walking, in truth almost stumbling into this hospital from this exact spot with Tom holding her arm to keep her from faltering. She recalled how she hated the smell of hospitals and the eeriness of the atmosphere around her. Her stomach, upset as they got off the elevator at the third floor, settled down some as she waited with several officers. Jim, Julie and the sarge all worried with Sammi to see if Dave would even make it out of his coma. It was very touchy for a while, but the support of friends and co-workers went a long way to alleviate her private pain. She read the thoughts of every hospital personnel that came into their little waiting room. The doctors carefully camouflaged their message and peppered it with encouragement although not as definite as she would have liked.

Then the word came down that he was out of immediate danger and she could stay with him in his room. When he finally opened his eyes five days later and recognized her, she had trouble containing her excitement. She had read his thoughts as they came close to the surface, but lost them as they took a deeper dive back into his subconscious area. She knew he was making a strong effort to make it up to the surface again. Still, when he finally made it, she was ecstatic.

The horn of Julie's car yanked her out of her reminiscing thoughts and feelings. It would be good to have Julie to talk to and share her concerns. They'd lived through fear together before and their closeness brought huge waves of comfort in the atmosphere around them. Besides, this time the scenario was much better than before, although being the wife of a police officer always brought extra worries and constant apprehension. Most days and assignments were unpredictable. Yet who better to share her unease and anxiety with than another police officer's wife.

***

Dave did need the surgery, although to everyone's relief, it was relatively minor. Dr. Keedman had found several minute tears in his pectoral muscle and taking the cautious road he decided to go in and fix it rather than chance it not healing correctly. Dave was home in four days and happy to be on his own again. He was on a strict regimen and not allowed to lift anything. His left arm was in a sling more as a precaution than anything else, and he expected this would probably last for a couple of weeks.

"At least I can see that you'll be a good patient," teased Sammi.

He laughed. "Yeah, this routine will drive me nuts for a little while, but I have to make sure that this shoulder heals as well as it possibly can. It also affects my left arm, so I can't have any pity parties right now."

"In a few weeks or so, you'll be glad that you did everything by the book."

Dave nodded and went back to reading the paper. There was another article about Senator Stedman's death in Hartford and he brought it to Sammi's attention.

"I saw it. They seem to be at a stalemate. That homeless man is still their main suspect, maybe even their only suspect."

"I wonder if Ben got down there yet. I'll be interested to hear what he has to say about this."

"Yeah, me, too," Sammi said, "The paper seemed to repeat the same old stuff again. It doesn't seem that there's anything new going on."

"Or they aren't saying it in the newspaper. This one's got me a bit curious."

The phone rang and it was Ben Collier. It was almost as if he knew they were talking about the case.

Sammi answered.

"Hi Ben. We were just reading an update in the paper; there doesn't seem to be any new stuff going on."

At this point Dave got on the phone as well.

"So what did you find out?"

"Nothing much at all. Actually, this trip allowed me to spend some time with his wife and kids and a few other officers I'd gotten to know over the years. It seems that the prosecutors are hooked on this homeless man and not checking out much else, but to be honest, the clues are minimal. They seem to think because this vagrant had the gun in his overcoat and a bloody handkerchief in his pocket that it's a slam-dunk. But I don't think so and neither do a few of the officials I've talked to."

"A bloody handkerchief doesn't make sense. Do they think it's involved with this case? I mean the senator was shot from a distance, right?" asked Sammi.

"I don't think the tests are back yet. But they seem to think the handkerchief is important."

"You mean they aren't even looking anywhere else?" asked Dave.

"That's right. The mayor and the governor are pushing for a fast resolution to this case; you know the drill. The citizens are in an uproar because Mike was very well liked and had a spotless reputation as well as a persistent spirit known to get things done. He was a good and effective senator."

"It must have been an emotional time for you," said Sammi.

"It was and actually my wife came up for the funeral with me. She needed to be there as well and that helped me a lot."

"I'm sure it helped Mike's family that you were there. Friends always help at a time like this."

When Ben went quiet for a few moments, Dave decided to tell him what had happened to his shoulder and about The Right Side Group.

"I've never heard of them. I'm surprised since you say they've killed a few cops and have gained this somewhat notorious reputation. I'd think the FBI should be aware of them."

"I just heard about them in passing in the last few years. I think they're starting to make a stronger name for themselves and this area is starting to take them seriously now. I'll keep you informed."

"As you've probably guessed I'm planning to go back in a few weeks. I've offered to help on this case and my bureau will let me go. I was hoping to have the two of you come up for a few days, but I can see now that won't be possible."

Dave said, "I'm in therapy three and four times a week right now, but Sammi could go."

Sammi looked over and smiled. That was a huge statement for him to make. He didn't always like her to be out investigating crimes unless he was around. She appreciated his comment.

"Yes, Ben. I could come. By then I'm sure that Dave will be doing much better, although he can't leave his therapy stuff. We've been lectured how important that is."

"I'm bringing in Jeff Slade as well, so you'd be with one of us at all times."

Dave reacted. "And you know that'd make me feel much better. This case does seem to be at a standstill. And Sammi is so good in situations like that. We'd seen the article in the paper before you called, and it certainly has my interest stirred up. I wish I could come myself."

Sammi said, "Maybe you can later."

"Well, in the meantime, I'm being kept abreast of everything that's going on, so I'll keep you informed as well. Something else may turn up, but if not, well, Sammi's the one who can discover clues that we all seem to miss."

"That she does. Keep us up-to-date."

"I will and thanks."

Sammi had picked up a lot more from the phone call than she was ready to reveal. Lately it seems that some of her abilities had sharpened up, but she wasn't ready to try to explain it to Dave. Sometimes, without any effort on her part, new thoughts came to her from individuals, thoughts that she hadn't made any attempt to hear. She felt that the universe helped her along with information that she needed to know. She was still at a point where it surprised her and she wondered what was happening. She was being edged along to new heights and although it didn't scare her, she took notice that possibly she had more work to do now than she did in the past. Presently, she felt best keeping this to herself.

Ben had more of a secret with this senator friend of his than he was willing to reveal at this time. They had a very strong bond because of something that had happened years ago. She didn't find out what it was, but knew that she would in time. She felt this was a preparation for her to be more aware of Ben's thoughts.

* * *

"I was very surprised to hear you volunteer me, but I'm happy about it."

"I'm beginning to think differently nowadays," said Dave. "I mean look at me. This was an incredibly unfortunate accident and if Roy hadn't been as good as he was, I could have been seriously hurt or even killed. I do worry about you all the time, but that's life. And I can't stop you from helping out in situations where you'd be valuable. You did it alone before I met you and all those years before we married and you're still okay."

"I really want to help out on this one," she said.

"I know and I thought you'd have had too much trouble saying no. Anyway, it sounds like Ben could really use your help, but I'm glad that Jeff will be there as well."

"Me, too. It'll be comfortable working with the two of them again. The good part is that they know I can get information, but they don't bug me about how I do it anymore. I like it best when you're around, but maybe before this is over, you'll be able to come up for a while."

"This will be your first visit to Connecticut?" he asked.

"Yes, and I'm looking forward to it. However, I'm not leaving until you're doing better and on a strict schedule. It doesn't sound like Ben will ask for me for a couple more weeks at least. He has a lot of groundwork to do."

"Yeah, he does and that takes time, but you won't have to worry about me. I'll have Jill and Julie and Tom and Jim and Roy and Amilio and Marlina ..." He stopped and smiled. "It's great to have good friends around, and you won't have to worry because if I need any help at all, they'll be here."

"I know. That'll make it easier for me when I'm gone. So what have you heard about the guys arrested for the shoot out?"

Dave took a deep breath. "This entire scenario is strange. I mean, they're an odd group as it is. We know many people don't like cops, especially if they're on the wrong side of the law, but this hate for anyone in uniform is scary. I understand the interviews have been weird, as expected. Roy and Jim were in on the first few. They said the look from these guys, especially one of them, when they even see a uniform is evil. It was pure hatred."

"You have to wonder about their life story ... like what got them to this point."

"True, Jim's having Julie run a detailed profile on all three of them to see how they all came together. We know these guys are just the little fish in this group. The kingpins never go out on the street and do the crimes. So we have quite a way to go up the ladder."

Sammi got quiet for a while, which prompted Dave to ask, "Okay, what's on your mind?"

She knew she'd been caught and said, "I hate things I don't understand. I'd like to be in on this one and see their profiles, maybe even be around them for a while. I'd sure like to see this Right Side Group get broken up."

"But you can't do everything. I do have a feeling that Sergeant Brady will ask for your assistance, but probably on a limited basis. It's funny you know," said Dave laughing as he shifted his position on the couch, "but the sarge still looks at me strange sometimes when he asks for your help. I believe he's still trying to figure you out, but he's too polite to ask out loud."

"I've tried to put myself on the other side and I know I'd always be curious about someone like me. But I'm glad they're used to me by now."

"I'm used to you, too," Dave laughed. "For a while I thought it was so weird." He stopped abruptly. "Not you personally, but what you can do. By all scales on earth, you are somewhat weird, or what you can do is weird. I think I'd better stop; this isn't coming out the way I want."

Sammi simply laughed. "I know what you mean. Honestly, the problem is that we're all so used to limiting beliefs. People aren't supposed to hear other people's thoughts; it doesn't fit into a solid category, therefore it's not considered possible. People thought the same thing about flying years ago. Think about it. One hundred years ago, how many people truly believed we'd ever make it to the moon? It's still all about believing as far as I'm concerned. Maybe I can hear people's thoughts because when it started for me at seven years old, I didn't believe it was impossible, so I did it."

"That's a thought. And you always bring in the belief theory. Why is that?"

"Because you have to believe something is possible before you can do it. That's one of the elements in my thoughts. If I could really believe that I could fly without wings, then I could do it. Come on, Dave; think back in history. The world is full of examples of people accomplishing unbelievable tasks because they ignored everyone who said it couldn't be done."

"Actually that's true of everything around us. In fact, everything that exists is the result of someone's thoughts, right? So you're saying that if I could believe that I could hear other people's thoughts, then I could do it."

"Yes, you could, if you truly had the faith. But many people live in hope and not in faith and that's the difference."

"I don't understand the difference between hope and faith, not really."

"The short version is that hope is always in the future. You hope something is going to happen sometime; you hope you are going to achieve or get something in the future. But faith is in the present, faith believes you already have it now."

"But you did it when you were seven years old. How did you teach yourself to believe it then?"

"Dave, seven year olds believe anything's possible. Actually maybe we could study the little children and that would give us a tremendous clue. They know how to enjoy the moment, live in the moment and believe in the moment. Kids are naturals."

"Yeah, kids are naturals and then we grow up."

"And go through years of having adults tell us that many things are impossible and to quit daydreaming. We're told to pay attention only to what we can see, hear and feel. Then we lose our ability to believe, and even lose part of our great imagination."

"That's sad, when you think of it."

"But I think it's possible to get a lot of it back."

"How?"

"That's a question that many philosophers have been trying to figure out for years. I'm tired, so let's keep that one for another day."

"Good enough."

CHAPTER III

Within the next few weeks, Jason Connors, Phil Anderson and Charlie Bowren were charged with three counts of attempted murder and presently being held without bond. Their interrogation did little to explain how The Right Side Group worked, and provided little light on the higher ups of this subversive club. Neither did it provide any other affiliations that would offer enough clues to be helpful. Julie was still trying to get a complete profile on these suspects, but some of their past seemed hidden enough to make one wonder if these were their real names. Although Dave couldn't participate in any official duties at this time, Sergeant Brady along with Jim Mucci and Tom Harrington asked that Sammi sit in on the next interrogation of Jason Connors. Of the three secretive and vigilant suspects, he seemed to be the leader and therefore the most obvious target.

Jason was back in jail, after spending some time in the hospital with a minor wound to his right arm, yet he was still under medical care. However, affiliation with their lawyers and other legal representation was getting increasingly complicated, as unknown sources in the background seemed to be in charge determining any outcome even before the initial steps began. Everyone assumed these nameless identities were the higher echelon of The Right Side Group.

Jim said to Tom, "When do you want this next interview with Jason?"

"I think we should do it this week, I hear that Sammi might be requested by the FBI to head down to Hartford for a while."

"What for?" asked Jim.

Tom related the story of the murder of Senator Stedman.

"No kidding; he's a friend of Ben Collier. That must hurt."

"Yeah, I think so and although Sammi has never clued them in to what she can do, they know she gets results. He's already asked her to be available."

Jim said, "Well, if anyone can find out anything I would think it would be her. Okay, let's set it up for Thursday. Julie's reports will be finished today and that'll give us a couple of days to study them. These suspects have a lot of missing gaps in their history."

Tom started to say something and hesitated. "Should I call Sammi or Dave? This is a little touchy I think."

"It could be ... but no, it should be fine. Okay, let's call Dave; he's home anyway and let him talk to Sammi. Then we'll talk to her later."

"Yeah, I like that. He's probably having a hard time being out of the loop right now, so we'll talk to him about this case and he can fill in Sammi. He wants to know anyway."

Just then, Sergeant Brady stopped by and asked when the interview would be. He seemed anxious.

"These lawyers are trying to make it harder and harder for us to get to these guys. They can't stop us, of course, but all of their damn protocol drives me nuts."

"We're trying for Thursday."

"And we'll bring in Sammi, right?" asked the sarge.

"That's the plan," said Tom.

"Okay, that's good. Let me know."

Tom and Jim watched him walk away shaking his head.

"You know," said Jim, "I'm glad that Dave will be back soon to take care of all this paperwork. I don't envy this boring part of the job and Sergeant Brady has a lot of political procedure to handle that wouldn't set to well with me either."

"Yeah," said Tom. "I'm glad we have the jobs we have. The sarge especially gets a lot more headaches than we do."

"Okay, is Roy coming to this interview?" asked Tom.

"Yeah, but he won't be doing any questioning. We want him to sit in the back row and make this guy nervous just by being there."

Tom smiled when he heard the plan. He agreed with that idea. And with Sammi there, they'd know what was on his mind.

* * *

Jim decided to give Dave a call to get him up to date and request Sammi for the interview. Although he was tactful, Dave saw through his charade immediately.

"You don't have to tiptoe around me. You could have called Sammi directly. But I get the impression you weren't sure what to do."

"I knew you'd want to know how this case was coming along anyway, but yeah, it did seem uncomfortable in a way."

"Thanks for the consideration, but don't worry about stuff like that in the future, okay?"

"Okay," Jim laughed.

"Sammi would clue me in anyway. I think discussing these cases helps as much as anything."

"We're sending over Julie's profiles of these guys later today. I wanted you both to have a chance to read them over. They're not as detailed as we'd like. Damn it, Dave, it seems that tons of stuff is hidden; hell, most of what we need is buried away somewhere. I'm sure Sammi will be a huge help there."

"I wish I could come to the interview, but the sarge would have a fit, although I think I'll start back on desk duty in a couple of weeks."

"Shoulder's getting better then."

"Oh yeah, I'm still on pain medication but the dose has been decreased a lot. Right now, I'm working on getting strength back to those muscles, but it's a slow road. If I try to rush anything, I could end up hurting myself again. It's so frustrating."

"I can imagine. Well, desk duty will be a start and you can do all those reports that you do so well."

Dave laughed. "You mean the ones that you and Tom hate to do."

"Yep, those are the ones."

"We want to have the interview on Thursday. We need Sammi and well, do you know when she might go to Hartford?"

"No, but we expect a call from Ben any day now. Then I think she'll be gone for a while."

"How do you feel about that?"

"I'm okay with it. She'll be with Ben Collier and Jeff Slade, but I hate it when she's gone. I better be back to work by then or I'll go crazy."

"Hope that timetable works out. That would be perfect for you."

"Yes, it would and I can take off when I need the therapy; that wouldn't be a problem. The sarge says I need to get the okay from the doctor. He's such a stickler for that."

Jim said, "And for good reason."

"True," said Dave pausing for a moment, "you're right."

* * *

By the time Sammi arrived home from work, the profiles had arrived and Dave seemed enthralled reading them.

"Hi honey. Sorry, I meant to start dinner, but I got hung up reading these reviews."

He updated Sammi about the interview request for Thursday and went on to mention Jim's hesitation.

"That's like Jim, isn't it? Trying to keep everybody happy."

Dave read for a few more minutes and said, "These profiles are skimpy at best and that's saying something because Julie can usually find even the most hidden information when we need it."

"Maybe they're using aliases."

"I think she's checking into that now."

"Which one are we interviewing on Thursday?"

"Jason Connors; he seems to be the ringleader of these three. Here's his file."

"Let me think for a minute."

Dave looked at her suspiciously.

"I'm wondering if I'd be better off going into that interrogation room without any preconceived opinions or if it would be better knowing something about him."

"I see. Well, let's eat and you can think about it. Bank schedule going okay?"

"Yes, things have been quiet, which is good for me at this time. I've already clued in my boss that I might have to go to Hartford for a while."

"Any problem?"

"No, he's used to me by now. He simply said to let him know so he can have someone fill in for me."

"How does that work out with the other workers?"

"Most don't seem to care, but a few get miffed when they have to pick up the slack caused by my absences. One approached me about it and I just said, Talk to Mr. Marconey."

"And?"

"That ended it. She never talked to him."

Dave seemed quiet and solemn creating a definite lull in the conversation.

"Okay, what's on your mind?" she asked.

He smiled, "I hate it when you're gone."

"I don't like being away either, but I need to help out on this case."

"Oh I know and I want you to do what you can; I'm proud of what you do, but ..."

"But?"

"I'm hoping to be back on desk duty by then. Just sitting around here with you gone would drive me crazy."

"As long as you're only on desk duty it should be okay."

"The doctor has to okay it or Sergeant Brady won't allow me to return."

"I've got a feeling that I'm going to hear from Ben soon. You're doing a lot better already, why don't you have a talk with Dr. Freedman? I'll bet he would okay desk duty. Does he want you to drive? If not, Jim or Tom would pick you up."

Dave smiled. He knew she understood his anxiety.

"That's an idea. I'll give him a call."

"Do that. Because even though your shoulder might take a little while longer to heal, you're mind is still as good as ever and that's what they could use around there."

"You always know what to say, don't you?"

"It's true, that's all."

* * *

Tom and Jim were waiting for Sammi when she arrived at the station for the interrogation of Jason Connors. She looked around, comfortable yet hesitant as she walked toward them.

Jim said, "Seems strange to you, right? Dave should be here."

She smiled, "I've worked without him many times, but I'm used to him being around these days. It's just different."

"I know he'd like to be here," said Tom. "Any idea yet when he might come back?"

Sammi clued them in on Dave's hope to return to desk duty soon. They both acknowledged that they'd like him around in any capacity. As soon as Roy joined the group, they headed down to the lockup area to interview Jason. Roy was hoping that they could find out something significant and Sammi was thoughtful with her notebook in hand, knowing she could get some helpful information that would help give these officers some new direction.

She had decided not to read the profile, but instead asked Dave to give her the highlights. That would be enough to fill her mind with appropriate facts, but not bias her in any specific direction. Jason had been in trouble with the law on many occasions, but he'd beat the felonies and got probation on the misdemeanors. He was twenty-eight years old and didn't seem to have any direction in his life except anger and hate for the police and prejudice against specific sections of society. His family wasn't mentioned, only his association with the few members of the Right Side Group that were known at this time. He'd graduated from high school with decent grades, which was surprising to her since he seemed to be using his brains in a subversive direction. Considered a troubled teenager when in school, his record mentioned that he could have benefited from some counseling, which his father refused to approve.

They passed Sergeant Brady on the way to the interview.

"Good luck to you all and let's hope we get somewhere."

He paused to talk to his group, putting a little pressure on their need to find a direction soon. As he turned around, he winked at Sammi acknowledging that he had his hopes pinned on her.

* * *

As planned, Roy sat in the back row with the idea that his presence alone might unnerve Jason. After all, he'd been in the middle of the action so if Jason tried to lie, he knew he wouldn't get away with it. And both Tom and Jim were two of Sammi's confidantes and knew that she could hear his thoughts, so they felt today could go a long way in determining what this Right Side Group was really about.

When Jason walked into the room, he seemed surprised and noticeably nervous seeing four people waiting to interrogate him. Immediately he took on a confident, self-assured attitude and sat down across the table from Tom, Jim and Sammi, exhibiting an arrogant look that conveyed he could hold his own against anyone. It was obvious from the beginning that he thought Sammi was only a note taker and as such, he dismissed her in his mind. Actually, Sammi realized immediately that he dismissed most women, as his mother was not one of his favorite people. She had abandoned him when he was a young teenager and he didn't have any use for her or any women since then. His determined attempts at rigidity brought along a sadness that he couldn't completely erase.

Jim began. "Okay, Mr. Connors, what have you to say for yourself?"

"About what?" he asked in a rather nonchalant cocky tone of voice.

"Let's start with why you were shooting up the neighborhood in Sweet Valley?"

"I don't think I should be talking to you without my lawyer."

"That's certainly your choice, of course. Do you have a designated lawyer? I wasn't aware of that," Jim replied.

"I'm trying to find one because I don't want any court-appointed one who won't have my best interest at heart."

"A court-appointed attorney is obligated to represent you to the best of his ability. That's his job."

"Well, I'm waiting to see if our group will get me one."

"You mean The Right Side Group?" Jim asked.

"Yeah, sure, that's who I mean."

"And who in your group would determine that?"

Jason let out an irregular audible smirk. "You don't think I'm going to tell you anything about our group. Is that what you're after? Well, it's not going to happen."

"Don't you think they should back you up?"

"Well, I'm not sure. This hit wasn't their idea. It was more of a spontaneous thing. We saw the uniforms and went for it."

"Then why did you hit Phil Pentin, the other guy that was there? He wasn't in any uniform."

For someone who had said he wanted a lawyer before he would talk, he seemed willing to speak as long as he felt he was leading the conversation. Jim intended to keep him in that frame of mind as long as he could.

Jason stuttered for a moment, paused, which made Jim wonder if he had pushed him too far. "He's helped out the law before a few times that we knew about and we wanted to teach him a lesson."

"And he was the real reason why you were in that neighborhood?"

"We'd been there before and missed him, but this time we got him, saw more uniforms and felt we'd hit the jackpot."

"You know you're in big trouble this time, don't you? You've been arrested for three counts of attempted murder."

This time Jason didn't blink or waste one second in his reply. "The only bad part is that I missed. Even if we had gotten all three, it wouldn't begin to make up for ...." Suddenly he shut up. Jason looked noticeably upset at what he had said. It didn't take more than a few seconds for slight sweat beads to start forming on his naked forehead near the loose strands of his blond hair that kept flopping toward his eyes.

He looked directly at Jim as he said, "I'm finished here until I get a lawyer."

Jim put up both his hands and said, "Okay, if that's your wish we have to respect it. We're done with you until that time."

Yet Jim wasn't too sad as he'd gotten him to talk quite a bit and knew that Sammi had probably picked up a lot more.

* * *

They had a little tête-à-tête after Jason left, and Roy was the first to speak. "You didn't get much out of him. It's a shame. A little more information and we could've had new leads to follow. But when he asked for a lawyer, you didn't have a choice; you had to back off."

Jim and Tom felt in an awkward position. They knew by the look on Sammi's face that she had information, but couldn't say anything. Sammi got them out of an awkward position.

"Let me type up my notes later today. Dave can give them to you tomorrow. I may have picked up a few innuendos that might help."

Roy turned to look at her in a strange way. He had been in the same room, watched Jason, and thought all of the data was cut and dried. Yet he watched Tom and Jim as they looked respectfully at Sammi as she spoke, and realized the confidence they had in her. He knew there must be some hidden agenda here, but didn't know what it was. He knew he was better off letting it go.

"Great, Sammi. We'll look forward to your report tomorrow."

After she left, Roy turned to Jim and said, "You really think that she might have picked up some idea. I sure didn't."

Jim said, "Sammi's very sensitive about people and can pick up clues that would surprise you. Sometimes it's an eye movement or a tilt of the head, hell, I don't even know how to explain it, but she's been quite effective over the years."

Roy added. "I know that Sergeant Brady speaks highly of her. How do you think she does it?"

Jim said, "I don't care, but I do know that when she's ready to release her findings, she's accurate and she's helped us a lot in the past. And now you can be as confused as the rest of us," he joked.

"Okay, so what do we do now?"

Jim and Tom relayed some other cases that needed their attention as they strolled back to the office. Yet Jim noticed that Roy still had a faraway look. He knew that's how he looked after sessions with Sammi before he'd been taken into her confidence. It was really something to watch her work. She never said anything in these interrogations; never spoke one word, but remained quiet and focused. And she was always writing something down. Yet when she left that room, she had more accurate information than everyone else combined; Jim was sure of that. He expected new leads by tomorrow.

* * *

Dave was restless in his attempt to fill his hours with anything substantial. He couldn't wait to hear what Sammi had found out. He hated being out of the loop and was edgy loafing around the house unable to do any real work and therefore, fidgety and tired of feeling useless. Again, he looked up at the clock. Barely ten minutes had passed since he'd checked before; time was inching along at an irritatingly slow pace. He was anxiously awaiting permission for desk duty. At least that would fill in his time and keep him abreast of what was going on at the station. He'd contacted Dr. Freedman earlier in the day and was waiting for a return call.

He loved his job and was committed to it. He'd worked hard and was as dedicated to the profession as was his father. Their motto of concentrating on the successes made their failures easier to handle because unfortunately, unsolved crimes existed. In fact, many crimes weren't even detected. Those were the ones that troubled him the most. Sammi helped enormously in those areas. He thought her talent was phenomenal although he hesitated in constantly telling her. He didn't want to get patronizing or overly complimentary, as she didn't handle that well. Yet she was amazing; she could actually hear other people's thoughts. What kind of a gift was that? He'd often tried to imagine himself in her position, and he couldn't. Sammi didn't act superior to anyone ever. She was unassuming and accepted her talent as part of who she was, someone imbued with a special gift to be utilized in a responsible fashion.

Kali surprised him and barked fiercely at the back door.

"Hey, girl, is something bothering you? What do you see out there?"

Dave couldn't see anything but Kali continued to growl at the door.

He opened the door in time to see a white cat escaping over their fence into their neighbor's yard.

"She was just visiting," he told Kali. "She's gone now and you can go back to sitting on your bed and relax. But you're a good watchdog. I appreciate you for that."

With a pat on her head and a quick scratch behind her ears, Dave went back to his earlier thoughts.

He often thought back to their college days. When he first met Sammi in an English class during his sophomore year, he liked her immediately. She was genuine and unpretentious, a quality not always easy to find, especially in college-aged girls. Yet before anything more than friendship developed between them, her friend Kelly showed up one day for lunch. It was no secret that Kelly liked him immediately and flirted with him openly and he wasn't opposed to it. Kelly was quite attractive, outgoing, and flirtatious as well as fun loving and charming. She was definitely aware of her feminine charm, but it didn't seem to matter so much back then. They began dating soon after their meeting. Looking back, he believed that he had detected some disappointment in the situation from Sammi's point of view, but she'd never said anything.

To this day, she admitted to nothing about her feelings during that time and that's when Dave wished at times he could read Sammi's thoughts. If he'd detected her disappointment so strongly, it must have been there. Still, Kelly was one of her best friends and Sammi eventually took the position of remaining best friends to both of them. However, Dave found it strange when she didn't stand up for their wedding. He knew that Kelly had asked her, but she declined. He never found out why. She did attend their wedding and was quite generous with her gift, but she couldn't handle being part of the ceremony. After five years of marriage to Kelly, it began to crumble and they were ready to split up; their lives had changed. They were different too, in many other important ways. Yet before the split happened, Kelly was shot and killed by a bullet meant for someone else. It took time for him to get over all the irrational feelings of starting to go through a divorce and then burying your wife. His double-edged sword was the fact that he was a police officer and supposed to save people and yet ...

He heard the key in the lock and Sammi came directly into the living room. She immediately detected the look on his face and questioned it.

"I was in such a reminiscing mood today. You probably wouldn't like where I was going."

She came to sit down next to him on their favorite couch and said, "We all reminisce; tell me about it."

"You're sure you want to hear this."

Sammi look confused at first, then a knowing look came over her as she said, "We've never had any secrets. Were you thinking of Kelly?"

"I should have known you'd know. Yes, I still think about her now and then."

"Well, so do I. She was my best friend and your wife for nearly five years."

"And even though we had decided to split up, I still liked her; hell, I cared about her a lot, but in a different way."

"I understand. Why would you think this would bother me?"

"I don't know. I guess I still think it's a touchy subject."

"Well it's not and it never will be, at least not for me."

"But I always wondered about one thing."

"What's that?"

"You wouldn't stand up for our wedding. I know that Kelly asked you because she told me. Why wouldn't you? I know you weren't mad because you came to the wedding, but you didn't stand up with us."

He saw Sammi stand up, actually put her hands on her hips, something she rarely did and simply stare directly into his eyes. Dave took notice. He put both of his hands up immediately and said, "I retract the question."

She laughed hysterically at that. "I was going to say that my personal reason comes under the same type of category as to why you, Tom and Jim won't tell anyone what the three referees is all about. Why won't you tell us?"

Tom, Jim and Dave had referred to themselves as the three referees for years, but wouldn't tell anybody what it meant. Even Sergeant Brady was in the dark on that one.

"I think we originally planned to tell everyone and really it's not that big of a deal, but then it became fun to tease you gals about it and we've just kept it going."

"I see," she said thoughtfully. "Mine is probably a little more delicate."

"So you did have a reason then?" he asked.

She pursed her lips as she said emphatically, "Of course I had a reason, but I didn't tell you then and I'm not telling you now."

Dave grabbed her with his right arm and gave her a quick kiss on the cheek and a slight hug.

"One of these days, I'll find out," he said teasingly.

Sammi gave him a doubtful smile.

Dave immediately said, "Tell you what. One of these day's we'll both come clean. You'll tell me why you wouldn't stand up for my first wedding and I'll tell you about the reason behind the three referees."

"Sure," said Sammi. "I can't imagine that ever happening, but then you never know."

Dave got serious and didn't laugh. He looked solemn for a moment.

She said, "Honey, don't be so serious. That's one secret about me that I don't feel you ever have to know. It's my own personal memory."

Dave looked surprised and had a comeback ready, but the telephone rang. He noticed it was about 7:30 PM as he picked up the phone. He listened for a few moments without speaking.

"Sure that's a great idea Dr. Freedman. I'll see you then."

He turned smiling and said, "I've got an appointment with Dr. Freedman tomorrow at 3:30 PM. If everything checks out, he'll probably let me get back to work, but for desk duty only, and he doesn't want me to drive yet. That's okay; I can manage that."

"I'm glad. I think all this time at home has you bored and restless. I'll be glad to see you back doing what you do best."

Dave looked at Sammi strangely. It was a long stare and made her ask, "What?"

"Someday I hope you'll tell me why you wouldn't stand up for my wedding to Kelly."

"Why is it so important to you now? You've never asked me in all the years I've known you."

"I never thought of it and it's something I don't know about you."

Sammi sneered. "We can just keep it under the category of something you don't need to know."

"But I'd like to know, and can't figure out why you won't tell me."

She smiled strangely hiding an unreadable emotion, "Maybe someday I will tell you, Dave. Maybe someday the moment will feel right."

CHAPTER IV

Sammi worked for over an hour getting her notes in order regarding the interrogation of Jason Connors. Sometimes she felt that her computer room was her entire world as she transcribed and conversed with a universe that few would believe she had access to. Yet she sometimes felt traumatized at some of the inner secrets revealed to her. At times her persona worked overtime to adjust to the information that the universe threw her way. Most of the time she could remain impartial; her position was not to judge but merely to relay known facts to Dave and let the legal force decide the plan of action. Yet sometimes it was difficult when she heard compelling stories. Jason Connors fell into that category.

He was an openly admitted cop killer; at least he wanted to be. That was a known fact. In the future if given any more opportunities, he'd no doubt try again. Yet his story was the stuff movies were made of. The police had killed his older brother Kyle during a liquor store robbery. Jason was barely five years old at the time and couldn't even remember his older brother anymore. His father never forgave the law for his son's death. He believed Kyle was only a stupid sixteen-year-old kid, who'd made a brainless mistake, which he couldn't be held totally responsible for. After all, he was only sixteen. He was convinced that the police didn't have to kill him and made sure that Jason always remembered the story.

Several lawsuits filed on Kyle's behalf, were all dismissed, one by one. His father's fury only grew over the years until he tried to murder the same cop who had killed his son. He failed, but landed in jail for his attempt and had at least ten years to serve before he'd be released. Jason's mother had all she could take by the time Jason was thirteen and although she tried to get her son away from his father's influence, which even from his jail cell was very strong, the courts didn't agree. They allowed him to stay in a home filled with anger, rage and fury on one side, and an attempt from his mom at saneness and logic on the other side. His grandparent's home, who shared his father's wrath toward the law, was his second residence. Jason knew nothing else. He was taught every day of his life how to hate the police, plan revenge on them and to succeed in undermining any official authority. Sammi wondered how he could have possibly ended up any other way.

"That's quite a story," said Dave. "I think it would be hard to undo all of the psychological damage that was done to that boy. And he's twenty-eight years old now; it's a sad situation."

"You wonder how he might have turned out if his mother had been able to get him away from that explosive environment."

"Yeah," he said, "You've got to wonder. But we have to deal with someone who'd kill another cop or FBI agent or any type of law enforcement in a second if he got the chance."

"Even if the court system gave him a chance, I don't know if he could be healed now. He's had too many years of hate ingrained into his mind."

"Did you pick up anything about The Right Side Group?"

"A little. His mind didn't go there much but when he talked about the top person, his mind thought about a Mr. Biltmore. Mean anything to you?"

"No, can't say I've ever heard the name," said Dave. "But that doesn't mean much; maybe he's on file for something else. We could have Julie look it up."

"And there was one other thought that crossed his mind a few times, and this one was rather telling."

"What's that?"

"His two buddies Phil and Charlie didn't seem to want to carry out this attack and he seemed rather miffed with them. He was thinking that they weren't nearly as dedicated as he thought they should be and this was something he'd have to make his father aware of."

Dave turned to look at her. "So his father is still involved even from the inside of prison. That's interesting."

"Is that even possible? When's his father due out?" Sammi asked.

"He just keeps screwing up, so he can't get parole. He's been in several incidents in prison and had more years tacked on to his sentence, so I'm not sure when he's due out. It will depend. Oh yes," he said, "to answer your question, many of the top guys still run the show from prison. It happens a lot."

"No kidding. I wasn't even going to mention that part because I figured I must be wrong, but whenever he thought about his dad he also thought of this Mr. Biltmore so maybe the two of them are running the show."

"That could be true; something to look into. Yet it could mean that his father hopes to become important to this Mr. Biltmore. Hard to say. I wonder how large a group this is."

"That's almost everything I got. It wasn't a very long meeting. He finally said he wouldn't do any more talking without an attorney," she said.

"Then we have to back off. That's okay. We should be able to get more information on the group and I'll have Julie track this Mr. Biltmore. Wonder if any of the other guys know about him?"

"Guess you'll have to wait and see."

"And if the other two guys weren't as enthused as Jason, they may be better targets to get information on the group. I'll pass it on to Jim; it's a thought."

"Do you want me to drive you to the doctor tomorrow?"

"Oh no, you stay at work. I'll get one of our guys to do it. Besides, if it works out the way I think, I'll need a designated driver for a few weeks anyway."

"At least you'll be back at work and know what's going on."

"Yeah, I'll be glad about that."

"Jim expects to get a copy of this report tomorrow, so maybe you could stop by and give it to him before you're appointment."

"Great, I'll do that. I'm tired and I'm turning in. You should too; it's been a long day for you."

"Yep, I'm heading there myself."

He put his arm around her, but she felt tension from him and she knew where it came from. She knew it bothered him when she had held something from him. He had a penchant for a solid base between them and that included no secrets of any important nature. Yet if he couldn't seem to figure it out on his own why she didn't want to stand up for his first wedding, she did not intend to tell him after all this time. It would be awkward and it wasn't necessary. There were times when it was better to keep certain things to yourself, and Sammi felt that this was definitely one of those times.

* * *

When Dave first stepped foot in his precinct he couldn't prevent the hesitancy that overtook him for a moment. Things looked different with everyone rushing around and busy with their duties and he had a sudden dispirited feeling that no one missed him at all. Things were moving along fine without him. Why did he feel so strange?

He took a deep breath being thankful that he was back here at all. The crime episode he was involved in could have turned out much worse. Another lucky break for him. His mind raced as he looked around wondering why he felt this way. For some unknown reason, there were times when he was more emotional than he used to be. He felt that when he reinjured his shoulder it brought back thoughts of the original sting operation where his involvement brought him close to death.

After that incident, he looked at life completely different. He knew that his feelings were usually on the outside now, instead of his customary habit of hiding them. Sammi had to make a big adjustment listening to him talking about his inner thoughts and feelings and expressing himself constantly. It was as if he had made a complete switch of personality in some areas of his life.

Today, for a second it brought everything back by simply walking into the station and taking a few steps toward his old familiar desk. He liked the position of his workplace over by one of the windows, yet not far from the mainstream of action. He didn't have much time to contemplate anything as Jim spotted him and came right over to his side.

He immediately put an arm on his back as he said, "Good to see you, buddy. Does this mean that you're back?"

"Not yet, but I've got an appointment with Dr. Freedman later today and I hope he'll give me desk duty for a while. But I already know that he doesn't want me to drive for a few more weeks."

"That's no problem. We have enough people around here to get you back and forth. And I need to pick your brain on this latest stuff. God, I'm glad you're coming back. When? Do you know yet?"

Dave felt energized simply talking to one of his inner group who was totally excited at having him back at work. Then Tom came over to join them and the three referees were together again. These were the ones who'd been his partners for years and they always watched out for each other, and these were also the ones he'd trusted with his life on many occasions. Feelings overcame him that couldn't be expressed, only felt with appreciation for their familiarity.

"Great to see you. Glad you're back. Didn't know it would be this soon."

Dave clued him in on his doctor's appointment.

"Well," said Tom. "You're walking, talking and moving; he'll probably okay you sitting at your desk helping us out for a while."

Although they smiled, they all knew that the unfortunate event could have had a different ending. Luck had been on their side one more time. Roy Dawson joined the trio. He had been singularly responsible for saving Dave.

"I can't thank you enough, Roy. You did great."

"Nothing you wouldn't have done for me," he said and as he looked around to the others added, "Anyone of you would have done the same thing."

On a lighter note Dave said, "Sammi wants to get me out of the house; I'm beginning to drive her nuts."

"How does the shoulder feel?" Roy asked.

"Pretty good as a matter of fact. Still a little sore, but so much better than last week. I'm feeling pretty good about that."

Sergeant Brady saw Dave and came out in time for the update. "It'll be great to have you back, but only if Dr. Freedman thinks you're ready. We don't want to rush this and have more problems down the road."

Dave expected this exact speech and gave him the proper response. "I agree. I'll follow doctor's orders."

He hated to say those words, but knew they were true. However, his gut feeling told him that Dr. Freedman would okay desk duty and probably feel it would do him good.

As he needed to leave in order to make his doctor's appointment, he turned to Jim and said, "Here are Sammi's notes. They'll give all us a little bit to think about. I wanted to discuss them with you, but I'm running late and I've got to go. We'll talk later."

With those words and a slight smile, he turned and left immediately.

* * *

Driving home from his appointment, Dave stopped to buy a bottle of Piesporter wine, Sammi's favorite. He was going back to work on Monday and he needed her to celebrate with him. True, it was only desk duty, but he'd be in the action again and see first hand what was happening with The Right Side Group. He felt encouraged and enthusiastic as he looked forward to resuming his career. Okay, so he needed a designated driver for a while, but that was all right, many of the rookie's were willing.

He'd made dinner, set up the wine glasses, and put on the final touches to his festive attempt when Sammi walked in the door. She immediately took notice and smiled at him, "You're going back to work," she said.

He came over gave her a long kiss and an emotional hug as he agreed. "Yep, still, I can't drive for at least two more weeks. But the doc said that I'm healing nicely although any sudden motion while driving could undo recent progress, so that's not allowed."

"Then you'd better not hug me too hard," she teased.

"I'm sure that's permissible," he shot back quickly.

She laughed at his quick reaction. "So things will be getting back to normal around here. That's good."

"Yeah, I was really getting restless. I'm used to going to work and this sitting around … well, it's hard. I can sit at my desk just as easily and be of some help."

"I'm sure Jim will be glad about that."

"Oh, that's right. He doesn't know yet. I'd better call him."

Sammi heard them laughing and joking for a few minutes, then he turned to her and said, "Jim and Julie are going to stop over later tonight for a few minutes. He wants to talk to you about your report."

"No problem," she said.

Later that evening Dave had to admit, "I'll bet we'll need you in two places before long."

"And I'm interested in both cases. Wish everything didn't happen all at once."

"I think the background investigation on The Right Side Group will take a while. Jim hinted at that. Then it takes everyone even more time to get their court cases in order. I think if Ben gets you out there soon that you might make it back here in time to be of help to us as well."

"I could always come home for a weekend."

"I wanted to talk to Ben about that," said Dave. "I was hoping we could have the same arrangement we had before. You could come home on Friday nights and get back there on Sunday night. I don't want you to be gone completely for too long."

She smiled. "I'll really miss you, too. That's a good thought and ..."

The telephone rang. It was Ben Collier. He always seemed to know when to call.

"Okay you two. I need some help desperately. They're trying to forge ahead on this case with that homeless person and I think they're wrong. They won't even look at anybody else. I can't believe their narrow outlook on this. It's ridiculous."

Dave said, "It's probably public pressure."

"And I can understand that to a degree, but they still have to do their jobs and they're not doing them. This case has been handled shoddily from the beginning; honestly, I think there's much more to this than I'm seeing right now. I don't want to yell cover up at this stage of the game, but it's what I'm thinking right now. And Jeff is on the same page with me."

Sammi said, "Sounds like there's an underlying reason why they aren't looking somewhere else. Just because they found a gun on this unaware person, well you know that doesn't mean that much. It could have easily been a plant. They must have thought about that; they're not stupid. I'm surprised at their attitude."

"Sammi, I'm shocked by it," said Ben. "It's very early in the process and they should be following up on all the leads, but they're not. I know they want the public to believe that they have the killer, but if it turns out to be the wrong guy, they're going to look pretty stupid. And I've got to wonder why they're buckling so early. That's not the norm. We're all used to public pressure and outrage. I know the police commissioner is solid, but he's listening to his sergeants under him. I think we have a problem with one or two of them. I need you, Sammi. We've got to find out who's shy out there right now and for what reason."

She looked at Dave and he nodded. "Okay, Ben. When did you want me to come?"

"Whenever you can. Jeff and I are leaving on Sunday. We've both been assigned to the case. We'll take care of all your travelling and lodging arrangements. We'll have you in the room next to us. And we'll watch out for her, Dave, I promise."

"I know you will and that's fine. But I was hoping we could have the same arrangement as last time. I'd like her to come home on weekends. First, I'd like it," he joked, "but also we've got that Right Side Group case starting to move and we'll need her occasionally to confer on that."

"No problem," said Ben. "We'll have the same charter availability set up to take you back and forth. Listen, we appreciate your help so much."

"Okay, then," said Sammi. "I've gotten used to those charter flights now and I love not having the hassle of a major airport. I'll plan to get out there sometime next week, but I'll have to let you know. I've got to clear up a few things at my bank job and ..."

Dave said, "And if we get to use her on this case in the next few days, I think we'll save time as well."

"That's perfect. It'll give Jeff and me time to nose around and find out what we're up against. That's great. Just let me know when you can make it and I'll have the charter ready."

"Okay, I think we can make this all work out. Talk to you later."

* * *

Dave look relieved; there was no doubt. He looked over at her with some pride but also with some calmness. "I don't think you really understand how important you are to all of these organizations. I know you like helping out, but do you really know how significant you are?"

She smiled, "Yes, I know simply because you mention it to me often. I have a gift, Dave. It's not something I chose or anything that puts me above anyone; it's a gift. And yes, I like it when I can get you police officers or the FBI looking in a better direction. I get very excited when we can all solve crimes together. I'm really energized about both of these cases right now. I don't think it's the homeless man either and I don't have a real reason for that thought."

"Me, too. I can't imagine how he fits into all this, but I don't see him as the killer. I think he's a convenient scapegoat for the police who want to calm down their districts."

Dave shook his head and puckered his lips as he added. "I'm interested to see what direction you'll get from all this."

She was about to answer, but the doorbell rang. It was Jim and Julie.

* * *

It took less than five minutes for them to settle down and get talking about Sammi's report. It was so comfortable for her with this group because they knew what she could do. She could talk openly and honestly without fear of slipping up. It meant a lot.

"Obviously I didn't get much," said Sammi.

"It was a very short meeting," Jim replied. "Honestly, it was less than five minutes into this interview when Jason felt like he slipped up on something and then he became very nervous and sweaty and said, 'I'm finished here until I have my lawyer.' Well, that ended it for all of us. I was surprised that you got this much. You're notes give some hints that I wanted to get into."

Sammi looked at Julie. "Did you get a chance to read them?"

She nodded that she had.

"Okay then. What part did you want to discuss?"

"First of all, it's a bunch of sad crap about this Jason guy. I mean his young life didn't give him much of a chance at living any kind of decent life. I'm hoping in time we can get to his father; he certainly has his hands in the mix, don't you think Dave?"

"Absolutely. I think his father and this Biltmore fellow are running a big part of the show, but we don't know how large this group is or how high up these guys are."

They both looked at Sammi. "No, I didn't get any hints in that direction. Yet I'm not sure about the connection with this Biltmore fellow. He could be the one giving orders or just someone important they want to connect with. I didn't have a feeling that they actually knew each other. I'm hoping to get in on more interviews later, but ..."

"You did great in that short amount of time," Jim said. "I wanted to know more about Phil Andersen and Charlie Bowren. You said that they had an attitude ... I don't think I said that right. It was Jason's thoughts that told you he wasn't entirely satisfied with how they were thinking about the raid, right?"

Sammi nodded.

Jim was trying to confirm his understanding. "They didn't really believe in it like Jason did and some of the higher ups. Is that what you meant?"

"Yes, that's right. Jason was concerned and thought he'd have to mention it to his father; he didn't think that Charlie and Phil were as dedicated as they should have been. It was almost as if Jason was disgusted with these two and disappointed that they weren't fanatical members."

Jim turned to Julie and said, "I'm going to have you concentrate on this Biltmore fellow. Trouble is we don't know where he's at. We don't know if he's around Scranton or even in PA."

"I'll see what I can find out," said Julie. "I can start by widening the search to anywhere in the U, S., and then start eliminating some by their history and other stuff."

"Right," said Dave. "It's not too likely that a Mr. Biltmore that was a college professor and on committees for advancing education would be involved in killing cops, so their lifestyle could give us a clue."

"And there are other ways," said Julie.

They all turned to look at her.

"I was thinking that their family history as well as their extra curricular activities and the people they pal around with could be another big sign. Your friends determine a lot about you."

Jim nodded, "I see what you mean. So maybe we could narrow this down more than we think."

"I wish I could've picked up a first name, but I couldn't. I even concentrated on it for a moment, but nothing came of it."

Jim said, "Sammi, you always get us way ahead of the game. I'm thrilled with any of the extras you come up with."

Dave smiled as he looked at her. "She always wants to do more."

"You guys are the same way," she said seriously.

"When are you going to Hartford?" asked Julie.

"I need to finish up a few things at the bank. And then Dave said that I could be needed here early next week, so I'm thinking I'll probably get up there after that."

"Or you could even wait until Sunday night and be there to start on Monday morning," Dave added.

"That's an idea," she said, realizing that could be the best plan.

"Hartford is an interesting city, well, most capitals are. But it does have a decent amount of history."

"You've been there?" Sammi asked.

"Only once a long time ago, but I remember thinking that I'd like to go back when I had more time."

Dave said, "Maybe we could all come up sometime for a weekend."

"That'd be great," said Sammi, then she got quiet.

"What?" asked Dave.

"I like it when we're all together. It helps so much for me to have someone around who knows what I can do, but I know it can't always happen." She laughed for a moment and added, "I guess I can't always get everything the way I want it."

* * *

Dave was back at his desk on Monday morning and it felt that time had stood still. He laughed as he looked at the blue paperweight that had been a present from a close friend for a job well done. He had inadvertently knocked it sideways as he got up in a hurry to join Roy on their assignment. He remembered at the time he thought that he'd have to clean up his desk when he got back; it had become too cluttered. Well, now, today, Monday morning he decided that it was the first job he was determined to do. It only took a few minutes to rearrange, discard and reshuffle several items. He felt better. Smiling at the paperweight in its proper position, he was glad to be back to get things in order again.

Sergeant Brady called his usual early Monday morning staff meeting and Dave found himself in familiar surroundings with his fellow officers.

"First, we have to welcome Dave back and it'll take all of us to keep him in line. He's on desk duty only. So pick his brain all you want, but he doesn't get to go anywhere yet."

Dave laughed. "That's true, but I get reassessed in another two weeks and I'm hoping to go up a notch by then."

"Glad it's going good, buddy," said one of the officers.

"The steps are slow right now, I know," said Dave, "but it's the safest way to go and I'm feeling pretty good right now."

"So we don't want to do anything to jeopardize it, right?" said the sarge.

They all agreed.

"I've been given some new information that I need to pass along. Our three suspects are in the process of hiring lawyers with some input from The Right Side Group, I understand. It may take a week or even two before they are satisfied with their representation. So we've been asked to leave them alone until then."

"Then I guess we have to leave them alone," said Tom. "Can't take a chance of screwing up everything by being too anxious, right?"

"That's right. And we don't want them getting off on some technicalities," said the sarge. "It's been suggested to me that this announcement was made in hopes that we'll cross over that line and give them reason for an appeal and a whole lot of other issues. So, here's what we're going to do. No police officer, detective, lawyer, consultant, prosecutor or anybody from the legal profession on our side can even see them until the lawyer situation is resolved and then we can't even get near them without their lawyers being present. It's the safest way. And the commissioner was very strong in his language on this one. We know we have to get them off the streets, so we have to tread very lightly right now. Understood?"

They all nodded. It was an important statement.

The sarge continued. "But when they've got their legal team in place, then we can start with the two newer members who are considerably less dedicated than some of the others and see what we can come up with. They might be willing to give us information for a plea deal, but until then, and I stress again, until then, no one goes near them. Understood?"

They all nodded again.

Jim asked, "Do we have any idea how long it will take for them to get their legal representation in place?"

"That's the tricky thing. They've told me the defense will delay this process and probably ask for more time as much as they can. We may even have to take them before a judge to force them to make a decision."

"Why?" asked Roy.

"Because the longer they take the more chance there is that we'll get frustrated and make a mistake that they can use against us ... or at least use in favor of their clients. We're playing with some pretty tough customers here, so we have to watch our every move. I can't emphasize this enough. The commissioner wants to be positive that every officer understands, that we stay away from them at this time. So, are we all in agreement?"

"Absolutely," said Dave and the others nodded.

The meeting broke up, but Dave stayed behind for a moment and then closed the door.

"If this is the way it's going to play out right now, there's no reason for Sammi to delay her other assignment in Hartford."

The sarge had been talking to Ben Collier so he was well aware of what was going on in the murder investigation.

"No, she might as well go. We don't know how long this'll take."

Dave nodded and then let the sarge know about the arrangement for Sammi to come home on most weekends.

"That's great. If we desperately need her, we can get her on the weekend or even keep her for an extra day or two. Ben would understand that."

"I'm sure he would. He's glad she's coming at all."

"Okay, we're all on the same page then. I think Ben has a real mystery on his hands. And I think there's much more to it than the murder of a senator." He looked over at Dave and added, "Just a gut feeling."

"We do, too. I'd like to be in both places myself, but I'm stuck. However, Sammi can help them out."

"I'm sure she can. She's one efficient person."

Sergeant Brady looked at Dave and half-smiled as he waited. Dave had the feeling that he thought Dave would say something more about her methods, but he didn't. Then the futile look crossed his mind as he continued.

"I know that Ben's got a real problem out there, but we do, too. All these difficult cases are hitting at the same time. This Right Side Group is a bunch of nuts and we have to clip their wings big time. We've lost enough officers to them."

"I hope this is the situation that does them in."

"And we have to follow the rules on this one. If we give them any ammunition at all to question or put on the front page of every newspaper and TV show, we might not be able to put them away for very long. I wasn't kidding when I said the commissioner is sweating this one out."

"I think we all are," said Dave as he got up to leave.

"Good point," said the sarge. "We've got to play this one by the rules."

* * *

Dave was still able to beat Sammi home from work. His driver dropped him off about five o'clock and he knew that Sammi was clearing up a lot loose ends this week; he didn't expect her home yet. Even though she thought she had another week to go, she started early in getting ahead of her game.

He was thinking that she'd probably leave this Sunday. He didn't like it. He never liked it when she was on some assignment by herself. Oh, he knew that Ben and Jeff would be with her, but it wasn't the same. He wanted to be there. He was her number one confidant and he liked that position. When she was on interviews, she could stumble on such interesting and important information, and being a part of that process was exciting. He never knew which details could turn a case around until she came up with some seemingly little clue, one that others may have ignored if they weren't paying attention, but one which she held as valuable in her notes. She didn't ignore or overlook anything that came her way through the thought world. She had told him that it might not make sense now, but experience proved to her that it would play right into the verification process later on. Everything needed to be acknowledged.

Dave knew she'd be calling him every night from Hartford, sometimes even in the middle of the day if she needed an objective opinion from someone who knew her ability. But it wasn't the same as being there. He drew a deep breath and waited. He had to clear his mind. He had to get himself under control. This was his life with Sammi; many times she was called away to help in difficult crimes. He knew that. He accepted that, but he didn't have to like it. He was almost finished beating himself up about this situation that he had no control over, when he heard her car pull into the garage. He didn't want her to know how he felt. He tried to keep it hidden. He didn't want to put any extra stress on her before she left.

"Hi honey," she said as she walked into the living room, "you don't even have the TV on and you're not reading the newspaper. Is something bothering you?"

He smiled and turned to look at her. She'd read his expression and then she'd know.

"I'm fine, but come and sit with me for a bit."

He put his arm around her and told her the update he'd received at the station. This would mean that she could go to Hartford by Sunday night.

He knew that now she would understand his mood, which was somewhere between self-induced depression with a hint of loneliness and unique pride in what she was able to accomplish.

"Don't forget I'll be coming home on weekends and I'll be calling you for your opinion on some of the stuff I find out."

"I know I'm being selfish, but I don't care. What I really wish is that the two of us were going out there together as we originally planned to do. I'd like to be in on that case."

"But this case here in Scranton needs you, too. I think it's good that you'll be on one case and I'll be on the other one. Then we'll both get instant updates."

"That's true. Guess I never thought of that. But we're a team and I like to work that way."

"And we'll still be a team."

She turned to look at him and he knew she was right. He was simply in a mood tonight.

"Just ignore me tonight. I don't know what's the matter with me."

"Maybe it has to do with your first day back at work. Were you disappointed that you'd have to wait a while before interrogating those suspects?"

"In a way. I really thought we'd be able to get to them and with you around we'd definitely get some new leads. But, we have to follow protocol. The commissioner is hot on this one and doesn't want any mistakes. So that's it for now."

"New stuff comes in everyday; you don't know what tomorrow will bring."

"That's true," he said as he hugged her. "Let's get together with some of the others on Friday or Saturday night. We need to give you a good sendoff."

He saw her smile. He was trying to shake his mood and he would. Tomorrow might bring other interesting specifics.

CHAPTER V

Sammi cranked her neck around as far as she could as the plane taxied out onto the runway. She kept Dave in her sight as long as possible and then had to give up and sit upright, take a deep breath and realize she was on her own again, at least for a while. It seemed strange in a way; they were always there for each other. Yet she had to admit that other times she rather liked being alone. It gave her more thinking time, more feeling time and precious moments of connection to her thought world. Being alone was a precious commodity to her.

She was used to the charter jets by now, and they made her life much easier. She could arrive at the airport fifteen minutes before takeoff; that's all that was required. Sometimes the jet actually waited for her. It was unusual for her to be the only passenger in the Blue Bell Air Piper Chieftain, which had room for ten passengers and was a perfect fit for the FBI, but today, she was alone and didn't mind it at all. She smiled remembering her first time on this charter jet. She was returning from Philadelphia to Scranton and another FBI agent had driven her and Bill Halley to the airport. She tried to hide her apprehension as they approached a plane that was incredibly smaller than she had imagined. It was one of the propjets that this particular FBI group used regularly and, although they tried to prepare her beforehand in words and explanations, her fear was showing for all to see.

"Don't worry," said Jeff. "It's sturdier than some of the larger planes and once you're used to it, I'll bet you'll like it even more than the larger ones."

She felt embarrassed as she responded. "It just looks so small."

"Well it is in comparison, but that's all. Bill here takes this flight all the time and he appreciates it by now. Besides, you'll seldom be alone."

She smiled, embarked with apprehension, as she couldn't quite shake her nervousness. After being seated for a few minutes, she surprised herself and relaxed. It was quiet and peaceful not to have to listen to all the chatter of other passengers, who were somewhat noisy and excited about their journey.

Bill said, "We all felt that way at first; in time, you'll love it."

She did. It didn't take long before this was her preferred way to travel. She was as relaxed as she would be on any other larger airline. There was the usual tension, but that was all.

She smiled remembering those first days. Now she was a seasoned traveler and it was Dave who had trouble getting used to her going away. She remembered today the resigned look on Dave's face as he slowly walked her toward the plane.

"Okay, here we go again, but you'll be home on Friday."

"Absolutely, and I'll probably be talking to you everyday."

"You've got a job to do and they need your help. I'll be interested to find out what this case is all about."

"So will I. At least I'll find out the basics, as far as the police are concerned and I'll probably find out what Ben and Jeff feel about the direction this case is taking. I wonder what they're planning to do."

Then they were at the plane. He gave her one final kiss, a hug and then she boarded. She always hated those moments; they seemed so awkward, but they happened to everyone. She hated the immediate emptiness she felt when something was finally over. Then the plane took off and her feelings settled in. She knew that some wives and husbands chose to take separate vacations, but they hadn't reached anything close to that yet. Somehow she didn't think they would.

Settling in her seat and getting comfortable almost wasn't worth it; the flying time to Hartford, Connecticut was barely thirty minutes. It was as if the plane went up in the air, looked around for a few minutes and started its decent immediately. Yet it was over one hundred and fifty miles, so driving wasn't an option. Because of the short distance, she had waited until Monday morning to leave. The charter jet made it easy to go back and forth quickly so she hoped to be helpful in both places as needed. She didn't feel that she was handling too much. Her mind and persona was happiest when it was involved and occupied.

* * *

Disembarking from the plane, she realized that her right foot had barely touched the ground before she heard Ben Collier's voice.

"Just like old times," he said. "I'm really glad to see you."

"That goes for me, too," said Jeff Slade.

"Having the two of you waiting for me is like old times, isn't it? I've rather missed our working association."

Ben said, "And we sure need your expertise around here. Are you up for breakfast? I thought we'd grab a bite and then we could get you up to speed on this case. I don't even know what to call this deception, except Jeff and I both think that this hobo is a scapegoat that can't even help himself. He's out in left field somewhere and seldom comes back to reality except for a few minutes at a time. And if this is his behavior and capability, well that's another reason why we don't think he could have committed this murder."

Jeff added, "And no one, even the police can figure out what possible motive he could have had. He has enough mental problems that would prohibit him from even thinking clearly. But the prosecutors say they'll come up with some type of personal reason."

"Seems like they're grabbing at straws to get someone in custody, right? I'd guess that they believe they need to pacify the public."

"For sure, but what scares me," said Ben, "is that there's some person or a subversive group out there who actually killed this senator and I'm sure they had a criminal reason to do it. We need to find out who they are and get them out of circulation as fast as we can."

At this point, Sammi only listened. She was hungry and trying to concentrate on what two rather excited FBI agents were telling her. As they sat down at the restaurant table, she took a deep breath. Ben took notice.

"My God, we haven't given you a chance to breathe. Let's eat first and then we'll start from the beginning telling you what the police have told us. We don't want to overwhelm you at the beginning."

Sammi smiled. "That's okay. I need to get up to speed fast if I'm going to be of help."

"And you will," Ben said, "but I'll give it to you in logical order and then we can discuss our theory. Believe me, it won't take very long. The police don't know much and aren't even investigating anyone else. The prosecutors seem to be totally absorbed in trying to get this person to fit the crime. It's really total chaos right now."

"So you two are assigned to the case and have access to what we'll need?"

"That's right. We can question anyone and investigate all we want. The police have their orders not to hamper us in any way. Actually, they don't want to. As far as I could tell they've been cooperative because they have no idea where to go with this case."

Sammi shifted in her chair and took a large sip of coffee. Jeff leaned forward on his elbows as he began. Sammi thought that he still looked young for his age and his light brown hair and blue eyes went a long way to create that affect. Some didn't take him seriously at first. Ben Collier, on the other hand, looked all business and seriousness with his more sophisticated demeanor and his serious dark eyes. He definitely seemed like the older brother although they were close in age. She thought they made a striking pair.

Jeff began. "To what we've been able to find out from the police is that everyone is convinced that this hobo is the killer. It only took two days to weed him out from the rest of the community with this gun on his person. And he had a bloody handkerchief in his pocket. Not sure, what that has to do with anything, but they're testing it now. I mean the senator was shot from fairly close range, maybe some twenty or thirty feet, not bludgeoned or killed with a knife, yet since he had this item on his person they think it's evidence."

Ben said, "We both think the blood will turn out to be his. To what I've heard it was older blood, more than a few days' old so that doesn't make sense."

"First," asked Sammi, "where was the senator killed?"

"Mike was killed as he left the Connecticut Convention Center in downtown Hartford. He was there at a fundraiser and had just finished up as he left for his limousine. There's quite a few steps to come down on the outside of the building, but he had his bodyguards with him and they were on the way to his limousine that was parked right at the bottom of the stairway. He only took about three steps onto the sidewalk and someone shot him twice, once in the back part of his head and another in his back shoulder area."

"You said the shooter was close. Was there only one shooter? Were the bullets from the same gun?"

"They had to be no more than twenty to twenty-five feet away. The two shots were in quick succession, so we don't know for sure. Rumors are that a car sped away quickly from the scene, but that was before anyone knew what happened. The bullets are still being tested."

Sammi said, "I doubt if this hobo was in that car. Why aren't they broadening the search?"

Jeff said, "Good question. Nothing about this entire scenario makes sense."

"So no one got a license plate or description of the car, right?"

"That's right. Everything happened too fast. In fact, I think it took a few seconds before anyone realized that Mike was shot and by then this car was gone. The immediate response was the shock that Mike had actually been hit and by the time that realization came forward and people looked around it was too late to get any information about the car or anything else unusual."

"Probably was strange to be at the scene of the crime," said Sammi.

"Yeah, I can imagine," said Jeff. "I heard that for some reason he went down slowly so no one even knew within that first critical moment that he'd been shot, let alone killed."

Sammi looked dumbfounded. "You mean Mike gets shot and it plays out in slow motion so that the car has time to get away before anybody realizes what happened? What about security cameras? A lot of those hotels have some type of surveillance, right?"

"We've been waiting on that. The police are definitely dragging their feet on this one because they believe the killer has been arrested."

Sammi smiled. They both looked at her. "I was thinking that Dave wouldn't work that way."

"Right, and neither would we," said Ben. "And you're just in time today to come with us. This'll be our first chance to view the surveillance tapes and we plan to get a copy so we can study them."

"Exactly where is this convention center?" Sammi asked.

"It's in downtown Hartford close to the Connecticut river. There's always a lot of activity in the area so even a car pulling away fast wouldn't attract that much attention until later. Now they all believe it was significant."

"And they believe this hobo was in this car?"

"I don't know. I made you a copy of the report and you can look it over tonight. It's quite skimpy I think, but it's all we've got. There are details about the senator, his position, where he fell, what time it was, people in the vicinity and the wounds he got. But there isn't much about anyone's theories regarding how or why this was done."

"That seems strange. Don't these reports usually go into some suggestions as to why the crime was committed?"

"Usually, yes, but this one doesn't. No one can think of a reason why this hobo would have committed this crime. They think he's a babbling nut, but since he was carrying the gun, they've jumped to the conclusion that he must be the one who pulled the trigger. So nothing is stated about the possibility of anyone else committing the crime."

* * *

Leaving the restaurant and heading toward the middle of town, gave Sammi a feeling of expectancy. They decided that they would walk around the crime scene, as it would give everyone a sense of being there. Ben and Jeff had been there briefly the day before, but they both knew that walking around with Sammi would trigger more questions and suspicions. In addition, Sammi wanted to take advantage of their familiarity with the area, and therefore feed her need to feel part of the scene.

Hartford was the capital of Connecticut and as such took on an importance of its own. With one of its own state senators gunned down on its streets, the city itself called for justice. It wasn't only the citizen's appetite for revenge either, because all involved realized that the total atmosphere of the place, life for years to come and the entire history of the metropolitan area would be affected forever and nothing could change that fact.

Hartford wasn't a large city, merely one hundred and thirty thousand people and the third largest city in the state. At four hundred years old, it was among the oldest cities in the United States and one of Mark Twain's favorites as he was heard to say, "Of all the beautiful towns it has been my fortune to see, Hartford is the chief."

Hartford did have its years of relative stagnation, but with the Connecticut Convention Center opening in 2005 and the Science Center following shortly after, there were ambitious landscaping projects attempting to rejoin the riverfront to the downtown district.

Standing quietly while looking at the Convention Center from a short block away, Sammi couldn't even imagine how huge it was. Ben saw the questions on her face and answered.

"It's about 540,000 square feet and if you look over there," he said pointing to the river, "that's the Connecticut River. And you can see that the Marriott Hotel is attached to center so it gave the gunmen a lot of walking space to discover exactly where the senator was and from which door he would leave."

Sammi took note. "With so many people in and around the area, no one would question anyone walking around; it was a perfect set up.

As they approached the area, she saw that the yellow 'Do Not Cross' tape was still there.

"They won't take that down for a while," Ben said. "I understand they're thinking of adding some sort of plaque or acknowledgement to him in time. But for now, you can see the position of the body when it went down and ..."

"What are you people doing crossing this line? Didn't you see the yellow tape? Don't you know that yellow tape means to stay out of this area," said one of the security officers walking over in obvious anger and agitation. His body language was quite excited and his arms began flapping instantly and didn't halt for a second until Ben took action. He took out his credentials and the officer backed off immediately putting his hands in the air. "Sorry, I didn't know."

"You're just doing your job; we understand," Ben said.

When someone else tried to enter the area, he pushed them back as well. They reacted in anger seeing other people inside the area. The officer looked over in disgust, but handled the situation effectively. He came back for a moment and said, "People want to examine this gory, horrific scene and take pictures no less. I think it's kind of sick in a way, but it's my job to keep them away."

"I don't envy you," said Jeff as he watched him walk away.

Sammi realized that the area where the senator had died was actually quite small. When you left the railed stairway and stepped onto the sidewalk, it only took a few more steps to get to the curb where his limousine waited. Someone had been quite meticulous to be in the area where he would only have a split second or two to make his move.

"Anyone figure out the direction of the bullet? The angle and impact could be quite important and telling," Sammi said.

"We don't have ballistics back yet, but his bodyguards confirmed that the shots came from the left side, so," Ben said as he turned around to point to the exact area, "They don't think it could have been much further than that second lamppost over there. I've been assuming that's where the car was parked."

"Does that angle fit?" she asked.

"We think so, but we're waiting for other results to confirm."

She nodded. It was still early in the game and the details were slow in coming. Still the parameters were in play and that could be enough.

"So where do they think this vagrant was at?"

"They have no idea and that's another peculiar thing. We know there was this car in the area that sped away, but it was about ten thirty at night and not too many people are in this area walking around at that time. Yet they still believe this hobo was here doing the killing. It's not even logical, but they won't let it go."

"All because of the gun," she said, "and most likely it was a plant."

"Sure it was, and it was probably wiped clean. We're told we should be getting all this information later today or tomorrow, except for ballistics. They may not be finished yet.

The report itself will be available for everyone by late this afternoon."

Sammi was still looking around the area trying to get an impression etched in her mind. So many thoughts were coming at her, some were impressions that both Ben and Jeff had on their minds.

"Okay, then, when can we get to see this suspect?"

"Not until Wednesday morning. Something tricky is going on because we have been given access, but he's undergoing various psychiatric and mental examinations so he's not available to us right now. I'm real curious to find out the results of those tests."

Sammi looked over at both Ben and Jeff curiously.

Jeff said, "Well you know that results of mental tests can easily be manipulated, sometimes to an unbelievable degree. I need to tell you again, Sammi, that when we talked to this guy he was as outside the wall of reality as I've ever seen. I know that people can fake it, but we saw him twice. He isn't even close to being rational, at least not the way most of us see it."

"Yeah, and he's not an alcoholic," said Ben, "and that's another strange thing. Many of these hobos who seem to be in outer space have taken risky drugs over time or have had years of drinking hard liquor, but this guy doesn't belong to any of those categories. We heard he tested clean on all counts."

"Here's the thing," said Sammi. "I need to see him to make my own assessment. I need to get the feel of him as a person, and see what I come up with. If it's the same as the both of you, we'll probably have to be the ones to start looking in another direction."

"Looks that way to me," said Ben. "Certainly none of the current investigators plan on extending themselves in any way. They think this one is a slam dunk."

"Has anything else strange happened to the senator lately, or even to his family? You know, like any threats or strange events?"

Ben said, "I know we have to start questioning the family. I was waiting a bit after the funeral, especially since they believe that this was a crazy killing done by this hobo. That makes everything sad, but palatable, especially if he's considered deranged."

"But it doesn't sound like the prosecutors want him to be insane, right?"

"That's right because then they couldn't prosecute him. The prosecutors are walking their own tight rope. For now, I'm going to get you settled in. We do have the room next to you at the Marriott, right over there. Later I want to get all the results we can get our hands on and then discuss them over dinner. Then we'll have to decide what course to take."

"Okay, but give me a few more minutes around this crime scene. I need to get a better feel of it."

"Sure, we want to pace again to where we saw the car and get an idea of how far away it was. See you in a few minutes."

Sammi wasn't sure why she needed to go back to the crime scene. Yet she had such a strong draw to the area where the body fell that she couldn't deny it. She went back and stood in the exact spot that Mike Stedman went down. For a moment, she was in a daze. She felt drawn into something she couldn't describe. Being mesmerized by the outline of where the body lay, a sudden coldness enveloped her. She stood frozen to the spot.

Then it happened. As she looked down to the position of where Mike would have been after he was killed, she saw in her mind a picture of the body and the face of this person she'd never seen. It was almost as if he twisted his body to look up at her and it gave her a chill. She would have walked away quickly, but she wasn't able to move. Then this Mike sort of turned to look at her straight in the eye and said, "Melanie Brooks; she knows something." Sammi heard these words the same way that she heard people's thoughts, loud and clear from mind to mind. She heard the words aloud and there was no denying the message. Mike Stedman thought that someone named Melanie Brooks had knowledge of his murder, perhaps was even involved.

She didn't know how long she stood there, but it was Jeff Slade's voice that startled her back to attention. She almost felt embarrassed and hoped she didn't offer any clue as to what had just happened to her.

"Sammi, are you ready? We'd like to get to the police station to view those tapes. We've got time to make it today."

"Sure, I'm ready," she said, feeling a new surge of strength come back into her character. "I'd like to see those tapes and compare it with what we've seen today."

"Exactly my idea," Ben said. "Now that we've seen the crime scene, the surveillance tapes should make more sense to us."

* * *

The police station in Hartford was a little smaller than the one in Scranton, which Sammi was familiar with, but it had all of the same services available. Ben was obviously recognized and given quick access to the reports and the tapes. They picked a quiet room and sat down ready to concentrate on these important surveillance tapes. They played them twice to get a total background and overhead view before they even slowed them down to get a more specific and detailed account of what had occurred.

"There's the shadow of a car leaving, but you can't tell anything about it, not even the color. And," Ben said pointing to one frame area that he had stopped, "this is where they believe the shots were fired from, exactly the same position of this car and then you can see the shadow of a car leave. Damn, too bad we didn't get a better view of this area."

"Doesn't leave much room for any mistakes. These shooters would have to be crack shots and I know they probably were, but they couldn't even get a good sight from there. In the area where Mike came out, there wasn't any lamppost within five feet so with a bunch of people coming out at the same time, how could they know which one was Mike? He had five bodyguards around him and it was dark; come on now. Something doesn't fit here."

Jeff scratched his head. "Nothing about this makes sense. And where would this hobo have been? He doesn't even walk solid and steady. He would have had to get away fast and go somewhere to hide. They keep saying he worked alone and there was no conspiracy. Why can't these people think logically about this? The hobo theory doesn't fit at all."

"Let's go on a bit further," said Sammi. "There were other people around just before he got hit. Not sure where they came from at that time of night, but notice … stop the frame. Okay, look here. Two seconds ago, no one was in this area here," she said pointing to a small area on the left side of the senator, "and now within one or two frames in this tape there are several people here on this left side area. Where did they come from?"

"Good question. I think we need blow ups of these frames. Let me see if we can get that to happen; probably not today, but hopefully by tomorrow. We need a better look at this. Good catch, Sammi."

She added, "This would put these people much closer to the senator, within five or ten feet. If one of them was the shooter, then the distance theory is wrong."

"Well, that's what it is, just a theory right now. Maybe the report will give us an idea of how far away he was from his killer."

"We need to identify those people. Can we do this?" she asked.

"We should be able to when the frames are blown up. And, we need to get some detailed information about that area. Maybe we can get it by going back there again when we figure out where these people were standing; I mean I want to know *exactly* where each one of these people were standing in relation to Mike."

"That's something we've got to know. The angle of the bullet, how far away was the shooter from Mike and how many people were in that little perimeter?"

Ben said, "We'll wait until tomorrow. I want to see these frames blown up and then maybe the computer system can give us details of the area that we need. We could get a virtual scenario that's just as good as being there and we could go over it as many times as we need. I think this is our starting place. We have to get this settled in our minds before we can move forward. And we're the only ones who would be interested in this theory right now."

They agreed they were finished for the day with Ben stopping at the desk with his new requests. They'd be back early tomorrow and while they waited for the new tape surveillance, they could utilize the computer system, which had been an early request.

* * *

Sammi was happy to have some time to relax in her hotel room. She unpacked and stared out the window for a moment.

She had a view of the crime scene and believed Ben and Jeff had the same luxury. A high profile case was never her favorite. She liked the quiet ones where she could work in secrecy. Here she felt that all would be watching her as she worked side by side with the FBI. This was not her favorite plan of action, but also not a decision for her to make. She had about two hours to herself before she'd meet Ben and Jeff in the Marriott dining room. That gave her time to relax some and call Dave.

Dave was not at his desk so she wasn't able to talk to him, but Jim talked to her for a moment.

"Don't imagine you've had much time to do anything yet?"

"No, but I did see the murder scene and got some perspective. We were even allowed to see the surveillance tapes late this afternoon, but they're inconclusive at best. Ben wants to have parts of them blown up; we all think that would help."

"Seems to me that you accomplished a lot for the first day."

"Doesn't seem like it. They say we can't see that suspect until Wednesday, so tomorrow I hope to find some way to get around some of the people involved in this investigation. We're going to be in the station anyway and I hope to meet some of these investigators. That's where I could possibly find out something."

"Understand," he said, "you have to be around people and interact with them before you can pick up information. Well, relax because you just arrived. There's only the three of you working together on this, right?"

"Looks that way. Everyone else believes the hobo did it and I think we'll have to do our own investigating; I think we'll be on our own."

"Will you get privy to all of the information and equipment that you need?"

"It seems that way, but we'll see. Tomorrow should tell us a lot."

"Look, I've got to run. I'll tell Dave you called and update him."

"Thanks."

* * *

Disappointed at Dave's unavailability, she turned her mind back to the crime scene that she had recently seen. Being in that area was surreal in itself. The experience she'd had was a step up for her and she knew it. She'd never received information in that way before. Although she was apprehensive, she knew that she was ready or she wouldn't have been given a new technique. What more was in store for her? Her curiosity was peeking, but her experience revealed all would come to her at the right time.

The position of the shooter's car that Ben had alluded to bothered her. She didn't think they could possibly have had a clear view from that spot, especially at night. There had to be another answer. Even though a car had sped away from the area at that exact moment, it could have been by chance and the shooter could have been somewhere else. She didn't want to limit the possibilities. She had to keep an open mind. How did someone manage to shoot him twice under those circumstances?

It did cross her mind that there may have been two shooters hiding in two different places. Ballistics could confirm or deny that scenario acknowledging whether both bullets were from the same gun. If not, that sounded like a conspiracy and one that was well planned. Her head was spinning; so many new possibilities were infiltrating her thought process. *What was this all about? Why target this senator? Did this mean that some of the other senators were in danger as well?* The police officers and prosecutors would only focus in one direction and that was another strange trend. *Why not look further? Wasn't this hobo a shaky suspect at best, even with the possession of a gun?* She'd never witnessed law enforcement and legal personnel acting in such a targeted manner before. They presumed he must be guilty and ignored anything else. Well, soon she'd find out more. She was somewhat anxious to read and study the reports. She still had thirty minutes before dinner and decided to utilize her time, but the telephone rang. It was Dave.

"Hi honey. Sorry I missed you. Everything okay?"

"It is. I have a nice room with Ben on one side and Jeff on the other. I'm in the room right between them."

Dave laughed. "That's good. What did you do today?"

She told him of her theories so far.

"You've got to wait, Sammi. It's too soon to figure out anything yet, but the crime scene does make you think. If they didn't have a clear view … it doesn't make much sense, does it?"

"No, it doesn't and remember the murder happened about ten thirty at night. I'm going to talk Ben into going back there at the same time of night and sit in a car to find out if we could possibly shoot anybody coming out of the Convention Center. It doesn't seem so to me. "

"Right; be interesting to see. And reliving the actual crime scenarios always helps."

"I got that from you. I never realized before how valuable it could be until we did it a couple of times together. Now I realize that I need to do it this time just to be sure. After that I think we'll be looking for another place where the shooter or shooters were."

"Right."

"Enough about that. How're you doing? Anything new at your end?"

"No, I was out grasping at straws with Roy and Tom today. We were backtracking on some previous stuff. This Right Side Group has always been secretive so it's slow going at best."

"They're letting you away from your desk?"

"Only for routine work."

"When will you interrogate those suspects? Any idea yet?"

"Not a clue, but it'll be a while. And when that happens maybe we can pull you back here."

"Shouldn't be a problem. I'm meeting Jeff and Ben for dinner here in the hotel. I have a copy of the report file but haven't read it yet. It's not very long. We'll discuss it at dinner, I'm sure. Hopefully it'll reveal something."

Dave laughed, "My little detective wife. Remember all those years ago when I wanted to hire you and you said no. I guess it was meant to be for you after all."

Sammi laughed as well. "And I do enjoy a good mystery. Actually, I enjoy solving them."

"Okay, then I'd better let you go. By the way, I hate getting into an empty bed. I do miss you."

"Oh, that's sweet. I love you, Dave Patterson. Talk to you soon."

"Love you, too."

Sammi hadn't forgotten about her new experience today at the murder scene. She decided not to tell Dave at this time. She didn't know what it was all about yet, but she found herself excited at the prospect of being trusted with even more ability.

Evil Thoughts Kill Dreams/Drouillard

CHAPTER VI

Sammi walked through the rather luxurious lobby of one of the most beautiful hotels in Hartford. The enormity of the Marriott's lobby reminded her of what it must be like to walk into the Taj Mahal. It made you feel small, yet necessary and as she looked around, she took in all she could with the elaborate decorations, large striking pictures on every wall and the cozy arrangements of small sofas for private meetings or discussions. She marveled believing that these extravagant decorations were ideas in someone's mind at one time and then brought into reality. Thoughts were everything to her.

Ben had found a rather secluded table near the back of the welcoming restaurant that would give them privacy.

"I've already ordered you a glass of Piesporter. You need it after this today."

Sammi smiled. "Yes, I'm getting known for my glass of wine, but it's a great relaxer."

Ben got serious for a moment. "I called a few people at the 10th precinct ... that's the one we were at today and asked for the use of computer equipment tomorrow and they didn't seem nearly as congenial as they were before. Suddenly, they seemed a little hesitant with us monopolizing their equipment."

Jeff said, "I think it's more than that. I got the feeling that if we were ready to investigate from their point of view in an attempt to make their case more rock-solid, everything would be available and open to us. But when we turned on the surveillance tapes and asked for blowups of certain frames, then they began to get suspicious and I got the impression that they didn't like our interference. Now they think we're meddling where we don't belong."

Ben said, "I noticed that, too. We were supposed to have a computer specialist at our disposal whenever we needed one. I had made this request before we got here, but now they seem like they're backsliding on that, too. I don't want to get pushy here, but we are the FBI and I could get priority over them anyway. But we don't usually get the most experienced people by pushing our authority."

Sammi said, "So that could make everything more difficult for us."

"Well, yeah," said Ben, "we always need researchers and people to check out things so, I'm going to wait until tomorrow and see what kind of reception I get when I make my requests again in person, and then I'll decide what to do. We're going to need more help than just the three of us and we'll get it, one way or another."

"I'd like to be there when you go," said Sammi.

"It could get nasty. They have their way of doing business and if they're already miffed by what they call our interference, well ..."

"But that's when I can find out things. If they refuse, maybe I could pick up an idea or two as to why they're in this locked position."

Ben pursed his lips. "Okay, then," he said, "let's all get down there together tomorrow. We both know you're very good at reading people so that might be as helpful as anything else."

Sammi took a deep breath and was relieved, but didn't let it show. This is exactly what she needed; she needed to be around people involved in this case and find out what was on their minds. Tomorrow may be the beginning, for her anyway.

"Okay, then everyone read the report?" Ben asked.

"I didn't finish it. Dave called and I got sidetracked."

"That's okay," said Jeff. "There wasn't much in it anyway; nothing new that I noticed."

"Nor me. Really Sammi, it was pretty much what we talked about. Actually, I must admit I'm a little frustrated already and downright confused. What's the matter with these people? Don't they want to solve this crime? I mean I know they think they have it solved, but they've been really sloppy and we've got to find out why."

After a moment, he looked at Sammi and said, "You coming with us tomorrow might be the best idea. I'd like to talk to Sergeant Wyman; he's one of the officers who is adamant about this hobo committing the crime. Maybe he's behind us getting us sidetracked here. And I'd like to hear why he won't look anywhere else."

Jeff added, "He's the one everybody wanted to check with today before they made any commitment, even about approving our request about the surveillance tape. Why is he so hard nosed about this?"

"He must be hiding something," said Sammi. "This certainly isn't the way Dave and his group investigate crimes. They stay open right until the end and sometimes that's when the best evidence comes in. Well, you both know that."

"Something is starting to smell in this investigation and I don't understand it. First, I can't imagine who'd want to kill Mike in the first place. He was a very effective senator, no known enemies that anyone was aware of and utterly fair about everything."

Sammi said, "But simply being a public official could gather him enemies."

"That's true for most," said Ben. "Yet for some reason his type of position didn't antagonize people even if they were on the other side of the aisle. He seemed to be able to placate people. I mean, he was a Republican, but had many Democrats who sang his praises. He was that kind of a guy."

Sammi nodded. "And that's hard to do, but some politicians manage to do it."

"I think we'll find out that his murder wasn't related to politics at all, at least that's my gut feeling," said Ben. Then he got rather somber for a moment and said, "I'm really going to miss that guy ... he just had a way about him." Then he stopped, rather abruptly and looked down.

Sammi picked up a little more about their friendship in college and got a clear hint at the reason they had such a strong bond.

* * *

The next day started out routine, meeting for breakfast and heading over to the 10th precinct in Hartford by ten o'clock. Ben needed to meet with a number of people today. He wanted to know exactly what the presence of the FBI on this case meant to those in charge. Were they happy about the extra support? Maybe they pretended, but it seemed like some were rather displeased and would like to discourage them quickly. Yet he knew that wasn't going to happen. It made Ben dig his heels in even deeper; it made him more determined than ever, so much so that he wouldn't let go until some answers were forthcoming. And this had all happened within three days. If they had acted more open and welcoming, even if they were giving them false information, he probably would have had a better opinion of their group. This new attitude wasn't about to be accepted, although he might keep his methods hidden for a while.

Sammi noted the sternness and the solid placement of Ben's jaw as they walked together into the police station. Walking up to the desk, he first requested the surveillance tapes that were promised for this morning. They weren't ready; he was now told it would be at least a couple more days. To his inquiry of why, a simple answer of 'I don't know' was returned. He was visibly upset. Next, he asked about access to a computer and again told none were available at present, but probably would be later today. The third request for a computer expert was also denied. He asked for a superior.

Almost as if it had been expected, another officer appeared.

"What's the problem, Mr. Collier?" he asked.

Ben repeated all three of his requests and wanted to know the reason for the delays.

"There is no delay that was done on purpose. We're busy right now handling other cases and will get to your requests as soon as possible."

"I'd like to see Sergeant Fred Wyman," he said.

"He's in a meeting presently, but should be available in about one hour."

"I'll wait," said Ben to the irritation of the senior officer.

Sammi knew, as did Ben that this latest episode was to deter them to the afternoon or even to another day. Continuing postponements would hopefully irritate and frustrate them enough so that eventually they would give up and leave. Sammi couldn't believe they really thought this tactic would work. She'd heard a few disturbing thoughts already. This senior officer had quite a negative attitude toward anyone trying to investigate this murder. However, she felt that he was only following orders, although he was quite adamant with his attitude that they could handle affairs in Hartford and didn't need any outside interference.

Less than twenty minutes later, they were called into Sergeant Wyman's office. It would be reasonable to say that he wasn't happy to see them, but was trying to put up a pleasant front.

"Mr. Collier," he said as he turned around acknowledging the others but not by name, "I'm sorry you've been frustrated by having to wait for your information, but you must realize that this happens at all police stations when we get busy."

"I'd like to have a computer expert available to me and then we can handle our own affairs."

"But your affairs have to do with this jurisdiction, so you'd need to work with us."

"I planned to do just that, but it doesn't seem I'm getting any cooperation at all from any of you."

Now Sergeant Wyman let down his guard. Sammi knew he hated them being here digging up information that might land them onto one Melanie Brooks. It was all she could do to hold her position. This sergeant was into this murder; at least he was connected to the name that Mike Stedman had revealed to her. And he was trying to tap dance around the reasons for the delays. He slowly realized that discouragement and underhandedness wasn't going to deter these people.

"Why is the FBI so interested in this case? It seems to me that the FBI has many other matters on their plate. What's so important about this one? Is it because he was a senator?"

Ben looked over at Sammi with fury in his eyes. What was this person hiding? He would have liked to know that.

"The murder of any state senator will give rise to an investigation by the FBI, especially if the local police aren't following protocol. You aren't even attempting to do a basic investigation on this murder. You grabbed one person, a hobo, because he had the gun on his person. You must know by now it had to be a plant. This vagrant is just an easy one to blame right now and you know it."

"We do have the right guy and this case shouldn't be a problem for the FBI. You don't investigate all political murders; I know that. What's up with this one?"

At this point Ben stood up. He had heard what he wanted to know. These guys didn't want them jeopardizing their perfect murder solution. It was a fast simple case and they wanted to keep it that way. Ben didn't know why, but Sammi had her suspicions.

"If you had played this by the book and cooperated with us, you'd know what we were up to every step of the way, because we'd inform you. But now, you'll be in the dark. I don't know what you're hiding, but I'll find out and you'll wish that you'd used another tactic with us. We're done with you."

"But, but ..." he said as all three of them arose abruptly and walked out the door.

Ben was livid and yet he seemed rather calm as they walked out to the parking lot. He turned to Sammi who said, "Let me type up some notes. I got some ideas from them, but I need time to sort them out."

"Where are we going to get you a computer?" said Ben. "That's the bad part. Listen, give me a few hours; I have a few things to check out. We need to find you a place to work. Come to think of it, with their attitude, maybe this was for the best. They could have been overshadowing us and ruining our information, but I want to get to his superiors. This guy's on the take or involved in something."

Sammi smiled, "That I can definitely agree with."

Ben smiled as well. "I'll be glad to read your notes, but for now, I'll tell you what. Why don't you and Jeff go have coffee or look around or something, I've got some calls to make and then we'll have a direction, I'm sure. My superiors will have a fit about this, but I think I want to keep it covert for a bit. Let our Sergeant Wyman think that we calmed down and decided to back off some. Then he'll let his guard down. In the meantime, I'm going full force ahead as soon as I get the okay. For now, just write some notes down, Sammi. I'll get you access to a computer soon."

Ben went back to the hotel while Jeff and Sammi decided to have a cup of coffee, and take time to unwind a little.

"Wouldn't the hotel give us access to a computer for a while? I'd only need about an hour to type up these notes."

Jeff looked over at her. "I don't know how you do it, but we need your notes. Let's get back there and ask. I think you're right. Besides, I could say we need use of one and they would accommodate us I'm sure."

"Okay, then we'll get some of this pressure off of Ben. He was so uptight, more than you or I. He's anxious to get going on this case and can't seem to get started. He's apparently had a long history with this senator."

Sammi nodded; she knew what it was. Somehow, she felt in the dramatization of events that had happened today, he would find a moment to clue them in, probably at dinner.

* * *

The hotel was more than willing to give Sammi use of a computer anytime and for however long she needed it. Apparently, since they were checked into some of the more expensive rooms, they extended every courtesy available. She began working immediately and told Jeff she'd check with him as soon as she was finished. Jeff, in turn, decided to find Ben and see if he could be of assistance to him.

Sammi found that curious eyes constantly cast themselves in her direction as she tried to block them out of her atmosphere. She was more distracted than when she worked in the privacy of her own home. She had to focus; she had to center her attention on the work at hand. Finally, she managed to ignore those around her and work in her own world. It had to do with concentration and being perfectly focused in one area. Her grandpa was the one who would have totally understood.

She decided she had to put in the names that she'd heard in her report, hoping that Jeff and Ben would keep to their old standard of confidence, and not question her. The lines seemed drawn around her and they usually accepted her findings without further inquiry. She was counting on it this time. This was the beginning of discussing some very sensitive data and it was at times like these that she wished her particular group was around her, especially Dave. She needed to bounce her ideas off someone and it wasn't the same discussing it on the telephone. She did receive the information easily enough, but with adjustment, it could become more useful and that could only happen if she had someone around who understood what she was doing. However, she couldn't complain. She had worked for years alone. Now, however, she was spoiled in having Dave and the others around helping her to decipher her findings.

She finished her report in less than an hour, surprising even herself. Once she began to focus, it seemed that everything else simply melted away. She let Ben and Jeff know she was ready and they were at her door quickly, and anxiously.

"Don't worry," Ben said, "I'm not giving you a rough time and Jeff is getting used to you as well. I can't imagine what you've got for us, but I've some data as well."

Sammi smiled. "Who goes first?"

"I think I will," Ben said, "because in the past I know once you get started we can go on for hours. Besides, mine isn't lengthy."

She laughed. "Okay, what have you got?"

Jeff said, "Ben is actually being modest because I believe he's been very effective this time."

"Certainly hope so. What I did is contact some of my superiors alerting them to the strange runaround we're getting here. I needed to find out what was going on, but I wanted to keep this Sergeant Wyman in the dark. I think he's involved in something … I see you smiling Sammi. Looks like I made a good guess."

"I made the same one," she offered.

"Okay, that's good to know. What I'll be doing from now on is working with Captain Malik. Their direct lieutenant works in the same 10th Precinct building so we don't want anything too close to him. Captain Malik works out of the 15th precinct and that works better for us."

Sammi asked, "Isn't that unusual?"

Jeff said, "Not really. Hartford has their top people spread out; it's just the way they do business around here."

"But whenever they try to block us out," said Ben, "we're suspicious. Sometimes their noses get bent out of joint because they think we're going over their heads, and that's understandable; I might feel that way sometimes myself if I were in their spot. Yet trying to keep data hidden from us is an entirely different matter. They aren't interested in getting this crime solved. They think they have the killer and that's it. Yet their case isn't even logical nor does it have solid evidence, so that put up a red flag as well. The fact that Mike's record is clean and his background is spotless as well leaves us to wonder again; who would want to do this and why? And we'll never find out by being blocked this way."

"So this Captain Malik will cooperate with us?"

"Definitely, he's worked with the FBI before and had a small role in some areas of our business. He's not thrilled with what he heard about one of his sergeants and he's very curious. It's not the way they're supposed to work. Anyway, we'll still need our computer specialist, but I think we'll work with Julie."

Sammi perked up.

"She can stay in Scranton for now, but if we need her later on, we'll bring her here. We need an expert to dig out what we need and she'll do fine."

Sammi was proud. "She is good."

"Oh yeah," said Ben. "She's one of the best, and I know we can count on her."

* * *

Ben ordered some coffee and when it arrived, they sat around for a few minutes talking about how they'd go about getting what they'd need. It was hard working away from your basic area of business; so much detail had to be worked out. Usually they had everything they needed, but here ... well, soon they'd have it as well.

"Okay, Sammi, what were you able to find out?"

She handed her report to them; she had made two copies. She had about five typed pages and saw their expressions change with interest as they found important facts previously hidden to them. Both went through facial contortions with brows puckered and lips pursed at different moments. At times, they both stopped to look at her and wondered how she did this, but they no longer worried about it. When Sammi presented her reports, the facts were correct and they knew it.

"God, Sammi, this is unbelievable," said Ben. "So you picked up on Sergeant Wyman, too. But you also mentioned a Sergeant Cullins. I wonder how they're connected."

Sammi said, "I'm not positive that they are related, but I think they might be. My main interest here is finding out whom Melanie Brooks is. Maybe she's connected to the two of them and might be the reason for Mike's murder. I'm just guessing here, but Melanie Brooks will play a real important part in all of this; keep that in mind. I'm not saying she's the shooter, but she'd probably know who is or at the very least some of the main characters involved. So with the treatment we've received from Sergeant Wyman, I'm thinking they must have some kind of bond with her."

"And a good one," said Jeff. "We're the only ones working from the point of view that the hobo isn't the killer. I want to keep an open mind. Possibly he was involved in some way but he certainly didn't work alone."

"He certainly doesn't seem to have the mentality for it. Okay," said Ben, "we've got two problems here. First, is Mike's murder and the second is something underhanded in this police department. And I know that Captain Malik wants to find out about that as well."

"When can we get to see this hobo?" Sammi asked.

"We were told we could see him tomorrow so I'm going over there. If we get the run around this time, I'm not to make a fuss, but to report to Captain Malik and he'll make it happen. I think we're going to have a very angry sergeant on our hands."

* * *

On Wednesday, Sammi, Ben and Jeff walked into the 10th precinct expecting to have access to the hobo.

The officer at the desk answered courteously but with ill-placed authority. His name was Officer Hogan and he'd only been on this duty for a few months. He answered as expected. "I'm afraid that's not going to happen today. Sergeant Wyman left orders that our investigation came first and the suspect is presently being given psychological testing and won't be available until it is finished."

"How long will that take?"

"At least a week, maybe more. We need to get this testing finished in quick order; otherwise, our case could be compromised. You'll just have to wait your turn."

Ben kept his cool but was busy reeling in this misguided officer who possibly was only following Sergeant Wyman's orders and trying to hide private reasons for undermining the investigation.

"I don't believe this is your idea. I want to know whose idea it is to keep us away from the suspect."

You could tell officer was annoyed. He wanted to act like the man-in-charge, the one who was making the decisions and he didn't take kindly for his authority to be questioned.

"I can't give out that information, but the protocol remains the same. We get to him first and then we'll see about you."

His tone of voice and attitude had changed into both gloating and rejoicing as he turned away, looking down on all three of his self-determined rivals. Glancing toward Sergeant Wyman's office, he quickly nodded and seemed to click his steps in victory as he walked on without one backward glance.

The group turned around and left, went outside and Ben placed a call to Captain Malik.

"You three stay where you're at. I'll be there in fifteen minutes. Wait for me in the parking lot. I'll take care of this crap right now."

True to his word, the captain arrived within his time limit.

"Let me go in alone first. I want to see what's really happening. Stay close to the door and I'll signal for you when I want you."

From their strategically hidden positions, all could hear the Captain as he stepped up to the desk. The officer on duty almost fell over himself getting Sergeant Wyman.

"I wanted to see our hobo now and find out what you've been doing with him. Is he available?"

"Oh yes, he's just resting in his cell. He's very out of it mentally most of the time, babbling on about things that no one can figure out."

"I thought he was going for psychological tests."

"He did, but they were finished on Monday," said Sergeant Wyman proudly, not realizing how far down into the hole he'd dug himself.

Then the captain's attitude changed. He signaled for the FBI people to come in and the look on Sergeant Wyman's face was nothing but total alarm. He was in shock and knew he was in big trouble. The sweat and slight tremor in his arms and hands didn't leave any room for doubt.

"Why in the hell is he available for me and not for the FBI? Who the hell are you taking orders from around here?" He paused for a moment, but his anger and frustration didn't lessen. "I'm waiting for an answer."

"Well ... I ... just didn't think they should be allowed to see him and possibly ruin our case."

At first, the captain didn't even answer but carried a look of disbelief on his face.

"How'd you ever get to be a Sergeant-in-chief here? Certainly not by following orders. As of now, you're being relieved until I look further into this insubordination. We're all about solving cases and new points of view can only help all of us; you know that. I think there may be other reasons for your misbehavior and I intend to find out what they are."

"I'm sorry sir. I really thought I was doing the right thing."

"No, you didn't. You know our agenda, and it's the exact opposite of what you've been doing."

He called over the other officer at the counter. "Officer Hogan, as of now, you're in charge. These FBI agents will be given access and support every time they come in here. I think some of you forget that we're all supposed to be on the same side of the law."

He turned to Sergeant Wyman. "What are you still doing here? You're relieved of duty. You're suspended until I get some answers."

One very angry and livid sergeant gathered up some papers and prepared to move on. Beside his dejected demeanor was a worry and fear that couldn't be denied. He felt that he had put this entire operation in jeopardy and he'd be held responsible.

* * *

Sammi had picked up many details during this angry encounter. She'd picked up a few more names and enough to realize that a conspiracy was definitely in progress. Yet she didn't have it all figured out yet. What was this conspiracy about? Why did the senator have to be killed? And what part did Sergeant Wyman and Sergeant Cullins play? Was this a conspiracy for political gain or more of a private motive? She knew she had a lot of work to do. She also wondered how this hobo fit into all this. Actually, she realized that she hated to call him 'the hobo'. Someone must have figured out his name by now.

As they slowly walked down to the private room where they would be able to interview the suspect, Sammi, with notebook in hand, felt a strange kind of nervousness. She knew that she was on the edge of a discovery that would probably take her into a world that would be a new revelation. She didn't know why, but that's how she felt. This would definitely be the turning point in this case as far as she was concerned. She agreed with the perspective that this man was a scapegoat, but a scapegoat for what. That hadn't been determined. She hoped his thought world would give them all a clue.

CHAPTER VII

After choosing a seat around a large well-worn conference table, they were congenially offered coffee in a total turnaround of behavior than was previously afforded them. They waited less than five minutes before the door opened and in walked a shackled, frail-looking prisoner who definitely had no common thread in reality with the rest of the world. He barely had the ability to focus occasionally and he did talk to himself in undetectable syllables that weren't even complete words. There was a fear in his eyes as he looked from person to person and finally landed on Sammi's face as she tried a slight smile to put him at ease. He didn't react. He was in his own world. The only question on her mind was why.

His chains and handcuffs were removed and he seemed to relax slightly, but with an air that connoted he didn't really understand what was going on around him. Sammi immediately entered his world of thoughts that mostly remained at surface level, which gave her access to his thinking. This was more difficult than anything she'd encountered before. His thoughts were confused, incoherent, sputtering and jagged. Yet she knew one thing immediately. This man was no babbling idiot. He had command of the English language to a remarkable degree, but his thoughts and ideas for some reason didn't translate outward into coherent words and sentences. Within a short time, his thought world was beginning to make sense to her, but she had to walk a careful path with only Ben and Jeff here. Would they give her the lead in time and let her take over? She had to be careful. She was walking a tightrope.

Ben began slowly to get this man's attention, and he did succeed to a tiny degree.

"What's your name?"

He babbled for a moment or two and then said, "Mr. Jim."

"Mr. Jim, do you have a last name?"

"Last name?" he said, looking confused, disoriented and lost with eyes that held questions and no answers.

"Yes, I'm Ben Collier; this is Jeff Slade. You are Jim who?"

His focus left him. He went back into his own world for a moment. Then he focused again and said, "Mr. Jim." But that was all.

"How old are you, Mr. Jim?" asked Ben.

Mr. Jim simply looked at Ben with unfocused eyes that didn't seem to have a meeting point.

"Where do you live?"

Same type of response; Mr. Jim didn't seem to have any thoughts of his own. It seemed that he could be led slightly, but to come up with an answer from his own thoughts didn't seem to be possible.

Frustrated Ben shrugged his shoulders and turned to Jeff. He tried as well with the same line. He got the same answer. By this time, they'd been talking with him for more than five minutes asking the same questions over and over in order to get to a starting point of conversation. Yet they couldn't even get him to focus enough to give his last name.

Ben said, "And they think this man shot Mike. Somebody is playing games here. And why? I don't know what to say about this man, but the report says that no one has been able to get any semblance of logic out of him yet. No one has been able to communicate with him."

"May I try?" said Sammi.

They both turned to look at her. Ben said, "Sure, give it a try."

Sammi's thoughts were all over the place speculating here and guessing there, but she did have his thoughts to work with. Although his thoughts were fearful and aloof, they were so much more sensible than the incoherent language he was presenting to the world. Even though she had this benefit, she was still playing a guessing game. This man's mind was in total shock and she wondered how long it had been that way. Did his mind blank out after he'd been arrested? Did something happen to this man sometime in the distant past that could have caused him to revert from an intelligent person to this state of confusion and perplexity? Her gut feeling was that he'd been hurt in some way, maybe a hemorrhage or serious concussion, one that needed medical assistance that he'd never received. For now, that was only a guess. She planned to ask questions to his thoughts and not his outer words. Her only pleasure at this moment was that it would probably confuse the hell out of Ben and Jeff.

She turned and looked at him, but he didn't focus on her, or on anyone else. He was thinking about his name, Mr. Jim and he liked it.

Sammi decided to answer that thought and said, "I think Mr. Jim is a nice name." That's all she said, but first he looked down and then he turned to look at her. Everyone noticed that for a quick instant, he realized someone was there.

Sammi listened to his thoughts. *I don't know where I am. I'm not home. I haven't been home for a long time. I don't even know where home is anymore. My head is sore. It's always sore, but I'm used to that. I have to stay here where I'm safe. I can't talk to these people. But I do like my name, Mr. Jim.*

Again Sammi continued. "I like the name Mr. Jim. Do you like it?"

There was a long pause. Then this man who'd been totally unaware of anyone since he'd been arrested and completely oblivious to anyone around him looked at Sammi and said, "I like Mr. Jim." He seldom answered a direct question, but muttered his own unrelated answers.

He spoke clearly and it was obvious that he was answering her question. Both Ben and Jeff were impressed. Yet Sammi knew that she had a long way to go. She didn't know if she could get this man to actually communicate with her. He groaned often and rubbed the back of his head.

"Does your head hurt, Mr. Jim?" she asked.

Ben and Jeff were in total confusion. They didn't know where Sammi was going or how she planned to get there, but there was a hint of communication with this man and based on the reports they had read, that was a huge step forward.

Mr. Jim nodded.

"Sometimes it's hard to think and talk when you're head hurts, right?"

He nodded again. Then he said a strange thing, "We cannot part with our friends. We cannot let our angels go." Again, he repeated, "We cannot part with our friends. We cannot let our angels go."

Ben and Jeff simply shook their heads. Still Sammi paid attention and wrote down his comments. She thought she'd heard that phrase somewhere.

About this time, the door opened and another investigator walked in with a few more pages of the report that had been missing. This precinct was now trying to be as cooperative as they could.

For a moment, the officer waited for Ben's reply and heard Mr. Jim say, "It was the best of times, it was the best of times, it was the best of times."

"I see he's at it again," he said. "Sometimes he goes on for hours with these little bits of nothing." He laughed, shook his head, turned around, and left.

However, this time Sammi's memory connected. She knew that line. It was the first line from Charles Dickens, "A Tale of Two Cities." This was an educated man. She hadn't figured out some of the other lines he'd said, but she planned to run them by Julie. This man had managed to keep some of his obviously favorite bits of literature in his mind. She wished he'd think about what had happened to him, but that seemed to be too deeply buried. Yet, she wanted to connect with him again before she left. If she could get the beginning of a rapport with him, he might remember something and want her to know. She decided to try.

"Mr. Jim, I know that story you began." Ben and Jeff turned to look at her confusedly. She continued. "It was the best of times; it was the worst of times, right?"

He actually focused to the astonishment of Ben and Jeff. Sammi continued, "It was the age of wisdom…" and then she cleverly paused. His thoughts told her that he knew the next line, which he repeated.

"It was the age of foolishness." Mr. Jim said this line with ease as he focused for a moment or two before he lost it again. Nevertheless, he had looked directly at Sammi, gave her a smile as his thoughts said, *You know I'm not an idiot. Thank You. But I am lost now; I've been lost for years. Can you help find me?*

Ben thought they'd accomplished all they could for today. He was ready to end the session. Jeff and Sammi agreed. Yet she had one more thing to add.

"It was nice discussing Charles Dickens with you. Maybe we can do it again?"

Mr. Jim got very excited. He shook his head up and down and his entire body took on a focus that had previously been missing. It didn't last very long, but they all realized that the possibility was there. As they left she turned to say, "It was nice meeting you, Mr. Jim. I'd like to come and see you again."

He smiled and he was definitely happy about her comment.

* * *

In the parking lot Ben said, "You do have your ways. I think you actually began to get a rapport with that man."

"And that man isn't a babbling idiot. I think he's quite educated and I wonder what happened to him. I have some ideas, but I'm going to type up my notes before I discuss them with you. I also have more ideas about our Sergeant Wyman."

Ben was pleased. "But this adds another mystery. There's no way this Mr. Jim was the shooter."

Sammi was happy that he'd referred to him by the only name they knew. It did show respect, and she'd expect no less from Ben Collier.

"So we need to look somewhere else, but where? Where do we start?"

"I may have picked up on something, but let me get my notes written up. It's all jumbled in my mind right now."

"Tell you what," said Ben. "Let's have a relaxing dinner. Then you can use the hotel computer to transcribe your notes. We all need some rest and tomorrow at breakfast if you're finished, we can continue."

"Sounds good to me, especially about dinner, I'm starved."

All the way to the hotel Sammi was rehashing the day's discovery in her mind. The only trouble that she detected was that she was going in several diverse directions, all at the same time. There was Sergeants Wyman and Cullins; they were involved deeply in this cover up and so was Melanie Brooks, whom she thought they were both protecting for some reason. They also needed to find out who the actual shooter was and Sammi had no idea. Then there was Mr. Jim. Who was he? Where did he come from and most importantly, how did he end up here? She was glad she'd be going home on Friday. She could talk to Dave, but she also had questions for Julie. She needed her help this time.

***

Dave found himself twiddling his pencil at his desk because his mind was so deep in thought that he couldn't bring it back to reality. Something about this case was bothering him, but he couldn't figure out what it was. Roy had told him that Charlie Bowren was the one who tackled him to the ground and inflicted this latest injury. Yet this guy had been running at him without a gun, without any cover and going wild to get away from there. It did seem that he was in total panic mode, but even so, getting back into the car and racing away from the scene would have made more sense. He could have possibly helped his buddies more by getting extra help rather than running aimlessly, and toward what? He didn't know. He must have known he was heading toward disaster; God, these guys hadn't thought out this attack very well. They were supposedly part of this swanky Right Side Group; that didn't make sense at all. Their reputation seemed more solid than that.

Dave was thinking it was time to read the reports again. Sometimes, when he was alone he could concentrate better, and words on the page would jump out at him. In this way, he sometimes got a clue to underlying activities that he hadn't noticed before. He laughed. Maybe that's how Sammi got some of her ideas. She used to say that you had to focus and be oblivious to anything around you. Apparently, he found that more difficult than she did. Still, he could get absorbed for hours reading reports that would lead him in another direction. And he needed to get a handle on this one.

Sergeant Brady sent word that he needed to see him. He went straightaway into his office.

"Okay, Dave, you feeling okay these days?"

"Doing fine. It's slow going, but definitely improving every day."

"What's the latest from the doctor?"

"I might even be driving by next week. We'll see, but he thinks I'm doing great and that I've lucked out again."

Sergeant Brady smiled. "You're one of my best, Dave, you always have been and I want to make sure you're doing things right."

"I am sergeant; I know it's important. My sling comes off by Saturday, at least on a trial basis. I'm still to favor this arm for a while, and I will. Sitting at a desk for a while longer is okay with me."

"Good, Good."

Dave could tell that Sergeant Brady had something on his mind, but was having trouble getting his thoughts together.

"Is something up?"

"Well, not immediately but I did want to run something by you. You know that we can't touch this Right Side Group now at all. It does look like their lawyers are purposely dragging their feet on this one; we figured they would. They want us to slip up, but you guys are following the rules; no contact at all, so we're okay. But we're at a total standstill here and it makes me nervous."

"Actually, Julie has been doing a lot of research on this group. She's fighting hard to get as much background on them as she can. She'll come up with something sarge, if anything's out there you know she'll find it."

"I know and I know she's good. Honestly, I just wish that Sammi was here, too."

"Sammi does her best work when she's around people. She can read them so well and that's how she works. Right now, we're not allowed to be near them. I think she'll be more valuable later on when the interrogations start."

Sergeant Brady took a deep breath. Dave could tell he couldn't settle down.

"I wish we knew what we're facing here. That's what bothers me the most. Is this a little group that works alone or are they connected with something bigger? I can't figure this one out. What are your thoughts, Dave? I guess that's what I want right now."

"Okay, sarge, here's how I see it. Somehow, I don't think they're connected with the mob. You know about Jason Connors' older brother being killed years ago and I think that's what started the entire hate thing. However, I do feel that they would like to be part of something bigger and they're killing police officers to gain attention. They hope to be recruited with other more established groups, but that doesn't seem to have happened yet. The father's still in jail though and info on him has been sketchy, but I think he holds a big key to finding out about the whole mess. However that Biltmore name keeps popping up and we need to find out about him."

"And Julie's working on this, right?"

"Right, but we don't have much. No first name, no location; hell, we don't even know if he's in this state. He's one I'd like to know about. We'll find out a lot through him. The father has his reasons for this criminal behavior, lame excuses as they are, but what about this Biltmore person? When we find him, it'll help a lot. Julie thinks it's a matter of elimination and it's tedious work. But I have confidence she'll find something."

"I want to be ready for them when the lawyers finally give us access to them. We need to be ready."

"And I hope we are, but either way, we'll get them."

Sergeant Brady sat back in his double-sized chair with his hands clasped behind his head and made an attempt at relaxation. That was something he seldom did. His job didn't give him any moments of luxurious breathing space. It was nice to see an occasional quick respite. Their eyes connected and they both understood.

"Thanks Dave, you always help me."

Then his phone rang and it was back to official business.

* * *

Julie was waiting for Dave when he returned to his desk. She seemed rather edgy.

"What's up?"

"I've found some information about five Biltmore characters. Only three are in this state, another one is in Ohio and another in New York. Now three have criminal records, but I was hesitant to eliminate anyone for a variety of reasons. I need to make copies of these reports and I'd like to sit down and go over them with you, Jim, Tom and whoever else you want. With no first name or other info, I could use some brainstorming. Sometimes the criminal minded aren't always obvious; some have a very good cover. When do you think you might have some time?"

Dave thought for a moment and said, "Sammi comes in tomorrow night. How about we all get together on Saturday? I don't think Tom and Jill are available, but the four of us could bounce ideas around. And I could update Roy, Amilio and Tom on Monday to see what they think. I know Sammi had hoped to get more than just a last name but she couldn't, yet maybe if we run these profiles by her, something will click. Can you and Jim make it on Saturday night?"

"Sure, we'll be there. That's a good idea. Sammi says that she reports on the most important thoughts because so many come across to her. Maybe by looking over all this stuff, she may remember something else that didn't seem to matter at the time, but will end up being important."

"That's what I was thinking. Maybe just a word or a circumstance can remind her of something else she heard. At least, it's worth a try."

"I'll tell Jim. Besides, it's been a while since we've been together."

"True and ..." Dave's phone rang and Julie left.

"Hi honey, how're you doing?"

She had called at the exact moment as if on cue. He told her what he planned to do on Saturday night.

"That's great. I need to talk to Julie anyway. Ben said that he might use her as our computer expert. We've got a lot of things that need researching and we're getting the runaround here."

"Hasn't that been resolved? Ben had hinted at that a while back, but I thought it was under control."

"He did get his captain over to Precinct 10 and suspended a few sergeants for now, but I think they're involved in a cover up and who knows how much further this fiasco goes. This case is really broadening out and away from that hobo. And his story is an entirely different issue."

"Sounds like you're making progress."

"Barely the beginning I'm afraid. Anyway, I'll be home tomorrow night about 5:30 PM. Can you pick me up?"

"Absolutely, I'll be there to pick you up. You had to ask? I've really missed you."

"I'm happy to hear that. So you want to get together on Saturday night. Honestly Dave, we have so much to talk about, it might take two evenings as it is. Maybe we should try for Friday as well."

"Not a chance. Friday night is for you and me, and that's not up for discussion."

She paused before she answered, "Yeah, you're right."

"We have to keep things in perspective. These cases will take a while, but we need our time and that's it unless we hit a catastrophe in the future. But for now, Friday evenings belong to us."

She laughed. "Okay by me. Got to go now. See you tomorrow night."

"Love you, Sammi."

"And I love you, Dave Patterson."

He laughed as he put down the phone. She always used his full name when she sweet-talked him. Once when he asked her why she said she liked how his named flowed together.

* * *

Jim wandered over to his desk and seemed to have his own agenda. He had many questions that were hot on his mind.

"Look Dave, Roy and I've been backtracking to the deaths of those two policemen over in Sweet Valley last year. I want to get over there tomorrow and see if I can get a copy of the death reports. I'm curious what ballistics will show."

Dave nodded. "Good idea. We couldn't be lucky enough to have a match on the bullets."

"Remember, they shot Phil Pentin and we've got those bullets on file here. I know it's a long shot, but if those other cops' death were connected to the Right Side Group in some way; well, it's a possibility."

"Absolutely, and we're going to try to connect them with everything we can. I can't believe it was these guys that killed those other cops; they're too sloppy. From what I heard those killings were well planned. Either way, we need to put them out of business or if we can find out who they're connected with, we might have some good news for Sergeant Brady."

Jim smiled. Yeah, Sergeant Brady would be waving flags if they could make a plausible connection.

"Jim, I want to see those reports. Do you know anything about those two police officers who were gunned down last year?"

"Nothing, that's why I thought we'd better start to study the details and find any connection that we can. Right now, there's no proof that they were killed by the Right Side Group, but speculation from Sweet Valley seems to think so. The officers out there all believe they're being targeted, so I need to find out more about this."

Dave shook his head. "I guess I'm still lost about this entire mess. Many people hate cops, especially the criminals, but most don't target them and this is what it appears we're dealing with. I mean, look at the attack on Roy and myself. It was as brazen as it gets. And we didn't personally ever have anything to do with them."

"It appears to be anyone in uniform and anyone who would help the police, like in the case of Phil Pentin. How's he doing by the way?"

"Better and he's gotten some feeling back in his legs, so that's good. Doctors say it's just a matter of time and he'll be able to walk again. But he has a ways to go."

Jim acknowledged. "You guys were all lucky. When you've got a bunch of nuts out there who'll kill just for the satisfaction, we've got a real problem on our hands."

"Sergeant Brady wonders if they were connected to any other killings. You just mentioned how they target people they think are connected to the police."

Jim was thoughtful. "I'll bet before this case is finished we're gonna have some big surprises. Are you going to get Amilio working on this one?"

"That's up to the sarge. Not sure what he has in mind for him."

"I thought you wanted him on this case."

"I always want him on everything as well as you, Tom, Roy … our group works so well together. But, like I said, it's not my call this time."

"Okay, I'm taking off for today. I probably won't see you tomorrow, but we'll be over Saturday night. I'll bet Sammi'll have a lot to talk about."

"For sure," he said as he watched Jim walk away. There was always so much in the criminal world and each had its own direction. Right now, there was a lot on everyone's plate. Sammi had her hands full with the senator's murder, and by her own assessment, possibly an amnesia victim who was not what he seemed. She was expected to help on the interrogations in Scranton when they occurred. In the meantime, his group was going in several directions with this Right Side Group. They targeted police officers, that was true, but any informant, aide and who knows who else would irritate them enough to become a target. This group was crazy and not one that could be ignored any longer.

* * *

Friday night seemed to come quickly after all. Dave was walking along the outside of the terminal building waiting for the Charter Jet to come in from Hartford. It was 5:40 PM., already ten minutes late. He wasn't worried yet, but he'd be glad when he saw that plane make its landing. He had a silly feeling for a moment; he felt so excited to see Sammi. He hadn't seen her in a week and felt like a schoolboy with a crush on someone. He laughed at himself. He'd found so much satisfaction in his relationship with her that it was hard to express. As she would say, the universe must have had a big part in getting them together. He snickered. It was now 5:45 PM and no plane yet. Seeing nothing in the sky, he went into the terminal and up to the information desk.

"Nothing's wrong, sir, but there has been a stronger headwind than anticipated causing a slight delay. It is now estimated to arrive in about ten minutes."

"Thanks," he said and went back outside more confidently.

He walked around for a few more minutes, lost in thoughts about his life. A bullet meant for someone else had killed his first wife Kelly. Their marriage had changed dramatically after only one year and although nothing turned nasty between them, it didn't hold anything meaningful anymore. They both hung on for four more years before they made the decision to end it. Dave realized shortly after they were married that their matchup wasn't solid. He sometimes wondered if Kelly knew it as well. He had met Sammi first and they had a good friendship going, but Kelly was exciting, beautiful and very flirtatious as well as the stronger personality and she completely overshadowed Sammi. He sensed a disappointment in Sammi, but she seemed to step aside gracefully; Kelly was a good friend of hers as well.

They had all remained friends, but Sammi wouldn't stand up for their wedding, which lately was a theme he kept coming back to. Why not? He liked to think that she had a crush on him back then. Yet, they'd never dated seriously. Knowing Kelly had invited her to be a bridesmaid, he'd asked her a few times why she'd refused, but she wouldn't tell him. And he'd never asked Kelly; at the time, it never crossed his mind. He thought about it now, and he wanted to know. He wondered if he could find a way to trick her into answering him. Maybe he could.

He saw the small plane approach for a landing and pushed the thought back into his mind. Someday he'd find a way to coax it out of her; he was good at that.

There were only three passengers on the charter this time. When he spotted her, it seemed that the wind blew her hair in every feasible direction, but she didn't seem to care. She was looking for Dave and he was next to her in a second.

After an emotional hug and a satisfying kiss he said, "God, it's great to see you."

She laughed. "This kind of reception makes everything worthwhile."

"I missed you a lot. I don't like it when you're away, and I'm excited when you come back. There's no way I can hide it." Part of his boyish personality was showing.

"I know and I'm glad to be home."

They stopped for dinner at their favorite place and decided not to talk about their cases until later. They wanted to relax with frivolous conversation and catch up on little tidbits that were usually overlooked. Arriving home before nine, she was greeted excitedly by Kali. Dogs always showed their emotions openly and Sammi felt wanted in this atmosphere. Home meant so much more to her than when she was a child; she was now in a loving environment and not one of constant turmoil, anger and disruption.

"So you now know that the hobo isn't the murderer, right?"

"That's right. He's definitely not the murderer, and Ben and Jeff know it as well. We're all wondering what they're trying to pull over there. There's no way this mixed up, confused, unfocused person could have done it, let alone anything else that required any type of concentration."

"Okay, then maybe those two sergeants are involved and they're trying to cover it up, but they can't be the only ones looking into this senator's murder. A senator killed is big news around the country; it's probably earth shattering around Hartford. Why are the prosecutors going along with this? Their reputation depends on convictions. Do they really believe they can convict this man?"

"I can't imagine what they're thinking. But Dave, if you saw this guy … he's confused, seems like he's babbling unclear sentences and can't answer any direct question."

"Maybe they'll say he's faking it."

"They'll have a long road to go to prove that one. Besides, I talked to him from his thought world and did get a few brief reactions. His responses were very short and then he'd go right back into his protective shell."

"What did you mean when you said he seemed like he was babbling unclear sentences?" he asked.

"Okay, Dave, here's what I think. I think this man is highly educated." She waited a moment allowing time for that sentence to sink in. "In his thoughts he complained about his head being sore for a long time, which he confirmed to me aloud."

Sammi stopped to take a deep breath. She was excited to finish her theory. "Those babbling sentences that everyone accuses him of repeating in nonsensical intensity are well chosen. I recognized one of them and it was the first line from 'A Tale of Two Cities' by Charles Dickens. He kept repeating, 'It was the best of times,' and I wrote down a few others that I didn't recognize but hope that Julie will know. Personally, I think he was in an accident or was mugged or robbed or something and has been wandering around for a while. It's hard to tell how long he's been like this; possibly a very long time. Trouble is that I can't determine when it happened or where? But I know he didn't kill the senator. Once we solve that murder, we'll have another dilemma on our hands."

Dave was thoughtful. "That's a lot to deal with. Are Ben and Jeff still confused by the way you work?"

"Yeah, they are. Sometimes they look at me with that wondering expression, but they leave me alone. They've accepted me now and just work with the information I give them."

"I figured that's what would happen. But I still think Ben thinks you're psychic and probably Jeff, too."

"You're right. I listened to both of them and they think I'm definitely psychic, but since they know I don't like the term they don't use it. But that's all right; I can live with that."

Dave laughed, "I keep forgetting that you can hear their thoughts as well, so of course you'd know what they thought of you."

Sammi yawned. She was tired; it had been a long day.

"Let's get to bed," said Dave then added, "I'm glad that I'm not getting into an empty bed tonight."

* * *

The next morning Sammi woke slowly and was happy that she had the luxury of sleeping in on Saturday. It was good to be in your own bed, your love beside you and man's best friend close by. She welcomed the comfort of relaxing, stretching and daydreaming in a quiet atmosphere with no alarm clock shocking your intentions. She looked over at Dave. He slept peacefully. She liked that. She missed him when he wasn't around and she liked to watch him sleep. Of a sudden, his eyes opened.

"You're watching me sleep again, aren't you?" he said.

She laughed. "I am, but only for a few minutes. I just woke up myself."

"I must admit that when you were gone, I pictured you being here with me, so I guess this puts me in the same category as you."

CHAPTER VIII

Saturday evening seemed to come very quickly. Sammi had spent the day getting her notes straightened out, reclaiming her wardrobe, making sure that she'd be ready to leave Sunday night, although she thought Monday morning would work as well. The charter jet was great in getting her back to Hartford by nine o'clock in the morning. She ran the idea past Dave.

"I think I'll leave on Monday morning. Ben thought it would be fine as long as I get there before ten o'clock. He wants to have a short meeting before we again get over to Precinct 10. They should have the blow ups of that surveillance tape and then we want to compare our findings and conclusions from the weekend."

"Great," he said, obviously pleased.

"So Julie wants to talk about this Mr. Biltmore? What's she found out so far?"

Dave was about to tell her, but the doorbell rang. It was Jim and Julie.

It took less than five minutes to get the preliminaries out of the way, how much they missed each other and working together and were glad to be able to be together tonight. Dave got the drinks and they settled in the living room ready for a discussion they hoped would help each one of them.

Julie started, "I wanted to talk about this Biltmore fellow. I've found five of them that could be possibilities, but I want some other ideas."

Sammi was into the discussion immediately. "Do any of them have any history? Were you able to find out about their past? That could tell us a lot."

"I'm looking into that and I've got some info on the three around our area, but little about the other two that are out of state. I'm still working on that. I made a copy of my report for all of you."

They all took some time looking over her notes.

Jeremy Biltmore, age 54, was a trucker for Allied Van Lines. He spent quite a bit of his time travelling and he'd been arrested a few times in his youth for aggravated assault and battery, but plead guilty to misdemeanors and was let off on probation. His profile said that he had a bad attitude toward police officers. He was divorced twice and had three children. He did graduate from high school but dropped out of college early on. He spent much of his time on the road, as he was a long distance truck driver.

Leonard Biltmore, Jr. age 37 was an executive in the medical area of an insurance company. He didn't seem to have a criminal past and was married and the father of two. His life on the surface seemed to be of a model citizen. He graduated from college with a degree in Business and even began studying toward a Master's Degree, but as of yet hadn't completed it. His wife is also a college graduate and active in the community.

Leonard Biltmore, Sr. age 63, worked for the same insurance company as his son. It wasn't exactly a family business, but several other relatives were involved. Father and son had a special affiliation in business. They were partnered together most of the time and spent time together on business trips for special projects. He was a college graduate as well and active in the community as was his wife. He had no criminal record of any kind and even his driving record was clean.

George Biltmore in New York City worked for a brokerage firm. He was 55 years old and information was limited about him at this time. It was the same for Jerome Biltmore of Ohio, age 60. He was a mechanical engineer and had worked for a supplier of engine products for over twenty years, seemed settled in and solid. Both of these men needed further investigation.

Dave was the first to speak. "Of course my mind goes right to the guy with the criminal record but I can't afford to be prejudiced. Yet, his record would show that he has enough anger to be associated with our suspects."

Sammi said, "I wonder if they're all related."

Everyone turned to look at her so she explained further. "They all live in this area and they could be related; that's all."

"True," said Julie, "I never thought of that. I'll look into it."

Jim was more thoughtful. "Somehow something doesn't feel right here. I don't know what it is." Turning to Julie he said, "Can you look up the background of this Jeremy Biltmore again and see what else you can pull up? I'm with Dave, here. I don't want to head in one direction only, but he'd definitely be my first guess."

"Wait a minute," said Sammi. "I remember when Jason thought about this Biltmore fellow. He had a quick thought about having to wait until he got back."

They looked at each other and she continued. "It could mean that he was out on a driving job and wasn't back yet."

"True," said Jim. "That would make sense."

"Or," she said slowly and thought some more.

"Come on; out with it," said Dave.

"Well, I was thinking that Jason could have been referring to one of the Biltmores in another state and talking about waiting until he visited. If the connection is with a Biltmore from Ohio or New York, they probably come to visit and have meetings with their group, don't you think?"

"Yeah, that's right," said Jim. "It could be either one."

"I wish I had heard more, especially a first name, but I didn't."

"And we can't go near anyone right now so we'll have to wait and do more of a background check. I'm going to talk to Sergeant Brady. Maybe we could utilize Amilio. He finds out a lot by nosing around and since you're pretty booked, Sammi, he could be helpful."

"And I'll broaden my search. These are the only ones I've found so far."

Dave said, "We need more background on these guys. It may be that none of them are involved."

"Biltmore doesn't sound like a nickname to me," said Sammi. "But could it be a first name?"

"That's a thought," said Julie. "I never thought of that. I could take a run on that."

"Is there a record on the guys from Ohio and New York?"

"Not that I've found, but I really have a lot more checking to do."

Then Sammi remembered something. It had been such a quick flash in the mind of Jason that she hadn't bothered writing it down and to be honest, she forgot about it. But now, with this discussion she remembered.

"Wait a minute," she said, "give me a moment here."

Everyone remained quiet as she tried to focus back to being in the interview room with Jason. She closed her eyes and concentrated, although everyone could tell that the tension was rising within her. Patience was everywhere in the room to give her time to renew her thoughts and memories. She slowly opened her eyes and smiled. Dave knew immediately she remembered something she considered important.

"I need to mention something first. As you all know, I hear a lot of thoughts coming across someone's mind and I write fast and furiously," she laughed. "But, as Dave would say, I can't get every single thought written down; there are too many. I do the best I can but sometimes I don't remember all of the important ones because truly, at the time, I'm not even sure which the important ones would be. Yet I did remember something more about Jason's thoughts and it's our discussion tonight that brought it up. I think this could be significant."

Sammi took a deep breath. It was obvious that she felt she had failed this time and Jim couldn't let that feeling pass by.

He said, "You're so hard on yourself, Sammi. You've told us before how this mind thing works and all you can do is the best you can. You always give us good stuff; don't be too hard on yourself."

"I think we're all hard on ourselves when we're trying to get a job done, but thanks."

Sammi had three people smiling at her in understanding and waiting impatiently for the newly remembered data.

"I can't imagine why I didn't write this one down; I must have gotten distracted. Okay, when Jason talked about this Biltmore fellow, a few other things crossed his mind. One was that he thought about being close to New Jersey."

"So that would mean the guy from New York is the one," said Jim.

Sammi put up her hand. "Wait a minute, there's more. He also thought about him having a relative in Ohio. It sounds like they're related, but I don't think that's the most significant part of all this. The most important thing I heard and I can't believe I didn't write this down was Jason's thoughts about this Biltmore person. He said, 'He's our main supreme resident.'"

Jim's chin dropped. It was obvious he was shocked to total alert. "Holy Shit," he said. He was quite excited and agitated. He turned to look at Dave and said, "Do you know what that means?"

Dave nodded. "We've got some real problems here and it probably goes nationwide."

Julie asked, "I've heard the term and they're a bunch of rebels or terrorists all over the country who hate policies and laws, aren't they?"

Dave looked over at Sammi and asked, "Do you know about these groups?"

"I've heard the phrase and I know they're against government, policies and stuff like that, right?"

"Let me tell you what I know … we know," he said as he included Jim. "It's much more than that. Let's talk about them for a bit and make sure we all understand what we're up against."

Jim said, "Good idea. We all need to understand this. Gees Sammi, this is a big clue you've given us. I never would have guessed that one." Then he waved to Dave to continue.

"Okay, this 'supreme resident' movement is not a large or organized group by any means, but more like a loose collection of little groups, none very large, who believe that virtually all existing government in the United States is illegitimate and they want to restore some type of minimal government that never really existed, except in their own minds. Now that's the basis for what they do, as I understand it. To this end, these little groups, who are not necessarily affiliated with one another except in their beliefs, wage war against the government and any other form of authority using harassment and intimidation tactics and more often than we care to admit, they will resort to violence."

Sammi and Julie looked at each other. This was bigger than they thought.

Sammi said, "I thought they were mainly people who would antagonize authority by disruptive demonstrations trying to create chaos and confusion."

Jim said, "They do a lot of that as well. They send letters and data over the internet trying to get people angry and rise up against the government. And there's other similar groups with the same goals such as sovereign citizens; I think they're mainly on the same page but don't affiliate much with each other."

Dave said, "There are so many examples of crazy things they do. I remember reading about one angry resident in Michigan who wrote a letter to the Michigan Department of Natural Resources stating that he was no longer a "citizen of the corrupt political corporate State of Michigan or United States of America. He said that now he was only answerable to "common laws." Then he said that he revoked his signature to any hunting or fishing licenses which he viewed as contracts that fraudulently bound him to the illegitimate government of Michigan."

Dave was silent for a few moments, shaking his head in disgust.

"This sounds crazy, Dave," Sammi said. "I've only heard a little of these groups and thought they didn't want to pay taxes and obey laws, but this sounds like people who have studied the law and contracts and plan to act as subversive as they can get away with."

Dave half-smiled as he turned to Sammi and said, "It's all of that and much more. If these guys we've got in custody are part of a group with these goals, then I think we're going to have to look into the death of those police officers in Sweet Valley last year. That and the attack on Roy and me cast an entire new light on these troubles around here."

Julie said, "So they resort to murder as well. They have no fear of going to prison?"

Jim took this one. "Two police officers were killed in Arkansas a while back by fellows who were involved in anti-government supreme citizens tactics. They simply believe in their cause and will do anything to promote it. And they believe they are above the law because the laws are illegal."

"Wow," said Sammi. "This is scary stuff."

"They're just like extremely angry terrorists who fight against the U.S. government and all it stands for," said Julie.

"That's exactly right. They claim they are not subject to most taxes, are not citizens of the United States and cannot be tried for anything except in "common law courts" which is mainly a people's tribunal with no lawyers." Dave continued, "Most refuse Social Security cards, they won't register their vehicles, carry driver's licenses or use zip codes."

Jim said, "I know they sound wacko, but they really believe in their philosophy and have their own interpretation of what the Founding Fathers had in mind for this country when they wrote the constitution. They're very dangerous and some areas of our country have had to take them quite seriously lately."

"You two seem to know a lot about these groups," said Sammi.

"I've run across a lot of officers who've dealt with them over the years. The 1990s showed a rise in violent activities within these groups which is a detour from the way these groups prefer to operate. They like to use what is called "paper terrorism." That's the use of fraudulent legal documents and filings as well as the misuse of legitimate documents in order to intimidate, harass and coerce public officials, law enforcement officers and private citizens in any way that they believe will hold up."

"They sound like they'd be very difficult to deal with," said Sammi.

"That's for sure. When you arrest them or capture them, unlike others who immediately call for their lawyers, these people will deny you have jurisdiction over them, quote all these interpretations of our country's documents and won't respect the courtroom, judges or anything else."

All were silent thinking about what this meant to their individuals cases. Dave, Jim and Julie were deciding how this would affect their present case.

Julie said, "I'm going to be digging into my files to see if I can find any connections with these subversive activities. Their conversations should be very telling and might lead us in a new direction."

Dave started to say something, and then stopped.

"What's on your mind?" Jim asked.

"I was thinking that this would make much more sense than everything being directed from that father in prison because his son was killed almost twenty years ago. I could have seen him trying to get revenge back then, but he waited almost ten years before he attempted to murder that police officer. That connection never made sense to me until now."

"Right, but we might have some proving to do, although some of these guys are very proud of what they do, and might discuss it openly." Jim turned to Julie. "We need to get the transcripts of the father's arrest and trial. His attitude could tell us a lot."

"I see that first thing Monday morning I'll have a lot of work to do."

"If all of plays out the way we think it might, I'd like to get over to that prison and talk to Jason's father." He turned to Sammi, "but I'd like you to be there."

Dave agreed. "Maybe we could plan it for next Saturday. We'd only need you in on this one interview to let us know where his thoughts are. We need you in both places already," he joked.

"That's okay. We can plan it when I'm home and that should work out just fine."

They spent the rest of the evening delving into how these supreme citizens worked. It seemed that in the 1990s violent confrontations were on an increase with even traffic stops resulting in death. Because of their high visibility, they were more vulnerable to concerted efforts by police officers, so these tactics decreased. However, the filing of frivolous lawsuits and liens against public officials, law enforcement officers and private citizens remained a favorite harassing strategy. These paper tactics seemed to intimidate their targets and had the beneficial side effect of clogging up the court system, which the supreme citizens believed, was illegitimate anyway. This gave them enormous pleasure.

As Dave and Jim thought more about the very great possibility that they were dealing with people who wanted to cause havoc and didn't believe in the laws of the United States, a shiver went through all of them. What were they dealing with? They knew their basic philosophy, but in outside practice, they didn't know what to expect from these people. Were they calmly yet methodically creating havoc while waiting for the right moment to kill officials of the law? That was the most difficult part. Who could know how to protect and defend yourself against these types of dissenters? And, most importantly, how could you get to the core of them and put them out of business?

***

Sammi walked slowly back to the sofa after bidding Julie and Jim farewell. It had been an anxious evening with the discussions taking astonishing turns in unforeseen directions. What were they dealing with? How could people like this be stopped? And, most important to her, what happened in their lives that twisted their thought processes so much that hate, anger and killing were the main topics on their minds?

"This was a very interesting and informative night," said Dave. "Jim was thrilled with the information you got this time. We need to know what we're dealing with and I think you found it."

Sammi didn't say anything. She was in her own world and Dave knew it. He continued, "I couldn't believe that those suspects attacked us on the street without provocation. I should have made the connection myself. I knew about these groups. Most law enforcement groups are well aware of them. Trouble is that they use so many tactics, most of which are not violent, that we forget about the sadistic ones. Yet it seems that more violent crimes have been happening in the last several years. Sounds to me like they may be changing their methods and heading for a new type of operation, a much more dangerous one."

Sammi still hadn't spoken. She was listening to Dave, but with a faraway look. Finally, he said, "Sammi, you're too quiet. What's on your mind?"

She looked startled. "Sorry, Dave, I was listening. You think they're turning to more dangerous methods now."

"I want to know what's on your mind."

"I'm trying to figure out the difference between the groups and why."

"What are you talking about?"

"I'm talking about the difference between people like Jerry Macey and Linda Saunders, you know those people who are close to the mob, but not exactly in it and these people who think of themselves as supreme citizens."

Linda Saunders and Jerry Macey were two people who tried to infiltrate the government offices in order to take over some areas of the government and make a profit. They were presently serving time for fraud, money laundering and attempted murder.

Sammi continued. "Linda and Jerry believed in the government and what it stood for but tried to use it for their own gain. These supreme residents don't believe in most of our government regulations or policies at all, and try to stand up against them to eventually knock them down. Am I right?"

Dave nodded. "Yeah, you've pretty much got the idea. Linda, Jerry and the others involved in that scheme are common criminals trying to manipulate people and places to serve their own purpose, usually greed. They seem to be fairly well organized and although they work in smaller groups all seem to have allegiance to others higher up in their own organization. Now, these supreme citizens work differently. They don't seem to have allegiance to anyone outside their little group. However, they do acknowledge that there are others out there who believe the same way they do. For some reason, they all run their own show and don't seem to want to merge together. It's a good thing, too, since they could get very powerful that way."

"They must know that, Dave. Why don't they organize?"

"They've had enough trouble now when they vent their views and cause problems; they're too much in the open that way. Even small groups are arrested when their extremist views are exposed. And I know they don't hesitate to relay their ideas when arrested. Still, they've kept a low profile on violent behavior unless confronted. Then, for some reason, they don't back down, but will sputter their opinions and views for hours to all who'll listen."

"It's so weird, but I had another thought about all this," she said.

"What's that?"

"Remember, this is only a thought." She paused and looked directly at Dave's eyes when she continued. "Do they hate senators, too?"

Dave looked over at her quickly. There's no doubt that he knew what she had in mind.

"It's a thought," she continued. "If they hate government officials, well, senators certainly fall into that category. And we know that this hobo didn't commit the murder so what if for some reason that senator irked someone either in person or maybe by a vote he cast or something like that."

"That's certainly something to look into. These two cases could be connected in a strange sort of way."

"What do you mean strange?"

"The group that works around here certainly isn't working in Connecticut. That would have to be an entirely different group."

"But they seem to have a connection with this Biltmore guy in New York. There's a hint of a relationship between the New York Biltmore guy and the Ohio one. Maybe some groups are in connection with each other, but keep it in the background. I'm not saying they're real well organized, but they may confer with each other more than we think they do."

"That's a thought, especially since Ben seems to be coming up empty for suspects."

"I'm going to ask Ben to check out Melanie Brooks' background. Let's see if there's a Melanie Brooks who might have done some subversive actions in her past. I think that would be something to look into."

"Good idea," said Dave.

"I don't know anything; it's just a gut feeling. I hope we can find her and talk with her. I think she's going to tell me a lot."

Dave yawned and stretched out. "I'm beat and getting ready for bed. How about you?"

"Yeah, me, too. You go first. We forgot to look at the mail. I put it on the kitchen table and then Julie and Jim came over earlier than we thought."

"Bring it into the bedroom. I'll look it over if you want to take your shower first."

"Okay."

* * *

When Sammi got out of the shower, she saw a disgusted look on Dave's face. At first, she thought it had to do with the heavy conversation that seemed to go on for hours earlier. She looked at him and he held out his hand for her. She sat next to him on the bed.

"Look what we got in the mail today."

She looked at a letter from the dreaded Linda Saunders. It had been close to two years since they had any direct contact that they definitely knew was from her. Linda had a fixation on

Dave especially after she went to prison. She tried desperately to coerce him into writing and visiting her in prison. She didn't care that Dave had married Sammi and felt she was only a substitute until she was free. She was convinced that Dave was her true love and wouldn't back down. Her fixation was a problem that had caused them both hours of apprehension. Yet her contacts had been a problem for her as well.

She had orders that she couldn't write, phone, contact Dave or his wife in any way, or have anyone else do it for her or she would have more time added on to her sentence. At this time, she wasn't eligible for parole until she'd served thirty-five years for the attempted murder of a police officer. With her ill thought out attempts to contact Dave and Sammi, she already had two years and three months added to her sentence. The extra three months were added for having a big mouth with the warden, a situation that didn't seem to surprise anyone.

"You want me to read it?" she asked. Sometimes she felt that Dave didn't realize that she could handle anything regarding Linda Saunders. She was an unpredictable spurned female and that's why anything she did didn't surprise Sammi anymore.

"No, I'll read it to you, but I have to warn you that it's not exactly bedtime story material." His face paled somewhat realizing that this part of his life story would probably never go away.

Sammi laughed. "At least you're getting a sense of humor about this. You used to get so upset."

"I still don't like it, but it is part of our lives and probably will be while she's in jail. The only good thing is that she'll get another year added to her sentence for this latest letter which will make her ... seventy-eight by the time she has her first chance for parole."

Sammi shook her head. "Such a loss in a way. She is a beautiful woman and has a real good brain in her head. She simply used it in the wrong way most of her life. Too bad she didn't keep her thoughts clean and working for her. Such a shame."

Dave laughed suddenly and caused Sammi to ask, "What?"

"Some people wouldn't take such a kind outlook for her. Wait until I read you this letter, you may change your mind." Then Dave started to read.

Dear Dave,

I have to admit that I'm really pissed off at you. You haven't even tried to contact me and I've been stuck in this God damned prison for several years now. I have a feeling that your crappy wife has something to do with that. But you should remember what we meant to each other. Don't pay attention to her. She's a real bitch anyway. I'm very disappointed in you. I thought you were stronger than that.

I had to get that off my mind. It's really been hurting lately knowing that you're not missing me as much as I miss you. And after what we meant to each other. I don't understand. I couldn't have misread your feelings for me, could I? No, I don't think so. I remember those wonderful times when we made love and you couldn't have faked that. We were meant to be together because you never had it so good, and neither did I.

I wish my life had turned out differently. I wish I'd had more advantages like that mousy little wife of yours. Maybe then, I'd be there instead of her.

I'm sorry this letter is so hateful, but that's how I feel right now. It's hard being locked up like this. I didn't even mean to shoot you, so I got this long sentence for an accident. But that's how my life's always been – UNLUCKY.

Anyway, you'd better write me back this time or else. I won't stop writing to you regardless because that's the only way I can feel close to you. I talk to you every night before I go to sleep. I know you miss what we

- 114 -

had, and I know you miss me but in time, we'll
get it back again.
I love you, always have and I always will.
Hope you're feeling okay by now.

Love always,
Linda Saunders

Sammi sat for a few moments and didn't say a word, but
the expression on her face gave her away. Finally she spoke.

"That letter certainly has a different tone than the others.
Now she's angry, vindictive and lashing out. But you can tell
she's hurting a lot being locked up. It's no surprise to me that
she won't give up on you."

"I told you this one would be difficult to hear. I'm sorry
about that."

"What are you sorry about? Don't blame yourself about
her. I still feel bad because I know she has a clever mind and a
strong disposition and she could have done so much good had
she directed herself in another direction."

Then for some reason, Sammi started to cry. Dave held
her and let her cry out her feelings.

"I'm not crying about the letter, believe it or not. But I
hate a waste of human potential. You have to admit it Dave,
whether you like to or not; she wasted her talents in the wrong
direction. And I can't help feeling sorry for her."

Dave nodded. "I know what you mean. But we could say
that about Jerry Macey and some of the others, too."

"We could. I know they made their own choices, but you
have to wonder why they went in that direction. Someday I still
would like to know something about Linda's past; I'll bet we'd
get some surprises there."

"You always look at the total picture, don't you? That's
not always as easy for me to do. This latest crime spree where
these people want to kill police officers, senators, lawyers and
anyone connected to the establishment just because they
disagree with them is too dangerous to ignore. There's many
things in this world that I don't agree with, but I don't cause
chaos and I don't harm people or kill people because of it.
Okay, I'm law enforcement but there are many other people
who hate some things about our country. None of us agree

about everything, but we don't do what these people do. That's what causes me trouble in having the same perspective that you do. I simply can't see the picture the same way."

Sammi was quiet for a moment before she said, "That's okay, Dave. You and I are never going to agree on everything either. I can't always forgive and forget, but I like to try because I don't always know what brought people to the point in their life where they think and act criminally, that's all. I'd like to give myself a chance to understand."

"I know you do, honey, and I admire you for trying, but sometimes I can't do it at all."

"And that's okay. You have to protect and uphold the law which puts you behind a different barrier."

"And you, dealing with the universe, always have a different or should I say unique perspective."

"Well, not always. I don't like Linda Saunders talking about her times with you, but I have to tell you that she's definitely in the past and I'm your present and future. She better get used to that."

Dave smiled and grabbed for Sammi. "Even if she were out of prison, she'd never have a chance against you. But I never knew it bothered you."

"Of course it bothers me. I just don't like to admit it to you out loud, that's all."

Dave smiled. It was something he seldom heard from Sammi. Some thoughts and feelings she usually kept deep inside; they were her own private business.

CHAPTER IX

Sunday was a busy day with endless little nothings that refused to be ignored. Somehow, Sammi liked being caught up in the boring routine occasionally as it kept her mind off the tension-filled days that were happening with more frequency than desired. Dave had gone down to the station for a few hours. He and Jim had details to work out before Monday morning. This new information needed to be sorted out and a plan implemented before they brought in Sergeant Brady and the rest of the group. Dave especially needed to have everything solid in his mind, which wouldn't be easy to do with this supreme resident theory. Jim was concerned how this theory would play out.

"How the hell are we going to get information on that group? All I know is what we read in the papers and that's mostly guesswork from the reporters. It's good to know what we're up against, but I'm still not sure how to find that out."

"Don't forget we've got Julie. She'll start on Monday finding out everything she can and I'm sure she'll come up with some type of theory on this group. And we have Sammi. When we can get another interview, we'll target our questions in a different way and get them thinking in a designated area. They'll try to hide what's on their minds because they'd never want to say anything out loud, but Sammi'll get what we need anyway. Then we'll have some type of clue of what we're up against."

"Yeah, you're probably right."

"You've got to settle down, Jim. You always want all the answers right away and that's unrealistic even when we've got people like Julie and Sammi working with us. We do have a huge advantage, but it still takes time to work itself out."

Jim sat and smiled for a moment. "You've got me pinned down again," he laughed. "I do try to get it all done right away. I've always been like that."

"Well," said Dave, "I've always liked your enthusiasm, that helps a lot, but you've got to spread it out. These guys aren't going anywhere. All in good time."

They both spent more time reading the reports and highlighting important material that they wanted to talk about in the early Monday morning staff meeting. They needed to bring the others up-to-speed as quickly as possible. Dave wanted Amilio here and was worried that Ben Collier might tag him for Hartford. He had worked as a double agent many times and was considered one of the best. Although he was mainly a police officer, the FBI used him frequently as well. They tried to get him in and out of cases with them quickly so nobody totally thought of him as working for the FBI. That was important. He needed to be known as a police officer.

"I think I've got these reports where I want them," said Dave signaling he was ready to leave.

"I'm working with Tom on a home invasion and I need to look over the notes he left for me. Haven't had a chance to do that yet."

"Okay, I'm leaving. Sammi doesn't have to leave until Monday morning."

"Really?"

"Those charters are great. It leaves at 7:30 and she'll make it to Hartford shortly after 8:00 AM. This works out great."

"You still don't like it when she's gone, do you?"

"No, I do miss her, but we also like working cases together. She's out there working with people who don't know what she can do and it makes everything harder for her."

Jim nodded. "But she's good. She can do it."

Dave agreed as he closed up his desk and left, but his lingering thoughts confirmed that this issue never left his mind.

* * *

Sammi was enjoying her time alone and the luxury of packing up again slowly, thinking her own thoughts while lost in the maze of her mind. She liked to let her thoughts wander in any direction they decided to go in leisure time and found out she usually picked up great information that way. She still thought of her Grandpa Logan. He had her gift as well and the conversations she had with him couldn't be matched by anyone else who hadn't experienced their flair for the other side first-hand, no matter how hard they tried. Life had given her his company for the first fourteen years of her life, the last seven of which he guided her and answered questions about events that she didn't understand. At times like this, when she was alone and thinking, she knew he was close around. And that always felt good.

The phone rang causing a slight disappointment in her experience. It was one of those times that she enjoyed being alone with her own thoughts and fantasies. She smiled realizing that there would be other times.

"Hi Julie, what's up?"

"Jim went to the station to join Dave and I found time to look up some of these sayings that your hobo kept talking about. I don't think I'm going to have much time this week."

"That's true, I'm sure. We're all keeping you quite busy."

Julie laughed as she said, "I'm so busy that I can't give justice to everyone, and that's not good. Sergeant Brady is thinking of getting me some help."

"Really," said Sammi, "that sounds like a great idea."

"It is and I guess the budget can afford it now. But back to our hobo friend, I agree with you totally, Sammi. This is one educated man and his mind has been holding on to to thoughts from Emerson, Thoreau and a few others, as well as Dickens, which you already figured out. Let me tell you; the first one, 'We cannot part with our friends. We cannot let our angels go.' That's Emerson right in the middle of his Essay on Compensation, and the second one is one that I used to have trouble with, 'Our moods do not believe in each other' ...' that's from Emerson again, in his Essay in Circles. This guy seems to have memorized entire parts of some of his works. Whoever thought he was a babbling simpleton wasn't familiar with some of the classics in literature. And one more thing; I was able to find that one that you felt sounded a little more familiar, but simply couldn't quite place. Well, Sammi, that was Dickens again from A Tale of Two Cities, the very last line 'It is a far, far better thing that I do, than I have ever done ...'"

"That's right, I remember it now," she said feeling rather excited, "and the rest was 'it is a far, far better rest that I go to than I have ever known.'"

Sammi was quiet for a moment before she added, "Yes, I remember the character was Sidney Carton from that Charles Dickens' story. I studied that book in my first year of college in my literature class." Then Sammi added, "So if this is what is on his mind now, possibly years after his dilemma, that means that this was something of extreme importance to him at one time and he is holding on to it as his last link to reality."

"I'd have to agree with that. If this man went through any kind of trauma or shock, I would think that his mind held on to something that was soothing and calming to him. This alone is quite a puzzle that needs to be solved."

"Yes, but the senator's murder is the first thing I have to concentrate on. However, since this hobo is connected I hope before all is over that we can help him as well."

"It sounds like he's been stuck in a nightmare for a while."

"Thanks for taking time to do this; I appreciate it. I realize that you've got a lot of work ahead of you this week."

"But at least we have a direction to go in and hopefully can round up some of these supreme residents before they do any more damage."

* * *

Sammi was back in Hartford before she realized how fast her Sunday evening had passed. Her weekend was behind her now and she was in Ben's hotel room with Jeff Slade entering only a moment after her.

After Sammi had updated Ben and Jeff on the latest theories for the senator's murder, she decided to tell them about their discussion of the supreme residents.

"Oh my God," said Ben, "I wonder if they could be involved in this. It certainly could fit in this picture."

"I'd like some investigation done in two areas," said Sammi. "First, I want this Biltmore character in New York looked into. His background and extra curricular activities could be very telling. Also, we need to find Melanie Brooks. I'm quite anxious to interview her and see if it's even possible that she's connected with this group. I feel she was involved in the senator's death, but I'm not sure how at this point."

As she talked on for a few minutes, both Ben and Jeff seemed in awe of what she was sharing. They were eager to follow up on her leads.

Sammi knew that Ben especially was quite pleased. He was thinking, *Where the hell does she get this information and how does she do it? I should be beyond this by now, but it still crosses my mind. It does give us a unique place to start and either way we can get some info on this group that's been a prickly thorn in our sides for a while.*

Sammi, too, mesmerized Jeff. *She's cool and so very sharp. She amazes me, but all I can say is that I'm happy she's on our side.*

Ben said aloud, "This is terrific, Sammi."

She said, "But we need more help and we need a place to work ..."

Ben interrupted. "That was my latest news. The FBI appreciates our dilemma here and we'll be working out of our headquarters in Hartford from now on. We'll have use of all the equipment we need. Captain Malick will remain in the picture; he's very interested in the behavior of his sergeants. I'm not sure if they're aware of the fact that they may be in real trouble. They probably think it's just a disciplinary action, but George Malick believes there's more involved. He won't say, but I do have to report to him of anything out of the ordinary that we experience at that station. I'm taking him into my confidence about the supreme residents group. I think he needs to know that."

Jeff jumped on that one. "Do you think these two sergeants could be involved with them?"

"Hell, I don't know anything at this point. But their behavior was totally against protocol, and they're hiding something, so who knows? Anyway, we've got our job to do and the Captain will keep us informed as well."

"Now that's how we all should be working--together," said Jeff.

* * *

Sammi was satisfied as they walked into the FBI headquarters in Hartford. Here they were treated as part of a team and given a great atmosphere of cooperation. It did make life simpler. Given time and a computer, she decided to look up

Melanie Brooks, although Ben said he had someone working on it. They were playing a waiting game as it was and this kept her interest and curiosity at its peak. Ben knew that he had to interview Mike's wife and children, but seemed to have a hard time doing it.

"Sammi, I think tomorrow I'm going to talk to Sarah, Mike's wife and I'd like you to go with me."

"Sure, I'd like to meet her."

Ben hesitated for a moment. He almost walked away from her desk twice and then retraced his footsteps. She knew what was on his mind, but waited until he found the right moment.

"This is tough for me," he said. "Sarah thinks the hobo committed this crime; that's what everyone's led her to believe. Hell, half of the city believes that, including law enforcement. It will be a shock to her when I have to open up this discussion with her. I'm sure her kids are probably still home from college – or maybe not. Maybe they've gone back to school by now, especially if Sarah thought it was best."

"She'd find out sooner or later anyway, Ben. Better now and from you than later after the news breaks. It'll give her more time to adjust."

He smiled. He knew she was right. "Still, I'll have to ask some pointed questions and I don't want to upset her or make her think we have any ulterior motives."

"Again, someone has to ask those targeted questions. It happens in every murder investigation. She may surprise you. Possibly, she's been waiting, even expecting some type of interview. After all, her husband was a senator and all areas must be examined."

"You could be right. Jeff will be on something else, so it'll be you and me. I'll let you know later what time."

"Sure."

"Anything on Melanie Brooks yet?" he asked.

"No, I've just started. There are several with that name in this area alone. I mean, Brooks is a common name, but I've got a feeling and I want to see if any of them has a tie to our Mr. Biltmore. Do we know his first name yet?"

"I don't know. I'll have to check with our researcher."

As he walked away, again he almost came back. He had something on his mind that he wanted to tell Sammi. She knew what it was and was hoping that he'd get it off his mind soon so he could relax. He needed to tell someone.

She began to plug in Melanie Brooks' name again. She wanted one in this Hartford area and surprisingly, five came up. She read quickly through the histories of each one and settled for a Melanie S. Brooks, age forty-seven. She had a background in law and was presently working at the brokerage firm of Hayden, Lawton and Biltmore. She couldn't believe her luck. This had to be the connection she had been looking for. Although she didn't have any solid proof, something inside her kept egging her on toward an association between these two people. Dave always told her to follow her gut feeling; that's where he got many of his new directions. She was the only one who knew about Biltmore and Melanie Brooks having any connection to these murders or the attempted murders in Sweet Valley. She felt appreciative that Ben and Jeff took her at her word, otherwise nothing would be pursued.

She was so deep in thought and concentration that she didn't hear Ben reenter her office. He shocked her to awareness as he called her name.

"Sorry, Ben. I think I may have found a connection."

She told him what she had just discovered. "I know we have to make sure that we have the correct Melanie Brooks, but this one feels right."

Ben looked at her strangely as he asked, "Where did you get this name anyway?"

Sammi didn't answer and kept working. Ben didn't pursue his question.

Yet he couldn't hide his excitement. "I'll get our researcher to get us a complete profile on this one."

Sammi said, "I wonder if Mike's wife ever heard of her."

Ben looked over with a thoughtful expression covering his face. "That's one question I'll make sure to ask her, maybe she could add something. That would be a break if she knew her."

* * *

On the way over to Sarah's home, Ben was unusually quiet. Sammi knew he had a fight going on inside and was quite sure who the winner would be. Sheepishly, he began a conversation that would lead to a type of confession on his part.

"Mike and I go back a long way. We met in college ... actually just before college and have been good friends ever since. He was a great guy."

Sammi nodded and waited. That's all she could do.

"There's something else," he began. Sammi was relieved. He was finally going to get something off his mind and take the weight off his guilty feelings. He seemed to put up tremendously high standards on himself and he was the only one who could bring them down a bit.

"Mike and I've always been very close. He'd been such a good friend to me. Back in college I did some pretty stupid things ..." He looked over at her and his conversation collapsed for a moment. Sammi felt compelled to say something.

"We all do stupid things in college and in our younger years. Actually stupidity isn't even delegated to younger years, is it?"

Ben nodded, smiled a bit, took a deep breath and continued. "Back then I did a lot of drinking, way too much, to be honest. I've been under control for a long time now, but back then, if I drank too much I was scary. I wasn't the same person at all; in fact, I went nuts and exhibited crazy behavior. I didn't even realize it until it happened a few times. Actually it was others who told me about it the next day because I didn't remember most of it."

Sammi simply listened. She knew Ben didn't want conversation at this point; he wanted an audience. She was more than willing.

"Once, at a party, my girlfriend at the time started making out with another guy. I was devastated and started drinking. I ended up putting my fist through a window. It was a mess and there was a lot of blood. Mike took charge immediately, cleaned me up, paid for the damage and got me out of there. The next day I couldn't believe what I'd done. Another incident happened a few months later and Mike was there again."

At this point, Ben choked up and a tear slipped from behind a well-protected eyelid. He was embarrassed; there was no doubt. At first, Sammi waited and gave him time to control himself, but then she realized that she needed to say something.

"It's hard, Ben, when a close friend dies. You have a lot of memories with him. Remember when we thought Amilio was dead. Dave went through a rough time just like you are now."

"But this is different. I could have messed up my life forever, but Mike and I together began studying why alcohol affected me the way it did. I wasn't the usual alcoholic we discovered, but after a certain limit I went totally crazy."

"What did you discover?"

"That no one has all of the answers. I hesitated going to AA because I was planning a career in law enforcement and Mike was going into law with an eye on politics. But he was my rock. We both realized that if I only had a couple of drinks I was okay, but I could no longer go to those all night drinking parties, which were rampant at college. I couldn't do those all nighters like some of the others were doing and still make it home okay. So we both stayed away. Mike didn't go either; can you imagine that? I made it through because of him."

"And because of you, too. I'm sure his support helped you, but you had to have tremendous willpower."

"I couldn't become a law enforcement officer who goes to AA, at least not in those days. As I said, I wasn't the usual type of alcoholic. For some reason if I drank modestly, I seemed to be okay. Whenever I drink now, I never have more than two drinks ever in one evening and I've been okay for years. Actually it's never happened again."

"That's great, Ben."

"Mike never told on me. Hell, it could have kept me out of law enforcement; it's been a secret between him and me all these years. Now if he had continued going to those parties, I think there would have been many questions about me, but we started doing other things and the suspicion dropped away from me totally. It was one of the luckiest breaks of my life."

"At least you took advantage of it."

"I learned from it as well. I learned how we're all susceptible to something. I've never been drunk since those two episodes, but I have to watch myself and I've done that for years."

"Do you think his wife Sarah knows?"

"I doubt it. We've never talked about it, but I don't think he told her. He met her shortly after our senior year began and by then it was one of those bumps in the road between us. It was something never to be forgotten, but not our main topic of conversation."

"It's great to have friends like that."

A few more tears escaped Ben's eyes. "I'm just so emotional about him."

"Dave was like that about Amilio, and he did some serious crying. He loves him like a brother."

"Yeah, some of the best relationship aren't blood ones. Thanks for letting me dump this on you. I needed to tell someone; I feel better now."

"That's good. And yes, Ben, it's between you and me."

He smiled. She knew it was something heavy on his mind and she needed to ease his burden. He was carrying a tough enough load as it was. Yet, Sammi knew there was a hint of another secret between the two of them. This time Sammi felt that it was Mike who had the secret. She couldn't determine what it was. The thoughts didn't rise that high up in his consciousness, but she did feel that it was extremely significant. Now that Mike was dead, she wondered if she'd ever find out. Well, she could find out, but only if Ben thought about it enough. He'd have to be concerned enough about the thought so that she could read it on his mind. Somehow, she wasn't sure this would ever happen.

***

Mike Stedman's home was beautiful, and what you'd expect as the home of a senator. It was pretentious and ornamental with plenty of large rooms for parties and gatherings, part of his positional necessity. A large two-story home with seven bedrooms, a tennis court, lovely gardens situated on two acres of prime land in the most prestigious area of Hartford, which left nothing else to be desired as far as Sammi could tell. As they pulled into the circle drive, Sammi had a moment of remembrance of the governor's mansion in Harrisburg, PA. It had the same circle drive, the same four white pillars making a dramatic statement of prestige and status. Only the front door seemed different as this one displayed strong ornamental features and a more decorative design whereas the Harrisburg mansion exhibited a firm wood design, majestic in its beauty, but with a more solid and functional appearance.

"This is quite lovely," said Sammi as her appreciation surfaced.

"Yes it is. My home is much smaller and not nearly as eye catching, but I love to call it home."

Sammi laughed. "Ours is the same way."

"My wife is so happy with our home," he said laughing, "and she's made it very clear that she doesn't want a bigger one."

"Where did you meet your wife?" she asked.

"At college. Actually, she and Sarah were casual friends so I have another reason to be thankful to the Stedmans."

By now, they had reached the front door. Ben pressed the bell and they waited. Sammi could see an instantaneous nervousness cross his demeanor as he rocked on his heels a few times before a very serious butler let them in.

"Mrs. Stedman is waiting for you in the library."

Sammi thought this was playing out like some movie scene she'd watched a number of times. As both of them looked confused as to which way the library was, the butler tactfully said, "If you'll follow me, please." He was totally serious and comfortable in his position, which he performed very reservedly.

Entering the library, Sarah Stedman stood up and walked over to Ben, gave him a warm welcoming hug and waited gracefully as Ben introduced Sammi.

"Welcome to both of you. It's so good to see you again Ben. Today is better than the last time." Turning to Sammi she added, "The last time was at the funeral."

"It was a lovely service and it showed how many loyal friends and associates that Mike had. He sure could make and keep friends," he said.

Sarah smiled. "He was always like that, as you well know."

Coffee was offered as Sammi took notice that Sarah was an attractive blond, about five feet nine with a casual and comfortable way about her. She guessed her about late forties and the years had been kind to her. She exhibited a reserved manner more than an outward open approach, which led Sammi to believe that it was probably her that had hired the butler. Yet she still presented a warm and friendly style, although it was over a restrained and carefully choreographed appearance. She had a distant look in her eyes, which could no doubt be excused due to the recent loss of her husband.

"How are you doing?" asked Ben.

"I'm okay ... honestly. It's quite a shock to get used to, but Mike had talked about the possibility on several occasions. In political life, you always have enemies, even if they aren't always obvious."

"I take it the children have gone back to college."

"Yes, they left at the beginning of the week and now the house seems unusually empty. Yet, I wanted them to get back to their lives and education; it was really the best for them."

Ben nodded. She continued. "I'm going to stay here for a while. We have an interim senator and he doesn't need this space. Luckily I can take my time to decide where I'd like to move."

"This is a lovely home," said Sammi.

"It is," she said with memories crossing her face, "but it always seemed so large to me. I won't mind downsizing at all. Mike and I had planned to do it as soon as his duties changed."

Sammi noticed that Sarah didn't talk with any sadness and she wasn't looking for pity from anyone. She seemed prepared to move on with her life. She was a strong woman.

Ben started slowly as he said, "This murder is a tough one to understand," he said using carefully chosen words. Sammi knew where he was heading immediately and felt his selected light steps would soften the blow.

Sarah picked up on his comment immediately. "What do you mean 'tough to understand'?"

For a moment, she looked anxiously back and forth from Sammi to Ben, but her eyes ultimately landed in Ben's direction.

Sammi sensed how Ben hated this moment and he faltered. She had picked up some horror thoughts from Sarah, *My God, how could this be any worse? Why should it be tough to understand?* She decided to intervene.

"Sarah, every conscious detail about this unfortunate and vindictive murder is unimaginable to most of us. We know what a fine job your husband did and how he could pull people together to accomplish important goals. Yet, we did find some discrepancies in the facts surrounding the murder scene and need to follow all clues."

As she began explaining their situation, she heard Sarah's thoughts turn to interest and wonderment and not fear or disappointment. She had a strong desire to see her husband's murderer answer for his actions, whoever it was.

Ben started to say something but Sarah interrupted him.

"Do you mean that you're not positive that this hobo is the murderer?"

As Ben hesitated, she shot another question at him. It was obvious by her excited manner that she wasn't angry and she wasn't upset, but she wanted to know the truth.

"Please Ben, I want to know the truth. You owe me that. I can take it no matter what. I've already lost Mike, that was the hardest thing, but I need to know the truth. Are you sure this hobo is the murderer or not?"

At first, Ben looked down, but he quickly began speaking. Prolonging what he needed to say wouldn't help anyone, least of all Sarah.

"Some of us have our doubts," he finally offered.

Sarah quickly looked over at Sammi. She wanted an answer from her as well.

Sammi accepted her challenge. "I have to be honest with you, Sarah."

"Of course," she interrupted, "that's exactly what I want from both of you."

"I rather doubt that this hobo killed your husband. Nothing fits as far as I'm concerned."

Sarah leaned back in her chair, calm, relaxed yet extremely focused.

She needed to know something before they continued. "I'm not questioning you, Sammi, and I mean no disrespect, but I guess I wonder who you really are and why Ben brought you into this case."

Ben turned to Sammi and said, "Let me answer this one. I met Sammi several years ago when I was working on some cases that completely confused and baffled most of us and managed to bring the entire FBI group to a standstill. She has a strong and surprising reputation and she has a way of finding out information that none of us can figure out. But that's okay. Her methods are her own. Yet when she's around, hidden clues always seem to turn up and she's been used by the FBI on several occasions with impressive success. She's the one who helped us solve those kidnapping cases in Philadelphia, along with her husband, Detective Dave Patterson."

"Wow," said Sarah, "I remember those kidnappings; everyone said that they were very tough to solve. I'm really impressed."

Ben said, "And we were lucky to find out where these kidnappings had spread across the country. Again, it was Sammi who figured that out."

Sarah sat quietly for the moment. Then she focused her entire attention on Sammi and asked, "And you don't think this hobo murdered my husband?"

Anyone could tell that Sarah had a new interest now. Her fascination for Sammi was obvious and she hoped that she could help the FBI solve her husband's murder. Her anxiety in awaiting Sammi's answer was noticeable.

"Sarah, I don't think he could possibly have done it. I'd like to tell you why."

Sarah nodded and was now leaning forward toward Sammi not wanting to miss a word. Sammi related the situation of this Mr. Jim, his unsteadiness, confusion and lack of memory. She ended by telling her that she didn't think he could focus long enough to accomplish anything.

After a deep breath, Sarah turned to Ben. "Why in the world does our police department here in Hartford have him in custody? To what I've been hearing, they aren't even looking for anyone else, am I right?"

"Totally," he said. "And I don't have an answer for you. We've been completely confused as to why this investigation is fixated on one confused, disoriented individual who couldn't plan anything if his life depended on it. It doesn't make any sense to me. That's one of the reasons I brought in Sammi. I feel that someone is hiding something and we intend to find out what that is."

Sarah looked whipped. She resembled someone who had just been hit in the stomach and had no power left to defend herself. She remained quiet. Sammi took advantage of the moment.

"I'd like to ask if you've ever heard of a woman named Melanie Brooks?"

There was no doubt as to the answer since Sarah had an immediate startled reaction. "Why yes, we both knew her. Actually, Mike knew her much better than I did. Let me explain. Although Mike seemed to get along with everyone, he did have some enemies, as you'd expect in politics. He didn't always vote the way some wanted; he just couldn't please everyone. A Milton Biltmore who heads some legal firm around here was particularly furious about a ruling last year that would cost legal institutions either more money or entice them to be more open about their methods and procedures. I'm sure I don't have all the facts correct, but there was a big campaign about it and Mike cast the deciding vote. Milton was livid and made it known. Okay, that's one part of it."

She stopped for a bit, gave everyone a refill and continued. "Part two is this. After we'd been married a short time, maybe a year or two, this Melanie showed up at one of the parties we frequented because of politics and made a very obvious play for Mike. They had dated for a time long before I met him and apparently, she'd never gotten over it. It was embarrassing and totally unnerved Mike and me because something like that is hard to handle. People would think he had something going on, which he didn't. It did settle down some after a while, but it was frustrating and irritating, but I don't think Mike ever thought she was dangerous. He felt she had a mission to forever make his life miserable because he had ended their relationship."

"Did she ever threaten you or Mike or the children?" asked Ben.

"Oh, no no, nothing like that. If she saw us at social gatherings, she'd find a reason to be friendlier to Mike than he wanted. He was always trying to handle the situation carefully; I mean, he didn't want bad publicity or any negative insinuations floating around out there. She usually totally ignored me. After a while Mike usually had his bodyguards tactfully keep her away."

"What do Milton Biltmore and Melanie Brooks have to do with each other?" asked Sammi.

The answer to this question presented the most surprising twist to this story.

"They were married for a brief time."

Ben and Sammi looked at each other in shock. Neither one had made that connection.

"That's what I heard, at least. They worked together for quite a while; she works at his law firm. Apparently, he always had a thing for her, but she was fixated on Mike. They got married, but it only lasted a few years. Rumor had it that she still wanted Mike and Milton's ego couldn't take it. Surprisingly, she still stayed on at the firm after the divorce and they've remained friends. They were a strange duo anyway, but apparently had a good working arrangement."

"That does sounds like an unusual combination, but why do you think strange?"

"I thought they were odd people, both of them. A few times at these parties, I was close enough to them to hear some of their conversations. They didn't seem loyal to the United States government, if you know what I mean. They didn't agree with many of our laws and always seemed to be in movements to repeal some of the regulations that they opposed."

Ben took a deep breath and mentioned to Sarah that he thought that sounded odd as well. He didn't mention to her about the supreme residents and didn't intend to. Sammi picked that up right away. She also picked up the fact that Sarah and her husband were both concerned about the attitude of these people and they'd had some serious discussions regarding them, although nothing much ever came of it.

"I'm glad we didn't have much to do with those two," said Sarah. "Somehow there seemed to be something underhanded about them." She quickly looked at both Ben and Sammi as she added, "Just a feeling."

Sammi said, "Sometimes that's where I get my best information."

Sarah smiled. It was obvious she was building a rapport with Sammi, one of definite admiration but also one of knowing another woman who was making a very impressive name for herself.

As they got up to leave, Sammi heard thoughts on Sarah's mind. She was heartbroken at losing her husband, whom she'd been with since her third year of college. She was wondering how life would play out without him after she'd gotten over the shock of his death and expected loneliness. She wondered what she would do with the rest of her life.

But there was one more thing that baffled Sammi. Sarah had a secret and it concerned her husband and Melanie Brooks. Her thoughts didn't come near high enough in her mind for Sammi to even pick up a direction, but still she knew something was there.

At the door, Sarah thanked them both for coming and making her aware of what was ahead.

"This will give me a chance to let my children know ahead of time so they won't be too shocked by the developments that will be forthcoming."

Ben said, "I was hoping that telling you now would make it a little easier. And if you get any other thoughts that could help, please let me know."

She then turned to Sammi and said, "Thanks so much for helping out on this case. I appreciate anything you can do."

Sammi smiled, nodded and added, "When you get over the loneliness and shock, I think you'll be a strong force in Hartford." Sammi purposely used words from her thought world, knowing it would make her comment special.

Sarah, immediately got a strange look on her face. She felt that Sammi knew what she'd been feeling and gave her a knowing, yet mystified smile.

Her final comment to Sammi was, "I can see why you're so effective."

Sammi nodded as she left. Ben was aware of something, but he wasn't sure what.

"You two made a real connection there at the end. I felt it, but I think I missed something."

Sammi said, "Ben, it was girl talk, that's all."

Ben had a sly look on his face but decided to leave it alone. Sammi was usually way ahead of him on some things as it was.

* * *

"We obviously need to get to Milton Biltmore and Melanie Brooks," said Ben. "The tough thing about this is that I don't want to tip our hands. It's not like they're going to tell us that they were involved in Mike's killing, but it seems to me at this point that they were."

Sammi was thoughtful. She finally offered. "I don't think it would be a great idea to let them know our suspicions at all, do you? I mean we're still guessing here."

"What do you have in mind?"

"We need someone to find out about that company that Milton Biltmore is partnered into. Do they have regular functions or any kind of activities where we could get involved? We may find out what we need to know that way and whether they should even be targeted or not. I feel Melanie Brooks is involved, but I don't know how yet. We could also learn about this Milton. How can we find out what they're involved in?"

Ben said, "This is where Captain George Malick can help us. He must have connections around town. That worked so well at those political parties back in Scranton a few years back. Good idea, Sammi. Let's see what party we can get ourselves invited to."

CHAPTER X

Back in her hotel room that night, Sammi felt empty inside. This case was a slow one. She needed to be around the right people; she could always get information that way. The good thing was that Ben seemed to try to give her what she needed, but she missed Dave. He knew her routines and her techniques and helped her navigate parties and gatherings, a difficulty that she'd never learned to manage as well on her own. Yet, when she was attending a party for a specific outcome, her focus and concentration overtook her shyness and timidity. This was exactly when her mental acuity sharpened. She smiled thinking, *when she was on a job, she could handle any situation.*

She was restless; there was no other way to say it. She missed Scranton, her friends and most of all Dave. Then the phone rang. It was Ben.

"Sammi, Jeff got some news today. He's been nosing around into the background of those two sergeants, and it seems that in their younger years, they were connected with this Melanie Brooks. And on top of that, they once had a connection with this supreme residents group."

"Wow," she said, "no kidding."

"It's not a big connection, but there was a small link a while back."

"Maybe they got more cautious and covered their tracks better in later years."

"That's a thought. Anyway, we're gonna watch them. I'm going to be talking to Captain Malick to see where his investigation has gone. Possibly we could give them some leads that could help them out."

"This is an interesting little group. This Melanie seemed to be a loose cannon for years with her fixation on Mike. People are dumped all the time but usually get over it one way or another. Melanie didn't handle her frustration well at all. She's the one I'm real interested in."

"Tomorrow Jeff wants to go over some files he recently had access to and thought you might be interested. I'm meeting with George Malick and hope he can find out something for us, especially about the activities of this law firm. It may take a few days, but he should know what's happening in his own town."

"No doubt. Okay, tell Jeff I'll be at the office by nine o'clock or earlier if he wants."

"Let's all meet for breakfast around eight o'clock and set up our plans then."

Great. Good night Ben."

* * *

Sammi's mood still wouldn't lose its grip on her. She decided to take a hot bath and relax her mind as well as her body. It worked for a while, but later on, her mood came back. She turned off the television and simply looked at the walls in this hotel room, which made a spectacular attempt to entertain its guests. The colors were subtle yet on target to relax anyone interested in pursuing their attempts at leisure.

Somehow, reality escaped her for a few moments as she lay there relaxing and trying to make sense out of a senseless situation. Of a sudden, she heard something over her left shoulder. She turned expecting to see someone there. There was no one. She again laid her head back against the headrest of the lounge chair thinking her day had been in and out of reality so what could she expect. Again, she heard a voice, this time a little clearer. She was puzzled as to what was happening. Hearing voices or thoughts from people was a common occurrence for her, but usually there had to be a person physically nearby in order for that to happen. This time, she was alone in her hotel room, but she'd heard a voice twice. She decided to work with it and let her thoughts know that she was ready to listen to anything that was coming toward her.

Melanie Brooks, she heard, *investigate Melanie Brooks. She can lead you to who pulled the trigger, but several were involved. Many wanted to silence me with the upcoming elections. I was their biggest distraction.*

Sammi mentally asked the question, *Biggest distraction on what?* She waited but heard nothing further. She felt frustrated. However, the voice confirmed to her that Melanie definitely knew something or at least had suspicions. Other suggestions inferred that a few others were involved. She wished she'd heard more, but was now convinced that being around Melanie and Milton Biltmore would get her all of the evidence she wanted. The trouble would be to prove it. How in the world could she accomplish that? This was proving to be one of the toughest cases she'd had in recent years.

The phone rang. She almost leaped up from her chair. She'd been so deep into her thought world that reality came as a shock.

"Hi Dave, is something wrong?"

"No, I just wanted to hear your voice."

"That's nice. I'm glad you called. How's your case going? Anything new?"

"Not yet, but some activity seems to indicate that the lawyers are beginning to dance around each other. It'll probably be in court by early next week to see when we can finagle some interviews with the suspects. Apparently, the defense lawyers have run out of excuses and the prosecution is beginning to push very hard. So we should get to these suspects before too long ... and we'll need you for these interviews."

"I'll be ready. I'm anxious to see what I can find out. On Ben's case, I may be able to confirm what I've been hearing. Melanie Brooks is involved in some way and knows something. It seems that more than one person was involved."

"No kidding, where did you hear that?"

"Let's just say I heard it for now. Okay?"

"Of course. You can explain later if you'd rather."

"I would. It does seem that Mike was involved in something that these people wanted him silenced about. Haven't figured out what yet."

Sammi explained to Dave that Ben was trying to find out about some of the activities of this firm so they could get in physical contact with these people, maybe at a party without sounding any alarms.

"That should work for you. You've been waiting for that, right?"

"Absolutely. I'm anxious to see what I can pick up from these people. They certainly hold the key to the murder and other suspicions around here."

Dave was silent for the moment. It prompted Sammi to ask. "Is something wrong?"

"No, not really, but I miss you. I don't like it when you're gone. That's number one. Also, we usually work cases together; it works so much better for me that way. I'm used to you being around and I'm in a bitchy mood right now."

"Oh, I'm sorry honey. I miss having you around, too. Some of the stuff I found out today I can't discuss with anyone and that makes it harder for me, too. I'm just lucky Ben takes me at my word these days."

"I'm looking forward to Friday; I guess that's all I wanted to say."

"I love you, Dave Patterson."

He laughed. He liked the way she always used both of his names. "And I love you, Sammi Patterson."

That was the last word either one of them said. It was enough.

* * *

During breakfast, Jeff Slade seemed to be the one most concerned about Milton Biltmore. He felt that the entire case depended upon that one person, and whether or not he was truly a supreme resident as suggested. He felt the conspiracy started there and ended up with the murder of Senator Mike Stedman. Somehow, he determined that this was a much more organized group than earlier believed and his entire focus was from that one perspective.

Ben had a broader view. He still included Melanie Brooks in the fix, but wondered whether the duo together had conspired to kill the senator for presently unknown reasons. He thought of them as possibly the ringleaders in a scheme to get rid of the senator and thereby balance the voting scale in their direction.

Sammi had mentioned to both of them that the senator seemed to be a big distraction to the cause of the supreme residents. Yet no one knew what that meant. She had been unable to pinpoint the exact legal references that Mike had been working on.

"We should be able to determine that from his office staff, right?" asked Sammi. She knew this was important and might lead somewhere.

"I'm going to be talking to Captain Malick first thing today and then I want to get over to Mike's offices. If I don't get enough of a clean reception, I may call his wife Sarah to come with me. Her approval would mean a lot to his staff."

"And we've got to finish up these files," said Jeff looking directly at Sammi. "If there's anything in them, we need to find it now."

Sammi was slightly disappointed. She did better getting information by being around people; something she couldn't tell either one of them directly. Yet, if they could find out more about the activities of this law firm, well, that might be enough for now. Captain Malick would work on one end and Jeff and Sammi would be looking at the other end. Details should alert them as to what was going on in that company.

* * *

Ben met Captain Malick at his office. He was ushered in and offered coffee and made to feel as comfortable as possible. This settled with him well. It was the total opposite type of treatment that he'd been experiencing at the other station. He felt they were on their way.

"These sergeants are still on suspension and will be for a time. We know they have connections considered subversive to the United States. They seemed to have done well getting themselves in key positions with access to very sensitive information. It's amazing that no one suspected anything. From what I've been able to find out, they have quite a bit of sympathy for these supreme residents. I can't even understand that. How can they be police officers and think like they do?"

"Obviously they gained access to their present positions to gather information?"

"But their records are first-rate and show excellent police work on several occasions. That's what I don't understand."

"They had to make it look good, George, so that no one would suspect them. You used the term 'sympathy.' Are you saying that they were full fledged members or not?"

"My findings so far have suggested that they might pass along information and make the group aware of certain things, but were relatively inactive themselves. We can't find any instances where they were physically involved in foul play. That's the hard part."

"Okay, well, at this time I need to find out something about that law firm of Hayden, Lawton and Biltmore. I want to know about their activities and functions and whatever else they're involved in. We need to be around them and maybe finagle some invitations to their regular events. Can you help me out?"

"Sure, I don't have anything right now, but I'll put some people on it and you'll have something within a few days."

"Great. It's nice when we cooperate with each other."

George smiled in a rather odd manner, Ben thought. He quickly dismissed it because George had a lot on his mind and needed to move on. It was a much shorter meeting than he'd planned; he had a lot more questions and explanations that would have been beneficial to him that he felt George would know. Yet he'd put in his requests which were accepted immediately. As feelings come and go, Ben felt a suspicion rise up inside of him, but he quickly gave it up. He thought it was probably a leftover from the station when the sergeants ignored them totally. No, he thought, Captain Malick has been forthcoming and the confirmation would be verified in a couple of days when he found out the activities of the firm, which were critical to them at this time.

"Sorry, Ben. I've got so much on my plate right now. Don't mean to rush you, but I've got two meetings within an hour. Maybe we could meet again later in the week if you need me."

"I'll be fine as long as you get that information to me as soon as you can."

"That I'll be able to do. Until later then."

Although it was polite and congenial, Ben realized he'd been dismissed. George Malik was a very busy captain and Ben realized that his concerns were an extra added to George's regular heavy schedule. He thought maybe he should feel lucky that he gave him any time at all, and didn't pawn him off on another who didn't have his sensitivity. He headed back to his office to join Jeff and Sammi.

* * *

They were still deep into the files of both the supreme residents and searching for information on Milton Biltmore and Melanie Brooks. The connection was solid, but they needed to expand their knowledge. They didn't yet have any detailed information on those two and they needed that before they confronted them in any way.

"How'd it go?" asked Jeff.

"Fine," he said, deciding to keep his misgivings to himself. He still wondered what was wrong with George. Possibly, he was having an off day. "We should have some information regarding this company within a few days."

"That's good," said Sammi. "We need to meet with some of these people, casually if possible."

Ben's concerns were not lost on Sammi and listening to his thoughts, she realized his disappointment in Captain Malick's attitude. She made note of it.

"Yes, it would be better if they believed we had some legal business or connection with their firm. That would be the best way to handle this entire mess."

"Amilio would be a great person to have around at this time. He can become best friends with anybody at a moment's notice. I wish I had his knack with people," said Sammi.

"I agree, but unfortunately I believe he's on some other project right now. However, you do just fine with people from what I've seen."

Sammi smiled. "What's on our agenda for tomorrow?"

"Pretty much the same as today. I'll be waiting to hear from Captain Malick so I thought we could just continue searching for more information on that law firm. I was hoping that we could discover something vital on our own."

Sammi's face said it all. She had something on her mind that wasn't lost on Ben.

"Okay," he said, "what do you have in mind?"

"I'd like to get back over to the jail and talk to our Mr. Jim. He might have more to tell us. Besides, I'm trying to find out who he really is."

"That's a good idea," said Jeff. "It would give us a break from all this tedious stuff and we probably won't have that much time later. When it gets closer to trial, I have a feeling that the prosecution will protect him from us in some way."

"No doubt," said Ben. "The people here in this city are a different breed."

* * *

The next day as they entered the interview room next to the jail area, Sammi felt more prepared than the first time. Mr. Jim was a fascinating person to her and one who had obviously been wronged in some criminal way. He needed help to get back to his previous life and he no doubt had a family somewhere who had probably been mourning him for some time. This was one interesting puzzle she hoped to solve. Yet she knew there would be significant difficulty communicating with him considering the fact that his mind was definitely not working anywhere near full capacity. Still, his ideas and mental ability were functioning adequately and she felt spending more time with him, while talking to him from his thought world, would trigger hidden memories and cause them to rise up where she could deal with them.

Ben and Jeff had decided ahead of time that Sammi would be the lead person in this second interview. She had definitely gotten some focus out of him the previous time and they believed that if anyone could get some flash of reality to occur, it would be her. He almost had a look of recognition on his face as he entered the interview room and shuffled unsteadily forward to his chair. He was looking at the same three people he'd seen last week, yet his faraway gaze was forever crossing his eyes as if it had earned the right to be there.

"Hi Mr. Jim," said Sammi as she began. "It's good to see you again."

His thoughts hadn't yet had time to adjust to the surroundings, but she knew there was a hint of acknowledgment in his mind. His thoughts rattled on with some of the same phrases she'd heard before. 'It was the best of times; it was the worst of times.' That was followed by 'Tis a far, far better thing I do …' Sammi was waiting for another thought to cross over so she'd have a new topic to present to him on his personal terms. Finally, it happened, but it wasn't in thoughts only as he spoke aloud clearly and distinctly to all three of them and it had nothing to do with literature.

"I didn't kill any senator," said Mr. Jim. "I was just there."

Then he added a surprising statement, "But I know who did."

The words came out of his mouth rapidly and shocked his audience. They hadn't even asked a question yet and he blurted out an important answer. Sammi knew the thought had been heavy on his mind.

Ben and Jeff both jumped on that phrase.

"Who killed the senator, Mr. Jim? Who killed him?"

This time he pulled himself backward and away from the pointed question that was thrown at him from both of the men. He cowered to the furthest point of his chair, and stopped talking, as he began rocking his body with his arms enveloping his entire person and looked down at the floor. His hair, which had begun its change from the slightly gray world into the silvery white arena, still had plenty of dark brown in it. Sammi thought it was hard to guess his age, but put him around fifty-five. His large brown eyes could stare through you, especially when he seemed to be retreating into another world.

Ben said, "I think we scared him. We lost him again."

Jeff said, "Sammi handles him better. Sorry. We'll let you work this one out."

She listened to Mr. Jim as his frightened thoughts began to settle down. He was thinking, *I didn't kill that senator. I was there, but that's all. But I saw the person who killed him. I don't want to get in trouble so I'm not going to tell anyone. They kill people for doing things like that.*

Sammi lowered her tone of voice as she remembered last time he responded better to a calm and slower delivery with a soft and gentle quality.

"Mr. Jim," she said pausing before she continued. She said his name again forcing him to look up at her. "Mr. Jim. I like your name."

She waited. His thoughts again confirmed *I like my name.*

She gave that idea a moment to settle. She tried a different technique this time. "I know that you're a proud man, Mr. Jim. You're proud of all the classic authors you've studied, right?"

She got his attention. He looked directly at her and smiled. His thoughts told her that he liked his authors.

"I, too, like Charles Dickens, Emerson and Thoreau. I've read them, too."

She got a wide smile from him. Ben and Jeff looked at each other and were amazed at the fact that this confused lost soul had actually focused for a long moment on what Sammi had said.

"I like 'There is a time in every man's education when he arrives at the conviction that ...'" Sammi paused hoping Mr. Jim would pick up the thread. And he did.

"Envy is ignorance ... imitation is suicide ... he ... he must take himself ..." then he stopped. For a moment, he returned to his unfocused, lost shell, but he returned quickly to reality this time as he said, "You know, Emerson?"

"Yes, I like him."

Mr. Jim smiled and waited. Then to a shocked threesome he asked a question in perfect diction, with faultless clarity and no confusion; his question was completely lucid as well as audible. "You want to know what I saw that night."

Sammi slowly so as not to deter him said unhurriedly, "That would be most helpful to us because we know that you didn't kill the senator, Mr. Jim."

"You ... you believe me?"

Mr. Jim looked surprised as he waited for a reply.

"Yes, we do."

"Why? No one else here believes me?"

Then as quickly as he came out of his shell, he strolled back into his safe world and rocked on his chair for a few moments. Sammi gave him time and then she asked. "Would you like to tell us what you know?"

He nodded and stuttered as he said, "I don't always remember ... things good. I've been forgetting things for a long time. Forgot my whole life. I'm very sad ... I'm sad about that. But I remember that night because ... I was scared."

"Why were you scared?"

He looked searchingly at Sammi's face, and then replied, "I was close ... heard guns, two of them. People running and screaming." He suddenly started waving his arms up and down and was obviously reliving the scene of the crime.

"Did you see who the shooter was?" asked Sammi.

"I saw the person with the gun."

"Was it a man or woman?"

"Man – I'm sure it was a man."

That stopped even Sammi. She was trying to get him to talk aloud and wasn't paying as much attention to his thoughts. She tried to remain casual, but it was difficult. Then Mr. Jim continued without any further prompting.

"Policeman came up and gave me a gun. I took it, but I didn't shoot the senator."

Sammi asked, "Did the policeman shoot the senator?"

"No, No," he said very emphatically, "man in a dark suit. He's the one that did it."

Ben and Jeff did a double take. Sammi had already heard the thoughts. A police officer was involved in the killing.

"Did you ever see this policeman or the man in the suit before?" asked Sammi.

He shook his head at first, but then stopped. They had to wait a few more minutes. By now, all three of them were getting used to him. He came out of his shell and talked, and then he seemed to have to go back in for a bit. They waited until they saw a changed expression and then Ben asked a question.

"What about the other person?"

"Saw him on TV once. Maybe in the paper, too. Sometimes I read the paper, you know."

"Would you know them again?"

He hunched up his shoulders. "Guns scare me, but police scare me, too."

Mr. Jim was overwhelmed and slipping off again. He wasn't answering any question directly. They waited for his mind to clear, but before they had a chance to continue, they were interrupted.

The door from the hallway opened and a police officer came in grumbling and exhibiting unpleasant behavior. He needed something signed by Ben and then he left quickly.

When Sammi turned back to Mr. Jim, he had retreated deeply into his inner world again and he was shaking.

"I think this might be it for today."

With that, they decided to end the interview. Sammi gave Mr. Jim a very warm smile and he almost held eye contact with her for a second. She ended with a familiar phrase. "I like your name, Mr. Jim."

***

On the way out to the car, Sammi shared some of her feelings. "I've got a feeling that these officers might give us a tough time if we ask to see him again."

"Really?" said Ben. "We've got Captain Malick backing us up."

Sammi didn't answer, but she had heard something in Mr. Jim's thoughts that led her to believe that possibly those sergeants weren't working alone either. She didn't want Ben to trust anyone with all of their newfound information, but she needed a solid way to tell him. That could be a hard sell, yet she had to try.

"I'm getting some feelings about things around this department," said Sammi.

They both turned to her.

"Oh, it's nothing concrete at this time, but something doesn't feel right around here. I think it goes beyond those two sergeants and that we'd be wise in keeping a lot of this new information to ourselves."

Ben nodded. "Yeah, I didn't plan to share what we heard today with anyone, not even with Captain Malick. God, Sammi, I'm not sure about anyone around here anymore." He turned to look at Jeff and added, "It's just the three of us. It's as if it's very hard to know who you can trust around here. For now, it's just the three of us, okay?"

They all felt comfortable with that statement.

Sammi got a strange look on her face and Ben noticed. It wasn't something that was meant to be verbalized, but something that was passed on internally from person to person.

"I don't think we know even half of the story of what's going on around here. We still have some shockers ahead of us."

Jeff nodded and took a moment to reflect. "Usually when we can trust our own, then it's like the good guys against the bad guys. But right now, we don't even know for sure who the good guys are, if you know what I mean."

Ben couldn't stop shaking his head. "These criminals are getting so clever these days. It's so hard to tell whom to trust, hell, I'm really confused on this case. I long for the old days when we knew what we were up against. But now, you can never tell."

"More reason to be very cautious. We know who to trust, really and it's just the three of us. I'm glad you've decided to put Julie as our computer expert. That cuts down on some leaks as well. Dave, his group and the three of us is all I'm comfortable with now."

"That's it, then," said Ben. "And I should mention that I had a few negative feelings about George Malick earlier today. Something about him wasn't right at our latest meeting. It's nothing he said, just a feeling."

"That's where I get my best information," said Sammi. "I know this makes our job a lot harder, but it also makes their job harder, too. And it does put us in a good position."

Ben looked surprised. "How's that?"

Jeff looked at Sammi strangely. He needed an encouraging moment.

"Well, think of this," said Sammi. "First of all, George thinks he's got us. Although it's true that we rely on him for some information, we have other sources as well that he doesn't understand. This is the important part, we can feed them whatever we want and I don't think they'll doubt us. Can you see how important that might be?"

Both Jeff and Ben smiled while they nodded.

Ben said, "I like working with you more all the time."

Jeff added, "My kind of investigator."

Sammi couldn't hold back her laughter. "You know that we have to use every situation to our advantage. Therefore, if no one knows what Mr. Jim told us, we're ahead of them already. And I have a feeling that we can confuse them as much as they've tried to confuse us. Don't you think?"

As they all slowly started to walk away from their huddle, their steps were lighter and their bodies showed a renewed enthusiasm.

CHAPTER XI

Melanie Brooks usually steered away from joining anyone for lunch. She was a loner, both by choice and by definition. There weren't many people in this world that she trusted and wouldn't spend her relatively few free moments chatting away about nonsensical crap that didn't interest her. She'd always been like that. It was her choice. There were a few times when she was in middle school and high school that she tried to mingle more with other students in an effort to broaden her experience. She was bored to death. She couldn't believe what the girls wanted to talk about and the boys were just as immature. Of course, it was true that her young life had made her grow up fast. And it was also true that she felt somewhat sorry for herself to this day, but she had learned to cover her feelings and not many people would ever suspect that she was anything but a confident, self-propelled starter who was on a whirlwind path to success.

Having a little extra time today, which was an occasional luxury for her, she had that extra cup of coffee in her office and didn't even bother to sign into her computer or look at her mail. She didn't want to. Her mind was teeming with little droplets of information that were unrelated to each other but crowded in on her attention. She was slightly depressed, yet she was noticing a feeling of exhilaration and didn't know how the two feelings could live within her at the same time. Her record of accomplishment in this company was quite impressive and her record was above most of her male counterparts. She could always show those guys that she was their equal. They didn't even question her anymore but she still pushed on and on. She was always proving something to herself; it was a necessity that she'd done all her life. She was never good enough, not in her own estimation and never in that of her parents.

She leaned back confidently in her large brown leather chair knowing that she'd arrived, but her mother would never acknowledge it. Her father had passed on years ago and she had never been able to impress him, not even when she won awards for excellence. She took a deep breath and a sip of latte coffee that pleased her taste buds. Again, she took a deep breath. It was finally relaxing her.

Her phone rang. She barely glanced at it and decided not to answer. Then, out of the corner of her right eye, she saw the red light. That was her private line that only four people had and rarely used. Her boss and ex-husband, Milton Biltmore and her secretary knew to use it only on urgent matters. Yet there were two other hidden people from her secret past who were allowed to contact her in this way. Always this phone line was important and she knew she had to pick up.

"Hi Milt. This must be important to use this line."

"Absolutely," he said, "We've got an urgent matter on our hands."

Melanie thought that Milton had a way of dragging any otherwise ordinary and commonplace occurrence so far out of proportion that she hardly recognized it. Yet, he was one of her bosses and remained a surprisingly congenial friend considering she once had been married to him, so she gave him the courtesy of focused interest.

"You sound worried. What's up?"

"It's the senator's murder. Look, I know you said that you didn't have anything to do with that, but are you telling me the truth? If you're not, we could all be in big trouble around here."

"Why? What's going on?"

"Okay, Melanie. One of my spies tells me that they've brought in the FBI and a few other special investigators to solve this thing quickly."

"Wait a minute; wait a minute. They brought in that homeless person and he's under arrest as far as I know. The police told me that they believe he committed the murder and can prove it. I thought that was a done deal. "

"I know; I know, and so did I, but apparently, not everyone is convinced so the FBI is starting its own investigation and that could mean trouble. I don't want anyone nosing around here. They think we're a reputable firm and I want to keep it that way."

"We are a reputable firm, Milton. All of our work is legit and above board. Why are you sweating this one out?"

"You know why. If anyone finds out about our extra activities, we could lose everything. They'd consider us subversive and un-American and God knows what else ... just for expressing our opinions in a legal and non combative way. That's supposed to be our right."

"It is our right. I know we've pushed the envelope right up to the edge a few times, Milton, but we've never crossed that line. Everything we've done is legal; we shouldn't have any problems even if they do investigate us."

"Yes, I guess you're right. When I heard about the FBI, I figured they'd look into us and a few others around, but I want them to move on fast."

"I'm sure they will. It should be boring for them around here."

"But you didn't answer me. You didn't kill Mike Stedman, did you? You weren't involved in any way."

Melanie took a quick deep breath realizing that she was amazed at Milton's insinuation. "Milton, Milton. After three years of marriage you don't know me better than that."

"It wasn't a very good marriage, Melanie and we didn't confide in each other at all."

"That's true, but it wasn't only me."

"I know, I know. Okay, we'll have to keep on top of this one. If anyone talks to you, let me know immediately."

"Relax, we'll be okay."

"Hope you're right this time."

"I usually am."

* * *

Then Milt abruptly hung up. She let out a sigh. He kept pushing her about the murder of Mike Stedman. She gave out an involuntary smirk. She was quite sure he didn't realize that she hadn't actually answered his question. She was good at clouding up the issues and subtly ending up on a different note so that Milt went along with it, not realizing what had happened. But he kept pushing harder all the time. One time, probably in the not too distant future, he would pin her down and then she'd have to look him right in the eye and convince him. That might be more difficult to do.

Her other telephone rang. She answered it and took care of some office business, nothing important, just a routine matter.

She gave an automatic response without realizing it. Her mind was on several other matters of greater urgency. She was thinking back about Mike Stedman. He had been the love of her life back in college and still held a special place in her life, if she admitted the truth to herself. She had dated him for well over six months exclusively on her part and thought he was as serious as she was. He had said so, well, maybe not in so many words, but she believed his actions. He fulfilled in her the feelings that had been so lacking in her life.

She felt she had a best friend that she could trust, and he took the place of her uncaring and indifferent father as well as fulfilling the role of lover and confidante. She had never been happier in her life. Yet he didn't seem to be as totally committed as she was. She hated to admit it to herself but she remembered a typical conversation during this time when he seemed to be pulling away. It scared her and left her angry as well as confused.

"We're on for this weekend, right? I so look forward to spending time with you," she said.

"Sure Melanie, all this weekend belongs to you. What would you like to do?"

"Just spend time with you. I love you so much. I need to be close to you."

She loved to talk to him like that, but knew that sometimes he seemed to back off. She wasn't pushing too hard, was she? He almost winced a few times at the word love. He was timid regarding any assurance of their future together. Yet he'd come back and respond favorably.

"Sure, I'd like to spend time with you, too. Remember, though, next weekend I'm going back home for a while."

"Can't I come with you? I've wanted to meet your family."

That was the first time that she noticed he definitely pulled back. She tried to pin him down a few times on making a further commitment, but he was never ready. She was more than ready herself, but she thought she'd give him all the time he needed. She knew the time would come when he'd be ready to commit to her. She hoped it would be soon.

"I have to meet your family sometime. Why not next weekend?"

"Well," he said, definitely making another convenient excuse, "we've got family business to discuss and it would be too awkward for you to be there."

As she pouted some, he tried to soothe her feelings.

"Look, Melanie, we've got a great friendship going. We can't push things, okay? Let's enjoy wherever it takes us."

She looked at him stunned. He was definitely giving her a message and it was one that she didn't want to hear. It hurt so much looking at his face and hearing words that were noncommittal. At the time, she knew she had to try harder. She felt she'd take the time when he was away, reassess the situation and be ready with a better plan when he returned.

Her phone rang again, but it wasn't her private line. She ignored it. She had mixed feelings about her reminiscent thoughts. He had loved her, hadn't he? There must have come a time when he really loved her. They were together at least part of every weekend for six months. She knew that she'd been the one who pushed the relationship in the beginning, but he wasn't exactly reluctant or unwilling. She was the leader, she knew that but she had that type of personality where people just moved aside and let her walk through. She relished the thought. People noticed her that way, something that had never happened in her early life. In her family, she knew she was an afterthought. Her parents didn't even want another child, let alone a girl so she acted aggressively and found out that was the only way to get attention. That type of behavior carried over into her personal affairs for the rest of her life. It had done her well. She'd moved up the ladder in a firm that boasted of male priority, but learned to accept her as an equal.

Her secretary buzzed her.

"You've got your staff meeting in ten minutes in the main conference room."

"Right," she said. "Thanks, Angie."

She could always count on Angie getting her where she needed to be on time. She grabbed her notes giving them a once over. She felt confident, but then she always did. She knew her job, how to handle and comprehend any part of it. However, there was this murder of Senator Stedman that had everyone looking in her direction. It did make her nervous, because anything connected with Mike hit an emotional note, but she'd handle it like she did the rest of her life.

She hadn't yet taken the time to really think of Mike Stedman as dead. He was gone and part of her knew it, but another part wouldn't even face the possibility. She still loved him in a special way, but as the years passed, she realized her love was more of a friendship. Milton had hinted to her a few times that he wondered whether she'd killed him or had anything to do with his murder. Milton didn't know her as well as she thought. She still would have done almost anything in the world for Mike Stedman, mostly for old time's sake. Mike had always been her anchor for something or other, usually that supportive male figure that escaped her in her early life. Even in later years, she used him as that support, even though she knew he was happily married to someone else.

There was her buzzer again. It was Angie.

"Three minutes before your staff meeting You've got to leave now."

"Thanks Angie, I'm on my way."

She had another secret regarding Mike Stedman. But she had no time to think about it now. She put her thoughts about Mike in a special category in the back of her mind. It was as if she had a filing cabinet in her brain and could close the drawer on any thought whenever she wanted. She had always been able to do that. She'd done it all her life. Whenever something bothered her too much she'd bury the thoughts away in her mind in special places and bring them back only when she wanted to face them. She was good at that.

* * *

The meeting went over the standard business matters and Melanie, as usual was on top of it. She gave her brief presentation of the accounts she was responsible for and there weren't any questions from anyone. She was always completely thorough. Later, coming out of the meeting, she had Milton on her tail again. He never gave her a minute's rest on this murder.

"I've been summoned for a meeting with the FBI for this afternoon. Damn, Melanie, I wish I knew what was going on."

"What do they want to talk to you about?"

"It's got to be the murder and I don't know anything at all. You better not be holding back on me."

"I'm not. I don't know anything either. Why the hell don't you leave me alone? It's like you're making me the main suspect."

"Knock it off, Melanie. You'd been wild about him all of your life. That's what ruined our marriage. Maybe your crush finally pushed you over the edge. I know you would do anything for him at any time and you never got over your anger and pain when he'd be in the news with his wife. It always ate away at you. You couldn't hide it."

She stopped in her tracks, put her hands on her hips, stared him directly in the eyes, and didn't even blink when she answered.

"You've got to be crazy. My obsession was in your imagination. Sure, I loved him years ago, but I did manage to get over it. You're the one that didn't. You used to ask me to play up to him at parties for information, but that was your request, not mine. Don't you forget it. "

"Like hell. It seemed to me that you certainly enjoyed the attention from him. I can't figure out if you're fooling yourself or trying to fool me. That's the one thing I felt sorry for you about ... the only thing."

"You're an idiot. If I wanted him that bad, I could have gotten him back. He wasn't nearly as important to me as you thought."

"We'll see who the idiot is if you had anything to do with his killing."

Melanie stared at him in disbelief as he turned to walk away. Did he really believe what he was saying? She had to admit that the pain in her heart and the anger within her being had lessened to a large degree over the years. Yet, it had never completely disappeared. She felt she hid it well, but was at a loss to make it go away totally. She finally reasoned that it was one of those happenings in life that everyone experienced in order to teach them lessons, and the recurring pain was a reminder to make you stronger. In a way Milton was right; she had married him because a married position would be more comfortable to her at that time in her life. Yet Milton hadn't lived up to his end of the bargain; he was overly jealous of her whenever other men showed interest in her. He was especially unbearable when they met Mike and his wife at parties. She was still staring at him as he walked down the hall and suddenly he turned to face her.

"You be in my office as soon as I return. Hopefully, I'll be back by five o'clock. I expect you to be there."

With that he turned the corner and was out of her sight.

Damn it, she thought. I'm having more problems with him now than when we were married; this entire relationship with him is still crap and always was.

The rest of her day she spent in intimidated anticipation of when Milt would return. If she had known what he was like, she'd never have married him. Before he seemed so independent and strong in areas she needed, but he turned out to be more of a wimp than any guy she'd ever known. She was disgusted.

* * *

Marvin Antwerp walked into her office. He always seemed to be around and she hoped that he hadn't overheard her and Milt go at it again. But it really didn't matter, not much anyway. She was sure that he'd overheard her and Milt during their many heated discussions that often took place in the hallway. It was a regular happening.

Marvin was sort of a breath of fresh air to her most of the time. At seven years her junior, he'd been with the firm for the last five years and had the light congenial attitude where he took life in his stride and had a positive approach to solving any problem. She'd had dinner with him a few times, only as a business partner, but she enjoyed him. There was talk that he had a slight crush on her, but she doubted it. She'd seen him around with plenty of other women.

"I have the notes ready on the Frazier account and need you to okay them. I think they're in good order, but I'd like you to get a chance to read them and let me know if I need to make any changes. It's a big account."

"Of course," she answered

"When do you think that you might get a chance to do this?"

"You caught me at a good time. I've got to stay here until Milt returns so I'll spend my time looking over your comments."

"Great," said Marvin. "He sure is miffed about that meeting with the FBI, isn't he?"

"Everything is touchy that has to do with the Stedman murder."

"I heard you used to date him," he said.

She turned and gave him her most surprised look. "Who told you that?"

"Sorry, but it's common gossip around the water cooler," he joked. Yet she was thinking that she did detect a rather sad, confusing look on his face.

"It was such a long time ago."

"I still remember my first love; it's the one that usually hurts the most, don't you think?"

"Yes, I guess so. We're much more open to believing in the impossible when we're younger so that when breakups happen, it's harder to handle. But that's how we learn to get tougher and grow up, right?"

"Yeah, it is. That's life." Even though Marvin said the right words, somehow Melanie wasn't convinced of his sincerity.

He turned on that remark and made it all the way to the door. He turned and said, "But it's one of the hardest ones to get over."

And with that he was gone. Melanie had to reflect on his words. Sometimes it was the one that was impossible to forget.

* * *

Milton Biltmore had been so nervous about the meeting with the FBI that he angered himself. He had nothing to hide about the murder; he didn't know anything about it. But he had other things to hide, namely his association with The Right Side Group. That was his biggest concern. Yet the meeting never touched on that subject much to his surprise and delight. They seemed satisfied that he wasn't involved in the murder and didn't know who was. He had been grilled about Melanie; she was their next target and he wondered how she would handle that. He would get pleasure in telling her when he returned to the office.

He was furious when Melanie wasn't waiting in his office when he returned. He forgot that she had taken his place in a meeting with the Board of Directors and blasted her as she walked through the door.

She answered by matching his anger. "If you don't change your God damned attitude I've no problem walking right back out that door and never giving you the results of the board's meeting."

Milton was embarrassed. "The meeting slipped my mind. Sorry."

Melanie was shocked. Milton never said he was sorry about anything, not during their marriage, not after and nowhere in between. His apologetic attitude was the only reason she decided to sit down at all, but she was ready to move out at a moment's notice if he reverted to his usual authoritarian and condescending self.

"Look, I'm sorry, okay?" he said knowing she hadn't completely forgiven him. He wasn't always sure why she irritated him so much. Deep down he still cared about her, but was happy that his excessive jealously didn't have a reason to exist anymore. He now felt that he'd probably live longer.

"How did the meeting go?" she asked, since he wasn't bringing up the subject.

"Better than expected. I was able to convince them that I didn't murder the senator, wasn't in a conspiracy to murder him and didn't know who did. They asked the same questions in several different ways to throw me off, but it didn't work. I don't know anything. Also, they didn't even bring up The Right Side Group, so that made me very happy. I guess the senator's murder is all that's on their minds right now. But they asked a lot of questions about you, so be prepared."

She didn't believe his slight attempt at concern. "What did they ask about me?"

"They'll be talking to you, I'm sure. They wanted to know if I thought you might be involved and they knew you had a relationship with Mike in the past."

"Gees," she said as she looked down at the floor. Her dark hair landed over one eye and she had to push it back. This happened constantly. It was a nervous habit with her.

"Did they say when?"

"No, but I can't imagine that it would be too long. They're really trying to move forward on this one. At least, that was my impression."

Melanie looked a tad nervous but tried to hide it as much as possible. "Is that it for today?"

Milton nodded. She rose to leave. At the door, she turned and said, "And I won't expect you to be waiting for me when I return." With that, she left his office and closed the door with more force than was needed. It pleasured her to do that.

* * *

Ben Collier and Jeff Slade decided to postpone the interview with Melanie Brooks until Sammi was available. They needed all of the help they could get to decipher the truth from her. Sammi was always good at that. A few more days wouldn't matter.

"That Milton Biltmore was one nervous guy," said Jeff. "I wonder what he's hiding."

Ben said, "Some people get nervous when they have to deal with the police or the FBI."

"I think it's more than that," said Jeff. "I think he was afraid that we were going to question him on The Right Side Group."

Ben looked over thoughtfully. "That's an idea. Hey, Jeff, you're getting more like Sammi every day."

He laughed. "I wish she had been here today. She doesn't miss much. When is she coming back?"

"On Tuesday. They wanted her in court when the Judge was deciding if they could finally question those suspects. Sergeant Brady wanted everyone in that courtroom to back up their side as much as possible."

Jeff said, "I would think that Sammi needed to be there to get a feel of where the case was heading. She always needs to get a sense of the atmosphere around a situation."

Ben smiled. He knew that feelings were important to Sammi. "So we'll try to get an interview with this Melanie Brooks for Tuesday or Wednesday. She should be an interesting character from what I hear."

"I've heard that as well. She can be mouthy and pushy and she needs to be in control. I must admit though, from what I've heard, she's one smart woman."

"To compete in that company she'd have to be."

Jeff said, "Okay I'll see what I can set up for Tuesday or Wednesday and hopefully between all of us we can pick up what's really going on beyond the words she chooses to say."

"That's what we need."

* * *

It had been a working weekend for Sammi and Dave. Much background information and details needed to be worked out before they headed to court on Monday. After several meetings with the entire group, a plan was in place. Amilio and Sammi were the best point people they had. Putting them in strategic positions in the courtroom would best determine what was going on in the minds of the lawyers as well as the defendants. They needed to be aware of everything they could possibly find out, as the proceedings were finally moving forward. Since another delay seemed unlikely, the police and FBI needed to be ready.

The courtroom consisted mainly of the lawyers, defendants and pertinent witnesses that needed to be there. It certainly wasn't a packed room. Sammi looked over at Amilio who confirmed that he liked the way this situation was playing out today.

Judge Samuel Rosen came in and started the proceedings. He listened to the opening arguments by the defense lawyers and Sammi quickly realized that he had no sympathy for these defendants who'd been given every consideration possible. Still, he listened with as much of an open mind as he could muster.

The defense's argument was still that they needed more time.

"You still have almost two months before the trial begins. That seems time enough to me," said the Judge.

"But we need to be confidential in our approach until a few weeks before the trial," said the lead attorney Andrew Meadows.

"The prosecution needs to have access to these defendants so they can prepare their case as well," said the Judge.

The defense pounced on that statement. "Your Honor, that would give them unfair advantage."

Judge Rosen stroked his chin as he considered that comment. "In what possible way would they have unfair

Evil Thoughts Kill Dreams/Drouillard

advantage? I believe the unfair advantage card has been on your side of the deck for quite some time."

"But your Honor," he managed to get out before the Judge shut him down.

"I want to hear from the other side. I've heard your arguments almost exclusively in the last few months. I believe it's their turn now."

Mr. Meadows slammed his fist on the conference table. The Judge turned his eyes and stared at him as he remarked. "I'm going to guess that was an accident this one time, right?"

"Oh yes, I apologize Your Honor," said the lead attorney with sincere sentiment lacking in his tone and demeanor. His body deportment connoted a person who wanted to direct the parade.

It was so noted by the Judge who turned his attention directly to the prosecution. "And what have you to say?"

"Your Honor, we have a case to prepare as well. We've been allowed no contact with the defendants, except for a brief talk when they were first arrested. At that time, they wouldn't discuss anything without the presence of their lawyers so we've never had a chance to hear their side of the story or even question their motives. I think that part has been very unfair, but realize that the courts want to make sure that these defendants are given every consideration. Yet the time has come when we need to understand the entire situation of this crime and give the people a reasonable attempt at our justice system. We've been patient. We've not fought the previous rulings. Yet if we do not get to have complete and free access to these individuals now, we are the ones who'll be at the unfair advantage side of the scale."

The defense attorney couldn't contain himself. He jumped up yelling that he needed more time and that our justice system was built on the fact that every defendant was entitled to the best defense available.

"And that will be your job, Mr. Meadows," said the Judge. "There will be no more delays, no more dramatics in my courtroom as I've bent the rules in your favor long enough. As of next week, the prosecution and anyone else that they deem necessary will have complete access to these defendants to begin their investigation and make their own preparation for trial. It is so ordered," he said as the gavel came down. The defense attorney reacted in thought and action in a manner not fit for any courtroom, which got him another reprimand from the judge

"Your outbursts are hurting your case with me already; I want you to realize that."

A very sheepish as well as embarrassed look on the face of attorney Meadows said it all. He had to learn to control himself.

* * *

When Dave met Sammi's gaze, he knew that something was brewing. Amilio was still watching the defendants as they sauntered out of the courtroom. It was unusual that they appear in court today, but the judge wanted them to know first-hand what was happening with their case. He knew the lawyers would tell their side of the story, and that was okay, but the court had its own obligation and felt it would be met by having them present in court today. This served Sammi as well as Amilio quite well.

Amilio received impressions about people that were always well above and beyond the ordinary person's evaluation. He was actually quite intuitive, but also realized that Sammi came up with data that baffled him. *How did she do it?*

Dave said, "Okay Amilio, what did you think?"

"I think they're going to have a problem with that Meadows fellow unless he learns to keep himself under control. What's with him anyway? He should know that's no way to act in front of a judge?"

"He was trying to make a point," said Sammi. "He wanted to be as obnoxious as possible this time around so that when the trial comes up he plans to act demure and reserved and make an inroad with the judge."

Dave and Amilio looked at each other.

Amilio said, "Good strategy, I never thought of that."

Sammi added. "Well, you know that if he looks like he's learned his lesson the judge will take note of that."

"Yeah, yeah," said Amilio. "He probably would at that."

Dave had a questioning look on his face. "Do you think that would work?"

"Usually it probably would work quite well," said Sammi, "but this Andrew Meadows does have a tough time controlling himself and I can't see him making it through the entire trial without losing it again. When the proceedings start leaning in the prosecution's favor, I think our Mr. Meadows won't be able to hold it together."

Amilio laughed. "From what I've seen today, I'd have to agree."

"What did you think about the defendants, Amilio?" Dave was anxious to hear his assessment.

"I think the leader, Jason, is quite set in his ways. He really believes in The Right Side Group and their mission, so I don't think we'll get much out of him in questioning."

He turned to Sammi for a moment and grinned. "Of course that's from my point of view. You always figure out something. What did you think today?"

Sammi smiled as she said, "I always have to type up my notes first."

"That's right. You need your notes," he teased.

Dave asked, "What about the other two, Amilio? Do you think we have a chance with them?"

"I think they're both scared and want out. They might give out information if we offered them a good plea deal."

"Yeah," said Dave. "They didn't seem as determined as Jason at all. They were nervous and hesitant. I'm looking forward to questioning them next week."

He turned to Sammi. "We'll have to talk to Ben and work it out in your schedule."

"It should work out. Tomorrow we interview Melanie Brooks, which is one interview we've been waiting for. Then depending on what happens, we'll have more work this week. Let's talk to Ben. Maybe I'll stick around for Monday or Tuesday or for however long I'm needed next week."

"Are they still targeting that hobo?" asked Amilio.

"Seems that way. No one, other than the three of us is investigating anything else. I think they may all have quite a surprise later on."

"Do you have any idea yet?"

"A few, but they're only guesses right now. I'm hoping Melanie's interview will provide a new lead or two."

"Yeah," said Amilio, "it's tough to be working in the dark and sometimes it takes a while for a solid lead."

Sammi nodded.

Dave said, "I'm anxious for Sammi to type up her notes, so we'll see you later. I'll have a copy for you tomorrow."

Amilio gave them both a suspicious look. "I'm anxious to see her notes as well."

* * *

Dave put an affectionate arm around Sammi's shoulder as they walked out to the car. "I'm really curious what you found out about today."

She smiled, in a teasing way. "I know you are, but I'm going to type up my notes first. There's a few things I need to get in the right order so it'll make more sense. But there were a few bits and pieces that surprised me today."

Dave nodded. "Okay, I'll make dinner and you get your notes translated. It does seem that by next week we should be finding out what's really happening around here."

"Right now it's confusing, even to me. All three of these guys' thoughts were scattered and illogical at times. Even their defense attorney is in on something, but I'm not sure what yet. These defendants didn't work alone, not exactly."

Dave looked at her confused.

"Their thoughts were confusing, Dave. They were jumping here and there in their thought world so I really do need time to put it all together. It'll make more sense that way."

"Okay, I understand. Hopefully we can get some insight into what's going on."

"I think we will, but these guys are hiding so much, and I couldn't catch it all."

* * *

Sammi welcomed the time when she was in her computer room alone, investigating her private thoughts and ideas. No one could understand what she went through trying to catch all of the fleeting images that went on in the courtroom today. This had been a considerable challenge for her. Oh sure, she thought that the three defendants, sitting together and thinking toward each other would be easy enough, and that alone wasn't the problem. But there were many other dynamics taking place that needed her consideration. Some surprised even her and she needed to make some semblance of logic between all of them.

The attorney, Andrew Meadows was an entire subject that she could have spent all day eavesdropping into his teeming thought world. He was totally involved in these proceedings and a lot of others happening in nearby areas of Pennsylvania. However, his association with these defendants equally shared the importance in his mind with another subject of identical value to him, namely his desire to maintain a positive relationship with Milton Biltmore. In fact, it was a direct phone call from Milton that convinced him to defend these suspects. Yet Sammi didn't feel that these two men were friends, but merely business associates for a common goal. She was worried because she didn't have all of the facts collected yet.

Dave came in and surprised her.

"Just keep working, but I thought you could use a cup of coffee. I'll hold dinner until you're finished."

She smiled. He could be so thoughtful. "About another half hour and I think I'll have the major points settled that I was concerned about. But I need a good discussion with you so I can decide how you want me to write the report that we'll give to the others."

Dave nodded and slowly walked out.

* * *

After dinner, relaxing in the living room with a cup of vanilla bean latte, Sammi was ready to share some of her confusion with Dave. Today had been more difficult than she had anticipated and her notes were still not in completely logical order.

"Just tell me what you've got and we'll decide together what to do with them."

She nodded and began. "First of all, their attorney Andrew Meadows is involved in a lot of stuff. I'm aware that he's their attorney, but that's not what I'm talking about. He has some type of relationship with Milt Biltmore."

Dave was impressed as well as intrigued. "That's interesting considering that Andrew's reputation and career has been mainly in this area of Pennsylvania. Wonder where they met?"

"Don't know. It never came up, but Andrew thinks of him as a mentor who can lead him to good contacts. In fact I got the impression that he doesn't make any important moves without checking with him."

"And you said that Milton was the one who suggested that he represent these suspects."

Sammi nodded.

"Okay, why? Any ideas?"

"A few. First of all, even though I don't know where or when they met, I believe that Andrew has savored his relationship with Milton since they met. He thinks he's lucky to have him in his corner for discussions."

"He seems to be considerably younger than him so it's not likely they met in college or early in their careers. I wonder what the connection is."

Sammi asked, "How old do you think he is?"

"Early to middle thirties, maybe thirty-two, thirty-three. What do you think?"

Sammi said, "That's probably what I'd guess. We should have Julie find out about his background. That could help."

"And finding their connection could help as well."

"Possibly, but they both have a common link to Melanie Brooks."

Dave let out a whistle. "Really? It'd be interesting to find out what that is."

"I have no idea. Maybe when we interview Melanie later this week I'll have Ben ask her a few questions that might trigger something in that area. Personally, I think it's bizarre that they have a strong connection. Can't imagine what it could be; I mean Melanie is in her middle forties. That makes it unlikely that they had a close relationship."

"Unlikely but not impossible." said Dave.

"You've got a point. It could be they had a thing at one time, but somehow I don't feel that's the connection."

"We'll have to wait and see on that," said Dave. "My biggest surprise is that these two cases seem to be so closely connected. I'd have never guessed that at the beginning."

"Well, let me go on. Some of our suspicions were correct. Jason is the only strong member of this group. The other two joined as a fluke and were thinking of bowing out even before this attack on you and Roy, but this cinched it. They want out – both of them; they are wondering why they got themselves into this situation. I think they'll do anything for a plea deal, but they are nervous and plan to leave town as soon as they can. In fact one of them was thinking that if he went to jail at all, he'd request jail in another nameless state as part of the plea."

"They sure sound nervous, but that can be good, at least for us. It could work to our advantage."

Sammi continued. "But I don't really understand the connection in all this. Apparently, Milton has nothing to do directly with The Right Side Group, at least nothing that we could discover. He's heard of them, obviously, but what he does is not under an affiliation with anyone. Remember it was stated that many of these groups pop up sporadically here and there around the country, but they're not associated with each other. Milton is always very interested in what non-violent causes they are proposing. If it happens to be anything that could benefit his company policies, he's not beyond helping out in a disguised way."

"That's interesting. He obviously doesn't want to be connected with them, at least not in the open. Still, he wouldn't mind taking advantage of any policy change they could bring about. On the other hand, if they'd have to come out in the open and become well known, he wouldn't want to be associated with this subversive group, or any other for that matter. They own companies and businesses, which would probably suffer tremendously if they were considered un-American. Kind of a Catch-22."

Sammi added, "And this Andrew Meadows is somewhat of a hothead who can't always keep his temper under control. Yet, since he's associated with these secret groups, I'll bet he worries a few people."

"Could be or it could have been more of a show in the courtroom. Remember how we discussed that if he looked more penitent next time in front of the judge, he could win sympathy."

Sammi replied. "That's true, but his inner thoughts belied the fact that he doesn't always have control and some definite thoughts were working in that area."

"That's good to know. Someday we may need to push his buttons and if he did explode, well ..."

"There's a lot we can do with this kind of information."

Dave simply smiled. "What else did you get?"

"Jason was supposed to be laying low for a while. That's what his dad wanted. But when he saw you and Roy in the vicinity of Phil Pentin, he couldn't pass up the opportunity. He thinks his father is quite upset with what he did."

"Wonder if he'd have felt the same way if we'd been killed?"

"Don't know. But he hasn't had a chance to visit his father in jail and he's pretty upset about seeing him."

"So apparently this wasn't in his father's plans; probably too close on the tail of the murder of that senator. In fact, that probably put too much emphasis on the group; yes, I can see why his father would be upset."

"You see all I have are a bunch of innuendos. There's nothing here that's real concrete."

"Are you kidding? You'll have us going in a new direction now. This connection is very important, even though we don't know exactly what it is yet. And I'm going to get Julie working on digging up everything she can about Andrew Meadows. You did great, Sammi."

"Still, I like it better when things are more cut and dried."

"But you had a lot of people in that courtroom today to think about. Don't worry, I think we'll get a lot of mileage from this information."

Sammi yawned. She was tired and she had to get ready to leave on the charter Tuesday morning.

"You look tired. It's been a long day.

"Yes, it has, Dave. But tomorrow we'll start another chapter in Hartford. Hope I can get something out of this Melanie Brooks."

CHAPTER XII

They had chosen to interview Melanie Brooks in her business office for calculated reasons. Being in her natural work environment could induce relaxation and possibly help Sammi pick up what she wanted without needing to ask obvious questions. Also, being in her comfortable surroundings might cause Melanie to reflect back in time and Sammi knew that would be most valuable to them.

Just entering Melanie's office seemed to send out an unusual explanatory tone of its own, at least it did for Sammi. It conveyed the impression of a very strong and confident person, yet one who was also quite timid and untrusting, a trait that seemed to stay in the woodwork and didn't lend itself to the people who occasionally entered her office. She hid her real personality quite well and even Sammi had to be particularly observant to dig out some lower thoughts that she tried to keep as hidden as possible.

Being the shrewd executive that she'd manage to become, she extended every courteous pleasantry that she could manage from offering coffee to comfortable chairs and even went as far as to lower the blinds of the rather large bay window in her corner office, which would have given her the advantage in eye contact. They all knew immediately that they were dealing with someone who was much more astute than Milt Biltmore. He connoted nervous energy from the beginning, but Melanie Brooks tried to emit the casualness of a forthcoming and friendly meeting where all parties could relax. Although it was a gallant attempt, no one was fooled by her actions, not even Melanie.

"Please make yourself comfortable. I've sent for coffee and we can begin whenever you're ready. What exactly did you want to talk with me about?"

She held an expressionless look on her face, hoping to deter nosy comments. Yet her strong body position and the questioning tilt of her head suggested that she knew she was in for a tough grilling.

Ben was just opening his mouth to speak when the door opened and a silver tray with coffee rolled in on a serving table. It took only moments to serve everyone and this time when Ben began to speak, he was blunt.

"I should think you'd know that we're here to talk about the death of Senator Mike Stedman. That should be obvious to you. We know that you dated him a while back and seemed to make a play for him at various parties and functions in the last year or so. Let's put our cards on the table, Ms. Brooks, we're not here to play any games."

Ben had been purposely straightforward and direct because he didn't sidetrack the main issues. He usually started out his questioning sessions by diving immediately into the main topics. That way it was obvious to anyone that he didn't put up with any crap. It had already angered him from the beginning that Melanie tried to make light of the situation; he couldn't quite put his personal feelings aside. He waited for her to answer.

Melanie was caught by surprise at Ben's curt comments; that was obvious to all. She took a moment to sit back in her chair. She pursed her lips, looked from Ben to Jeff, and took a longer moment to try to figure out what Sammi was all about. Ben noticed and offered an olive branch, hoping that they could finally begin in earnest.

"You know that I'm Ben Collier and this is my colleague Jeff Slade." Turning toward Sammi he added, "and this is Sammi Evans who works with us as well."

It was obvious to all that Sammi seemed to fascinate her. However, with Ben's next question, her attention immediately focused on what she needed to say.

"When did you first meet Mike Stedman?"

The look of resignation on her face signified that she might as well get the basics over. "Okay, well, Mike and I knew each other a very long time ago. Actually, it was during our college years and a little after that as well. We were serious for a while, at least I was, but I wondered about him later on. I mean, he led me to believe that his interest was much more than simply casual, yet he had difficulty taking our relationship to the next step."

"So you were never engaged or anything like that?" asked Ben.

"To be honest, I would have liked to be. But Mike seemed to be unsure and I wanted to give him all the time he needed. I guess I gave him too much time or too much space because the next thing I knew he had met someone else. He wanted to remain good friends with me, but ..." she stopped and took a deep breath, "it broke my heart at the time." After a moment, she added, "But that was a long time ago."

She abruptly finished and although tempted, didn't say another word. She felt she had totally answered the question and Sammi knew that she didn't like to talk about that part of her life to this day. That was a failure to her. She didn't like to concentrate on failures and was waiting for more direct questions. Sammi felt her thoughts conveyed that she always had a soft spot for her first real love, but realized that it would never be. That didn't stop her from daydreaming once in a while, but she was a logical thinker and knew the line that separated reverie from reality.

"It's been noted by several people that you made a play for Mike at some of the parties which you both attended. Were you hoping to get something started with him again?"

She put out an almost silent smirk. "I, too, was married at the time and my husband was jealous enough. I didn't need any more trouble. No, no, but there were times that I would ... actually our firm here .... would have liked to know how he stood on certain issues and how he was likely to vote. That was my main goal, but I have to admit that I wasn't very successful."

Jeff asked, "Then you are saying that your pretense at flirting with him was mainly to get information?"

"Mainly, yes, but I must admit that it was fun for me as well. And it didn't bother me a bit that his Mrs. was irritated by my behavior."

Ben raised an eyebrow so she continued. "Well, she was my competition and she won. And she was such a Miss Goody Goody, if you know what I mean. I hated losing to someone I felt was beneath me."

"Did you hold any hard feelings for the way the relationship went?" asked Jeff.

She looked at him slyly as she said, "Oh I see. Did I hate him enough to kill him or have someone else kill him? Is that what you're getting at?" She again relaxed in her chair and enjoyed a satisfying grin. "No, definitely no. If that is what this interrogation is about then you really are wasting your time. Sure sometimes it still bugged me when I saw him on television or in the newspaper with his wife on his arm, but it was only a passing reminder of a long ago hurt. You know, you never really forget your first love. But that was a long time ago. There have been many others since then."

Sammi felt she had to get into the game. Melanie's thoughts were not totally honest. Something else had happened with Mike Stedman. She was keeping something concealed that required secret protection and her thoughts wouldn't allow that information to climb up near the surface. Yet she didn't mourn Mike's death as much as Sammi thought she should. She was sad that he'd been killed, true, but it seemed to have ended something for her that needed to be deemed finished. There was much more to Melanie Brooks than Sammi had assumed.

"And you were married at the time of these purposeful flirtations?"

"Yes, I was," she replied. It was obvious she didn't want to elaborate on this part of her life.

"To whom?" asked Sammi.

Again was that look of resignation so she consented to talk about that part of her life.

"I was married to Milton Biltmore, but I would have guessed that you already knew that. Yes, he was my boss at the time and yes, I really did feel that it would work out and fulfill something in me that was missing. He turned out to be very jealous, something he didn't show while we were in a relationship. And after a while, it didn't work out. Although we still to this day have some heated arguments, business arguments that is, we truly get along better now than we did when we were married."

"So Milt encouraged these flirtations?" asked Ben.

"Well, he certainly didn't object. Like I said, it was to find out some information that would help our company, that's all."

"It doesn't sound like you were too unhappy to hear that he had been killed; were you?" asked Jeff.

That stopped her for a moment. She wondered how she should answer that question. If she didn't feel too unhappy about Mike's death, then they might suspect her. Yet, she didn't kill Mike, but she did have a few suspicions of who would have had good reason. Sammi was hoping that her thoughts would reveal more.

"I did feel bad, but it wasn't like he'd been a personal friend of mine for years. It wasn't anything like that. Yet I did think he was a decent human being and in that way, I felt sorry that it had happened."

Sammi decided to get very specific. "Do you have any idea who would want him dead? Who do you think would benefit from his death?"

She had chosen her questions carefully and got something in Melanie's thought world that was not only unexpected but also quite shocking as well. She'd run it by Dave before anyone else.

Her audible answer was rather predictable. "Honestly, I don't have any idea who'd want him dead. He was very well liked for a senator, if you know what I mean. And who would profit? No one I could think of. He was an approachable-type of guy which would seem to benefit people rather than turn them away."

"Where were you at the time of the shooting?" asked Ben.

It was obvious that Melanie was surprised at the question. She thought that she had proved her case convincingly but she cooperated reluctantly.

"I was having dinner with a few friends and I'll give you their names, if you like. We were on the other side of town actually and I didn't even hear about the murder until it came on the news the next day."

"Yes," said Jeff, "we will need the names of the people you were with."

"Of course," she said, "I guess I would expect no less."

With that, she wrote the names of three people and their phone numbers on a piece of paper and handed it to Ben.

Since there was a slight lull in the conversation, she assumed that the session was over. However, Ben had a few more questions for her. He needed to push one of the issues even more.

"You say that your flirtatious actions with Mike were to get information from him. Since you said that your husband was jealous how did he handle this action on your part?"

Now she felt she had created a trap for herself. Milt would have a fit if she said it came mainly from him, but at this point, lying to the FBI was not anything she wanted to do. It would probably come out eventually anyway.

"Milt and I both considered the possibility that my flirting with him might result in some pertinent information. However, I must remind you that at the time of my flirtations, Milt and I were married and he was overtly jealous. However, whenever I came back with just a hint of beneficial information he was pleased and never bitched about it. Knowing what side of an issue Mike was on was always important for us to know if in any way it could affect the firm. Yet it was a known fact that Milt had a serious jealousy problem with Mike Stedman and it was tedious for me as he griped about it for hours on end. To me it was totally ridiculous."

"Do you know of any legislation that he was working on when he was killed?" asked Sammi.

Melanie gave her a targeted look. It was clear that she didn't want to answer that question, but she was stuck.

"Well, there was a tax compromise coming up. It didn't affect only our firm, obviously, because several companies had concerns. But it did seem that the vote would be close which made it all the more crucial for us to know how Mike was leaning."

"And how did the vote go?" asked Sammi.

"It has been postponed for a while. Not sure when it will come up now."

"How would it affect your company?" asked Jeff.

"To keep it basic, if the new legislation went through, we'd pay a lot more taxes toward city and state affairs, which had been raised just three years ago as it is. Many companies were vehemently against this type of policy."

Jeff said, "So Mike could have made a lot of enemies if people knew he was leaning toward voting yes, is that correct?"

"Definitely. Even if a hint was out there as to how he was likely to vote, there would be many people either out to get him or trying to get him to change his mind."

Ben had been writing notes throughout this interview. Sammi wrote notes as well and this activity seemed to worry Melanie some. She kept looking at their notepaper.

"But all politicians face this all the time. It's part of their job, but they don't usually get killed."

"Okay, that's all for today," said Ben abruptly. He liked to do that to keep suspects off their mark. "We'll probably want to talk to you again in the future."

At first glance, it was obvious that Melanie didn't like the idea, but she quickly relented. "Sure, if I can help at all, that'll be fine."

***

Assessing the meeting on the way out to the parking lot, Jeff was the first to speak.

"She certainly got a little nervous and edgy later on in the interview. At first, I thought she was a pretty cool person, but that sure changed down the line."

Ben added. "Yeah, when we got to certain points about her marriage or anything to do with Mike, she tried to be careful, but didn't manage to pull off her aloof personality that she started with."

Both men took a deep breath. Then they turned to look at Sammi. They knew she must have picked up information, after all, she always did.

She decided to join in the conversation, but hold back on a few incomplete items.

"I agree that she's hiding some stuff, but I guess that was obvious to the both of you as well. I have to type up my notes, but I may have a few more ideas later. I really don't think she killed the senator. Was she involved? I rather doubt it. Yet, I feel that she's in a difficult situation."

"What do you mean?" asked Ben.

"Not entirely sure, but I got the feeling that she's being told to do things, you know. Someone else is pulling the strings sometimes and she doesn't like it, but there's a reason she can't say no."

"Maybe someone is holding something over her head and forcing her. What do you think of that?"

"Could be. Something's not right, but I'm not sure what right now."

Jeff asked. "What did you think of her personally, Sammi?"

"Well, she keeps a lot hidden. She's not that strong personality that she wants everyone to believe. I mean, she can pull that one out whenever she wants and she can be totally convincing, but she also has a lot of vulnerable parts to her."

"Wow," said Jeff. "That's a surprise to me. She seemed that she could stay real tough, just like the guys."

"I think she hides things very well, but she definitely hurts inside. She'll be an interesting one to watch."

"Okay, well let's call it a day. Let's meet for breakfast tomorrow morning, same place about 8:00. Right?"

"Sure," they both said as they all turned slowly but Ben and Jeff walked on together for a few moments.

***

Ben and Jeff were quite serious and thoughtful. At first, both were rather deep into their own world and Ben almost forgot that Jeff was with him. Then Jeff coughed and brought Ben back to reality.

Jeff said, "I could tell by the look in Sammi's eyes that she's onto something. I might be getting to know her too well," he joked, "but I can almost tell when she's holding back."

"I felt the same way," said Ben. "That's probably what happens when you work with people over a period of time. Yet she needs to be so exact. She won't ever say anything unless she's had time to make sure she's correct. And she's usually correct."

"Don't you wonder how she does it? I mean, we were both there in the room with her, and we heard the very same conversation that Sammi heard, yet when we get her notes tomorrow, she'll have discovered things that I'll find impossible to believe. Of course, I know she's not guessing; she knows. Did you ever get a clue to how she does it?"

Ben smiled slyly for a moment. "No, but I occasionally still spend time trying to figure it out, although I try not to. It used to drive me crazy. I wish that she or Dave would just tell us how Sammi does it. Don't think that's ever going to happen, do you?"

Jeff shook his head. "But I have to respect her privacy. If she doesn't want people to know, I guess that's her business and she probably has a good reason for her secrecy. But I wish I was one of the people she confided in."

"So do I. She amazes me in every case we work on. Yet that first case, remember the one about the missing children, she outdid herself that time. We not only found the five or six missing children around Philadelphia, but also managed to get the files of the entire organization and found hundreds of missing kids all around the country. Hell, some groups in the FBI are still working on that one and another child was found just last week. I'm sure there will be more to come in the future."

"I'm just happy to be in her company. She's a marvel in her own right, and yet I feel like my own senses are keener and more focused when she's around. She certainly has a way about her."

When they reached their cars they were still trying to figure out the puzzle named Sammi and just smiled as they entered their vehicles.

"See you at 8:00 tomorrow morning," said Ben.

Jeff nodded and then they were off.

***

Ben watched as Jeff pulled away, but he sat there a few minutes longer. His mind has turned from Sammi and wandered back to the discussion with Melanie Brooks earlier. No mention had been made that the two of them had met briefly in college when Mike was dating her. Somehow, it seemed irrelevant. He could see what attracted Mike to her in college. She was a smart gal, attractive and her intelligence led to great conversations. Mike always liked that. He liked stimulating conversations, be it with man or woman. He knew for a fact that Mike had really fallen for her. Yet after he met Sarah there didn't seem to be any turning back.

Although Ben knew that Mike had doubts in some areas with Sarah, he also knew Mike was looking for someone who'd be a good political wife. That was a basic requirement for him.

Remembering some of their previous discussions, Mike couldn't see Melanie fulfilling that role and it did cause him many sleepless nights. It was too bad, in a way. Melanie was sharp in business and could have been a great ally. But he needed a more social wife, one who could create and complete social obligations that were necessary for his dream career. This role also consisted of his wife staying mainly in the background most of the time, and this was not a role that Melanie could play willingly or otherwise. It wasn't in her nature. Ben knew that throughout the years Mike at times had some regrets, yet he was mostly happy with Sarah.

Remembering the times that Mike had helped him during his drinking days in college, Ben had to admit that he had helped Mike over one huge hurdle. As in all marriages as Ben could easily attest to, there were some rough roads and since Mike travelled a decent amount of time leaving Sarah home to care for the children, he also had amassed a few secrets, which luckily had never made the news. Ben was never sure totally what they were in detail since Mike never said, but he seemed to have some quiet and reflective times that he needed to be alone. Yet, after a period of time, Sarah and Mike had a renewed closeness that lasted until the day he died.

As he turned the key in his ignition, he listened for a moment to the sound of the engine. He thought how confusing yet fragile life could be. It was so important to have close friends in times of need. Those who had managed to do this were the real successes of the world.

***

Sammi was thankful that Ben had called an end to their work routine early in the day. She needed to get her thoughts straight and to transcribe her notes. It was different when Dave was around. She could always start to discuss things with him immediately. She missed that. It always made her job easier.

She decided to order dinner in her room and begin to transcribe her notes without delay. She would type them up tomorrow immediately after breakfast, but she wanted to have them in some kind of order before she talked to Dave. She did have one bombshell that she couldn't wait to share.

A relaxing shower seemed the best idea after she ate. Her mind wouldn't settle down and for good reason. Some hidden information was starting to come through and many would be stunned. After all, she usually opened up her mind to all possibilities and felt she was ready for anything, but not this time. Perhaps she should have been more sensitive. She was just beginning to realize that none of us prepare or visualize enough to get ready for unforeseen events; they seem to catch us all by shock.

She had finished a great shower, put on her comfortable robe and proceeded to relax with a hot and satisfying cup of coffee, yet managing to keep her mind focused on today's events. Then the phone rang jolting her back to reality.

"Hi Dave, how are you? I would have called you in the next few minutes?"

"Glad to hear that. I've been thinking about you most of the day."

"That's nice to hear. I wish you had been here. I sure could have used you."

"What's going on?"

"Honestly, first I'd like to know what's going on in Scranton. Please humor me. Is anything happening?"

Dave laughed. "Okay, I know that probably means that you have something important to tell me, but you want to talk about other things first, right?"

"Right. You know me too well," she laughed.

"I should. We've been married for almost three years … my God Sammi, we're about to have our three year anniversary."

"That's right. It seems too soon to be three years, don't you think?"

"Yes, but we'll be saying that in 10 years and in 20 years."

She giggled. "I suppose so. I needed to be able to joke around with you right now."

"Do you want me to come up for a few days?"

"I would love it, I must admit, but I'm really okay. So tell me, what's going on with you?"

"Not all that much really. The court has told the suspects' attorneys that there will be no more delays. The trial is to move forward now. That means that we will be given all of the information that they have and we do the same. They've been really holding back some major information so we should be getting some pretty vital stuff. Also, and this is a big one, we'll be given total access to the defendants as of Friday so that we can prepare our side of the trial. I know Sergeant Brady will want you in on the questioning. I know I do. Now the real stuff will begin."

"Gee, that's quite a lot that has happened."

"Well, yeah, in one way. But it hasn't started yet. We've only gotten the okay. But you're right, that is one really big step."

"I'm anxious to be in on the questioning. I truly want to know how these guys think. Their inner world seems so warped to me. I mean even in the world of crooks and thieves their thinking is twisted, far away from the norm. Some clues or hints on the reasons why they believe as they do might really help us get into their world and then trick them. Know what I mean?"

"I do and I agree, but one step at a time. I'm not sure if we'll interrogate them all together or one at a time. We'll decide that later. Okay now, enough about that. I want to hear your news."

Sammi paused for a moment getting her thoughts straight. After all everything would change when she told Dave what she'd heard today. Of that, she was sure. This would create an entirely new set of obstacles and challenges.

"Ok, well, we interviewed Melanie Brooks today. She was cool at the beginning but as the questioning proceeded, her façade slipped. But more important, her thoughts began to scramble. She was really flustered inside, although her exterior seemed calm and unruffled. It was all I could do to keep up with her. Her thoughts were bouncing off the walls in so many directions that I had trouble following her. Finally, I picked up what her reason was. And it was a shocker."

"Okay, Sammi get to the point."

"Yes, well sorry about that. I was reliving the moment. It always helps me. She had a particular name cross her mind several times. She's very worried about this person. She apparently has something very heavy that she's holding over her head."

"Sammi, Sammi. Just tell me who it is?"

"Okay, it was Linda Saunders."

"What? You've go to be kidding. Linda Saunders kept crossing her mind?"

"Yep she did, and she was very worried about her. Every answer that came from her today she first ran by the fact of how Linda would react to it."

"Do you have any idea what Linda could have on her?"

"Not exactly. I was sorry Ben ended the meeting abruptly because I was starting to get important thoughts. But I do know it was from a long time ago. I get the impression that they were friends for a while, almost confidantes, but then something happened and everything changed. Melanie feels that she is really stuck. I think she would be a fairly decent person, but she doesn't have a choice right now."

Dave hesitated and then said, "Wow, wouldn't you know that Linda would be in on this in some way. Wait a minute, hold on now. Since Linda is not on the good side of the law anyway, could she possibly be involved with this Right Side Group?"

"I don't know, Dave. I didn't get anything specific in that direction. But I did pick up a few other little things."

"What?"

"Well, apparently Melanie has several phone lines on her desk for business. A few lines are for any business calls. Another is strictly Milt Biltmore, but her third private line is for Linda Saunders and for one other person only."

"This is getting thicker all the time. Who would have guessed this one?"

"Well, the third line is the one that fascinates me. This other person is totally hidden. She didn't bring it up in her mind high enough that I could grab it. She's very secretive in this area, but has very definite strong passionate feelings for this person that definitely surpasses anything she felt for her husband or Mike Stedman. I couldn't snatch enough information to determine anything, but I will.

"I'm still dumbfounded about all this."

"This Melanie has a lot of secrets. She seems fiercely protective about this other person, or persons, not sure why but she'll do anything to protect this part of her life."

"Okay, well, I'm sure Ben will want to talk to her again so that should help. If not, hopefully later I'll be coming up and between all of us, we'll find out. Any clues yet who killed Mike?"

"Nope, but after today, I have a lot more suspects to think about."

"Are you coming home on Friday?"

"Oh yes, this case will take a while. I hope we're starting to put some parts of the puzzle together. About now though, I must admit, that I'd like to get away from it for a while."

"I wonder where it will lead. So many twists and turns could lead anywhere."

"I know. Yet, it will seem logical when we get on the right trail. Right now, your guess is as good as mine."

Dave laughed. "Another complicated crime. Doesn't anyone commit a simple murder anymore?"

"This is what makes our lives dedicated. We stick to it until the end and then we feel good about what we've done."

"Guess so, but once in a while it would be nice ..."

"You can't fool me. You love a good mystery."

Dave joked, "You're right. I do love a good mystery."

CHAPTER XIII

Friday came quickly and Dave's group was given access to all of the information from the defense attorneys. Although their opponents were reluctant, they did provide background history, up-to-date records as to any violations these three suspects had committed and even more important the ballistic reports from the gun used to shoot Phil Pentin. Dave had wanted to run a comparison between this gun and the one used to shoot other officers in the past few years. That request got top priority.

"Now that we've got most of what they have, we need a system to proceed."

"Dave, what do you mean 'most of what they have'? They're under orders to give us everything," said Jim.

Dave looked up thoughtfully as he said, "I've never known defense attorneys who will cooperate fully when they are ordered to do so. There will be more, but we have enough to start with."

Jim nodded. "Yeah, I'm sure you're right. How do you want to proceed?"

"I'm going to assign two of you to each suspect. We are going to dig into their background and find out everything that's available. We don't want to leave out anything significant as the defense team has. These three guys acted as liaisons for The Right Side Group and that didn't happen by accident. This group is in many more things than we previously realized. So let's use this opportunity to find out what else they've ignited. We may find them leading us to some closed files."

"Really," said Tom. "Why do you think so?"

"Just a feeling right now. But this entire scenario seems weird and I want to find out the real story."

"You're sounding more like Sammi everyday," joked Tom.

"Don't I wish," answered Dave.

After giving out his special assignments, Dave wondered inwardly about nagging thoughts. The latest information from Sammi, which was covert at this time, had him wondering if the Right Side Group was somehow involved in the governor's problems several years back. He believed, as did Jim, that everything was connected in some way. By broadening his suspicions, he could only collect more data. He couldn't wait until Sammi got home tonight and he had a chance to read a copy of her latest report. Could it possibly be that all these seemingly disorganized groups had a lot more in common than anyone guessed? Well, more leaks were coming in all the time and soon they'd know. Hopefully, it would be in time to prevent more catastrophes.

* * *

Most operations shut down shortly after lunch on this particular Friday preferring to start anew and refreshed on Monday morning. Ben thought Sammi would be glad so that she could leave earlier for Scranton. Yet she had a request.

"Do you think we could get to see that Mr. Jim before I leave?"

Ben whistled slowly as he thought about it. "We could try. In fact, that's probably not a bad idea. I do think that shortly they will refuse us access to him until we get higher ups to approve it, and that could take time."

"My thoughts exactly and I'd like one more go at him."

They popped into Precinct 10 unexpectedly and found a rookie at the desk who gave them access to Mr. Jim. Ben was quite sure if anyone knowledgeable had been around, they would have been blocked.

"We'd better make good on this visit," he said. "It'll probably be the last one for a while."

Sammi nodded. Her inside feelings told her she was sure it would be difficult in the future, at least until the trial started. Even then, prosecutors would probably try to deny any contact with him. Even now, she knew that Ben was trying to see what he could do to make it happen, and she'd learned not to underestimate Ben Collier.

When Mr. Jim came in, he was confused as usual, but looked even more tired than before. Yet, when he saw Sammi, he perked up a bit. It was obvious to Ben as well.

Sammi didn't lose a second; she wanted to keep him in his top moment. "Hi, Mr. Jim. I like your name."

He actually smiled this time. It wasn't a weak smile that you had to guess about, but a wide grin that left no doubt of his momentary happiness.

"It's good to see you again, Mr. Jim. I hope you remember me."

Mr. Jim nodded and for some reason couldn't take his eyes off Sammi. He just stared at her and replied, "I remember you," wanting to make her happy. His thoughts wondered why she didn't come more often.

Sammi was waiting for this type of opening. She needed to plant some ideas in his mind that she hoped wouldn't be lost before or after the trial.

Sammi answered, "We cannot part with our friends. We cannot let our angels go." Then she paused for a moment to get his reaction.

He actually sat back on his chair quickly and looked pleasantly surprised.

"Yes, Mr. Jim. You are my friend and I won't let you go."

This time he smiled and shook his head with excitement.

"I think we understand each other, right?"

He said, "Yes, you are my friend. You are my angel."

Then he looked at Ben and then back to Sammi. She knew what he wanted to know.

"Yes, Ben is your friend as well. You can trust him."

He seemed pleased and actually looked over at Ben and smiled. He again rubbed the back of his head slowly and thoughtfully. He was always doing that.

"Is your head still sore, Mr. Jim?"

He nodded.

"Do you know how you hurt your head?"

He looked at Sammi with a warm, caring gaze. *She worries about me,* he thought. And Sammi picked that up very quickly.

"I care about you, Mr. Jim. I'm sorry your head is always sore. Do you know how you hurt it?"

This time Mr. Jim seemed to retreat inside a little. It seemed that he couldn't remember anything and it frustrated him.

"That's okay, Mr. Jim. Don't worry. Remember, I'm your friend and I'll help you."

His head remained in a downward position and Sammi looked at Ben. He simply shook his head because he had no idea where Sammi's ideas came from or where she was going with them.

Sammi decided to get bold. "Mr. Jim, I may not be able to see you for a while. I want to because I really like you, but I can't help it. Can you forgive me for that?"

"You won't come and talk to me about Dickens?" he asked.

"I will definitely come again, but not for a while. I want you to remember I'm your friend – don't forget that."

"Okay, I'll remember my angel."

"Okay and when I come back I'll be able to help you."

Just then, the door opened and a very aggravated sergeant came into the room. He walked heavily up to the table and stopped directly in front of Ben, glaring at him.

"How the hell did you manage this without our approval?"

"We just came in and asked if we could see him," he answered. "Your officer at the desk led us back here."

Ben was trying not to irritate this sergeant anymore than he already was. He knew everything would be reported.

"This meeting is over and probably won't happen again until the trial."

Ben simply said, "Okay, and when will that be?"

"Well," he answered smugly, "since we know we have the senator's killer they are moving ahead very quickly now and we believe it will start within the next few weeks, at least the preliminaries should start by then."

Mr. Jim suddenly exhibited a strong reaction to his words, which didn't go unnoticed.

"Look at him," he joked, "he acts like he knows what we're talking about. Yet years of booze and who knows what else has his brain fried to that of an idiot. Anyway, that's it, you have to leave now."

Ben stood up immediately to exhibit total compliance with this sergeant's orders. He didn't need a new enemy in this department.

The sergeant called in another officer to take a rather frightened looking Mr. Jim away. Before that happened, Sammi had a chance to utter a few more words to him.

"Your angel will not leave you, Mr. Jim. Tis a far far better thing I do ..." then she stopped. The sergeant shook his head in disgust, but Mr. Jim stopped totally in his tracks and said, "I cannot let my angel go and I won't."

The sergeant looked at Sammi and said, "You're as crazy as he is."

She smiled and answered, "It appears so. Goodbye Mr. Jim for now."

As they were walking out the sergeant said, "Don't you both know he's loony? Well, it won't matter. He's off limits to all of you until the trial. Those are my orders."

Ben asked, "Whose orders are they?"

He smiled but wouldn't answer the question. He simply said good day as he turned on his heels and left.

As they walked out Ben had to comment, "Today had to be our luckiest day ever. I don't think we can count on any further confusion allowing us another unwarranted visit until the trial begins."

Sammi only smiled. She didn't believe in luck.

"Well I wanted to ask him again about the officer that gave him the gun. He said that he remembered him. I'm wondering if he could pick him out for us. I only needed another few minutes."

"We're lucky for what we got. I know it may be awhile, but we'll have another chance. I can't pretend to know what you do, but you do have a clear connection with him. Of that, I'm sure, especially after today. It really is to our benefit that they think he's crazy so they aren't about to even attempt to talk to him logically." Ben paused for a moment then said, "I do feel sorry for him. He's trapped somewhere inside and I wonder how it happened."

"I hope when all this is done we can help him."

"So do I," said Ben, "so do I."

* * *

This time on the charter flight back to Scranton, Sammi didn't even try to figure out anything about Mr. Jim or the senator's murder. Her mind was so exhausted and fatigued that she decided for once to put her seat back and extended herself into a relaxed position. She let her mind wander freely and liberally without any direction from her.

Instantly she was back on her Grandpa Logan's farm when, as a young girl she enjoyed wandering around mostly by herself lost in her own thoughts. That was always pleasant for her. Her grandparents were fun people who truly seemed to care about each other and offered her a respite from her own family home where tension, anger and hostility were more common than not. She often wondered why. Even more important was the fact that her Grandpa Logan was the only other person she knew who could hear other people's thoughts. He had counseled her and instructed her as best he could so as to get her past the pitfalls as quickly as possible. And he wanted her to be responsible with her gift and use it appropriately. She smiled as she relaxed in her own body. She knew he'd be proud of her today. In fact, there were many times that she was sure he was still around guiding her and reminding her that she couldn't solve all the problems of the world.

At that moment, Mr. Jim crossed her mind. He certainly was a confusing puzzle to her. She could hear other people's thoughts, that was true, but his thoughts were so confusing. His mind was not at all like that of others who contemplated ideas logically in their thought world before they spoke aloud. His original thoughts were too deep and she couldn't get to them. Still, the thoughts that she had obtained had given her clues. Yet, he would be a full time job. There was nothing more she could do right now. As Ben figured out, they probably wouldn't even be able to talk to him for a while. Yet later, the time would come and then she'd be ready.

* * *

On the way to the station on Saturday, Dave clued her into what they hoped to accomplish. They would be interviewing Phil Anderson alone. He was considered one of the followers in

the Right Side Group, yet not one of the main members. As
such, it was hoped Sammi could pick up something. After all,
no one believed that he was a solid associate. In fact, rumor
had it that while being held he let slip a few things that
confirmed he wanted out of the group and thought it had been a
stupid decision to join in the first place.

"Really," said Sammi, "who got that information?"

"Everyone who had contact with him it seems. He's a
talker so be ready for this one. His thoughts should be fast and
furious. He's talked to the prison guards, the cook, and other
prisoners when he could manage it and it was always the same
story. He wanted to know what he could do to get himself out
of this situation."

"Seems like he'll be a good target."

Dave paused before he answered. "We hope so. I think
he's our best shot. Because the other one, Charlie ... Bowren I
think, he's very quiet and reserved. We couldn't get much out
of him. Of course, you could, I know that and that will be a
good thing. We've all been assuming that Phil is the best one,
but you never know."

"Who'll be there today?"

Jim, Roy, and us; I think Tom is out on another
assignment. I was hoping Sergeant Brady could stop by but
we'll see. He's so deep in the cop killings from last year, I
think he's buried."

"That's okay," said Sammi, "Let's see what turns up
today."

At the station, Sammi looked over a copy of Phil
Anderson's profile. She studied it for only a few minutes
before she put the file down in her lap and looked at Dave.

"What?" he said noticing her confusion.

"Do you realize the connection there is between Phil
Anderson and Charlie Bowren?"

"Well, no, but you've only got Phil Anderson's profile,
why are you talking about Charlie Bowren?"

"They've been connected since they were little boys. It's
vague on how they knew each other, but there seems to be a
strong connection between them that started when they were
quite little. This is going to be interesting."

"You're kidding." Dave seemed to be surprised and motioned for Sammi to let him see the file. About this time, Jim walked in and saw the confused look on Dave's face.

"Oh that's a new updated copy of Phil's profile. Julie was able to pull up more information on him. Pretty interesting, right?"

"Sure is," said Sammi. "Wonder what we can do with the connection these two have. Are you planning on bringing it up in the interview or not?"

"Depends on where the interview leads. We could use it if it seems like a good idea. You can pull ideas from him anyway."

"How and why did they end up together as kids? There isn't much information. Do we know anymore?"

"Actually Julie just ran across that detail accidentally," said Jim. "She plans to follow up as soon as she can."

"It'll give me something else to concentrate on in this interview. Wonder if he'll think about Charlie at all."

"Interesting thought," said Jim. He then answered his cell phone and found out that it was time for them to go. They'd know soon.

* * *

When Phil Anderson walked into the room, he looked around carefully to see who could be of benefit to him. From his almost six-foot height and broad physical stature, he seemed confident about his position in this room. Immediately Sammi picked up that he knew the police needed him and he was quite willing to cooperate, but for a price. He had a definite payment in mind that he kept upfront in his thoughts. He started talking immediately.

"Okay, okay, I know I'm in trouble. I did a stupid thing by shooting up the area, but I have information that you'd probably like to have. Maybe we can help each other."

"Maybe we can," said Jim as he took the lead. "But we need some information first."

"I don't give out information until I know if it will help me. Look, I'm not stupid. I know I did a stupid thing," ... he looked down suddenly and shook his head, "wish I'd never done it. Can't believe I participated in such a stupid move. Actually, I wish we'd ... I'd never joined that stupid group."

Tom jumped on this opportunity as he saw Sammi writing fast on her note pad. She sat on the left side of Dave, her usual spot. Phil almost dismissed her as a note taker and didn't seem to give her a second thought. That was another mistake he made and most other people did the same thing. Phil occasionally glanced at Sammi, but never gave her much attention.

"Why did you join the Right Side Group anyway?"

"It was an organization, a small one I know, but one that had connections into a lot of things. I thought they could benefit me."

Again conscious of Sammi's earlier thoughts Jim asked, "Did you join this group alone?"

"Huh?" he asked looking surprised at the question. "Yeah, who else would I join with?"

"Well, maybe Charlie Bowren."

Phil sat back in his chair, his eyes went from Dave to Tom thoughtfully, and he briefly included Sammi. His blond hair fell onto his forehead where it attracted beads of sweat. Obviously, he didn't want to talk about this part of his life. That was off limits as far as he was concerned. A certain nervousness began to show up in his confident demeanor and he wondered where he should go from here.

"I hardly know him. When did he join?"

"We thought you'd know that."

"Well, I don't. I've only been with this group about six months and I don't know many of the members. Look, why don't you just tell me what you can do for me and then I can decide what I should tell you, if anything. I need guarantees."

"The system doesn't work that way. We need to find out what you know and then we pass it on to our superiors and they decide what, if anything, we can do for you."

This comment didn't set very well with Phil. You could tell by his expression that he thought if he offered information, he'd get a sweet deal. Now he didn't know what he wanted to do. He tried to leave and give himself some time to think about everything.

"No, no, not so fast," said Dave. "We have questions for you."

"Can't I have a lawyer present? Maybe I should wait for that. I thought you'd want to hear what I know. I've known others who got a good deal. And I know things; probably a lot more than you think I know."

"Of course you are entitled to an attorney," said Jim. "And we can stop now if you like. But I thought you wanted to know what we could do for each other."

"Well, yes I do, but I need to know what you can do for me."

"I'm sure that's true," said Dave. "But we have to follow our rules. We can't make decisions about a deal right now, but we can take the information back to our people and I'm sure they'll be grateful if you help us."

Phil frowned. He didn't like the sound of this. "But I could tell you things and then I get no deal, right?"

"True, but that usually doesn't happen. If you cooperate you'll probably get a shorter sentence or be put in a better prison."

That shocked Phil. "You seem to think that we'll automatically get jail time. Really?"

"I need to ask you if you want to talk some more without a lawyer. Yes or No?"

"Well, okay to a point, but if I change my mind I'll let you know, right?"

"Of course. Now about getting jail time … all three of you probably are likely to face jail time. You tried to kill a citizen and two police officers. What would you expect?"

"But Charlie and I only shot wild. Jason is the one who tried to make the hit."

Jim pounced on this once. "How do you know that Charlie didn't try to kill?"

Phil was excited and not thinking clearly, as he answered, "Because I know Charlie and he'd never do that. Neither would I."

When he'd finished, he stopped. He knew that he'd said too much. His story had changed somewhat and he knew it.

"Okay, okay," he said. You could tell that Phil was irritated with himself. "I know Charlie somewhat. He's an easy person and would never want to kill anyone. He's not even very good with guns. This Right Side Group wants everyone to have a gun and be prepared. That's what they do."

Phil stopped for a moment. No one else spoke. They just waited and gave him enough time to recover his position hoping he'd continue. And he did.

"I'll be honest with you. I'm quite sure that the Right Side Group won't help us anyway. We're not solid members. We're total newbies to them and they don't trust us yet. They probably will help Jason because he has connections. I don't doubt that they'll send out some broken down lawyer and pretend to defend us, but they'll want us in jail and out of their way. What a nightmare this is."

"How did this group recruit you?" asked Dave.

By this time, the edge had been taken off of Phil's attitude. He wasn't totally friendly and trusting by any means, but his tone was somewhat more engaging and his sweat was disappearing. He was almost relaxing with these officers.

"I had met Charlie about a month earlier and we were at a bar drinking one Friday night. Jason was there with a few of his buddies and there was some disagreement between a few people. We just sat back and watched and Jason and his group did the same. Yet afterwards, he approached us and started talking. We saw him a few weeks in a row then he told us about a group for which he was recruiting. He said his group didn't like the underhanded things that the government did and were trying to protect society. He gave us some literature that sounded good."

He stopped suddenly. He was reluctant to go on for a bit. Then it seems that he decided this was probably his only chance since the Right Side Group wouldn't help them anyway. As he opened his mouth to speak, the door to the interview room opened.

"That's all for today. You don't have permission to interview this suspect," said an angry sergeant who glared specifically at Dave.

"We've got clearance," Dave answered. "We've been given all the rights to open interviews now and throughout the trial." Dave had slammed his folder on the table irritated by this interruption.

"I haven't received any such orders," continued the sergeant, "and until I do, this area is off limits to you. Now you have to go."

Dave decided to handle this situation another way. He had suspicions this was planned to confuse the suspect and ended up being congenial stating, "We'll be back with the proper paperwork and personnel."

This somewhat took the sergeant aback but Dave stated to Phil, "Hold your thoughts, we'll get this straightened out."

* * *

Dave knew immediately that this planned interruption was part of a plan and even though they were in safe territory, their opposition wanted to make their jobs as difficult as possible. It was true that none of the defense's pretrial winnings had gone down well with the other side, so even playing by the rules didn't always allow for a smooth road. They'd handle this situation the right way so it wouldn't happen again.

Jim was irate. "What the hell? That sergeant knows that we're allowed to see the suspects. What in the hell's going on?"

"Settle down, Jim. They just want to flex their muscle a little more. Soon, they won't have anywhere to go. Besides, I think it might be a good idea to give Phil a little room. We caught him off guard today. He does need time to get his thoughts together."

Jim was still angry but could see the benefit in playing it cool.

Dave turned to Sammi. "You never stopped writing. I'm assuming that you got quite a bit."

She smiled. "Yes I did. Did you notice how he was still covering up about knowing Charlie? He was still real tight-lipped about that. But I got quite a bit of details about their relationship. He was honest about the Right Side Group, though; they were rookies and would never get any special treatment from them. Anyway, give me time to decipher all my notes and everything will make more sense. Besides, we'll have a lot more information next time we talk to him."

Jim asked. "What about Charlie? When do we talk to him?"

Dave said, "Let's look at Sammi's notes first. That should give us a clue as to the best direction to take."

Jim nodded. He knew that was true.

"We can go back to the office, Jim. That'll give Sammi time to get these notes transcribed. Okay with you, Sammi?"

"Sure I'll get to it right away. Some ideas will probably be important to you."

* * *

Sammi was feeling somewhat delicate about the notes she needed to transcribe. Many times details were necessary in a crime, that was true, but today she had also gained access to personal details about Phil Anderson and Charlie Bowren. She felt rather sensitive about how much she should reveal. She thought for a moment about her Grandpa Logan. He'd be happy that she was concerned about other people's privacy. This case might involve a difficult decision for her to make. Give out the details that were required to help solve this crime, yet maintain the integrity she had worked so hard to achieve.

Arriving home, she immediately made herself a cup of herb tea. This time it was the Bengal Spice flavor that she chose and she let the aroma permeate the room for a few moments. She needed to relax and think about what she should do. Somehow holding her teacup high enough so that the aroma penetrated her sense of smell seemed to bring about a feeling of calmness. It didn't in itself solve her dilemma but it put her in a state of stillness that enabled her mind to draw from the atmosphere around her. She was ready to begin.

Phil Anderson's abandonment by his parents happened around the age of five. He moved from foster home to foster home experiencing the best and worst of adult human behavior. By the age of seven, his home was an orphanage and he stayed there until he was sixteen years old. Adoption almost happened for him twice, but somehow a kink in the system thwarted his chance both times. However, by the time he had reached nine years of age, Charlie Bowren came to live at the same orphanage. He was only one year younger, but had lost both parents to a traffic accident and his emotional health had suffered tremendously. He was a lost child who wouldn't speak, had to be coaxed to eat and cowered whenever adults came near.

Charlie's delicate behavior continued until they decided to move the boys into the same room. Phil seemed to make a connection with Charlie. He reacted to him positively which couldn't be said for any other caregiver, doctor or person in charge. Once they roomed together Phil was able to gain Charlie's trust and since neither one was adopted they clung to each other and became each other's confidantes.

Some of these details Sammi felt weren't necessary to put into her report. The fact that they had known each other since they were little was a necessary ingredient to know since they felt like family and would protect each other to the end. That she knew. They were always trying to find a place in life where they belonged; somewhere they would feel comfortable. They lived together immediately after they left the orphanage. As years passed, they found mediocre jobs but were able to earn a living. They seemed to be moving along in the right direction but they needed an extended family, so to speak. They were looking for some type of clan where they could feel a kinship, a feeling of belonging. When they heard of the Right Side Group, it instilled in them the idea of affiliation to an organization where they would feel wanted. In truth, they had no real idea what it was all about.

Sammi took a break about the same time that her phone rang.

"Hi Dave, what's up?"

"Nothing. Just had a moment and was wondering about you. How you doing on that report?"

"I'll have it done soon. Why? Are you that much in a hurry for it? You can't even see Phil again for a while."

"Sergeant Brady will give us the paperwork by the end of the day. For some reason, it's beginning to move along faster again."

"Well, okay, then I'll have it for you tonight. We can make our adjustments and give Tom and Jim copies by tomorrow."

"How do you feel about it?"

"Good information and I'll share extras with you; you can help me decide if some of the smaller details are necessary."

"Great, see you later."

* * *

Dave agreed that some of the lesser personal details in the lives of Charlie Bowren and Phil Anderson weren't pertinent and could be left out. Sammi was happy about that. She would never exploit the hidden memories of people unless absolutely necessary, since she felt that everyone had their right to privacy. Dave had been correct about getting the proper paperwork forwarded so that they would have legal access to the two suspects again, and that happened the next day.

Phil Anderson was still their main focus at this time and he had decided to cooperate with the police. He felt that he and his friend Charlie had the best chance at leniency in being cooperative with the legal side. Since he didn't have access to the inner workings of the group it was believed he wouldn't be emitting many of the small details that could be enlightening, however it was surprising that he did have some information that was valuable to them.

First, their main contact in Sweet Valley was Jason Connor, Sr. who gave out orders from prison. A connection to Milt Biltmore was insinuated, but never proven. Although Milt pretended to be on the outside rim of the organization, in truth he was knee deep in picking out the major irritating projects that would be advantageous to his company. He was not beneath using any underhanded techniques in order to thwart the government from regulating his company too much. Yet he was careful to stay on the right side of the law; he never crossed the line.

Melanie Brooks was in on the game as well, but she always confused Phil. She was passive and only followed orders if it suited her. Phil as well as Charlie believed that someone must have something on her, but never got a glimmer of what that could be. Most of the information they knew was from conversations they'd overheard, or a brief comment made in their presence. They were never trusted enough to attend high-level meetings.

"This game is coming full circle," said Dave. "Everyone seems to think that someone has something on this Melanie Brooks. Any ideas?"

"Not really, but I agree that's a fact. She didn't seem to have the emotions that would attach her to this group at all. In fact, she seemed a bit angry and frustrated that she couldn't get out of whatever was happening to her," offered Sammi. "I'm anxious to know where this will lead."

"You go back Tuesday, right? Does Ben plan to interview her again?"

"Eventually, I'm sure, but I don't know when. Not sure where we'll be heading this week."

"Right. There's still so much ground to cover. What about that Mr. Jim?"

Sammi said, "We can't talk to him at all until the trial. That's written in stone right now."

Dave smirked. It seemed that everyone had their problems with lawyers and the court system.

CHAPTER XIV

Melanie pushed herself away from the desk and relaxed in the brown leather chair made exclusively for her. She relished the thought that she was valuable enough to warrant this special treatment. Inwardly, she smiled. Yes, she had arrived.

She'd had another business dinner date last night with her protégé, Marvin Antwerp. In reality, she really didn't know how to think about him. It was true that she'd taken him under her wing the last few years, both at Milt's request and at her own inner urging since she believed he had talent that could enrich the company. Although rumor had it that he had a crush on her, she felt that was probably more hero worship. She was one of the top executives and that did muster admiration from men and women alike. Curiosity engulfed her for a moment so she reached for his file. She couldn't remember exactly what his total background entailed. She remembered he had graduated from Yale and had worked for one of their competitors for a while, but couldn't quite recollect exactly what ploy had been used to entice him away.

Wanting to begin looking further into his background, she found that it was skimpy at best. Some vague high school information was visible, but no details that would render him worthy of attending one of the most prestigious schools in the country. In fact, there wasn't much on his personal life either. After he'd left Yale there was at least five to eight lost years. It wasn't known what had happened to him during that time. She searched further back into the file. Surely, there was more information on someone who'd been deemed a very bright mind and scouted by several influential companies. Yet she found nothing. Now her curiosity was peeking and it couldn't be denied. She made a note to herself. She'd need to delve into this further. Something didn't feel right to her. She was hoping that maybe some data had been misplaced or even possibly lost. Most files on other employees were thorough and complete; this one wasn't satisfactory. Then her phone rang and she put the file away. It was one of her private lines.

She had just begun talking to a very important person in her life when Marvin showed up at her door reminding her of a meeting in five minutes. She paused, asked a significant question and relaxed, as the phone call had only been the monthly update she required. She signaled she'd make it to the meeting.

Memories rushed over her mind as she unwillingly began to recall happenings in her early life. They were not happy memories.

"Why would you think you'd ever amount to anything, Melanie?"

That would be her father, who alone was probably the most discouraging and disagreeable person she'd ever met.

"You're not that good looking, nothing in the brain department and certainly not from the best side of town. You're gonna be a loser just like the rest of us. You might as well quit reading all those books and stop pretending."

Melanie didn't answer, at least not aloud. She had stopped arguing with her father by the time she was eight years old. He loved to fight and the battles got increasingly nasty. She had learned to keep quiet and retain what dignity she could.

Her mother, on the other hand, was not outwardly disagreeable, although being encouraging and supportive was not her strong point. Melanie used to watch and listen to her parents, but never inwardly agreed with them. In fact, while they were spewing out their nasty comments, her mind was always busy refuting them. She remembers thinking, "I'm going to be an important person. Many people will think I'm smart. I'm going places and not because of you, but despite the both of you." She never said this aloud; that would have sent damaging sparks around the place for days, but she kept them in her mind and heart and slowly she began to believe them.

"Melanie, Melanie." That would be her secretary tapping on her window and calling her name. "Your meeting is starting you've got to leave now."

"Okay, thanks," she said as she cleared her mind. Now was not the time for daydreaming; it was the time for reality.

The meeting went very well. Melanie's presentation was on target as usual, but after the meeting, Milt cornered her again. He was getting to be boring, she thought.

"The feds are coming back. Did you know that?"

She looked surprised. "No, I didn't. What for?"

"Well, if I knew that I wouldn't be upset," he said unpleasantly. "I don't know what the hell they want now. I answered all their questions. I don't know anything. Honestly, Melanie, you'd better not be lying to me. You said you didn't know anything about that senator's murder."

"And I don't, you fool. You just don't get it, do you? I'm in the dark as much as you are. They're probably just double-checking with a lot of people. You know they do have a murder to solve."

Taking a deep sigh, Milt said, "I hope so. I sure hope so."

"That's what they usually do. Don't be surprised if they come back again. They will, you know. Until this murder is solved, you can count on it."

"Okay, okay, what are you up to now?"

"I've got a new employee coming in so I have to do the welcoming interview and get him started."

Milt looked surprised. "Who's that?"

"Don't you remember? You're the one that okayed me having another investigator to help me out on the legwork I need to do to stay ahead of the competition. You're the one that okayed it, Milt."

"Oh, alright. I forgot."

Then abruptly he turned and walked away. Melanie thought he could be so strange at times. She knew he hadn't forgotten, not really. He didn't forget much, ever. What game was he playing now?

* * *

Diego Garcia walked proudly into Melanie's office. She noted immediately that he had a secure air about him that couldn't be denied. He was self-assured, and carried himself lightly despite a muscular frame on his roughly five-foot ten-inch body. He accepted the chair offered with polite assurance and never once stooped to a subsidiary position in his stance. She knew he would speak to her on equal terms. She might be his boss and that seemed okay with him, but he was definitely her equal; there was no denying his mind-set.

He was definitely a good-looking man with his Mexican or Spanish heritage obvious to anyone. His jet-black hair was cut appropriately and although he didn't wear a suit and tie, his casual attire was acceptable and in good fashion.

"Okay, Diego," said Melanie as she opened his file. She needed to make sure everything was in order as a quick thought about Marvin crossed her mind and created an irritating frown. But she recovered quickly.

"I like to know my employees so I'd like to discuss your profile with you."

He nodded back to her. She couldn't seem to read his expression. Usually she was good at deciphering her staff's thoughts, but Diego seemed to hold his expressions mainly to himself. She might have to work at this one.

"Okay, it says here that you were born in Rosarito, Mexico. Is that correct?"

She purposely threw out a question at him since he didn't seem to be much of a talker.

"Yes, that's correct."

"Where is that?"

"It's very close to Tijuana. I spent many hours of my childhood in Tijuana."

He spoke casually and seemed relaxed, she thought. However, she wasn't getting a feeling of his basic personality and that's what she wanted.

"When did you move to the United States? Just tell me something about yourself and how you ended up here."

"Oh, okay, you want to know about me," he answered in a rather good-humored tone. His Spanish accent still shone through his words and gave his pronunciation a rather impressive sound.

"My family moved to San Diego when I was three years old. We stayed there for five years but then my father was having trouble finding work so we moved to Arizona. My family still lives in Prescott. I went to college at the University of Connecticut and began looking for work after I graduated. Actually I worked in the college library during my college years; I'm a reader and can't seem to stop so that suited me quite well."

She smiled and asked, "Where was your first job after college?"

I worked for the Chicago Title Insurance Company right here in Hartford. I did mostly investigative work, although they did use me in administrative areas as well. That was new to me. But they seemed to like my criminal justice background the best and that got me most of my extra jobs and promotions. I like to do research and I like to keep digging for answers until I find them. That seems to be what I'm good at."

He paused for a moment before he continued. Then, as if he had to get everything out in the open he said, "The only other job I had was working in connection with the police department in Farmington. I was referred to them by my manager at the insurance company as a person who could turn up clues whenever necessary." He laughed and said, "I guess that's my best talent."

He stopped talking suddenly just when Melanie felt that he was beginning to open up. She had taken an immediate liking to him. She wasn't exactly sure why. He was impressive in his enthusiasm for his work. He was quite personable. It came across very clearly in his explanations of a few of the projects he'd been working on. Melanie was impressed inwardly. This guy had a lot going for him. His mannerism and congeniality came through very well and she was sure she'd be glad that he was on her team.

Just then, Marvin came into her office unannounced thinking she was alone.

"Yes, what is it, Marvin?"

He stopped cold in his tracks when he saw Diego. His slight tap dance signaled that he didn't know if he should leave or stay.

Melanie took the reins. "Marvin, this is Diego Garcia. He'll be joining our staff and I was going to have you show him around when I'm finished here."

The two men shook hands but there was a definite iciness coming from Marvin. Melanie couldn't understand why. Diego seemed unaffected.

"My staff works closely together and I will have a get-acquainted meeting soon. For now if there isn't anything you need, Marvin, I'd like to finish up."

With that, Marvin nodded, barely gave Diego a glance and left the room quickly. It was obvious something wasn't right with him.

Their meeting finished quickly after the accidental intrusion and Melanie sent Diego back to personnel for further enrolling. And she contacted a friend in personnel to send everything they had on Marvin Antwerp.

Melanie didn't like loose ends of any kind. When she realized that Marvin's profile wasn't complete, she almost panicked. He'd been on her personal staff for over a year and with the company for a few years before that and she was usually proficient in making sure that all her people had the proper credentials with a complete background check. The background check on Marvin was missing.

* * *

Diego hadn't missed anything in the meeting. His obvious rebuff from Marvin was surprising but not totally unexpected as he surmised quickly that this was one dude who had a giant crush on his boss. It didn't take much imagination to figure that one out. Marvin had placed him in the category of competition in both the personal and professional areas. He didn't quite have it figured out, but there was something rather strange about this guy who seemed well-mannered and controlled on the outside yet Diego felt that on the inside he had an anger that wasn't always manageable. He laughed. Probably some of his legal training was surfacing again. It did that sometimes, but it usually kept him aware of impending disarray. He'd keep his eye on this guy.

For now, it was back to personnel. Although he usually found a new job interesting at the beginning, the idea of being scrutinized by everyone was particularly tedious to him. Yet, he could handle it. He'd done it many times before and that's what he was good at. He needed to find a way to fit in; he needed to have a strong rapport with his coworkers. That was his specialty and this time he needed to be particularly adept. There was a murder to solve.

Playing the new kid on the block usually helped him to manipulate people in opening up to him. There was a tendency for employees to help a newbie so he used it to its full potential.

"So you'll be working on Melanie's staff," asked Michael, one interested person with a curious look on his face.

"Yes, it seems that way," he answered. "Why?"

Diego couldn't let the expression pass without commenting. He didn't want to lose the opportunity as a few others seemed to share his opinion.

"You'll be working with Marvin, that's all."

"Oh, yes I guess so. Is that a problem?"

Michael seemed to squirm a little, but did throw out a tidbit since he had already subtly insinuated a predicament.

"Well, he can be strange, that's all. He's one to watch. He's very close to Melanie."

Diego added a little lightness to the situation. He tried to release the tension.

"If he wants to be her right-hand man, that's okay with me. I just need assignments and I'll not be in his way," joked Diego.

"That's probably the best way to look at it. He likes being number one with Melanie. Just to let you know"

"I already got that feeling," said Diego with a wink. "That's fine with me."

Information gained in his first week came easily to Diego. He had already learned much of the inner workings of this department from people who were more than willing to talk about the strange behaviors around them. The jealousy exhibited by Marvin was incredibly obvious to him immediately, but he was surprised that those on the outer edge of this department were also apprised and willing to talk about the situation. Many times these conditions were kept under cover and never talked about with new personnel. He decided that he'd put in a call to Dave Patterson tonight. Dave always worried when he did undercover work, but this seemed to be one of his easier assignments. The hardest part was that he kept changing names, so he had to make that mental note that from now on, here in this company he was Diego Garcia. But that was okay; he was good at pretending. He'd done it all his life and worked it to his advantage. This was another murder that needed solving and he felt the answer, at least some of it, was going to be found here, mostly with Melanie and this strange Marvin.

***

Early the next week, Marvin created a run-in with Diego. He insisted that all reports to Melanie came through him and that he would remain her right-hand man. Diego said that would be fine with him, but he'd have to hear that arrangement from Melanie. Marvin didn't like his authority being challenged and after many ill-fated arguments in his favor, he said he'd have Diego fired before he stormed off. At his first opportunity, Diego had a private meeting with Melanie.

"What's the matter already," she said rather flippantly. "This is only the beginning of your second week and already you have a problem?"

In his best Mexican accent, Diego exhibited a charm and persuasiveness that even caught Melanie by surprise. "Oh, no, Melanie," he said with a slight smile crossing his pleasant expression. "I have no problem at all. I'm enjoying my work here. But I do need to know who I'm supposed to report to."

She looked surprised. "I already told you. You report to me. And I'm hoping that soon you'll have something to tell me about the inefficiency of our mailing department."

"Actually, I'm ready to do that right now. First, I need to tell you that yesterday Marvin informed me that all my reporting would go through him and he would pass it along to you. If you agree, of course, that's fine, but I need to be sure that my reports will make it to your desk."

With that said Diego sat far back in his chair and waited for Melanie to lose the shocked and irritated look that had crossed her face. Annoying disbelief followed by exasperation gave a hint that she was aware of a problem, which was becoming more apparent everyday. Yet, she handled herself well.

"Okay," she said as she pursed her lips. "This is what I expect of you. You report to me and me only. You do not discuss your reports with anyone else. Marvin is becoming too important in his own mind and I'll have to talk to him. Okay? Are we clear on this?"

"Totally," Diego answered and proceeded to give her the report on the mailing procedure and where it could be improved. She seemed impressed, and somewhat surprised.

"You got this in only three or four days. That's a good piece of information. It does seem like something that I should have known about before now. You'd think someone would have brought this to my attention a while back. This is good work."

"I told you," said Diego, "digging up information is what I do best."

"But you did it so fast," she answered.

"I focus and I know where to look for information."

Melanie stared at him and realized that he wouldn't give up any more ideas than he already had, but she didn't care. He got results quickly and that's what she wanted with her newest investigator.

* * *

The meeting with Marvin didn't go well at all. Melanie was surprised at how much he seemed to think he was worth and it was nowhere near her assessment. Honestly, she could handle all the things he did herself; she'd have to work much longer hours, but she had done it before. Yet now that she was much more valuable in the company, assistants made her life easier. What was beginning to unnerve her was that she couldn't figure out what Marvin was all about anyway. Okay, maybe he did have a slight crush on her, but she felt there was something more. She wasn't a young schoolgirl believing someone was obsessed with her and trying desperately to please her. No, no, she had long passed those years. There was another reason and it alarmed her somewhat; she didn't like what she couldn't understand. Too bad she couldn't use Diego on this one. He'd find out something for sure. She couldn't chance it; she didn't know him well enough. Also, with Marvin's blank background check and surprisingly meager profile, she realized she had a problem. It was one she would fix herself and soon.

It was funny how life could be at times. Just when Melanie was trying to decide how to dig into Marvin's early life and find out what his interests and dreams were without sending up an obvious flag to him, he was called to jury duty. Melanie was thrilled. He wouldn't be around for a while and she could be more blatant in her search. Of course, he insisted to her that she get him out of this joke of government duty, but she refused. That wasn't the end of it and her telephone rang within ten minutes of her decision. It was one of her private lines.

"Yes, Milt I have decided that he should be on jury duty."

"What the hell, Melanie. He's been in here bitching and griping and he's furious at you and this company right now. I want you to get him out of it."

"No, Milt, and I have two reasons. Do you even want to hear them?"

"Damn, what? I don't want any problems here."

"Neither do I, so first of all," said Melanie thinking she would appeal to his concern about the company, "I think at this time it would look bad if we got anybody out of jury duty. The government always checks out those requests and we don't need that right now, don't you think?"

"Damn, that's right. I never thought of that. What's the other reason?"

"The second reason is personal with me. He's been trying to tell some of my subordinates to report to him instead of directly to me. He's usurping my authority and I'm going to have to watch him. Suddenly, I don't trust him. I'm going to look into his background again. How much do you know about him, Milt? It was your idea to make him my assistant."

Milt was actually quiet for a moment. This was an unusual occurrence. "Geez, I don't know that much. He came on a recommendation from someone. Okay, you convinced me after the first point anyway. We don't need the government checking up on why one of our employees shouldn't serve on a jury. But I want you to let me know what you find out?"

"I will. Shall you tell him or you want me to?"

"I think I will," said Milt. "I'll probably enjoy it."

* * *

Fate being on Melanie's side got Marvin selected to serve on a jury and would be gone at least two weeks. *What a stroke of luck*, she thought. She should have everything she needed by then. She decided not to waste any time and immediately put in a call to Yale to get his records faxed to her. It didn't turn out to be as simple as that. There was no Marvin Antwerp who graduated in the year given on his application. She tried a few years before and a few years after. There was nothing. She tried Antwerp with different first names. There was nothing. The only Antwerp during his given time history was a female and not from Cleveland, Ohio where he had claimed to have graduated high school.

Now, Melanie was intrigued as well as extremely concerned. Her call to Baxter High School in Cleveland produced no results. No one had heard of Marvin there either. She felt at a dead end. Who was this guy and where did he come from? He had worked for one of their competitors, but she didn't know which one; Milt had handled that. She had some very probing questions for Milt Biltmore and felt that he had better have some direct answers for her.

In the meantime, she had waived in Diego during her last phone call. As sharp as he was he would already have guessed what was happening, but he played it professionally.

"I wish you hadn't heard that," she said.

"I didn't," he answered.

By this time, Diego had worked closely with her on several projects and she had admiration for him. She wished she had known him before. Now he was a valuable and conscientious investigator and if she could have relied on him and taken him into her confidence, she had no doubt that she'd already be going in the right direction. What a shame.

"I'm embarrassed and I'm stuck. It's sometimes hard to be sure of people in this business or any other business for that matter. I must tell you that because this came to my attention a few weeks ago, I have already double-checked on your application and history.

"Of course," he said. "I've nothing to hide."

"I know," she smiled. "I guess most people don't."

Melanie was in deep thought for a moment. Then she said, "Look, I need to talk to Milt about something so I'm going to cancel our meeting and reset it for tomorrow. Oh, that's Saturday. Why don't we meet first thing Monday morning? I may have another job for you."

"Okay."

"How about 8:00 AM?"

Diego wrinkled his nose. "I guess you know by my file that I'm from Scranton, PA. My family still lives there and I was planning to visit them this weekend. I might not be back for 8:00 Monday morning."

"Okay, what time?

"10:00 would be fine. I'd appreciate that."

"No problem. Then 10:00 it is. That would probably work better for me as well."

As he got up to leave Melanie said, "You've done good work here. And I do agree with what you first told me. You do know how to dig out details. I might need you to do that next week."

"No problem," he said, "it's what I do best."

* * *

Diego had to admit that he was rather excited. Something inside was cluing him in to the fact that he was getting himself in the middle of some important business that would do him well, would help Dave and his group and possibly lead to a new direction in the murder of the senator. Melanie, he deduced was extremely nervous about this Marvin Antwerp, or whoever he really was. She had never used his name in discussing his possible new assignment but he knew; he figured that out quickly enough. It seemed more possible than not that he was using a fictitious name and wasn't the person he'd claimed to be on his application.

Diego laughed; this guy must be an amateur because he hadn't done a very good job. He hadn't even covered his bases in case someone checked up on him. That lead him to believe that his sponsors were so solid that they didn't think anyone would question him at all. Not a good idea.

Diego placed a call to Dave Patterson.

"Heh buddy," he said. "how's it going back in Scranton?"

"Heh Amilio. Oops, I mean Diego. I guess that's who you are right now. Well, we're moving along. The trial starts in a few weeks and we have all the paperwork we need to start with the interviews so we can finally get the entire story of this mess around here."

"Heh, that's great. Plus you'll have Sammi with you for the interviews so she'll get something. She always does."

"Well, so do you. I'd like to have you here too, but I think you might pick up something out there in Hartford."

"That's true. I'm coming home this weekend. I need to make everyone aware of a few things and I think we'll need Julie's help on this one. Things are moving fast here. Some of it's rather strange, but .... I think I'll save it for later. Where's Sammi gonna be?"

"She'll be home this weekend. Why?"

"I'd like to have a meeting with everyone involved. We all have to get on the same page. After that, it might be a while before I'll see you guys in person because I'll be watched. We have to get our system down."

"Ok. We'll make that happen. You've got me upbeat on this one."

"I'm really excited, Dave. I just fell into something and I think it's gonna work out very well for all of us."

"Have you seen Sammi yet? I don't think she knows about you being there yet."

"No, I haven't seen her. This job came about a lot faster than I thought it would. Sammi is a pro as well as Ben and Jeff. They'd handle it fine."

"Still, it will be good if they know about you and this weekend we can take care of all of that."

"Right. Okay, I'll check in with you later."

CHAPTER XV

"I get enough surprises everyday I don't need you showing up again without my knowledge," joked Sammi. She was sure that she could have handled it just fine, but couldn't resist poking fun at Amilio, now known as Diego.

"Hah," he said laughingly, "you would have probably given me a rough time just because you knew that you could."

"Never happen. Our games are dangerous enough as it is."

Although this get together was a lot of fun, they were here to get their plan of action exact, as precarious times loomed ahead of them and they never knew when all would become evident.

"Enough you two," said Dave. "How and when do you think that you'd see each other at that Biltmore Company?"

Sammi took this one. "Well, now that Amilio is working as an assistant to Melanie, it seems that he might be around when we interview her again. Ben is hoping to make that happen this coming week."

"And I hope to have some targeted questions to pass along to you before then so you can make her sweat a little. That should help you, Sammi."

"I don't quite understand how you got this job, Amilio."

"Honestly, part of it was pure luck." He sat back in his chair and laughed. "Okay, Sammi, I know that you don't believe in luck or coincidence. I got the basic interview that got me into the company because of our connections, but the only opening at the time was in the mail department and I wondered if from there I could even be effective."

Amilio took a deep breath before he continued. He wanted to get the details right.

"Okay, well, I know that they'd been having some tough times with their mailing procedures. It just wasn't working very efficiently and they were thinking of having one of those efficiency experts come in before it got any worse. However, they did ask for suggestions from the employees and I placed some very targeted and direct ideas that I saw would immediately help. I was hoping Melanie would take notice because if I got into a position where I would be in contact with her on a regular basis, well, that's what I was hoping for."

Dave interjected. "Yes, you're a lot like Sammi in a way. If you're around people you can usually get them to open up and trust you. That's what you're so good at."

Sammi smiled. She could hear Amilio's thoughts. He felt pride that Dave had compared him to Sammi. He always tried to figure out how she got her information, but so far, he had failed. However, he still thought they made a good team.

"I was already finagling as to how I could get out of the mailroom or at least get some assignments nearer to the top level floor. Then, because of my suggestions, she called me in. She was really impressed with my ideas to improve their problems in that department and saw immediately my concern about the downfall of the efficiency and how it could be corrected."

Sammi said, "It's good that you always spot things because it got you noticed."

"Right and at an opportune time. She was already having some misgivings about this Marvin Antwerp. Apparently, nothing in his application agrees with real life and after checking on some of his college work and references, the people and facts don't exist at all. She was on the phone so she waived me in and I overheard a few things that I don't think she wanted me to hear. She had already double-checked me and I think I'm about to become part of her inner circle. This will be perfect for us."

Jim said, "How will this Marvin take it? I understand he is very protective of her and a bit jealous, too, didn't you say?"

"He's a lot jealous of her. Either he has a gigantic crush on her or he plays her for reasons yet to be determined. He's a tough cookie to figure out."

"You'll probably have to protect yourself from this Marvin," offered Dave.

"At this time he still has a few weeks left on jury duty. They forced that on him and wouldn't get him out of it. He was quite furious, I understand. Meantime, I got the feeling that Melanie wants to check with Milt about this guy, because apparently he brought him into the company in the first place. She wants to know if he's aware of his lack of credentials."

"That should be one hot meeting," laughed Dave.

"No kidding," said Amilio, "even though they generally get along okay professionally, well, they used to be married to each other and there is definitely animosity there .... or something; I can't figure them out yet."

Sammi said, "Probably a touchy situation. When did they divorce?"

"Not sure, but it wasn't a friendly divorce."

"I don't think any of them are," said Jim.

"The point is," said Amilio, "when I get back there next week, if Melanie gets me to check into the background of Marvin like I think she will, I'll be watched like a hawk by her and Milt and the other top people. He could be a plant from somewhere and they want to find out as quickly as possible, hopefully before he returns. They will no doubt want to play it cool and not let him think anything is wrong. I'm sure they'll have their own agenda by then."

"And when we come back to interrogate both Milt and Melanie, Marvin won't know that they're on to him and Melanie doesn't know about the real you. Eh gads. This is a confusing situation."

"Right, so I need to make sure that we're all on the same page as far as I'm concerned and how we can possibly communicate with one another. I thought I'd use pay phones to contact Dave when I need to. No one should call me directly; it would be too dangerous."

"Okay, okay," said Dave. "That's the way we usually play it and now Sammi can clue in Ben and Jeff about you. But I think Ben probably knows, don't you, Sammi?"

"Not sure. This has happened quite fast so I'll make sure to let them know. We don't need any more surprises right now."

After all the rules were set, they relaxed for the rest of the evening. They still had Sunday to add any smaller points before Amilio had to go back. Everyone was getting somewhat anxious now. The trial was nearing, more interviews would be forthcoming in both Scranton and Hartford and it seemed that all that could be done right now was accomplished.

* * *

Dave decided to interview Charlie Bowren on Sunday while Sammi was around. This was somewhat out of order because everyone was expecting them to continue their interrogation of Phil Anderson.

Jim said, "Why switch to Charlie? Phil seems to be sweating some right now."

"Exactly, and a little more sweating won't hurt him any. In fact, I like the thought. Besides, of the two, Charlie is the meeker one. Even as young children, their file shows that Phil was always the leader and Charlie just followed along. Now that they have a strong bond with each other, Charlie does rely on him like a big brother. They are family to each other and as such I think Charlie will follow Phil's lead."

"Does Charlie even know what Phil's last interview was about?" asked Jim.

"Yes, by now I'm sure he does. We made sure that they got some time around each other during recess. I requested it. Let them compare notes and see what happens. In the meantime, before they decide to get a solid plan of their own to follow, let's talk to Charlie and see what happens?"

"Good idea. It can't hurt and it may confuse them both enough to want to make a deal. That's what we hope for, right?"

"For sure. I'm trying to keep both of them away from Jason right now. Hope we accomplished that. If he throws threats at them … well, who knows? I actually feel sorry for them."

"But remember, Dave, Phil said they wanted to get away from that Right Side Group. They seemed quite intimated by them."

"And I hope that holds. Right now, it's our best weapon."

* * *

Sammi was ready for Charlie Bowren as soon as he walked into the interrogation room. She was in focus and carefully concentrating, hoping to pick up as many of his thoughts as possible. A lot hinged on any new information.

In a way to Sammi, listening to thoughts was like writing a book. Each new page and most definitely each new chapter could send you in an entirely different direction. Sometimes you had to wait for the next page or chapter before you could take your next step. Actually, life was like that countless times. Before you could make your next move, you had to wait and see what was thrown your way. Just a big giant puzzle, she thought. One challenge following upon another and all you could do was to give your best to each situation as it arose. Oh yes, and hope was also part of the game.

She was aware that she had an extra advantage. Hearing thoughts put her ahead of the game in most instances. Yet, murderers always lied and tried to cheat the system, so any step you could get up on them was a plus.

When Charlie walked into the room, it was evident that he and his friend Phil were very different personalities. Phil had a confidence and an awareness that led you to believe he couldn't be fooled easily. He had a heart that had been hardened over the years and he gave the impression that he could take care of himself.

Charlie's personality was a great deal softer. He looked at all the people in the room and recoiled in experienced shyness. Sammi caught him thinking that he wasn't ready for an entire group to be asking him questions. He wished Phil was here. He always did all the talking. Charlie usually only backed him up when necessary. But today, he was on his own. He didn't like it. It made him feel small and somewhat fearful.

He instantly remembered when his parents were killed when he was eight years old. His memory was still quite sharp in this area. He felt so alone and terrified. He had spent many nights crying before sleep finally came. He often wondered what they would think of him now. He had actually done pretty well most of his life. He hadn't gotten into any real trouble and had learned to obey the rules of society. And he thought his mom would like Phil, especially for the way he protected him. Yet the Right Side Group was a big mistake for both of them. It was not at all what they thought it would be. They had wanted a solid group that would be like an extended family. Instead, they had inadvertently got themselves involved with a bunch of subversive crooks that were really weird and unpredictable. What a mess, he thought. What a horrible, nasty mess. They couldn't get out of it now. Sammi knew he felt like crying but held himself in.

Sammi sat on Dave's left side ready to take notes. Jim was there along with Roy, who was there for added value, and would sit in the back row as a listener. Sammi saw Charlie look over at Dave as he thought. *I'm sure glad he's okay. I really didn't mean anything; I was just so scared and I panicked; I didn't know what to do. I guess I'm cooked anyway. Probably jail for a long time. I mean, I hit a cop and they're not likely to go easy on that. I wish my dad was here. I don't know why it's still important that my parents are proud of me.*

"Okay, Mr. Bowren," said Dave in a rather obvious tone, "I'm sure you remember me and my other partner Roy." He gestured toward him. "And this other officer is Jim."

He nodded as he looked around the table. *Funny,* he thought, *they all look like regular people, probably friendly enough in their own way. But I know they're out to get me. Phil thought they might help us out if we had something to offer them. But they're not our buddies, I must remember that.*

"Charlie," continued Dave, "why don't you tell us why you and your buddies attacked our group."

"First of all, they ain't my buddies," he said but then quickly modified his statement. "Well, Phil is, but not Jason. I barely know him."

"Okay," said Jim. "Why did you and Phil and Jason attack the group?"

"It really was a surprise to me and Phil," he said. "Oh sure, I know that sounds funny, but we didn't really know what this group was about. We thought we had joined a fraternity-type group that did things together and watched out for each other. We didn't know they shot up police officers nor did other violent things. Honestly, we didn't know much about them. When we found out and tried to leave, we knew we were in big trouble. I know you won't believe me, I don't blame you. But that's the way it was."

Jim and Dave looked at each other. They even turned to Roy. There was something in Charlie's voice that was sincere and possibly a quality looking for hope. He was scared; there was no doubt about that and he was looking for an out. They decided to let him go further.

"Okay, so you got into this group by mistake. But," said Dave, "what made you guys attack us?"

"It was Jason's idea. Phil and I freaked out. We didn't know what he planned until about a minute before. But he raced the car and was out shooting before we even knew what was happening." His voice was getting shakier and more emotional. "Honestly, I didn't even shoot and dropped my gun somewhere close to the car and Phil only shot up into the air sort of like to pretend we were going along with him. We'd already been threatened about trying to leave the group. We tried to play it safe."

Charlie put his face into his hands and shook his head from side to side. It was obvious that he couldn't believe what had happened that day. Then without any further delay he said, "I'm so very sorry that you got hurt. I just totally panicked and when I came around that tree and saw you, I didn't know what to do. I'm very sorry and sure hope that you're okay."

"I guess it was a surprise to you that I was there."

"Yeah, it was. I was just hoping to get the hell out of there as fast as I could. I thought Phil might be right behind me and we'd get out of there and just keep going and get away from this group."

You could tell that Charlie meant to go on, but he stopped. Sammi knew that he thought all was futile and there was no way back. First jail, then this group would be at them again. He felt his life was over and he was only twenty-four. Sammi clued in Dave.

"You know, Charlie, there may be a way that we could help each other. I've looked over your record as well as Phil and the two of you have never been in trouble before."

"Oh no, and we've had some pretty tough times after we left that last foster home."

Then Charlie stopped abruptly. Apparently, he hadn't planned to bring up that part of his life. That was his personal business. Dave jumped on that one.

"Look Charlie. We know about you and Phil. We know that you've watched out for each other for years. Apparently, you've been quite good for each other. Nevertheless, this is serious business. You're both in a lot of trouble."

"I know, I know," he said as he finally sat back in his chair and exhibited the first bit of relaxation since he'd walked into the room. Although his body finally seemed to calm down, his attitude displayed tumultuous emotions of uselessness and hopelessness; he felt it was too late to rectify anything.

"What can you tell us about this Right Side Group?"

At this point Sammi started writing furiously on her writing pad. Dave knew he had struck some type of area in his memory and decided to stay right there and ask pointed questions.

"I don't know much, but I'll cooperate. I think they're very strange."

"Okay, just tell us what you know."

"Well, they don't like cops or the government or any legal type people, if you know what I mean. We didn't know any of this at first."

"What made you join the group?"

"It wasn't really joining exactly. It's not as if we made any kind of application and they accepted us. Phil and I talked about that later. It was just they asked us to come to a few of their meetings and after that they just expected that we would be part of them. We didn't really have a choice."

"So they don't like police or anything legal. Why is that?" asked Jim.

"I don't know the whole story, but it seems like Jason's father, who is in jail by the way for trying to kill a policeman, had another son that was killed by a policeman during a robbery. He was only sixteen and that started part of the hate."

"Part of the hate?" questioned Dave.

"Well, yeah. They don't seem to agree with many of the federal or state laws and cause trouble about them whenever they can. I told you they're a weird group."

"Hmm," said Dave and just waited.

"It didn't take them long before they realized that we didn't think like them at all and soon there was a meeting just for our benefit that said that they thought we knew too much to be let go. We had to stay in or we'd be sorry. And they weren't nice about it. I have to tell you we were both pretty scared. We had planned to play along just to be safe and after a while we'd make a getaway to another state as soon as we could."

Dave shook his head. He soon realized that these two boys had started out with a heavy load, no parents, and various foster homes and then they inadvertently landed into a subversive group totally unaware. Sammi could let him know if Charlie was being perfectly honest. But it seemed that he was. Still, he had to move on.

"Have you ever heard any plans or details that you think might help us?"

"Well, it's a small group around here, but they have affiliations with other groups around the country. I know one is in New York and another in New Jersey....." then Charlie stopped cold.

He looked upset as he asked, "If any of this information gets out, you won't say it came from me, will you? Cause if you do, I'm dead, in or out of jail."

Charlie looked around the group. His breathing was desperate, his forehead and hands were sweating and Dave could detect a slight tremor in his fingers. If this guy was acting, he was one of the best.

"Nope," said Dave to try to relax Charlie, an almost impossible feat at this time. "All of our information is confidential. And some of this stuff, we already know."

He seemed to take a deep breath. Without trying to hide it, a look of satisfaction crossed his face. He was definitely pleased.

Some type of protocol, a step from the other side that was not surprising anymore, suddenly interrupted them. This interview was over for now. They knew they'd talk to him again. In the meantime, they'd make sure that Phil and Charlie had access to each other. That could help them a lot.

* * *

"That crappy other side is playing games again," said Jim totally frustrated. "They didn't have to break up our interview. That stuff could have waited until later."

"I think they'll always exercise their muscles whenever they can. They want to make sure that we realize they are running the show. So, let's let them think that." Dave was satisfied.

"I don't know why this doesn't seem to bother you, Dave," said Roy. "I think they're very irritating."

"That's what they want. Anyway, we got plenty for today. It will probably be best if Phil and Charlie get a chance to exchange notes before we see either one of them again. They really do need a little time."

Sammi said, "And that Charlie, he's a very nice-type person. In other circumstances, he'd be considered a real conscientious and upright guy. Too bad they got themselves involved in these circumstances. Didn't get much help in their young lives I would think."

"Probably true, still, they could be a big help to us. Maybe more than they know." Dave seemed to be in deep thought. He was definitely looking toward the future and wondering what Sammi had picked up. She seemed upbeat.

"Let's meet tomorrow morning. I think Sammi will have her notes finished by then."

She nodded in confirmation.

"Okay, then we'll call it a day. A few things Charlie said do ring true. He said that he never fired his gun and just dropped it. That does check out. I do believe he panicked and dropped his firearm very close to the car. That gun was never fired. These kids are not full-blown criminals; I think they could make it all the way back."

Jim added, "I get the same impression. They've had a lot of bad luck."

Dave pursed his lips and tried to shake off the deep feelings that were still clouding his demeanor. "Yes, that's true. Hopefully they can still be helped."

"Okay, then," said Roy. "How about Dave's desk at 10:00?"

"Sure," interjected Jim. "Unless the sarge wants to hear the latest."

They all laughed at that one. These type of meetings usually ended up in Sergeant Brady's office.

* * *

Sammi and Dave decided to eat out. Sometimes they needed to clear their minds for a while. The drama of these cases was difficult to digest and for Sammi, well, she was the one that really needed a break. She experienced all of the outer feelings yet, also had to deal with the inner emotionalism. Long meetings could get to her. That was one reason why Dave hadn't minded that the interview was cut short. He could tell Sammi was exhausted and thought maybe it was a lucky break.

"Bet you were glad the meeting was cut short."

She smiled. "I didn't mind, that's for sure. I can always go on longer if I need to. I've sort of trained myself to do that now."

"Still, I get the feeling that you got a lot today."

"I did and for once, it wasn't too confusing. Charlie is very much a straight thinker. He isn't conniving or sneaky; he's pretty much what he appears to be."

"Then his words did agree with his thoughts."

"They definitely did. He's very upset that they got into a subversive group and according to his thoughts, it was an accident. He believes Phil is just as upset, but he doesn't show it as much. Phil doesn't even talk about it very much to Charlie. He apparently doesn't want to upset him. I guess they've discussed this lately. Phil still thinks of Charlie as his little brother and doesn't believe that he has grown up. He still comes across as a vulnerable personality but he has a strong underlying character. He really can handle things."

"Really? It didn't seem so to me. At one point, I thought he might shed some tears."

"You're right. He handles things differently and he will cry. Phil, on the other hand, will hold matters inside but he will be just as upset. Just different personalities."

"Will I find any surprises in your notes?"

"Not much. Charlie is pretty much what he seems to be on the surface. He really is a nice guy, mainly looking for a place that he belongs. So is Phil for that matter, although he is definitely a little rougher around the edges. Yet, considering the lives they were forced to live, I think they've turned out very well."

"So no real surprises? Everything is pretty much what we heard today. I saw you writing furiously at one point and thought maybe there were some new details."

Sammi had to laugh. "You know me entirely too well. I know you can usually read my expressions by now, but I didn't count on you knowing my writing habits."

"Well, you always sit right next to me. I can't help but notice."

"That's okay because you're right. There was one very interesting thought that crossed his mind several times."

Dave waited, then said, "Don't keep me in suspense."

"Okay, okay. First, I do want to say that although he didn't mention this aloud I think it's because the conversation didn't really go there. This was one of those thoughts that was somewhat low, if you know what I mean. It came toward the surface, but definitely wasn't way up there on top. I'm lucky I caught it at all. It could be significant."

Dave said, "And do I get to know what it is?"

Sammi looked confused, "Oh that's right, I haven't told you. I still get mixed up at times between what was said out loud and what I just heard through thoughts. Anyway, here it is. Charlie kept thinking about the name Bill Lueger. Mean anything to you?"

Dave shook his head.

Sammi continued. "I'm pretty sure that he is an important player in the Right Side Group. Both Charlie and Phil have met him. So they know what he looks like. It went like this. Remember those meetings that Charlie said they attended, well Bill was there at one of them. In fact, he was one of the speakers, but he doesn't work around here. I don't know where he's from; I couldn't pick that up. However, it seems like the people here felt honored to have him come to speak. Charlie seems to think he's a higher up."

"Funny he didn't mention it?"

"I don't think he was hiding it. I don't think the conversation today really went in that direction and as I said, this thought wasn't really up near the surface. But, and this is important, that meeting that Charlie said was for the benefit of him and Phil, well, this Bill Lueger was there and they believe that he was the one that didn't want them to be let out of the group. I know Charlie is very worried about him."

"Heh that is a good piece of information. I'll have Julie see what she can find out. Anything else?"

"Not that I can think of right now. I'll let you know when I type up my notes."

As Sammi finished her glass of Piesporter, she let out a deep sigh. She knew that she had captured some important data and felt satisfied. She looked into space for a moment and relaxed. She knew they were moving in the right direction.

CHAPTER XVI

Diego had mentioned to Sammi that Marvin still had another week at least on jury duty. Therefore, it was a surprise when he saw him at the office on Monday morning. For some reason the jury case was delayed until 1:00 PM that day so he felt he wanted to make his presence known. He still tried to avoid Melanie, since his anger at being forced into jury duty hadn't subsided yet.

"What's been going on around here, Diego? Anything that I should know about?"

Even though their previous encounters hadn't been anything close to friendly, Marvin still seemed to think that Diego would do anything to be his friend. He felt he still held the high cards as a person of authority.

"Nothing much." He kept his answer short, as he knew this would irritate him. And it did.

"Well, what are you working on?"

Marvin's body stance was showing irritation, as he knew he was not getting the respect he felt he deserved.

"Mainly I'm helping to reorganize the mailing department. That's not quite finished yet."

"Right, right," he said as he walked into his office. He was out quickly looking definitely upset.

"Has anybody been in my office? I want to know right now."

"Eh gaads Marvin. I'm hardly ever up here. I wouldn't know. Don't you keep your door locked?"

He muttered something under his breath as he turned and walked back in, but not before he asked, "What are you doing up here now?"

"Got a meeting with Melanie soon."

"Oh, what about?"

"Don't know. I'm sure I'll find out any minute."

Marvin's expression proved that he didn't believe Diego. In addition, Marvin's appearance belied another unforgiving trait. He felt that he was losing his grip on Diego, which he counted on for information. He was about to make a comment in an attempt to subdue him again, but an overheard comment made him make a quick exit.

"Heh, Diego, I hear that Melanie just arrived. She should be up here shortly."

There was no way to misinterpret Marvin's body language. He didn't want to see Melanie. More importantly, he didn't want her to see him up there. He almost fell over himself making his way to the distant elevator, which would definitely avoid an encounter.

And he was right. Diego enjoyed the entertainment of seeing Marvin scurrying off, yet barely making the elevator in time to escape. He watched as the elevator doors closed in slow motion as Melanie came around the other corner in her usually lively step strut anxious to begin her day.

"Good morning, Diego. What's wrong? You looked surprised to see me."

"Not exactly, but Marvin just hightailed it out of here as soon as he heard you were coming. He barely made it to the far elevator when you came around the corner. It looks like he was trying to avoid you."

"He was here? Is he out of jury duty already?"

She looked anxious. It was obvious she was hoping to make progress during this last week she expected him to be away.

"No, no. The case is still ongoing. For some reason, there was a delay and won't start until later in the day. He just stopped by to check on things, I guess."

"Oh," she said. "Did he talk to you?"

"Only because he had to. I was already here waiting for you."

"What did he want to know?"

Diego felt two people were using him as an information center, but that was okay with him. He got a secret look at two worlds and this could help him in the future.

"He was real interested to know what I'd been working on. And then he went into his office for a few seconds and came out demanding to know who'd been in there."

Melanie smiled. *He probably had his door silently booby trapped,* she thought, *so that it would be easily determined if someone had entered.* It would have had to be someone significant since he kept his door locked at all times.

"Give me about ten minutes. I'll get us some coffee and then I have business to discuss with you."

Diego half bowed to her and turned to walk away. He was happy. It was as he had hoped. He was being taken into the inner circle to dig up something on Marvin, whom he believed was a mysterious fellow.

* * *

Melanie unlocked her office door and walked over to her large brown leather chair that always pleasured her. She first checked her phone lines to be sure she didn't have any messages. Unlocking her desk brought back thoughts of the day's events. She'd had an early breakfast meeting with Milt. And she had been blunt and direct with him. Who was this Marvin Antwerp and why didn't they have any information on him? Milt was shocked.

"What the hell are you talking about?"

She relayed to him that his profile was lacking many important details and when she had tried to follow up on his college credits and past employment, no one ever heard of him. The only pleasure she got was the astonished look on Milt's face. Someone had pulled a good one on him.

"John Durant from Upward Managers recommended him highly and convinced me that he was just what we needed. John's always been tight with me; I had no reason to doubt him."

"Get with him today and find out what this is all about. I can't believe this one got past you. You're usually right on top of all these details. I didn't even check him out because you assured me he was okay. Now I can't even trust you."

It was obvious that those last words really hurt Milt. Usually he had a nasty retort for his ex-wife, but unfortunately, he understood her panic. He was feeling it as well.

Then in a quick moment of regret, Melanie added, "Look Milt, despite all our problems and anger with each other, I really do trust you. I'm just surprised and really, really nervous. What if he's a plant from somewhere? We have enough trouble now with the FBI investigating the senator's murder. We need to find out fast who Marvin is and why his profile information is false."

"Yeah, I know," said Milt still looking stunned. Then he sort of caught himself and said, "I'll find out and I'll do it today. I just can't believe that John would be involved in something subversive to us. Maybe he doesn't know anything either."

Suddenly, they just looked at each other caught up in their own thoughts. And the messages they were getting were quite scary. Milt was the first to get up and leave. He grabbed his briefcase and left without saying another word. None was necessary.

* * *

Melanie had the coffee ready when she called in Diego. She had to take a chance on him; she had no other choice. But she had him checked out thoroughly and he was completely on target. His specialty was digging up information on people. She hoped he could do better than she had.

"Well, Diego, here's the deal. It goes without saying that this is totally confidential and must be kept one hundred percent between you and me. Well, Milt is in on this one, but that's my call. You deal only with me. Got it?"

"Definitely," he said, happy inside because he knew what was coming.

"I need you to find out all you can about Marvin Antwerp."

Diego put a convincing surprised look on his face. He couldn't let Melanie know that he had already figured that out.

"You want an investigation on Marvin?" he answered. "I thought he was your main assistant."

"He was; he is," she said. "Oh hell, I don't know what to think or do."

She then relayed to him what she had found lacking in his profile and that even the provided information had turned out to be completely false.

Diego let out a long, slow whistle. "That does not sound good at all. Kind of makes you think he's probably a plant of some kind."

Melanie looked up obviously worried, but not surprised at his comment.

"That crossed my mind, of course. We need to find out who he is, and why he's here. There's a reason; that's for sure. He's not what he appears to be. Honestly, I've worked closely with him for the last two years and I'm shocked. He always was so eager to please me and very helpful."

Diego was about to say something but Melanie was musing aloud, almost muttering to herself, and then continued as if she needed to create a timeline of events.

"He always did act strange at times. I know that he isn't very well liked among the other employees. Many times, he seems to be in his own world and only steps outside if he needs to connect with me. At times, I must admit he concerned me, but then we hired him on a recommendation from another firm who had a spotless reputation with us. So I dismissed my thoughts."

"Sometimes a gut feeling needs to be given attention."

"True, true. Is that how you find out things?"

Melanie had suddenly taken a new look at Diego and he seemed to realize that she did respect his profile regarding his talent at being able to uncover a hidden agenda. He decided to change the subject a little to get the attention off himself.

Diego shifted in his chair and then said, "Rumor has it that he has a crush on you. Are you aware of that?"

"Yeah, I've heard that rumor, but I don't think so. I think it's more like a type of respect that I'm in a very high position in this company. He seems like someone who wants to move to the top. I think he thought I could be his mentor."

Diego was thoughtful. "That could all be true as well, but I got the impression that he kind of liked you when you first introduced me to him, remember? He wasn't at all friendly to me and I think he sort of felt that I may be cutting in on his territory."

Melanie sat back in her chair, a little thoughtful. "I'll have to consider the personal aspect more carefully. However, we need to find out what he's doing here and we need to find out fast. Can you do it?"

"I'll do my best, but I'll need a copy of his file and anything else that you know. I'll start on it right now."

As he got up to leave, he turned and said, "Any chance we can look in his office and get a clue?" As an afterthought he added, "Do you have access to his computer?"

"Let me do that. I'll give you whatever I find out right after lunch. Meet me back here about 2:00."

Somehow, by the time Diego left her office Melanie had the feeling that if anyone could dig up information it would be Diego. He had a calm assurance about himself that carried out into the atmosphere. He was already on the job.

* * *

Sammi was sorry that she couldn't be in direct communication with Diego. They seemed to share information so well and, as she had to admit, they were very well matched. Diego had his own way of finding out information and his inner circuits were usually on target. It was hard to fool him.

On her flight back to Hartford she had heard from Ben and it was decided that they would be analyzing data at least for the next few days. Apparently, it wasn't time yet to re-interview Melanie or Milton; she suspected they wanted to give Diego time to make a dent into their system. She asked if there was any possibility that they could finagle their way back to Mr. Jim. It had been a while since she had seen him and she needed to keep her rapport with him intact, since his frame of mind was so delicate. Therefore, even though the opposition made things as difficult as possible, Ben had decided to put some muscle behind his words. By Tuesday, they'd have another meeting with him.

During lunch with Ben, he stated, "They're not happy with us at all right now. We have pushed our agenda close to going public, which they don't want under any circumstances at this time. So in order to pacify us, they are giving us little crumbs to keep us from bitching too much. Yet, they know it's going to happen in the near future. The public in Hartford is screaming for more information about the case. They want to know what's happening. Still, for some reason the attorneys need to keep everything as quiet as possible right now. I really don't get it."

"Then why will they let us meet with Mr. Jim?" asked Sammi

"To appease us and buy more time. They want as much time as possible. We go to trial, at least the preliminary trial in less than two weeks and if they can have everything in order as they see it, they believe they will have a quick conviction."

"Surely they know that there will be a defense for him."

"That's been kept hidden for now. No attorney has seen him as far as we know. And he's not competent enough to ask for one. I think that they will try to get a very new court ordered attorney that they can push around. I know that they plan to make this a very fast slam-dunk. They think the evidence is there. I can't believe they're that stupid."

"You know, Ben. I don't think they are that stupid. I think they want this done fast and clean for other reasons."

"Yeah, I'm sure you're right. What do you think?"

"Well, of course, to pacify the public is one reason, but what if this was not a random shooting and it was planned. I know we both believe that. Well, the sooner they get someone in jail and convicted, the safer they think they are. I really think they believe this will all go away if they convict Mr. Jim."

"Yeah, but the FBI has now authorized us to get him an attorney. Nothing is out there yet, and they will have a fit when they find out. We better get our meeting in with Mr. Jim before they find out or we're gonna have a tough mountain to climb."

"When can we see him?"

"I'm trying for tomorrow morning. I plan to get all the time we can because as we go forward it may be hard. His attorneys probably won't relish the thought that we want to see him. They'll have their own job to do. So get everything you can this time; it may be our last for a long time."

"Okay, it's good if we can get to see him one more time. It might calm him down to know that I'm back again. We need to keep him on our side. We know that he doesn't think that well right now. Why hasn't anyone had him checked out medically? I know they've had psychiatrists check him over, but I think his physical problems are where the answers are at."

"That may be true but we have no jurisdiction there. It could be a suggestion that we could give to his lawyers."

Sammi smiled in a knowing way.

"What's on your mind?" asked Ben.

"Well, I was thinking that if we were really lucky, maybe we'll find the real killer before the trial takes place."

Ben smiled. "Yeah, that would be the best solution."

* * *

Tuesday morning went so smoothly that it worried Ben. He made the appointment to see Mr. Jim and when he and Sammi arrived at the jail, they were escorted into the interview room with no problems, no sarcastic remarks and definitely no irritating delays. Coffee was even provided which made Ben marvel at their turn of behavior. All that was asked of them was that they didn't go public with anything right now. That Ben could promise, at least from his point of view. When the attorneys hired by the FBI, got into the case, he had no power over them. Yet that was their secret.

When Mr. Jim entered the room, it seemed to be a repeat performance of the last two interviews. In fact, the police escort, who brought Mr. Jim into the room and smirked at his usual nonsensical remarks, painfully reminded her that nothing had changed. Yes, thought Sammi, he's still living in his dream world.

"Hi, Mr. Jim," she said. "I like your name."

Mr. Jim reacted to that. Actually, he seemed like he remembered a few things, which surprised both of them. Sammi wondered if the prosecutors had noticed.

"Hi," he answered immediately with definite focus. "You came again. I've missed you."

"I wish I could come more often, but I can't. But you are my friend," she said as she smiled at him. He definitely seemed to keep focus much better this time. Sammi decided to push him further.

"Do you remember Ben? He's your friend, too."

Mr. Jim shook his head in the affirmative. "I remember him." He turned in a friendly familiar gesture and asked, "How are you?"

Ben looked at Sammi in surprise. He definitely had improved.

"Do you remember what happened to you? When did you hurt your head?"

He rubbed his head, paused for so long that Sammi thought she had lost him. Maybe she had pushed him too far. Then he answered.

"Long time ago. My head still hurts and my car is bad."

"Did you have a car accident?"

"No, I didn't. Someone stopped me."

"Where were you going?"

"I was going home. I always go home after school."

He was amazing today. Sammi didn't know if this was a short spurt or if he was slowly improving, but they could communicate better today than they ever had. Then Ben stepped in.

"Can I ask you questions about the murder? Do you remember that?"

His head slowly moved up and down, but his expression and body language changed. He was now upset and noticeably nervous.

"Yes, but I ... didn't do it. I ... didn't kill anybody. I was just there."

His body language was angry. He was not happy at this moment.

"Everybody asks me that. They say ... I did it. I didn't do it ... but I saw who did it."

Ben moved excitedly forward in his seat. He had made this statement before, but now with his new clarity of mind, would he get more information out of him?

"Who did it? Can you describe him?"

"Man ... in a coat. Saw him on TV once ... Don't know his name."

Then in a quick moment, Mr. Jim seemed to go back into the same world he was in before. "My head hurts. I can't think anymore. 'Tis a far far better thing I do ... I miss Nappa. I want to see Nappa."

Sammi jumped on that one. "Who is Nappa?"

He looked at her bewildered that she didn't know.

"Nappa, my best friend, one of my angels; he's my dog."

Mr. Jim became especially silent after that. His focus was gone. Ben and Sammi sat silently trying to give him a few minutes. This time it didn't seem to help much. His attention span was gone again. They looked at each other amazed that they had talked to him during a few lucid moments. It showed that with help, he could regain his clarity again.

Sammi tried again; she was still hopeful. "Can you describe the man who shot the senator?"

He looked toward Sammi, but he didn't seem to see her. There was a very long pause during which time Ben signaled that maybe they should go. Then surprisingly, Mr. Jim did have another thing to say.

"The one who gave me the gun ... he didn't shoot the senator."

Ben was shocked. "There were two men?"

"There were a lot of people there."

"But who shot the senator?"

Mr. Jim smiled. "I saw him on television."

As a big smile crossed his face, Mr. Jim added a comment that he didn't even know meant anything at all.

He said, "He was standing next to the senator."

"Which senator?" said Ben in shock. "Do you know who the senator is?"

"Of course I do," he answered, "it's Senator Stedman, Senator Mike Stedman." Mr. Jim said this with much pride. "He's handsome."

And he was right. Yet this time Mr. Jim slipped far away. Even with all of the probing and carefully constructed questions, nothing could bring him back. Sammi listened to his thoughts which were sluggish and tired and wouldn't come anywhere near the surface anymore. Mr. Jim needed rest and a lot of it. He probably wouldn't be back today. This was probably it for them.

* * *

On the way out Ben was speculating about their conversation with a man who was in and out of reality without any choice on his part.

He said, "God, we could almost have a regular conversation with him today. How could that happen?"

Sammi answered. "I think it's very obvious that this man has brain damage or a concussion. He talked about a car so it was probably a car accident. He did give us some clues as to his identity that we might be able to follow up later. But we did learn one other thing. There were two men involved in the senator's murder. It's not much more info, but it's something."

"Yeah," said Ben. He was incredibly disappointed that he couldn't get more out of him today. It was obvious that this man was improving, but it could take forever. It wouldn't happen any time soon and definitely not in time to help him in his own trial.

Ben went on. "It's sad to think that he's probably been roaming around like this for years, just needing medical treatment. Hell, he's still not getting it."

"True, but maybe when his lawyers come on board they can insist on some type of medical examination. What do you think?"

"I'm sure of that." Ben was nodding his head. "It will probably happen automatically. After all, the defense lawyers will have his best interest at heart. The prosecution only wanted some psychiatrist to say he was sane enough to stand trial."

"Maybe the trial will be postponed until that happens."

Maybe," said Ben, "but where does that leave us now?"

"Remember Ben, we have Diego/Amilio working one angle and Dave and his group are working on the Right Side Group. Something will turn up. This wasn't random; somebody wanted him dead. Could be about legislation in Connecticut or something else political, but we have to focus on what he was working on. I think that's the key."

Ben rested his shoulders. "I think you're right and I believe it more than ever right now. If the murderer was standing next to Mike on TV, well, obviously, he knows him and it's probably political. The answer is right here and we haven't seen it yet. It's probably right in front of us. And I always believed that there is no such thing as a perfect murder."

"I do agree. There's always something …."

"Wish we could follow up on the thought that this guy was on TV next to the senator, but we don't know even when or where. If only Mr. Jim could have helped us more."

"But he did help us some. It is a known person, one who goes on TV politically, at least some of the time. I know that's a wide clue, but it's a clue. Someday all of this will fit together."

"Well, I'm back to the office … there's always more data to figure out. What are you doing?" asked Ben.

"I'm meeting with Jeff. He had something he wanted to update me on and then hopefully some lunch. I'm starving."

* * *

After lunch, Jeff clued in Sammi that he had gotten some background information on Melanie Brooks. He wanted to know when they could interview her again.

"Well, Diego is working closely with her this week. Marvin is still on jury duty so they are both trying to figure out who he is and I'm waiting to get the word that we can get to her again."

"Oh, that's right. Diego got into her inner circle. That's great, but it doesn't seem that any of them know what's going on with him anyway. Right?"

"That's true, but I think while he's gone they will check his office and computers and see if they get any hints as to his true identity."

"Everything is so complicated. I mean, Melanie is a kind of mystery herself. About six years ago, she left the company for a while; at least she worked from somewhere else. It seems to be a mystery where she went and why, since she's always been such a 'hands on' person."

Sammi remained silent. She had pretty much figured out what had happened to Melanie, but wasn't ready yet to give out the information. She needed to talk to Dave first and the group back home. It wasn't detrimental if that info was kept silent for a while.

Noticing her silence, Jeff said, "Anything particular bothering you?"

She always had to be careful as to what she revealed, unless she was around Dave.

"I guess sometimes I like to sit and contemplate the data we already have. If something doesn't fit for me, I have to go deeper."

Jeff smiled. "And that's how you figure out things, right?"

"To a degree, that's true. When some of the facts don't seem right, I keep going over things and then something usually jumps out at me."

"Like what?"

She smiled and decided to give him a few crumbs that he may not have thought of.

"Well, okay. Melanie has several phone lines on her desk. One is for usual business. Another line is linked to Milt so that he can get her at anytime. When that line rings, she always answers it no matter what. Yet there is a third phone line that intrigues me. I've gotten some hints as to what it may be about, but I'm only speculating."

"Care to speculate out loud?"

She laughed. "Not yet. It's not a strong feeling so I'm just guessing. I'd like to see where it takes me. Surely Jeff, you do the same thing when you go over clues, don't you?"

"I do, but you certainly seem to get better and faster results."

"Guess I'm just lucky."

Jeff gave her one of those looks that said he realized he'd never get her system out of her. A few more calculated looks concluded that they had each established a barrier line. Both felt comfortable behind it.

Jeff continued his appraisal of Melanie. "I'm not sure if she was an orphan, but she didn't seem to have any parents around after the age of eight or ten; at least none that I could find. Her parents were not good parent material anyway and to what I could glean out of her past they were fighters, drug users and drinkers, rather mean and not very encouraging to her. Any positive endorsement she received came from her teachers in grade school. They actually felt sorry for her."

"So she pushed on in spite of them, not because of them."

He nodded almost instinctively as he added, "She apparently worked hard at school but was pretty much of a loner; not many friends and no relatives that we know of. I don't think she had anyone to lean on. So, for her to get from there to where she is now, she had to be a strong person."

Sammi had to agree with that. "She puts up a façade of a strong-willed person, but if you remember in that first interview, she does have some vulnerable spots. I think you may have found the answer of why in her childhood."

"I guess that's where all of us get our strengths and weaknesses. Well, I hope to get more from our next interview. At least we can get into some areas that might be touchy with her. That should help."

"Yes, that's true."

"I wish we had a way," said Jeff with a wink, "to find out about that third phone line."

Sammi laughed. "I'm sure we will in time."

CHAPTER XVII

Sammi liked it when she had a chance to be on her own for a while. Some things she just couldn't relate to Ben or Jeff and, although she was around them physically, she didn't confide in them completely. Yet she felt comfortable about that since she knew that the FBI always had some hidden agenda that wasn't passed her way. That was fine with her. She didn't spend any effort trying to find out since she had enough things on her mind.

She was waiting to hear from Diego. For some reason, Marvin Antwerp was frequently on her mind. She was very anxious to find out something about him. She was thinking that possibly the FBI should interview him. He was another interesting person.

Dave had called her during these reflections and commented on her laid-back attitude.

"You seem so matter-of-fact about all this. What's up?"

"Oh, not really, Dave, but there are so many facts that are whirling around in my mind, I'm just wondering which ones I should concentrate on. I'm interested in Milt and Melanie, but this mysterious Marvin has been on my mind since Diego brought it up. Have you heard from him yet?"

"No, I haven't and to tell the truth, I've been wondering, too. Anyone hiding something in that company has to be investigated."

"Exactly what I thought."

"Wait a minute, Sammi. Are you thinking that you and Ben should be talking to him?"

"Yes, I do; just a gut feeling really, but something doesn't feel right. I know I'm pulling at anything unusual right now, but we only got a little more information from Mr. Jim. And that will probably be our last shot for a while."

Sammi related their last interview with Mr. Jim. She mentioned how excited they were over his lucid behavior, the first they'd ever seen.

"You think this will all fit in?"

"I really do and something low in my mind keeps nagging at me. I don't think we've talked to enough people in that company."

"Have you told Ben?"

"Not yet. I'm waiting to hear something from Diego. I want to know what he found out about Marvin. I'm meeting Ben and Jeff for dinner tonight. Maybe I could mention something to them at that time, but I'd like to hear what Diego found out first."

"Well, I think the sarge is hoping to hear from Diego real soon." Then Dave suddenly let out a laugh.

"What?"

"Most of the time I just don't know what to call that guy, that's all."

"That's true. I'm just glad he's with us."

* * *

Melanie was ready for Diego when he walked back into her office at 2:00 PM. She studied his face directly, but it didn't give a trace of anything. He seemed to cover himself very well.

"Well, what's up, Diego? Anything at all."

"I was hoping you'd have something for me," he said. Melanie look disappointed; she couldn't hide it. "Did you check out his office and computer? That would be the best for now and maybe give me a direction to go."

"Well, okay," she said realizing two hours was not much time for him to do any real investigating.

"I did find out that he actually did go to Yale. That's what his file had said. Yet he didn't go during the years that he'd recorded. It seems that he was there more than five years before."

"So he's probably older than we thought he was."

"I think so. But that seems to be a stupid thing to lie about."

"Right."

"So after digging further, it seems to be the case that he also had a wife that he didn't mention, but he is divorced. He stated on his application that he was single and never married."

"Why would he hide that fact? I mean a lot of people are married and divorced" – Diego laughed, "Probably half the country."

"Why did he lie about being married? I'm as confused as you are. And he seems to be from somewhere in Arkansas, but that's all I've got."

Diego was disappointed. "Did you check his computer?"

"Yes, of course I did, but nothing much there. He has some private documents that are under secret passwords but I couldn't get to them."

"You've got to get to them. I did find out something interesting about him," he said giving Melanie a pleasant moment. "Marvin doesn't seem to like the government. He did get into a scuffle at Yale about some government rules and there is a report identifying him as an enemy of the government and someone who should be watched."

"Really? Any police report?"

"Doesn't seem to be, but this seems to be something that the college handled themselves while he was there. I didn't get the impression that it went any further."

Melanie was quiet and in deep thought. Diego was sure the anti-government reference upset her a lot. It was obvious anyone would be wondering why he was working here.

Diego decided to speak frankly. "Kind of makes you wonder why he is here, right?"

Melanie still didn't speak. She was obviously upset and nervous.

Diego continued. "Do you have a computer expert that could get into those files? That could help."

"We've already had problems with anti-government legislation being introduced into our company. Nothing has ever come of it, but Milt is always worried. I'm sure you know that we've been interviewed by the FBI concerning the murder of Senator Stedman. It has been hinted at that some subversive people might be involved since Mike was working on legislation that would tax and encumber companies on our level."

She looked over at Diego. "Yes, we were one of them. But there were many others. Since all of us had our taxes raised considerably three years ago, we felt this one was just a smoke cover for something else. Regardless we would lobby against it, but that's all we could do."

"But you must be wondering if Marvin was in some way connected with subversives; he had to have a reason to be here."

"Yes, that's what I'm wondering. This is beginning to smell real bad. Milt is checking on the company that referred him to us. He should have something by tomorrow. Maybe they'll know something; maybe not."

Melanie made a decision. "I'm going to get someone to infiltrate his computer. But I'll have to do it at night; no one must know."

"I think Marvin will know."

Melanie looked upset.

"If he bothered to put a secret password on those documents, I'll have to bet that anyone who breaks in will be documented. He's playing it safe from all angles."

"True, but we have to chance it. We have to find out what's on those files."

Diego thought of Julie, back home in Scranton. She could get in and out without being detected. If Marvin had implanted a protection device, she'd be able to put in back in place without anyone knowing. She was that good. But she wasn't here.

"It's worth the chance. You could always blame the cleaning crew."

Melanie looked at him questioningly.

"Well, look, if your computer expert finds anything incriminating on those documents, he should make a copy then destroy the computer. He could smash it on the ground or whatever he has to do to make sure that the hard drive is destroyed. Then we could say it was an accident done by the cleaning crew."

"You've been involved with this stuff before?"

Diego smiled, but didn't answer. Of course, he wasn't new to this. Yet wasn't that why she'd taken him into her confidence.

"Do you have any suggestions? Do you know anyone?"

She surprised Diego with her request. Of course, he knew someone. If she bought it, it would be great. It would be someone that Ben could send in disguise, directly from the FBI. Wouldn't that be something?

"Let me make a few phone calls. I'm sure I could get someone over here, maybe by tonight, if you want."

Melanie was pensive for a moment. She was in deep already and she didn't want to run this one by Milt. This was her decision alone. She may as well jump in both feet. She needed a break – and knowing who Marvin was could be the beginning of a streamlining of her department and the company.

"Okay, Diego. See if you can find a real expert, but I want to be there and I want you here as well. I'll make copies of any important information that we find and if we can put the computer back together, I think we'd be ahead of the game."

* * *

Diego contacted Ben quickly and set up a computer expert. It was a go for Wednesday night after hours. Only Melanie, Diego and the computer expert from the FBI would be there. He was able to get Ben to communicate this information to Sergeant Brady who then forwarded it along to Sammi. The pieces were falling into place, and it was about time. If Diego could trust his gut feelings, Melanie and Milt were both caught in a destructive web that they did not create. Although they might push decisions to the limit to get legislation that would be in their favor, they were not subversive themselves. They had never intentionally broken the law, although they were close on occasion. Diego now wondered whom, if anyone else in the company was working with Marvin. Part of the answers might be on Marvin's computer.

* * *

Ben was extremely excited when talking to Sammi and Dave. He wanted to be sure that they were aware of what was going on.

"It's a go for Wednesday night. I want to wait until we find out what Diego gets, and then we can interview Milt and Melanie again. We're sending out a person named Cameron. He's one of our best and should be able to get in and out of that computer without Marvin even knowing."

Sammi couldn't help but comment. "I want to interview Marvin when he gets back. I think he might have some answers for us."

"Yes, I've been thinking of that as well. Being interviewed by the FBI might unnerve him a little. We'll definitely add him to the list for next week We're finally moving forward. Can't be too soon for me."

"We've gotten about all we can get from the two suspects here," said Dave. "They really didn't know as much as we'd hoped for. Kind of feel sorry for these kids. They just got themselves involved in this revolutionary group and later discovered the mistake they made. They are really sweating it out."

"You don't think they are hardened criminals, then?" asked Ben.

"No, no. Not at all, they're just scared young kids trying to find a safe place in the world. They simply wanted to belong somewhere. They really made a bad mistake."

Ben added, "Dave, if I didn't know any better, I would think that you had a soft spot for these two, despite them causing your injury."

Dave laughed. "And you'd be right. I think they have a good chance of becoming good citizens, with a little bit of luck."

"Okay, if you feel the same way when this is over, maybe we can do something for them."

"That would be nice. Sammi got good impressions from these guys as well, didn't you honey?"

"Yes, they were just looking for somewhere solid to belong. Neither one has any family or relatives that we know of. They grew up in foster homes. I think they were lost and looking, if you know what I mean. I really hope we can do something for them later."

"Okay, when this is over, let's see what we can do. We see the rotten side of crime and punishment often enough, it would be nice to be part of something good."

No one spoke for a moment, but one could hear a few satisfying sighs. It was like when you stayed on the positive side of the universe, there was always something good to report.

That ended the conference call. Ben hung up and gave Dave and Sammi a few minutes to talk alone.

* * *

Melanie had turned her chair around to face the window and get a look at the outside world with its beckoning blue sky and welcoming sunshine. She needed a moment to relax. She was upset and livid about the fact that Milt couldn't get any information from Upward Managers as to why they had unconditionally recommended Marvin Antwerp to them. He was clearly a subversive character who had now infiltrated their company for several years. She thought back on the times that the government had had them in court on questionable activities. It was true that they had won every case and were in the clear, but some of their activities surprised even Milt. He was supposed to clear any new business within this company, yet someone had passed him by and they still didn't know who was undermining them. Their conversation on Wednesday morning had been unpleasant and disagreeable at best.

"Milt, we're in the middle of some nasty business and you don't even know why? Are you serious?"

"Hold on, will you? I'm looking into several things. I've hired some private investigators to get to the bottom of this, but I'm afraid that someone is trying to use our company as a cover for some malicious transactions."

Melanie sat back in her chair, obviously more shocked than she was a few minutes before.

"And you're not in on any of this? I need to hear you say it."

"God, no Melanie. I'll go to whatever length I have to in order to get the best for this company, but breaking the law is not one of them. You should know me better than that."

She shook her head in the affirmative. "Yeah, I do. But somebody is doing something, and I'm very nervous about it. I mean, we already have the FBI nosing around here. Where will this all end?"

"With us helping the FBI and getting us on their good side, if I can help it." Milt had a determined look on his face, one that connoted using this infuriating experience to get a better relationship with the law enforcement agencies.

"Well, I'm using that new guy Diego to help me find out what I can. He has a spotless reputation and believe me, I've checked him out. And he's good."

"Ok, because right now we have to do all we can to find out what's going on. The feds think we might be involved in that senator's murder and that's bad enough, but now it seems that we are in the middle of something else, and we don't even know what it is."

"To think we used to be on top of everything. And I'm talking about both of us. How could this happen?" Melanie knew that the outside world had changed dramatically and it was definitely more dangerous than ever before.

"It's a new world of criminals now and I think we got caught just like a lot of others. Nothing they do is obvious. We'll find the underlying cause of this and soon. You do whatever you can and so will I. Anything significant turns up and we have to compare notes. Agreed?"

"Yes, I agree," she said, but it was clear that Melanie had been thrown for a loop like never before.

It seemed strange to Melanie to have her and Milt on the same side. They were usually at each other's throats about everything, yet now they had a compatible goal. They needed to keep their company healthy and viable. And she was thinking for the first time in recent memory, *that they would have to work as a team.*

* * *

Diego was pleased with Wednesday night. 9:00 PM was set up for the time to hit Marvin's office and computer system. Cameron, Diego and Melanie went in with a mission and all were hoping to get what they needed quickly, get out and not be detected.

Cameron worked for only a few minutes on Marvin's computer. He turned to Diego and said, "This is not very sophisticated at all. It is blocked for the normal person, but for any computer person like myself, or even less informed, it can be hacked."

"Will he know we got in?" asked Melanie rather nervously.

"Oh no, not at all; but I can make him nervous if you want."

Melanie looked shocked. "What do you mean?"

"Well, I'll put everything back the way it was so he will be sure that no one got into his computer, but I can finagle a few things that will make our Marvin wonder if he forgot something important. I think he'll get very nervous."

"I don't know," said Melanie. Then she turned to Diego. "What do you think?"

"That could play in our favor, but I can see you don't seem to like the idea. It's not new, right, Cameron? This is a ploy used sometimes to get criminals off their game. They think they've done everything perfect, but then discover something that only they could have done is out of whack. Works good, but why don't we wait to see what we find. That might help you make up your mind."

She agreed and Cameron went to work. He was in the secret files easily and quickly. They began making copies of the reports to review later. Actually, there were only about three secret files, and all of them had the initial W.L. as the author.

"He must be using an alias," said Melanie.

"Or possibly that's his real name," said Diego.

"Oh, that's right. Nothing much has checked out on him anyway."

Diego stopped for a moment. His gut feeling was kicking in. Usually, it never failed him. He just stood there for a moment not moving. Both Melanie and Cameron turned to look at him.

"What's the matter?" said Cameron.

"I've got a very strong feeling that this office is bugged. We better find it fast."

And find it they did. That had to be dealt with immediately. But Diego wasn't happy. His gut feeling hadn't gone away yet.

"I think there's another one. This guy is the nervous type and will have his bug covered with a back up."

The second took longer to find but was handled accordingly. Now everything was obliterated and put back in place so Marvin wouldn't be the wiser.

At this point Melanie spoke up. "I think I do want to make him nervous. Do whatever you have to do? But you said he won't know, right?"

"Oh, no, he'll never be sure and that's what usually gets them."

"What exactly will you do?" she asked.

"Well, this is computer stuff, somewhat complicated to the amateur, but it'll make him very unsure of his computer system and what he's been doing with it."

Melanie smiled. "I like that. And you're right, I probably wouldn't understand."

Diego said, "We all have our own expertise."

Their goal had been accomplished, the bugs were back in place, the computer was in its original condition and Marvin's door was locked. It was finished.

Cameron left; his job was finished. But Melanie and Diego went for a late snack and took time to read the reports. Some were definitely in a type of code, but the senator's name was mentioned several times in the weeks before his murder. Pending legislation on the taxes to be raised in the northern part of the state was mentioned, underscored and highlighted. That was what Senator Stedman had been working on and was within weeks of casting the deciding vote.

"Sure looks like he was involved in the senator's death. I wish I knew who W.L. was," said Melanie, "it would go a long way to clear the picture."

"I'm sure that will come in time. What do you plan to do with this information?"

"Well, that's a problem right now, isn't it? I'm not sure. I can't just turn it over to the FBI because they'll wonder how I got it and if they're not ready to arrest Marvin on something, I could have a real problem on my hands."

"That's true. I'd just hold on to it right now. When the time comes, you'll know."

Melanie smiled. She had a good feeling about Diego. He seemed to know what to say at the right time to put her at ease.

"So, on Monday and until we decide what to do, everything goes on as normal. I'm trying to decide what to tell Milt about this. I suppose I have to tell him."

Diego's eyebrows crossed somewhat. His question was obvious.

"I know, I know. You're wondering why I would be hesitant at telling Milt. I'm not sure, honestly. We don't always see eye to eye. He has some investigators looking into things, but I wanted to know what was on Marvin's computer. Maybe I'll tell him later, when it's necessary."

Diego noticed her smile. He understood their relationship was unique. He let it go.

"Next week I think I'll find some project that will bring you on our floor more. First, I know that it will unnerve Marvin and I like that thought, but also I know you pick up things. What do you think if I put you working with Marvin on a few assignments?"

Diego laughed. "I think you have a spiteful sense of humor?"

"Would it bother you?"

"Me, not at all. All part of a day's work," he smiled.

"Marvin wouldn't like it, but it would help keep tabs on him. Might be hard on you, though."

"I'm okay." Diego suddenly had a feeling about Melanie. Possibly, she was trying to play both ends and see what happens. On the other hand, she perhaps felt better having Diego around. It was hard to tell. Still, it would be interesting.

* * *

Diego had been able to get a copy of the documents to Ben. Actually, Cameron did that. It was important for Dave and Sammi as well as the sarge to be aware of the latest. Sammi went back to Scranton on Thursday as nothing was happening until the next week in Hartford. Diego had reason to call Dave and luckily, Sammi was home.

"Hi amiga," he said. "It's good to talk to you. I want you to know that I'll probably be around next week when you interview Melanie and Milt. Melanie wants to bring me up on the executive floor to keep an eye on Marvin. So I might see you then. Just be prepared."

"Okay," she said. "You've done a good job getting into her confidence."

"I think so, but I think she's still leery of me. Just my gut feeling, but I really don't think she trusts anybody right now."

"Understandable, I'm sure."

"Yeah, I've reread those documents and you know what Dave, I think this guy is knee deep in subservice. Not sure if it's that Right Side Group or not, but he's kind of a weird guy anyway. He might be a good one to interview."

Dave laughed and looked at Sammi.

"What are you laughing about? I heard that sneaky laugh."

"Well, it's just that you and Sammi think so much alike. We just put him on the list of people to be interviewed by Ben and Sammi."

"No kidding. Ha, Ha," he thought. "See amiga, you and I are so much alike. But I've met him and heard people talk about him, and that made me suspicious. How come you think so?"

"His name has come up a few times too many for me. Just a gut feeling," she laughed. "I get them, too."

Diego laughed. "That will really make him nervous. I can't wait. When will you interview him; has Ben said?"

"I think he's trying for early next week."

"Are your suspects there in Scranton giving out any more?"

"I really think they've told us all they know. We'll have to wait and see."

"Next week should be very interesting. Maybe I'll see you, Sammi."

"Maybe you will," she laughed.

CHAPTER XVIII

Melanie was happy that her interview with the FBI had been brief and direct. When asked, she had expressed concerns about Marvin, although she didn't know why they'd be asking about him yet since she hadn't made them aware of her findings. Still, she answered truthfully and honestly not wanting to be caught in any suggestions of lying or hiding the truth. Actually, Melanie had a delicate secret of her own. It was a big one, but no one had found out in seven years and she didn't plan for anyone to find out. It had nothing to do with the company anyway so she felt she was on firm ground.

Melanie realized that her life was an open book to most, but she did have some chapters that were closed. However, she was surprised when Sammi kept asking her about the third phone line on her desk. She had been caught off guard on that one but kept her answers logically above board, yet considerably brief in order to rise beyond any suspicions. Still, she thought Sammi was a very sharp woman, uncanny and one to be watched.

Milt, she knew, had been questioned before her and he couldn't wait to run to her office after they left. He wanted to compare notes with her, but she remained aloof. He didn't like it.

"Nothing new, I swear, Milt," she said. "Why are you always in such a panic about the FBI?"

"Because of that Marvin."

"Did you talk to the FBI about Marvin and what you're doing?"

"Of course I did, but I don't want him to find out. Who knows what he could do? Hell, we still don't know who he is."

"True, but with the FBI on the case I'm sure everything will be out in the open soon."

"I don't want our company to be in trouble of any kind."

"Why would we? We haven't done anything wrong."

Milt was quiet and brooding as usual. He did that a lot lately. It was obvious that he was losing his grip on many things and it unnerved him. In a funny way, Melanie felt sorry for him.

"Just relax. I hear that Marvin is supposed to be interviewed tomorrow."

"You're kidding. I didn't know that. When did you hear that?"

"They asked me for some contact information and said he was next on their list."

"No kidding. I'll bet he'll have a fit. Does he know yet?"

"I have no idea, Milt. Really, I don't."

Milt finally sat back in his chair and took a deep breath. Melanie couldn't believe that this Milt, whom she'd been married to for three unpleasant years, and who was considered a tyrant around the company, was becoming a nervous, edgy individual. In a way, he was crumbling and his personality was diminishing before her eyes. She hoped he'd keep it together until this senator business was over.

* * *

It was less than two minutes after Milt left her office that Marvin was at her door asking for entrance. She looked forward to this.

"Melanie, I just got a call from the FBI. They want to interview me tomorrow."

Now his comments were most interesting to Melanie. This was late Monday afternoon, the first day that Marvin had been back to work since his two week jury duty and he wasn't asking if anyone had been in his office or rummaging through his stuff. It didn't even cross his mind, so they must be home free there. Diego and Cameron had done an excellent job.

"They've been interviewing several people around here. I just got interviewed for a second time."

"Really, but you're an executive in this company. What do they want with me?"

"How should I know? What's the matter with you? Just answer their questions truthfully. You don't have anything to hide do you?"

"No, no, of course not. But I have private matters that I keep hidden. Don't you? We all do."

"They're still investigating the senator's murder." Melanie paused on purpose and Marvin did blanche somewhat, so Melanie threw out an obvious remark intended to totally alarm him. It did. "So unless you personally killed him, they are probably only looking for information."

Marvin was speechless. He actually stuttered, which was something he never did. Usually he was much more in control of himself. It made Melanie quiver and tremble for the thoughts that were beginning to cross her mind. My God, could he possibly have had something to do with the senator's murder? Before it had only been words on paper, but now he looked so suspicious. She was visibly shaken.

"Guess I'll have to wait then," he said, unsatisfied with Melanie's lack of concern.

"When is your interview?"

"Tomorrow morning at 10:00."

"Okay, then. That's when you'll find out."

* * *

Marvin went back to his office totally demoralized and anxious. On the one hand, he knew that he could handle the FBI and they didn't really scare him, although he assumed that Melanie thought they did. But he had done a lot for her and she didn't even seem to appreciate it.

Actually, he had to admit that she really didn't know what he had done, only one other person knew, but that was not the point. She should be acting more appreciative toward him and realize how much he cared for her and how he made her job much easier to handle. He went out of his way every day for her and here she was passing him off as just another employee. Could he have been wrong about her? He did care for her and thought she returned his feelings? Maybe before long they'd had to have dinner again and get some matters straightened out between them. He'd have to let her know that she really owed him for a few things and then she'd probably act differently.

He sat back in his oversized chair and began reminiscing about Melanie; he remembered the first time he saw her. He liked her immediately. She was pretty, that was true, but that had little to do with his infatuation of her. She had worked her way up to the top of this company, and she had done it with her brains. She could stand next to anyone here and be their mental equal. Marvin wanted to be one of those people someday. By that time, he hoped to have some of the government regulations repealed and they could both enjoy running a company with no limitations that he considered unfair and unjust. He began thinking, *Maybe we won't have a total love relationship, but that's okay with me. I want us to be the top in this city and state. When we go to meetings together people will look at us with respect. And I will be glad to have that woman on my arm eating dinner next to me.*

Marvin had had a difficult early life himself. He seldom talked about it. Actually, he seldom even thought about it anymore. That was another thing he felt that him and Melanie had in common. She'd appreciate him soon, he thought. He knew for sure that in the near future their relationship would change and be on more congenial ground.

* * *

On Tuesday morning, Marvin had another surprise that was not to his liking. Melanie had told him that Diego would be working on two projects with him. He didn't like that at all. He had plans for these projects and another set of eyes would simply mar the outcome totally. He tried to talk her out of it, but she was adamant. Now he was sitting in his office with Diego, and he knew that his unpleasant thoughts were showing on his face and there was nothing he could do about it.

"I really don't like this idea at all. However, Melanie is my boss so there's nothing I can do about it. What the hell do you have on her? I've always worked alone before."

Diego sat there completely unaffected by Marvin's rude and offensive behavior. Finally, Marvin attacked him directly.

"I asked you a question; what do you have on her?"

"Oh was that a question," he said. "I wasn't sure. I really don't have anything on her. I think she just wants another pair of eyes to oversee these projects. Why does it bother you so much?"

Marvin was livid. He wasn't going to let this inferior person ask him any questions and expect an answer. He kept moving papers on his desk and then went into his computer. His face suddenly changed. He was shocked and it showed. His demeanor totally changed.

"Okay, if I have to work with you I guess I will. But the FBI are interviewing me soon and I need to prepare."

"Why would you need to prepare?" asked Diego.

He definitely got a look of fury in return. Then, Marvin's control took over and he said, "Are you being interviewed?"

"Nope," Diego responded. "Guess they don't think I'm important enough."

Surprisingly, that seemed to satisfy Marvin as his thoughts of Diego being a second-rate individual took over.

He said smugly, "Well, I guess they see me differently. So I'll let you know later when I need you."

As Diego left his office, he ran directly into Ben and Sammi who were on their way in. Of course, he ignored them but was secretly satisfied that Sammi would get something out of Marvin. She was the one who always came up with information.

* * *

It was obvious that Marvin didn't plan to extend any social etiquette to his unwelcomed visitors. When Ben and Sammi entered his office, they were expected to take whatever chair was available and sit and wait until he was finished moving papers around on his desk. Ben only allowed that for a very short minute.

"I'm sure anything that you are doing can wait. We need your attention now."

"I'll only be a few minutes," he answered in return as he entertained a frustrated look on his face as he puttered with his computer.

"You're finished now," said Ben, "or I'll pull the plug on your computer."

When he finished making his warning, Ben sat far back in his chair with a look of total satisfaction. His authoritative manner was shining through and even Sammi was surprised. Marvin decided that it was to his advantage to cooperate. Getting on the wrong side of the FBI wouldn't get him any favors.

Ben introduced himself and before he had a chance to introduce Sammi, Marvin said, "Who's she? Why does she have to be here?"

"She's my associate and I want her here. That's all you need to know."

Ben had almost spit out his words and finally Marvin realized that the FBI was not fooling around. It was time to settle down and cooperate.

"I don't know why you even want to talk to me. I don't know anything about the senator's murder or anything else."

"Really," said Ben. "And why would you think that's what we wanted to talk to you about?"

"Well, Melanie told me that you talked to her about that, so I figured ...." Marvin's voice trailed off which made him wonder if he had goofed. He decided to shut up and just answer questions.

Sammi had already picked up a lot, especially after Marvin's comment about the senator's murder. Most of his thoughts were out there and she was writing feverishly.

"What is she writing down? Why does she have to write things down?"

Obviously, Marvin was nervous and little sweat beads were already forming near his receding hairline. Ben looked assured. He looked over at Sammi who hadn't stopped writing and yet, the interview had only begun. He wondered how she did what she did.

"I make a record of all my interviews," Ben said smugly. Then he waited. He wanted to give Sammi time to catch up on her notes, but he also enjoyed seeing Marvin squirm. He acquired an immediate dislike for him.

"Where were you the night that Senator Stedman was murdered?"

Marvin almost started to cry. He wasn't prepared; it was obvious. He didn't know what to say. He just sat there looking at Ben as if he hadn't even asked a question. He tried to keep his facial contortions under control; his difficulty was apparent. Ben helped him along.

"I asked you a question. Must I repeat it? Well, okay. Where were you the night that Senator Stedman was killed?"

"I have to think back, give me a minute. I didn't know you were going to ask me about that."

"You said at the beginning of our interview that you assumed that we were going to ask you about the senator's murder. Now you say you are surprised. Which is it?"

Marvin realized he had dug himself into a hole and didn't know how to get out of it.

"Let me think about where I was," he said trying to appear more cooperative. "I'm sure that was the week that we were having late night conferences on new regulations. I may have even been at the Connecticut Convention Center, let me check my notes."

"Go right ahead. I need to know where you say you were."

Looking over at Sammi, Ben realized that she was slightly agitated. That only happened to her occasionally when she was receiving pertinent information. And she had never stopped writing. This was a good omen. Ben couldn't help but wonder, even after all these years -- how did she do it?

"Yes, yes, that was on a Wednesday night. I was at the Convention Center for conferences."

Marvin stopped abruptly, assuming that he had given Ben all the information he wanted. Yet Ben continued.

"I will need you to account for your whereabouts for that entire evening, particularly around the hour of 7:30 to 8:30 PM."

"Why? I don't think I can do that. I was attending meetings like I told you."

"And there were meetings between 7:30 and 8:30?" he asked.

"Well, yes, there were."

"And who can account for the fact that you were at these meetings."

That stopped Marvin and it upset him as well. It was easy to hear his mind jutting back and forth trying to figure out who would remember him.

"I don't know right now. I'll have to check and find out who else was there. We could probably vouch for each other."

"I'll need that information," said Ben.

"Well, I don't have that at my fingertips. I go to a lot of meetings."

"I'll wait," said Ben.

Although he was trying to keep himself under control, Marvin's façade was slipping. Those little sweat beads on his forehead were more prominent now.

"You want to sit here while I go through all my notes. That could take a while. I could email them to you."

"No, no. We'll wait."

Marvin was not a happy person. His mind was trying to figure out how he could manage to cover his tracks that night. Finally, he decided to take the notes of the meeting and offer it as evidence. After all, he was one of the speakers that night.

"As you can see, I did give one of the speeches."

"What time was that?"

"Most likely, 6:30 PM to 7:30 PM. It's hard to remember exactly what time I finished."

"I'm certain that the speaker who followed you should remember what time he started his speech. Who was it?"

Marvin's eyes became intense and relaxed at the same time. He knew that he was backing himself up into a corner and he didn't like it. After all, meetings were sometimes unpredictable and who could expect him to remember everything to the minute. He had counted on that for his alibi. He paused and hoped for a better idea. Sammi finally asked.

"There must be notes kept from the meeting or even a video. That would give us the information we want."

That didn't sit well with Marvin. A woman who was only an associate of the FBI was drilling him. He felt he deserved better.

"Well, I probably could get that. But it might take time."

"Was Milt Biltmore at the meeting?"

"Yes, he was," answered Marvin. He didn't like Milt being brought into this discussion.

"We'll get the tape from him."

Marvin gulped as he said, "I should be able to get it off my computer, but it's not working right today. Something's wrong. I'll have to get it checked out."

Sammi experienced a feeling of satisfaction. Diego had done a good job in two areas. Marvin was concerned about his computer and it wasn't working right in his estimation. Now, they could watch him squirm.

Ben's phone rang. After listening intently for a few moments he finally said, "That'll be it for now." He turned to Sammi and said, "We're needed somewhere else."

Abruptly, he got up and told Marvin, "We'll finish this up later today or tomorrow. You should have the video by then, right?"

Marvin agreed but his mouth never closed. He hated the fact that this meeting wasn't finished and they'd come back. He'd be worried until it was finally over.

* * *

Upon leaving the office, Sammi asked Ben where they were going.

"Oh," he laughed, "just to meet Jeff for lunch. I just wanted to upset our friend Marvin even more."

Sammi chuckled. "You're really good. He was pretty upset having to account for his time. And I think I know why."

"Are you telling now or do I have to wait?"

Sammi smiled. "Well, I think you already realize that he was certainly involved in Mike's murder. Not being able to account for his time will be a big obstacle for him and I can tell you right now, he can't account for his time. He may be able to line up some people on his side to vouch for him, but we'll have to knock that down. He was involved."

Ben's eyes got very wide. "So, he did it."

"Let me get my notes together. There's a lot I need to talk about, but as usual, I need time to put everything in order, even in my own mind."

"But you think we're getting somewhere."

"I do, and I might need to get Dave in on this," said Sammi with a definite tone in her voice that Ben took to be positive.

Sammi couldn't wait to talk to Dave. She needed to prioritize events and he always helped her to do that. She had some major events to sort out this time. Proving it could be difficult, but she knew who killed Mike. However, the why was a huge surprise to her. That might be the toughest obstacle to climb. She was sure that Dave could help her with that. She wanted to present the information to Ben in a logical, reasonable format.

* * *

Unfortunately, Dave wasn't in his office when Sammi called. His cell phone was off. *He must be in an important meeting,* she thought. She took this time to take a quick shower and relax. It had been an ugly meeting with Marvin from her side of the room. His thoughts were angry, manipulating, evasive and calculating. Plus, his ideas were moving at lightning speed. The loose ends that he thought were covered were coming back to disturb him. Sammi knew what he was thinking. It was flight or attempt to lie his way out of the situation. She wondered if he would even be around for the second interview. He had connections, but she wasn't sure yet if they were happy with what he had done.

Her phone rang and startled her out of her interesting contemplation.

"Hi Dave," she said. "You must be busy."

"Yeah, well, right now for some reason there's a lot of activity here. What's up with you? Everything okay?"

"Ben and I just had a meeting with Marvin this morning."

"Oh, and how did that go? I think you're anxious to tell me something, right?"

Sammi laughed. "You always know."

Dave reacted. "Well, you have a certain tone of voice that I pick up. I'm right then?"

"Oh yeah. I've pretty much figured out everything by now. I've got two requests."

"You miss me and you want to come up to Hartford?"

"That's true. I do miss you, and I do want you to come up here. Could you make it?"

"I was kidding, but you're serious? I'm sure the sarge would give me a few days off. What's up?"

"Everything is going to be exposed real soon. I haven't shared anything with Ben and Jeff yet, but I'd like you to be here when I do. It'll take most of tomorrow to get my notes together, so if you could be here by Thursday, it would help me out."

"Okay, but you said two requests. What's the other?"

"I'm quite sure that our Marvin Antwerp is Bill Lueger." She heard Dave let out a long, slow whistle. "I'm going to have

Ben fax you a picture of him and I'd like you to show it to the suspects in custody. If they identify him, as I think they will, we will need to move quickly. He's going to run."

"No kidding. Wow! Things are opening up then?"

"Right and I want to get my notes in order before I say anymore. As usual, it's complicated."

"Okay, then I'll let the sarge know. Now if Bill Lueger and Marvin Antwerp are the same person, then that company has had a plant in their surroundings for a while. But why?"

"Mostly it has to do with political legislation, but other things as well."

"Let me know when you send the picture. I'll be most interested in finding this out."

"And if I'm right, a lot of things will begin to make sense."

"Yeah, I can see that. Okay, I've got to go. I'll plan on being there Thursday morning."

CHAPTER XIX

It was no surprise to anyone that Marvin Antwerp and Bill Lueger were the same person. As usual, Ben and Jeff were stunned at Sammi and even though they still hadn't figured out how she obtained information so quickly, they were gratified that she was on their side. Sammi didn't hold back on that part of the information and informed Ben that Marvin needed to be watched. Ben agreed and already had someone tailing him.

By Thursday morning when Sammi and Dave walked into the restaurant, Ben and Jeff were eager to hear the rest of the information she had obtained.

Ben jokingly said, "My favorite investigator."

Jeff agreed and they all relaxed over a cup of coffee and decided that now was the time to get everything out in the open, and set up a plan.

"I got a lot of information from Marvin at our meeting, Ben. Part of it was a leftover from the data I got from Diego after they got into his computer. Putting everything together took a little time, but now I'm ready to move forward. First of all, we know that Marvin Antwerp is Bill Lueger. He only took on the new name when he applied at this company. He thought his name would be recognized."

"Really?" said Jeff. "I'd never heard of him."

"Me, neither," said Ben.

"But you haven't been digging into that Right Side Group or his name would have come up. He didn't want to take any chances. That group is truly strange. It has little pockets of people here and there around the country, but no real main group that governs them; they are quite disorganized. Yet, there seems to be enough people who are anti-government to make it work."

"So he was there on some sort of anti-government agenda?" asked Ben.

"Mostly, yes. His part in the scheme of things is to make sure regulations of the government are rolled back as much as possible. His people don't believe in federal laws at all and want as many repealed as possible."

"Yeah," said Jeff. "We have a lot of unpatriotic rebellions occurring, but this one seemed so blatantly open."

"More so than usual," added Dave. "They were quiet and peacefully rebellious for a long time, but now with the occurrences in and around Scranton, they seem to be getting braver and creating more attention to themselves."

"And I'm not sure that's what the entire group wants. Marvin had a separate agenda. I'll get to that in a minute, but I think he's in disfavor with the group big time. That's why he's thinking of running. And I'm not entirely convinced that he'd get much help from the group for that."

"Why? You'd think they'd be happy that he had infiltrated a large company and could keep his hand on the pulse of happenings concerning federal regulations."

"That part is true," said Sammi. "But it was his idea alone to kill the senator. His group had a fit that this murder is taking center stage around the world. It was not at all what they wanted."

"Why did he do it? Did he want to come off as a big guy within the group?"

"Good question. He had a separate personal agenda, but I still think he took a big chance."

Finally, Ben said, "Ok, I give up. What was his personal agenda?"

Sammi sat back in her chair, took a sip of coffee and began.

"Marvin's personal life reads like a weird novel. I'm not sure he was ever married at all."

Jeff jumped on that comment. "But his personal profile not only refers to his marriage, but there is an official marriage certificate confirming that."

"That's under the name of Marvin Antwerp, which is not his real name. I don't think Bill Lueger was ever married."

Ben let out a whistle. "That's right. We're talking about two different people and need to find out their separate histories. This is getting complicated. We'll have to have Julie straighten this out for us."

"Exactly," said Sammi. "I'm not sure right now whose history has what facts to back it up. Now Marvin's reputation confirms that he is not smooth around women. Since that's who he is pretending to be, let's concentrate on him at this moment. Most would think that he didn't have that much interest in them. Yet he really fell for Melanie Brooks. His long-range plans were that some day he will win her over and they will be together to rule companies and be important people in the regulation business. They'd had dinner several times in the past and apparently, he thought they had something going. From Melanie's side, she only thought of him as an associate."

"Okay, okay," said Ben. "But was he the one that actually killed the senator?"

"Yes, he did it. But he had help from Sergeants Wyman and Cullins."

"Wait a minute," replied Ben. "Those were the sergeants that gave us a rough time when we tried to see Mr. Jim. God we've got a dirty police department as well."

"Hold on for a minute," said Sammi. "Let me continue. The reason that Marvin wanted Senator Stedman out of the way is even more bizarre."

Now Sammi had everyone's attention. She was always able to gather the small details that put the finishing touches on a case.

"It has to do with that third phone line on Melanie's desk. I was always interested in that line and wondered why it was necessary. Now we know that Melanie was married to Milton Biltmore for almost three years; I think they've been divorced a little over a year. Melanie has a daughter around six years old that she keeps hidden for her own personal reasons and that extra line is so that they can get in touch with her at any time."

There were blank faces around the table for two reasons. First of all, this was startling information, but also Ben and Jeff were shocked that she had obtained this information at all. After a deep breath, Ben waived her on.

"Obviously she had an affair with someone and created this child as a result. However, Marvin thought that Senator Stedman was the father."

"What?" said Ben. "This is all crazy. What the hell is going on here?"

"Remember Melanie and Mike had quite a romantic relationship during their college years. Marvin knew all about it. He made it his business to know almost everything about

Melanie. The thing is that he found out that Mike and his wife had briefly separated about seven years ago and during that time Melanie and Mike were spotted having dinner a few times. Marvin figured they had an affair and the child is the result. After all, the timing is perfect."

About this time, the waitress came around with more coffee. Everyone nodded automatically so as not to miss any detail of this story.

After a welcomed break and a satisfying sip of coffee, Sammi continued. "Marvin was furious for a couple of reasons. He was afraid that Melanie might still have a thing for Mike and because of the child, they would always have a connection. He wanted Mike eliminated and since he wasn't politically favoring the Right Side Group on any important piece of pending legislation, he thought it was the perfect thing to do. Sadly, the truth is that Mike and Melanie had remained friends over the years, but they were only friends. He is not the father of her child."

"No kidding," said Ben. "Who is the father?"

"I don't really know, but I have another fact I need to mention here. Dave, I only recently got this information and haven't had a chance to tell even you. The name of Linda Saunders has come up a few times."

"Both Ben and Jeff were surprised, although her name was always surfacing during illegal activities.

"I was trying to figure out what Linda had to do with Melanie. She sometimes uses that third line of hers. She knew Melanie years ago and they were never friends, but associates on a few projects. That's all I know about their association. She had found out about the baby and for some reason, she also believed that Mike Stedman was the father of Melanie's baby. She used this data to try to keep Melanie on her side."

"But the information wasn't true," said Dave. "Why didn't she put a stop to her?"

"I'm guessing here myself. I don't think that Melanie felt Linda was a threat to her. Yet, she always kept her baby a secret. Although the name of the father was wrong, Melanie didn't want to bring up the subject at all. She wanted to keep it quiet, so she let Linda think she had something on her."

Sammi stopped. She needed a breather. Most of the important details were out of the way and the remaining ones would be discussed shortly. She wanted to give Ben and Jeff time to digest this complicated and thorny information.

It was quiet for a few moments around the table. Ben was the first to speak.

"So Marvin actually shot Mike, but it was probably a policeman who planted the gun on Mr. Jim."

"I think so. I think it was Sergeant Wyman."

Ben was troubled. The murder of one of his best friends wasn't even necessary except in the sick mind of this Marvin person. Yet he also had to contend with dirty policemen. He sat there with his face in his hands shaking his head.

"There's still a little more to it, Ben," said Sammi.

Dave had been quiet; he already knew the story and it was an emotional time for Ben.

"What more could there possibly be? Mike is dead because of some nut and we have to deal with corrupt police officers. Geez, I hate this."

"Well, I'm not sure how you'll feel about the policemen when you hear the rest of the story."

"It had better be good."

"It is," said Sammi. "Sergeant Wyman was a participant but one who was totally unwilling. He has a son away at college, which Marvin had managed to rough up brutally a few times. He threatened to kill him if Sergeant Wyman didn't cooperate. Now I know he did wrong in helping with the cover up, but he really believed that his son would be killed. That needs to be looked into and taken into consideration."

At this point Sammi looked over at Dave. They had discussed this aspect of the situation and knew that it was a tough spot for Sergeant Wyman.

"Wow," said Ben, admitting as a father, "I'm not sure what I would have done in his position." He looked around the table, "Honestly, I don't."

"And Sergeant Cullins wasn't part of it. Yet his attitude to give us a rough time came from his superior Sergeant Wyman. He wanted to be seen as cooperative since Marvin had him watched."

"Yeah, I see," said Ben. "What a bunch of crap this is. Mike was really killed for nothing."

Sammi added, "And you do have a tail on him, right?"

"And I'm going to double it right now."

Ben made a few quick calls to that end.

"We have to make sure that that kid of Sergeant Wyman is protected and out of harm's way before we continue. I need to find him now."

Ben was already pushing back his chair and attempting to stand up. He paused and asked, "Anything else I should know right now?"

"No, get that kid safe and I think that Sergeant Wyman will give you a lot of information proving that Marvin killed your friend."

"Right. Okay, I need to move on this. Again, thanks Sammi. You're amazing. We'll meet again, maybe even later today. Come on, Jeff, we've got work to do."

In a moment, they was gone leaving Dave and Sammi to consult among themselves.

* * *

"This case sure didn't end up how we thought it would," said Sammi.

"That's for sure. And it's not finished yet. I'm wondering where Marvin is right now. You know he was already spooked and you say you thought he'd run."

"I wouldn't be surprised if he has already made plans. Hope the tail on him is complete. We can't afford to lose him now."

"Do you want to talk to him again, Sammi?"

"I'd like Ben to catch Marvin, and then see what Sergeant Wyman has to say. I would imagine he knows all of the details."

Dave simply nodded his head in agreement. Sammi liked to cover her tracks, which meant that she didn't want to overdue her welcome and give any further hints of information that came to her. She was ready to retreat back to Scranton to be among her confidantes; she was more relaxed there.

She looked over at Dave who knew what she was thinking.

"You're ready to go home, right?"

"Yeah, I am, but I still have things to do here."

"This might be over within a day or two."

"But I want to solve the mystery of our Mr. Jim. He's been in isolation for so long; I hope he can make it back."

"Do you have an idea about him?"

"Yes, I do. And when we find out what happened to him and where he belongs, I think a lot of people who thought he was a bumbling idiot are going to be shocked."

Dave smiled and thought for a moment. "Maybe we could see him in the meantime while we are waiting."

"I don't think we should try until Marvin is arrested, do you?"

"That's a thought. Probably we should check it out with Ben. When is Mr. Jim's trial supposed to start?"

"In about five days. It would be great to have those charges dropped before then and start searching for his real identity."

Dave's phone rang. He listened intently for a few long minutes before he turned to Sammi and said, "Marvin is on the run, but they have him tracked down and are closing in. He tried to get on a flight out of the country, but ran when he saw the FBI net starting to close in. He's driving somewhere now; has changed cars three times, but they still have him cornered. Ben will let us know. It should be any minute now."

"Does anybody know where he would head to?"

"Actually they asked Melanie, who is in complete shock by now. He had told her about a secret place he had and he seems to be heading there. But ...."

Dave's phone rang again. He nodded and smiled. "They've got him and they say he's acting strange."

"What do you mean acting strange?"

"Well, the way it sounds, he and Mr. Jim would have a lot in common."

"No kidding. Maybe it's an act."

"I'm sure the FBI can sort it out."

"Any problem with us going back to the motel for a while," said Sammi. "I'm exhausted and could use a long nap."

"Not at all, honey. You had better rest up for tomorrow. I think it will be a long day."

* * *

The next day had a lot of busy bits and pieces on the agenda. Ben had already safely retrieved Sergeant Wyman's son and he was safe. An interview with him was on the schedule and Ben wanted Sammi there. This did seem to be the first step, but they had to know what Sergeant Wyman could tell them before they could continue.

Walking into the interview room Dave and Sammi walked over to Ben, who was waiting for Sergeant Wyman to arrive.

"I hope this isn't going to be a waste of time. I mean, we do have his son and he is safe. But I think the sergeant will be embarrassed about cooperating and that could pose a problem."

"Let's just wait and see what ......" Dave was saying when the door opened and in walked a worried looking Sergeant Dan Wyman.

Ben set his mind at ease at once. "Look Dan, we have your son and he is safe. We know that you were an unwilling participant in all this. So just relax."

"My son is okay? Where is he? Can I see him?"

"Right now, he is on his way to a safe haven with several of our people. He is okay."

"No offense, Ben, but I'd feel better if I could just talk to him."

"Of course," said Ben. "I understand. I'd probably feel the same way. Let me see what I can do."

He walked out of the room and within a few minutes came in with a cell phone.

"Your son, Justin is on the line."

After a few minutes, and a few satisfying tears shed by Dan, he hung up the phone. Then, he really let go and cried. He couldn't help it. This ordeal had had a weakening effect on his strength for a long time. As he started to apologize, Ben hushed him. In the meantime, Sammi knew that he was sincere and that his thoughts matched his words and emotions. He was one relieved father.

And so the story began. "I was approached by Marvin almost two years ago. At first, he wanted to find out how loyal I was to the police force and threw out hints about my allegiance to our government and federal agencies. I thought he was a weird one at that time, but he was a friend of Milt Biltmore so I paid attention to him."

Dan paused, taking a deep breath, after shedding a few more tears that were involuntarily, which he pretended they weren't even there. Dan had a habit of running his right hand through his dark blonde hair and when he was finished all his hair fell back into perfect arrangement as if ordered to do so. Yet relief was still visible on his face as he continued.

"He made me nervous whenever he came into the precinct and Sergeant Cullins thought he was someone to be guarded against. It all changed for me about a year ago. You see, he couldn't get me to be interested in that Right Side Group. Yet, after he talked to me about it quite a few times and determined my disinterest, he warned me to keep quiet and hinted that he knew I had a son at Penn State University in Harrisburg. Now that made me sit up and take notice."

"Geez," said Ben. "So he had taken the time to find out about your life and see where you were vulnerable. Do you have any other children?"

"Yes, I do. I have a daughter who is twenty-five, married with two kids. My wife died a few years ago."

"Sorry, about that."

"Well, he had mentioned the fact that he knew I had a daughter once, but never mentioned her again. I think he thought that Justin was a better target. Kids away at college are more at risk anyway. Still, he did make me nervous about my daughter as well."

"So after that," said Dave, "he began to make demands on you."

"That's right. He wanted information that only the police department was privy to and he really seemed to have an agenda."

Dave and Ben looked at each other and realized that this was a familiar ploy. Dan continued.

"At first, I told him no, I wasn't going to do it and he'd just laugh. He told me that he knew how to make me cooperate."

"And that was roughing up, Justin."

"Yes, but that didn't even cross my mind. Honestly, I just thought he was a punk trying to make a name for himself and I really ignored his statements after he left. Sergeant Bill Cullins and I thought he was an irritating character that we had to put up with occasionally."

Dan accepted a glass of water, but his hand was still shaking, a fact he tried to hide.

"One day he walked into the precinct again and Bill and I simply eyed each other. We were thinking 'here we go again.' This time was different. He wanted some private information on people who were involved in the regulations department of our state. I said No. Then he insisted on talking to me privately and he had pictures. They were of Justin and they had done a thorough job of disfiguring him. I immediately gave him what he wanted."

Dan took pictures out of a folder he had brought in. They showed Justin's face with a black eye and bruises all over his face. He was also holding his right arm that looked like it could be broken.

"After that, I usually gave him what he wanted. But one time I wasn't thorough enough and I got this next picture."

This time Justin had a sling on his right arm and more bruises on his face. This second attack had occurred almost two months after the first.

"Marvin said that if I didn't cooperate fully from now on that my son would be sent to me in little pieces. My heart sank because I did believe he would do it. He's a very evil man."

"And it's continued on all this time, almost a year?"

"Yes, it has. I've probably helped him out ten to twelve times and in between visits, he'd call me to make sure that I hadn't forgotten about him. I didn't know what to do. You probably think I should have reported this and maybe so, but he warned me so many times that he'd kill Justin. I was too afraid to take the chance."

Ben nodded. "Okay, what we need from you now is testimony as to what happened to you and your son and anything else that you might know. Are you willing to cooperate now?"

Dan did hesitate for a moment. Then he said, "I'd like to see that bastard pay for what he did to us and what he was doing to our state. But I need to make sure that my daughter and her family are safe, too. He didn't work alone. He worked with this Right Side Group."

"Understood, we will protect your daughter as well. But we know that it was his idea alone to kill Senator Stedman and that the Right Side Group are not happy with him right now. It's not likely that they would be helping him."

"Really, I guess that's good. You know the night of the murder I was informed I had to accompany him to the Connecticut Convention Center and stay with him. I swear I had no idea that he planned to kill anyone. I didn't even know that he had a gun. I was caught totally off guard."

"So you were with him when he shot Senator Stedman?"

"Yes, I was standing right next to him. It happened so fast. We had left the meeting room and he was walking quickly toward the west exit, you know, where all those stairs are. I noticed a crowd and then saw the protection squad and knew someone important was in the area. He grabbed my arm and yelled, 'Stay with me,' and he literally ran to the bottom of those steps to get ahead of the squad unit. He went to an area that was somewhat darkened and then he pulled out his gun and shot the senator twice. I was shocked."

"Did anyone else around you see what happened?"

"Yes, I do believe that one of the men in the senator's squad looked over at Marvin and recognized something. But then he quickly was busy trying to help the senator."

"Even though it did happen quickly," said Ben, "sometimes memories stay with a person. He didn't hesitate, right? He moved fast?"

"Yes, it happened in a second. At first, the senator stood upright like everything was okay. He went down very slowly and that's when everyone realized he'd been shot. At that moment, that one guard of his looked around and saw us. I'm sure he noticed both of us."

"Were you in uniform?" asked Dave.

"Yes I was. I thought I was on an official duty that night. Even though I was caught in Marvin's web, I thought I was on police duty that night."

"Then what?"

"He turned to me, stuck the gun in my hand and said, 'Get rid of this.' I was still in shock and he walked away and got himself out of there. I saw a vagabond nearby and he was clearly drunk, so I put the gun in his pocket. Don't think he was aware of anything. He said something like, 'Present? Did you give me a present?' He was really out of it."

Dan put his head down on the table. Recalling the murder scene had been quite emotional for him. He shed more tears and seemed quite worn out.

"If I had known, I like to think I might have been able to prevent it. I think my policeman's brain would have taken over, but ..."

At this point, Dan stopped. He was finished for now.

Ben had a few questions and he had to ask them now.

"This guard on the senator's squad, would you recognize him if you saw him again?"

"Sure, I've seen him several times. In fact, one time when Mike came into our station he was one of his guards. Sure, I'd know him, but I don't know his name."

"Okay, he could be another witness. We have you and him as well as the homeless man."

"The homeless man? You really think he'd be any help?"

"Actually, he's already been some help. We don't think he's what he seems to be. Anyway, that's another story. With your testimony and the guard, if he's on our side, plus a few more people who could be of some help, we should have a good case. We need to put this guy away."

"I'll cooperate, like I said, just make sure my kids are protected."

"Absolutely. We'll talk again soon."

* * *

Leaving the station, Ben, Dave and Sammi paused for a moment. Emotional as this meeting had been, especially for Ben, focus had to be on the facts and the witnesses.

"Seems we've got a solid case unfolding here. I'm glad. I really wanted to catch Mike's killer, but this Right Side Group is getting too strong and too dangerous as they come out in the open. Dave, you could have been killed back there in Sweet Valley as well as Roy. You were both lucky. We have to beat these guys back into submission. I don't think we can get them to dismantle entirely, but if they went back to demonstrations that were peaceful, that's okay. They have a right to do that."

Sammi had been quiet for a while. Dave sensed that something was on her mind but hesitated to call her on it since she might want to think about it for a while. Then, to his surprise, she spoke.

"You know Ben, Dan was very emotional and feeling guilty about this entire episode. He had a lot on his mind, but I think that he knows more about Marvin than he remembered to tell you tonight."

"Really? You think so. Why did he hide it? Does he know something else that could help us?"

"I don't think he meant to hide it; he simply had so much to say. Next time ask him about Marvin's interest in Mike's home life. He was obsessed with him because of Melanie. I think he questioned Dan about it constantly. It's another fact that should be brought into the open. We need to check out his computer more thoroughly. He had plans to hurt that entire family because of the Melanie's connection. Killing Mike at the convention center was simply an opportunity that came up and he grabbed it. I think he planned to kill the entire family and had something on his computer to that effect. That might be even more proof."

Ben looked at Sammi with a certain admiration. He didn't know where she was getting this information, but it made sense. If it were proven true, it would be even more proof.

Catching Ben's thoughts, Sammi said, "Just a gut feeling really, but this guy was so out of contact with the normal world that he wanted to annihilate everyone who was in his way. Anyway, it's something to think about."

"Sammi," said Ben. "I learned a long time ago that anything you say is something to be investigated. Thanks. Are you two going to be heading home soon?"

Dave said, "We do want to decide what we should do about our suspects in Scranton. They have been helpful and I believe if given a fair chance, could become good citizens. What are your feelings on that?"

"Let me look into their backgrounds again. I tend to think in your direction, and I'd like your sarge to check them out and give me his opinion. I'm all for saving youth who should be given a second chance."

"But we're staying for a while, Ben. We'd like to help out Mr. Jim."

"That's right," said Ben. "I'm sure they'll delay the trial for now. It might take a couple of weeks, but I think they'll cancel it totally. Still, it could take a while to sort things out so he'll no doubt stay in jail a little while longer."

"I want to find out what happened to him. I think he was hurt, maybe in a car accident or something a while back and he's been wandering around ever since. I'd like to get him back home if we can find out where that is."

"From what you've said, he's educated and moral. Good luck on that one, though; it could be a long shot."

"Do we have your permission to talk to him again?"

"Sure, I don't see any harm now. Give it a try. Knowing you Sammi, the information will come. It always does when you're around."

Sammi smiled and Dave joined in. Yes, the universe had a way of helping Sammi since she knew how to cooperate with it.

CHAPTER XX

Sammi was excited to get over to the jail and see Mr. Jim. It had been a while and she knew that he needed her in his environment to feel her genuine concern. Dave hadn't met him yet, but Sammi had clued him in on everything she had understood and surmised about him. Now Dave could help her to understand and interpret his actions.

Walking into the jail she said, "I know that he's a very intelligent man so it's been eating away at me as to what actually happened to him."

"His thoughts didn't help you?" asked Dave.

"At times, they did. Yet, he seems to have had a concussion or some damage to his brain. His thoughts are well below the surface most of the time and occasionally when they manage to come up to consciousness, I've been able to catch a few of them. However, I think I told you that the last time we were here, Ben and I both were surprised at how lucid he was for a longer period of time. Before he was only aware for maybe a few seconds, but last time he actually had a few minutes where we could talk to him and he made sense. That was quite a breakthrough."

"So we'll hope he's doing better today. I don't think we can tell him much about the case yet."

"That's okay. I'm not sure how much he'd understand anyway. I do like to repeat to him that I believe that he didn't murder the senator; that seems to set him at ease."

"Here we are," said Dave. "Let's hope for the best today."

Both were quiet as they waited for Mr. Jim to arrive. The light colored cream walls seem to have special significance for Sammi. As she focused on them, her thoughts became serene and she tried to put out positive energy into the atmosphere. She felt an urgency somehow and she didn't know why. Mr. Jim was in a much better position now than he was a week ago. Marvin was arrested and being held on 'no bond'. It wasn't likely that he'd get out of jail before the trial. He'd already tried to run, so his chances of any leniency or trust were slim. In addition, the evidence against him was abundant and solid. Things were looking up for Mr. Jim and suddenly Sammi was able to take a deep breath and relax. She hadn't done that for a while.

The door opened abruptly and in walked Mr. Jim, still unsteady on his feet and in handcuffs. The officer removed them immediately and he had a happy facial expression when he saw Sammi. But was he lucid today? It was hard to tell.

"I like the name, Mr. Jim," she began. "It's good to see my friend again."

"It's good to see my angel again," he said. Then he looked over at Dave.

"This is Dave Patterson, Mr. Jim. He's your friend, too, and he's my husband."

It took a moment for those words to sink in so Sammi said again, "He's your friend, too."

That seemed to relax Mr. Jim and he sat back on his chair with a comfortable posture.

"It's been a long time," he said.

"I know and I'm sorry. The police wouldn't let me come. I know you didn't kill the senator."

He nodded. He understood that.

Then he started, "Tis a far, far better thing I do …."

"than I have ever done," said Sammi. Then she stopped and smiled.

"We like the same people," he said.

"Yes, we do. How do you feel, Mr. Jim? Does your head still hurt?"

"Yes, it's still sore. It hurts all the time. I want to go home."

Sammi jumped at this statement. "Where is home, Mr. Jim? Do you know where home is?"

"No, no. I don't remember anymore."

"Okay," she said, as he looked worried. "Don't worry; maybe we can help you find your home."

"Really? I haven't been home for a long time."

Sammi decided to throw in a few familiar statements that he had already told her.

"You miss your dog, Nappa, don't you?"

He looked at her in surprise. "Yes, you remembered my dog. He's an angel."

"Do you know where you were when you had the accident?"

"No, but it wasn't an accident. Some boys stopped me."

"Oh, I see. You said you were going home after work. Do you remember where you worked?"

He shook his head, but added, "I worked with Emerson, Thoreau and Dickens. Remember, we talked a lot about them."

"Yes, I remember."

For some reason, Mr. Jim suddenly sat back on his chair and his body became increasingly tense. Sammi asked him two questions, which he either didn't hear or couldn't answer. He was gone again for a while.

She turned to Dave who had been studying him. "It seems you get through to him. Can you hear his thoughts?"

"Only some of them – the ones that come higher up once in a while. Other than that I just guess what he's thinking."

Mr. Jim did perk up for a few moments, but his eyes showed that he was somewhere else. He kept rubbing his head and saying, "It hurts. I'm tired of my head hurting. Hurts all the time."

"I'm sorry," said Sammi.

Mr. Jim focused for a moment and answered, "I cannot let my angels go. You are my angel."

Next, Mr. Jim put his head in his arms and rested it on the table. It seems that today was a little more difficult for him. His eyes showed tears and his thoughts were only on how much his head hurt.

Sammi thought they should stop for the day. "Let him go back and lie down. I think rest is the only thing that helps him right now."

As he arose and walked unsteadily toward the door, he turned to Sammi and said, "Thank you for coming." Then he turned to Dave and said, "You, too."

He shuffled out the door and he stopped again before he went totally through it. This time he was focused on Sammi, smiled and said, "There are voices we hear in solitude, but they grow faint and inaudible as we enter the world."

Sammi was in shock. That was the longest, yet most profound statement she had heard him say. He had a strange look on his face, and then he was gone.

"Wow," she said to Dave. "His memory has obvious moments of clarity. I want to run some of his statements past Julie again. I'm so convinced this man is very educated. What do you think?"

"He's no vagabond," Dave answered. "He met with some tragedy and he hasn't been the same since. We need to look into this."

* * *

Sammi was unusually quiet on the way back to the motel. Her thoughts were in constant disarray as to what the next step should be. She didn't think it was right to keep Mr. Jim in jail where he wasn't getting any medical attention. That could be the key to his recovery and he didn't have anyone fighting on his side. His newly hired attorneys were on hold since the new developments regarding Marvin Antwerp, and it was delay after delay for him again.

"Okay, what's on your mind?" asked Dave. "You're too quiet."

"Well, I was thinking that since Mr. Jim isn't the main suspect anymore, that we could do something for him."

"Like what?" asked Dave. "He's still in custody."

"I know, but remember, when we thought his attorneys would be on board, we hoped he would get medical help. But now, that's not happening."

"Yeah, he's sort of in limbo."

"I wonder if Ben could pull some strings for us."

Dave smiled. "What do you have in mind?"

"Okay, okay," she began. "I know that Mr. Jim needs to be in custody until he's officially cleared, and that could take time. I'm okay with that. He doesn't have the capacity to make a run for it or take off in any way. He also can't take care of himself so he needs to be where people can take care of him. I was thinking of talking to Ben and have Mr. Jim released to our custody."

Dave raised an eyebrow.

"Wait a minute. Hear me out. I would like to take him back to Mercy Hospital in Scranton. He could still be in custody and have police outside his door. We know he needs and deserves medical help. He should have had it a long time ago, but no one cared to do it for him at those precincts. That's a shame. If anyone had a physical injury, he'd get help immediately. This man has a head injury and I think we would have a sympathetic cohort in Ben. We could tell him that he might even be a better witness if they took care of his head injury. What do you think?"

Dave paused for quite a while before he answered. "I have to agree with you especially on a humanitarian aspect. He should have had medical help before now. The prosecuting attorneys only had him checked out to see if he was sane enough to stand trial. Other than that, they didn't care about him. This has been shameful when you think of it. However, the FBI only got custody of him a few days ago, but I think we might be able to move on this. Let's talk to Ben and see what he says."

* * *

After listening to an impassioned plea from Sammi as well as Dave, Ben wanted a little time to think about it. He also would talk to his superiors and see what they would advise. He did agree with his friends, but didn't know how higher ups would view these circumstances. He asked them to come back the next day after he had time to talk to a few people.

"Well, the news is good. They do agree that Mr. Jim should have had more health evaluations. I think we talked about the fact that his attorneys were planning to have him totally evaluated, so that's not a new idea. The problem was sending him to Scranton with you. Yet, with Sammi's involvement in the situation and with the idea that she has been a marvelous help to the FBI in the past and we hope she'll be of the same frame of mind in the future, I was able to convince them that Scranton is the best place for Mr. Jim at this time. I also mentioned your idea that he might be a better witness in the future, but honestly, that's splitting hairs and we all know it. Yet evaluating Mr. Jim was on their agenda so we will supply police escorts at the hospital until he is released and that will be at the expense of the FBI, so your sarge will be happy about that."

Sammi had involuntary tears slipping past her eyelids; she couldn't hide them. It caused Ben to make the comment, "I've only seen you cry once before and that was when Dave came out of his coma."

"I think Mr. Jim has been through hell, and someone has to help him get back to reality. He deserves that."

"He does indeed," said Ben. "We all want to know who the man really is and what happened to him."

"Yeah," said Sammi sadly. "I'm sure he has a family who will be most appreciative."

Everyone nodded.

"The papers are being drawn up right now so you should be able to take him back with you by early next week."

"That's great news," said Dave.

"If I need you here Sammi, I'll let you know. I'd like you to be in on the interview with Marvin."

"Oh yeah," said Sammi, "and Dave, too. We wouldn't miss it for the world."

* * *

Sammi and Dave went back to Scranton immediately to prepare for Mr. Jim's arrival. They had a meeting with Dr. Ken Freedman, a physician who'd saved Dave's life on one occasion and restored him to good health on another. He wasn't a brain surgeon, however, but Dave wanted him to evaluate Mr. Jim's entire condition and then recommend the best brain surgeon for his condition.

After hearing his story, Dr. Freedman was extremely interested. "So this man could have been roaming around the country in this condition for a while."

"Yes," said Sammi. "We have no way of knowing how long, but from the scant conversation we got from him, it seems that it must have been quite a while."

"Of course, that means that his brain injuries, whatever they may be will have somewhat healed in probably unsatisfactory conditions. What I mean is, you can have concussions or even worse and when you get no medical treatment, the body will do what it has to do to survive. Yet many times this means that healing has to be redirected to get the patient healing properly. It gets complicated, but it's been done often in modern times. I know a few surgeons who will be most interested in his case. In fact, I'll follow up as well. This man could be one to be studied."

"Yeah, if only he remembered more and could have talked to us, that would have helped."

"Head injuries and amnesia go hand in hand. What type of amnesia he has will be interesting to interpret. Sounds like a combination of a few types. Definitely traumatic amnesia since it sounds like he was possibly mugged and beaten up. Also, retrograde amnesia which is when you forget your past or who you are. Nevertheless, he does seem to remember a little background, like his first name and his dog, and if that proves to be correct, the brain is probably in a healing process. Hopefully we can help it along. When is he due here?"

"Within the next couple of days and he'll have FBI escorts."

"Okay," said Dr. Freedman since he knew the story from Hartford, Conn. We'll be ready. We may need you, Sammi since you seem to have a rapport with him. We need to make him as comfortable and trusting as quickly as possible."

"Of course, I plan to be here."

* * *

Dave got back to his routine within the next few days. He'd missed working with his little group and was interested in how the suspects were doing.

"Just biding their time until they find out what will happen to them," said Jim. "Honestly, Dave, they seem like decent young people. I hope we can work out something for them."

"Ben is looking into it, so we'll see."

Amilio wandered over. His assignment in Hartford was over and he was on duty again with Dave's group.

"That Marvin was one weird dude. Some people are just bad through and through but I think this dude has a messed up mind, maybe a sociopath or something. He was so controlling. I mean everything had to be under his control or he went nuts. What do you call a guy like that?"

"Not sure, but he sure caused himself and a lot of other people trouble. And he killed the senator for no good reason," said Dave. "What a shame."

"I think Jason Connors will get a jail sentence. This kid has no brains," said Amilio. "Even in custody he yells about killing policemen and harming other government officials. He really is a nut."

"His father's influence really runs deep. What about the others, Phil and Charlie."

"You know, amigo, I believe they really are good kids that got caught up in something by accident. They don't have a bad attitude about life or about us police officers. In fact, Charlie has been saying that he wished he could get a degree of some kind and maybe do some kind of police work. He liked the idea that we're sort of a family around here. Those kids' lives are rather sad."

If everything works out okay," said Dave, "I was hoping we could get them probation and community service with us. That might give them a new direction."

"Ah, amigo, you've got a good heart."

* * *

By Thursday, Mr. Jim had arrived at Mercy Hospital in Scranton, PA. He had two police escorts and a medical assistant with him. After being thoroughly evaluated it was determined that some high potency pain relievers would be in order. Sammi came in to see him shortly after.

"My angel," he said, "I was hoping you'd come to see me."

"Yes, Mr. Jim, I plan to be around often now."

Mr. Jim looked over at the police officers. "They'll let you see me now?"

"Yes, Mr. Jim. These people are your friends."

"My friends? Police aren't my friends."

"These police officers are your friends."

"How come?" he asked.

Sammi simply smiled. She didn't know how to answer that question.

"How's your head? Does it feel better?"

Mr. Jim smiled. "Yes, that woman in white gave me a pill and now it feels better. This is the first time it has felt better in a long time."

Sammi noticed that Mr. Jim was talking better. He was using complete sentences. She wondered if it was because his head didn't hurt as much. Yet, suddenly he seemed to regress a little.

"Tis a far far better thing I do ...." Then he trailed off.

At that moment, Dr. Freedman walked in with a Dr. Maloney, a brain surgeon.

Introductions were made and Dr. Freedman explained how Sammi had maintained a rapport with Mr. Jim.

Dr. Maloney turned to his new patient. "Well hello, how are you today?"

Mr. Jim said nothing but looked nervously at Sammi. Everyone waited, but Mr. Jim didn't answer. Sammi heard his thoughts and realized that he was very nervous about this new person. His thoughts became cloudy and started to descend; this wasn't a good sign.

Finally, Sammi said, "He does better if you call him by his name. He likes to hear it. Let me show you."

She stated, "Mr. Jim. I like your name."

He smiled and began to show focus which was not lost on Dr. Maloney.

The new doctor smiled at Sammi and began in her frame of reference. "Mr. Jim, I'm happy to meet you. I like your name, too."

That did it. Mr. Jim sat up straighter in his bed and gave Dr. Maloney a slight smile.

Sammi continued, "This is Dr. Maloney. He's your friend, too."

"My friend?" He looked at Dr. Maloney and said, "She's my angel. We cannot let our angels go."

Dr. Maloney looked slightly confused. They decided to have a small conference in the hallway and Sammi clued the two doctors in about how she felt Mr. Jim was an educated man and kept repeating quotes from Emerson, Thoreau and Dickens. It must be something he remembered from his past. Today, he had held his focus much longer than usual which seemed like a good sign to her.

Dr. Maloney was impressed. "Maybe the meds helped but I need to have a meeting with you and have you tell me everything you know about this man. In the meantime, I need some total body x-rays and some head x-rays, CAT Scan, EEG,

MRI, the works. I need pictures of his head from all angles. We need to know what happened to his brain and how long ago. The healing process should tell us that."

And so the medical evaluations of Mr. Jim began. Someone would finally know what had happened to him and determine his method of treatment. With Sammi nearby, he would trust and she would be by his side whenever needed.

* * *

Within a week, Mr. Jim was a free man with all charges against him dropped. Marvin had halfway confessed to his crimes and was acting somewhere between a controlling, demanding tyrant to being a confused little child. He was being evaluated by several psychiatrists, and although he was trying to be considered 'not sane enough to stand trial' his true sanity came into play often enough to deter that prognosis. His would be a confusing case. After Sammi and Dave had returned to Hartford with Ben to sit in on some interviews with him, her report was able to pinpoint his propensity for lying and his inclination to confuse the truth. With the help of Sergeant Wyman, his insanity plea was not allowed. This was one of the biggest reasons why the charges against Mr. Jim were dropped much sooner than expected. This opened the door for Sammi and Julie to work together and put out information to begin determining where Mr. Jim was from and what had happened to him. The FBI was helpful and Julie had access to all of their missing persons' files. Yet, the task was still overwhelming. They first needed to determine where he was from and the information was not very plentiful in that direction.

Julie said, "There are no missing men between fifty-five and sixty in Connecticut in the last ten years that fits his description."

Sammi was strong. "So we go to surrounding states. The news will get his picture out there by the end of the week. Something will turn up. I'm sure his family has been desperate for a long time."

Sammi took a long deep breath.

"What?" asked Julie.

"Well, the doctors seem to think that he will need surgery on his brain. The x-rays showed he had some bleeding on the brain and some clots are lingering around there. In addition, he did have a significant skull fracture, so they need to make sure no bone fragments are causing problems. The constant soreness that he complains about could be that or a bunch of other things. Honestly, Julie, it's so confusing. But we need to try and find someone in his family who can give consent for this operation."

"Okay, he's got good doctors now. I'm sure they can keep him comfortable until then."

"Yes, and he's talking better now. Yet, I still can't get more information out of him."

"Everything takes time. Keep talking to him. Maybe a new statement will come out."

Sammi smiled. That's what she'd been hoping would happen. She spent time each day talking and visiting with him. The doctors needed her to try to keep him trusting and cooperative. Still, while he talked to her, she couldn't help hope that maybe one day he would say something that would give a clue. She felt the universe would help this lost man, who needed to be found soon.

* * *

Sammi had dosed off on the couch waiting for Dave to get home. Everything about Mr. Jim continued to cloud her thoughts. It haunted her. Who was he? Someone must be missing him. But who? And where? Hints to either one of those questions would be a tremendous help.

Yesterday, the media got his story with pictures and all the personal data that could be released. It was too soon for any responses yet, but Sammi was an optimist. She could almost hear the telephone ring with a positive reply.

Suddenly, she was awake. It was Dave tugging at her shoulder.

"Sammi, let's get you to bed. You're exhausted."

"Hi sweetie. I'm so hoping for some answers soon."

"I'm sure they'll come, but get some sleep so you'll be ready for tomorrow."

She smiled. "Yes, that's a good idea. I'm sorry, honey. I didn't ask you about your day."

Dave laughed. "It was fine, but I'm tired, too. We'll handle all this tomorrow, but tonight we need rest."

CHAPTER XXI

It was eight days since the news media got the story of Mr. Jim and not one clear or dependable clue had surfaced. Oh sure, there were the usual calls from people that wanted their name in the paper and made up something which unfortunately had to be looked into. Most seemed like a waste of time and they were. Mr. Jim was facing brain surgery by next week at the latest and Sammi hoped that he had some family there to console him before and after. It didn't seem that was going to happen.

"Good morning, sweetie. What are you up to today?"

"Just the usual routine. Sometimes I'm happy about that."

"Me, too."

Sammi was drinking her coffee and making breakfast conversation. Her mind was so heavy with conflicting thoughts that she sounded rather mystified. She was trying to sort through them all.

"You going to work today?" asked Dave.

"Yes, I am, but I'll stop by the hospital to see Mr. Jim later."

"I know. You go every day. Is he doing okay?"

"Actually, he is. He seems to talk better most of the time, but his memory hasn't kicked in that much yet. I was hoping he's think of something. I just need one little bit of information and between Julie and I we could make sense of it."

"Well, hang in there. Today could be the day."

She smiled. "There's not been one phone tip that made any sense at all. Do they ever come in later?"

"They come in constantly. Don't think that they're over yet; it's only been a little over a week."

She nodded. "That's good. We'll just hope for the best."

After receiving a phone call from Roy, Dave left in a hurry. Sammi was alone again. She looked up at the sky knowing that the answer was somewhere in the universe and she wished she could find it soon. She was fighting discouragement; it was something she didn't believe in. She'd rather keep her thoughts on the positive side since that's where all the answers were. She concentrated on her grandpa. He always made her feel comfortable and serene.

* * *

Walking into the hospital room she found a sleepy Mr. Jim. The nurse said that he was nodding off a lot lately. It wasn't a bad sign; he was on a lot of medication. The surgeons were hoping for some results in his brain region before the operation.

Sammi walked around, looking out the window and was captivated by the blue sky with particularly bright white clouds. It was a spectacular sight holding her interest for a few minutes. She tried to keep her thoughts calm until Mr. Jim woke up. He needed to see her as often as possible. She had become his link to sanity.

She turned to the voice that said, "My angel, you're here."

"Yes, Mr. Jim. Did you have a good rest?"

"Yes, I did. I was thinking that in the jail the beds were hard and uncomfortable. Now, I'm treated so well."

There were those long sentences again and in perfect grammar. Mr. Jim was slowly inching along in the right direction. Today, she thought she would try to get some new recollections out of him. She would use some of his favorite memories to begin.

"Mr. Jim, did you take Nappa for walks? Did he like to walk along with you?

Mr. Jim smiled. "Oh yes. He tried to get me to walk faster and faster. I'm sure he would have liked to run, but I didn't do that much."

"How big was Nappa?"

"Oh, not too big. He weighs about thirty-five pounds and he's a golden color. My angel is so beautiful."

Well, that was new. He remembered how big his dog was and he remembered the color. Maybe she hadn't been asking the right questions before. She decided to talk only about past memories and see where he'd go. His thoughts were rising higher now, but they were still unclear.

"What did Nappa like to eat?"

For the first time, Mr. Jim let out a vocal laugh. He actually laughed aloud for a long minute. Then he said, "Well, he ate his dog food, but his dessert was whatever was left on my plate. Not the best I know, but I loved my angel."

"We do that for our little angels. I have a dog named Kali and I give her some of my food, too."

Mr. Jim said, "You do. Yeah, it's hard not to. God loves them so much."

Now there was a new thought again. He spoke of God. Now he was thinking about open spaces and his thoughts went to figures or statues, but she couldn't hear which ones. She decided to ask.

"Where did you take Nappa for walks?"

This time he thought for a few minutes. In fact, Sammi thought she had lost him, which hadn't happened for a few days now. He finally answered with an amazing statement. "Well, Nappa loves the Wildcat. It's only a statue, but he barks at it every time. I try to explain it to him, but I think he is just practicing his barking."

Mr. Jim had a twinkle in his eyes now. He was remembering something. Sammi pressed on.

"Where is the Wildcat statue?"

He looked over at her surprised and answered. "Well, it's at the same place as Thompson Hall; you know the one with the flag. Lots of interesting things around there."

Sammi felt she had grasped something personal, and she was ecstatic. Because now, Mr. Jim was getting tired again and he was yawning. The nurse came in with more medication and she knew he'd be asleep soon. Along with everything else that was going on, the doctors still felt that lots of sleep was good for him. The body can heal itself better with adequate rest. She tiptoed out of the room shortly after he fell asleep.

* * *

As soon as she got to her car, Sammi put in a call to Julie. She told her of the new memories and asked for her opinion.

"Well, let me look them up. Could give us a clue to a town somewhere. Many towns have statues and most buildings have names. Maybe we'll have a direction to go."

"Great. I'll get on my computer when I get home, too. I feel good about today, Julie. I'll talk to him tomorrow and keep pressing on memories. Wouldn't it be great to find out something?"

"You'll get there, Sammi. I can feel it."

"Thanks."

Driving home was difficult. Sammi couldn't get the new thoughts out of her mind. She felt she was on the edge of a discovery, but not quite there yet. She couldn't wait to tell Dave.

"Now that sounds like something," said Dave. "Let's get Julie on this."

"Oh, honey, I already called her. Hope you don't mind. I was so anxious."

"That's fine."

"I'm getting on the computer right after dinner. We could have a breakthrough tonight."

Dave looked over at Sammi's hopeful face. She had worked so long on this case. Right from the beginning when she first read that newspaper article, she'd had a feeling about this man. So far, she'd been correct. He was no murderer and he'd been the victim of a mugging or something and wandered around for a long time, possibly years. Finally, they were close to finding out his identity. He could feel her excitement and eagerness. It had taken a long time to get to this point.

"You know ...." Dave was cut off by the telephone. It was Julie and she was excited. Sammi put her on speaker.

"I think I may have found something. Not for sure of course. But the University of New Hampshire in Durham has a Wildcat statue on campus. The next part is important. The first building ever built on their campus is named Thompson Hall and it has a flag on top of it. Now Thompson Hall could be a common name and there probably are more around the country, but that along with the Wildcat Statue seems worth checking out."

Sammi had tears as she said, "Julie, that's great. It fits. I'll bet he was a teacher there."

Julie's excitement came through the telephone. "You're right, Sammi. All of his talk about Emerson, Thoreau and Dickens; maybe he was a teacher in Liberal Arts at the university. It's possible. What do you think, Dave?"

"I'd have to agree. It's late tonight, but tomorrow I plan to call the university. I mean this is a missing person so I'd like to make an official inquiry. Did they lose a teacher or professor and how long ago?"

"I guess we have to wait until tomorrow," said Sammi.

"It's after nine, honey. I want to talk to the President of the University or his representative."

"Right, that's best."

Julie said, "Tomorrow as soon as I get to work I'll start checking out missing persons in that area and see if anything comes up. Dave, I may have something for you when you get in."

"Great, I think it'll be a long night for all of us."

When Sammi put the phone down, she turned to Dave and started crying. All of the tension, worries and strain over this Mr. Jim was finally spilling out.

"I'm glad you're crying. You've needed a release for so long."

Sammi laughed in the middle of her tears. These were not sad tears but welcomed ones that would heal her body. It was great to have Dave to share this moment.

* * *

The next day was filled with surprises. Dave had everyone working on this assignment for the first part of the morning. Even the sarge spared these officers and opened up their schedules hoping for a quick conclusion to a long dilemma.

Julie had found three missing males in the general vicinity of Durham. One was a man by the name of Jim Applegate, but he was only thirty-nine and his body was recovered about a year later. That had happened in 2005. However, in 2009 there were two interesting cases. John Seymour disappeared and left behind a wife and two children. He was fifty-one years old. But, he was a millwright at one of the local foundries, uneducated and rather a crude character. Rumors swirled around the fact that his extra girlfriend left with him. Neither one was ever seen since that time.

Then there was John Montague, Professor of Education at the University of New Hampshire in Durham. He specialized in Literature and English. He had disappeared in 2009 and no trace of him was ever found. He had left the college after giving a lecture that ended at ten o'clock at night. Two students walked out to the parking lot with him, waived goodbye and that was the last anyone ever saw of him. Everyone figured this was their Mr. Jim.

Dave put in a call to the university and talked to Mark W. Middleton, the president of the university. They talked for a while and Mr. Middleton was shocked to hear the reason for Dave's call. Mr. Montague had disappeared in the spring of 2009. He was heading home and never made it; there was no trace of him. The local police had found some kind of scuffle on the road he was likely to have taken. There was a bumper and a broken headlight, which matched up to the professor's car. But that was it. His car was never found and the professor was never seen again, despite a huge manhunt that lasted well over two years. All feared he had died. Although still considered an open case, no clues or any new information had been collected for the last few years.

"I can't wait to talk to his wife and children. They will be so excited."

Dave cautioned him. "I don't want you to talk to anyone about this yet. We don't want to get their hopes up until we're sure. Can you send us a few pictures of him? Although this man has been through a lot for the last few years, I think we could find a resemblance. Also, I want to check his fingerprints with the local police."

"Oh, okay. I do understand. It will be hard to keep quiet but we do need to make sure we have the correct person. Mr. Montague was a favorite teacher around here. He was very caring and went out of his way for his students. They all loved him. Many people mourned him; some still do."

"You say he was a married man."

"Yes, his wife used to teach here as well, but chose to retire and spend more time with their children. The entire family are graduates of the university. You can imagine how hard it must have been because no one knew what happened.

The family was very devoted and no one ever thought that he just left; everyone figured he met with foul play."

"I understand. Send me those pictures quickly. As soon as I get a positive identification, I'll let you know. The FBI has been involved in this case as well. We'll have to follow their lead to tell the family. I'm sure they'd appreciate your cooperation."

"Of course. I'll be anxiously waiting."

* * *

When Dave got the pictures later in the day, there was no doubt. He brought them home to Sammi whose hands immediately went up to her face. Mr. John Montague was a very handsome man, distinguished and his intelligence seemed to show through a welcoming smile. Even in his present somewhat deteriorated state, the likeness was unquestionable. Sammi's thoughts were all over the place.

She began with the 'what ifs'.

"Dave can you imagine? What if I hadn't read that article? What if Ben hadn't gotten us involved in this case? What if we'd never had occasion to meet Mr. Jim. No one else seemed to have any interest in him. What if …"

"Stop, Sammi. Settle down, honey. You're the one that doesn't believe in coincidences."

She paused for a moment. "That's right; I don't. I'm just so happy right now."

"I need to call Ben and see how he wants to handle this. We need his family here now. He may recognize them; with a bit of luck, he will. And they have to be here for the surgery."

With Ben on the phone, the plan seemed to progress. "I'll rush the fingerprint identification. I'll get it to you by morning. I'm sure the FBI will fly them to the hospital where I want you and Sammi to take charge. You'd be the perfect couple to walk them through everything. This is fantastic. Sammi, you should be so proud."

"A lot of people have worked on this, Ben. You included."

"I'd like to get them down there tomorrow. You know, in a case like this, we'll probably never find out what really happened unless Mr. Jim gets his memory back."

Just then, Ben laughed aloud.

"What?" asked Dave.

"I'll probably always call him Mr. Jim, thanks to Sammi."

"So will I."

CHAPTER XXI

Dave and Sammi anxiously waited for the Montague family to arrive at Mercy Hospital. They were in the lobby checking out everyone that came in. It wasn't necessary though as Ben had decided to send Jeff Slade with them to make the transition easier.

Mr. Middleton, the university president, said that Mrs. Montague almost fainted at the news. He tried to present it to her delicately, but after three and a half years, there really wasn't an easy way to tell her that her missing husband was found alive. Luckily, his son and daughter gave their mother the strength she needed. This was unbelievable news.

Sammi recognized Jeff Slade coming in from the parking lot. Mr. Jim's wife was an attractive woman, blonde, about fifty years old who looked expectedly anxious. His two children, both in their twenties walked quickly to enter the lobby. Dave and Sammi met them immediately and led them to a room where they could have privacy as they all discussed everything they knew.

Jeff helped them to understand the facts.

"Sammi here is a confidante to the FBI and helps us out quite often. And she's amazing. She developed a rapport with your husband when no one else could get through to him."

Turning to Sammi he said, "I think they'd like to hear your end of the story. I told them all about Hartford and the murder and how he got involved in this."

They confirmed that he loved Emerson, Thoreau, Dickens, Chaucer and all of the masters. After all, that's what he did. He taught classical literature at the university.

"You must have been pretty sharp to pick up the fragments that he talked about."

"Oh, it wasn't just me."

"You don't have to be delicate. Jeff told us that the police thought he was just a crazy, drunken vagabond. It took someone with special talents to figure out what he was trying to say."

Jeff jumped on that statement. "Sammi does have special talents. Most of us can't figure out how she gets her information and believe me, we've all studied her."

He winked at Sammi, but the session was getting close to the end. Sammi wanted to get up to Mr. Jim's room.

Standing outside, the family looked at him through the window and there was some shock on their faces. He was so thin and bony looking.

"Of course," said his wife Sandy. "It's been a long rough few years for him."

Sammi walked in first and the family could hear her and the wonderful rapport she'd developed with her Mr. Jim.

"Hi, Mr. Jim. I like your name."

He turned to her and said, "My angel is here. I cannot let my angels go."

"Mr. Jim, I brought some visitors to see you. Maybe you'll remember them. You knew them a while ago."

"Really? Some people are here to see me."

Then Sandy and her two kids came into the room. The look on Mr. Jim's face was sudden shock and it was also recognition. He looked at his wife and said, "Hi Sandy, did you bring Nappa?"

She walked over and gave him a big hug and he accepted it lovingly. He also remembered his son and daughter.

Dave leaned over to Sammi and said, "Love is such a strong bond. I wonder if he would have recognized them back in the jail cell. I think he's come a long way since then."

"Yes, I think so, too. The doctor says that after his surgery next week, he should make an almost complete recovery. A few elements might remain, but he will teach again and regain a normal life."

"That's like a miracle, you know," said Dave. "From when you first saw him to now, is a miracle."

"It's so great being a part of all this."

As they were leaving, Mr. Jim called to Sammi, "Where is my angel going?"

"Oh, I'll be back to see you Mr. Jim."

"Okay," he said, "I cannot let my angel go."

The last thing Sammi and Dave saw were Mr. Jim and his family all smiling at them as they left the room.

Sammi said, "I think my heart will burst."

Dave nodded and understood.

* * *

Several months after the surgery and a lengthy rehab program, a dinner was held for Mr. Jim and his family before they headed back to Durham, New Hampshire. Most of his motor skills were intact although he would continue physical therapy in Durham indefinitely. Sammi had mixed feelings. She was ecstatic that Mr. Jim was well enough to go home, but he'd been part of her life for so long now, that something deep inside ached at the thought of him being gone.

Dave said, "This is the greatest end result, Sammi. He gets to go home and regain his life. I'm sure there are many students who will benefit from him returning."

"I know, but I feel like I'm losing a friend. Well, maybe not losing a friend, but you know."

He smiled as he said, "You don't want to let your angel go."

Mr. Jim came over and gave her a long hug. Then he took a few minutes to have a necessary conversation with her alone.

"You know there's no way I can thank you, but I also know that it's not necessary. You and I have gained a friendship and something more that few can understand. I do remember many things in those first few days when I was so thrilled that someone knew I wasn't crazy. It's hard to describe in words, but it's here in my heart."

"I think I know how you felt; at least I know how I would have felt. You were so trapped inside and couldn't get anyone to understand."

"But you understood, Sammi. You understood and that was amazing. You know that I deal in a lot of philosophy, which of course enables me to entertain the other side of our world. I mean, I love being human and experiencing earth, but I like to keep one foot on the other side of the universe."

Sammi smiled.

"I know you understand me and are with me every step of the way. I've had a lot of time to think about how you could have possibly figured me out. I think I know. The only thing that makes sense to me was that you were answering what I was thinking. I've known that for a while."

Sammi didn't answer. She was surprised and yet believed Mr. Jim probably knew.

"I've dealt with a lot of philosophical and psychic people in my time, some true and believable and others total fakes trying to make a name for themselves. My experience came in handy. You see, I remember when you'd answer what I was thinking. In my mind at the time, it was so wonderful; I can't even describe it. The universe talked to me, too. But you became my link to the outside world."

Sammi let out a knowing expression as she said. "There were times by the look on your face that I felt you understood."

"It's a marvelous gift you have, and it's safe with me."

"Thanks. I'm valuable because a lot of people don't know."

Mr. Jim nodded. He understood.

"But you have a wonderful gift as well. I'm sure many people will be glad to see you back in Durham. Sorry, but I'm not one of them. I'm gonna miss you."

"As I will you. But I plan to keep in contact. It's something I have to do. I'd like you and Dave to make the trip down to see us in the future when you can. What we shared together during my difficult time is a treasure and I know I'd like to talk about it again."

"I would as well. How the universe steps in and makes things happen is always astonishing to me."

Just then, a few more people came up and their cherished conversation was over for now. Sammi's sad thoughts converted to happy thoughts realizing that she'd been part of an amazing journey that wasn't over yet. It was:

~~TO BE CONTINUED~~

Other Titles in the Sammi Evans Mystery Series

by

Jeanne L. Drouillard

*****

Thinking Out Loud

*****

Sinister Thoughts Kill

*****

Thoughts Can Be Murder

*****

Thoughts Can Be Deadly

*****

Your Thoughts Can Trap You

*****

Evil Thoughts Kill Dreams

About our Author

Jeanne L. Drouillard graduated from Madonna University with a Bachelor of Science Degree in Business with minors in French, computers and Sign Language. Other recognized studies and experiences have included handwriting analysis, bible studies, love & logic parenting, attachment disorder and other adoptive issues, listening skills as well as various seminars in leadership, self-improvement and psychology. She has published many articles dealing with the positive side of human nature and emphasizes what can be accomplished with a strong belief system coupled with tenacity.

Her first book, Thinking Out Loud, was conceived because of her fascination with the world of thought and how it relates to our lives. Sammi Evans, her heroine, is in a unique position to study the inner and outer environment of people and to monitor their success and failure while relating it to their thought world.

The second book in her series of Sammi Evans mysteries was Your Thoughts Can Trap You, followed by Sinister Thoughts Kill, Thoughts Can Be Murder, Thoughts Can Be Deadly and Evil Thoughts Kill Dreams. Being caught up in the inner thoughts of other people gives her a unique understanding and ability to grasp how feelings and thoughts affect our lives and the lives of others around us.

Jeanne L. Drouillard presently lives in Michigan, after being transplanted from Canada as a teenager. She's experienced the wonderment of strong and deep roots of belonging as well as being the new kid on the block. She is thankful for all the thoughts and feelings she's gathered along the way, as she draws on every one of them when she writes.